THREE TRUMPS

THREE TRUMPS

A Nero Wolfe Omnibus

Rex Stout

THE VIKING PRESS | New York

Contents

The Black Mountain

WARNING

In a way this is a phony. A lot of the talk I report was in languages I am not on speaking terms with, so even with the training I've had there is no use pretending that here it is, word for word. But this is what happened, and since I had to know what was going on to earn my keep, Nero Wolfe put it in English for me every chance he got. For the times when it had to be on the fly, and pretty sketchy, I have filled it in as well as I could. Maybe I shouldn't have tried to tell it at all, but I hated to skip it.

ARCHIE GOODWIN

1

That was the one and only time Nero Wolfe has ever seen the inside of the morgue.

That Thursday evening in March I barely caught the phone call. With a ticket for a basketball game at the Garden in my pocket, I had dined in the kitchen, because I would have to leave the house at ten to eight, and Wolfe refuses to sit at table with one who has to pack it in and run. And that time I couldn't eat early because Fritz was braising a wild turkey and had to convey it to the dining room on a platter for Wolfe to see whole before wielding the knife. Sometimes when I have a date for a game or a show I get things from the refrigerator around six-thirty and take my time, but I wanted some of that hot turkey, not to mention Fritz's celery sauce and corn fritters.

I was six minutes behind schedule when, as I pushed my chair back and got erect, the phone rang. After asking Fritz to get it on the kitchen extension and proceeding to the hall, I had got my topcoat from the rack and was putting it on when Fritz called to me, "Archie! Sergeant Stebbins wants you!"

I muttered something appropriate for muttering but not for printing, made it to the office and across to my desk, lifted the receiver, and told it, "Shoot. You may have eight seconds."

It took more like eight times eighty, not because Purley Stebbins insisted on it, but I did after he had given me the main fact. When I had hung up I stood a while, frowning at Wolfe's desk. Many times through the years I have had the job of reporting something to Wolfe that I knew he wouldn't enjoy hearing, but this was different. This was tough. I even found myself wishing I had got away two minutes sooner, and then, realizing that that would have been tougher—for him, at least—I went to the hall, crossed it to the dining room, entered, and spoke.

"That was Purley Stebbins. Half an hour ago a man came out of a house on East Fifty-fourth Street and was shot and killed by a man waiting there in a parked car. Papers found—"

Wolfe cut me off. "Must I remind you that business shall not intrude on meals?"

"You don't need to. This isn't business. Papers found on the body indicate that it was Marko Vukcic. Purley says there's no doubt about it, two of the dicks knew him by sight, but he wants me to come down and give positive identification. If you have no objection I'm going. It won't be as pleasant a way to spend an evening as going to a ball game, but I'm sure he would have done as much . . ."

I would have preferred to go on talking, but had to stop to clear my throat. Wolfe had put down his knife and fork, quietly and properly, on his plate. His eyes were leveled at me, but he wasn't scowling. A corner of his mouth twitched, and after a moment twitched again. To stop it he compressed his lips.

He nodded at me. "Go. Phone."

"Have you any—"

"No. Phone."

I whirled and went.

After going a block south on Tenth Avenue and flagging a taxi on Thirty-fourth Street, it didn't take long to roll cross-town to the city mortuary on East Twenty-ninth; and, since I was not a stranger there and was expected, I was passed through the railing and on in with no questions asked. I have never cared for the smell of that place. An assistant medical examiner named Faber tried once to sell me the idea that it smells just like a hospital, but I have a good nose and I didn't buy. He claimed that there are rarely more than one or two cadavers on the premises not in the coolers, and I said in that case someone must spray the joint with something to make it smell like a morgue.

The Homicide dick who escorted me down the corridor was one I knew only well enough to nod to, and the assistant ME in the room we entered was one I hadn't run across before. He was working on an object that was stretched out on a long table under a strong light, with a helper standing by. The dick and I stood and watched a minute. A detailed description of the performance would help only if you expect to be faced with the job of probing a corpse for a bullet that entered at an angle between the fifth and sixth ribs, so I won't go into it.

"Well?" the dick demanded.

"Yes," I told him. "I identify it as the body of Marko Vukcic, owner of Rusterman's Restaurant. If you want that signed, get it ready while I go use the phone."

I went out and down the corridor to the phone booth and dialed a number. Ordinarily when I am out of the house and phone in Fritz will answer after two or three signals or Wolfe will answer after five or six, but that time Wolfe's voice came before the first whirr was done.

"Yes?"

"Archie. It's Marko. Shot twice in the chest and once in the belly. I suppose Stebbins is up at Fifty-fourth Street, at the scene, and maybe Cramer too. Shall I go up there?"

"No. Stay where you are. I'm coming to look at him. Where is it?"

He had been making a living as a private detective in Manhattan for more than twenty years, and majoring in murder, and he didn't know where the morgue was. I told him; and, thinking that a little *esprit de corps* wouldn't be out of place in the circumstances, and knowing how he hated moving vehicles, I was going to suggest that I go get the sedan from the garage and drive him myself, but he hung up. I went out front to the sergeant at the desk, whose name was Donovan, and told him I had identified the body but Mr. Wolfe was coming to take a look and I would stick around.

Donovan shook his head. "I only got orders about you."

"Nuts. You don't need orders. Any citizen and taxpayer can enter here to look for the remains of a relative or friend or enemy. Mr. Wolfe is a citizen and taxpayer. I make out his tax returns."

"I thought you was a private eye."

"I don't like the way you say it, but I am. Also I am an accountant, an amanuensis, and a cocklebur. Eight to five you never heard the word amanuensis and you never saw a cocklebur."

He didn't rile. "Yeah, I know, you're an educated wit. For Nero Wolfe I need orders. I know too much about him. Maybe he can get away with his tricks with Homicide and the DA, but not with me or none of my guests."

I didn't feel like arguing. Besides, I knew Donovan had a lot to put up with. When the door opened to admit a customer it might be anything from a pair of hoodlums wanting to collect data for a fake identification, to a hysterical female wanting to find out if she was a widow. That must have got on his nerves. So I merely explained it to him. I told him a few things about Marko Vukcic. That he was one of the only ten men I knew of that Nero Wolfe called by their first names. That for years he had dined once a month at Wolfe's table, and Wolfe and I had dined once a month at his restaurant. That he and Wolfe had been boys together in Montenegro, which was now a part of Yugoslavia. Donovan seemed to be listening, but he wasn't impressed. When I thought I had made the situation perfectly plain and stopped for breath, he turned to his phone, called Homicide, told them Wolfe was coming, and asked for instructions.

He hung up. "They'll call back," he informed me.

No bones got broken. His instructions came a minute before the door opened to admit Wolfe. I went and opened the gate in the railing, and Wolfe stepped through. "This way," I said and steered him to the corridor and along to the room.

The doctor had got the slug that had entered between the fifth and sixth ribs, and was going for the one lower down. I saw that from three paces off, where I stopped. Wolfe went on until the part of him that is farthest front, his middle, was touching the edge of the table. The doctor recognized him and spoke.

"I understand he was a friend of yours, Mr. Wolfe."

"He was," Wolfe said a little louder than necessary. He moved sidewise, reached a hand, put fingertips under Marko's chin, and pushed the jaw up so that the mouth closed; but when he took his hand away the lips parted again. He turned his head to frown at the doctor.

"That'll be arranged," the doctor assured him.

Wolfe nodded. He put fingers and a thumb into his vest pocket, withdrew them, and showed the doctor two small coins. "These are old dinars. I would like to fulfill a pledge made many years ago." The scientist said sure, go ahead, and Wolfe reached to Marko's face again, this time to place the coins on the eyes. The head was twisted a little, and he had to level it so the coins would stay put.

He turned away. "That's all. I have no further commitment to the clay. Come, Archie."

I followed him out and along the corridor to the front. The dick who had been my escort, there chinning with the sergeant, told me I didn't need to sign a statement and asked Wolfe if he verified the identification. Wolfe said he did and added, "Where's Mr. Cramer?"

"Sorry, I couldn't tell you."

Wolfe turned to me. "I told the driver to wait. You said East Fifty-fourth Street. Marko's address?"

"Right."

"We'll go there." He went, and I followed.

That taxi ride uptown broke a precedent. Wolfe's distrust of machinery is such that he is never in a condition to talk when he is being conveyed in something on wheels, even when I am driving, but that time he mastered it. He asked me questions about Marko Vukcic. I reminded him that he had known Marko a lot longer and better than I had, but he said there were some subjects which Marko had never discussed with him but might have with me—for example, his relations with women. I agreed that was logical, but said that as far as I knew Marko hadn't wasted time discussing his relations with women; he just went ahead and enjoyed them. I gave an instance. When, a couple of years previously, I had taken one named Sue Dondero to Rusterman's for dinner, Marko had cast an eye on her and contributed a bottle of one of his best clarets, and the next day had phoned to ask if I would care to give him her address and phone number, and I had done so and crossed her off. Wolfe asked why. I said to give her a break. Marko, sole owner of Rusterman's, was a wealthy man and a widower, and Sue might hook him. But she hadn't, Wolfe said. No, I agreed, as far as I knew there had been something wrong with the ignition.

"What the hell," the hackie grumbled, braking.

Having turned off Park Avenue into Fifty-fourth Street, he had made to cross Lexington, and a cop had waved him down. The cab stopped with a jerk that justified Wolfe's attitude toward machinery, and the hackie stuck his head out and objected.

"My fare's number is in that block, officer."

"Can't help it. Closed. Up or down."

He yanked the wheel, and we swung to the curb. I paid him, got out, and held the door, and Wolfe emerged. He stood a moment to take a deep breath, and we headed east. Ten paces along there was another cop, and a little farther on still another. Ahead, in the middle of the block, was a convention: police cars, spotlights, men working, and a gathering of citizens on the sidewalk across the street. On our side a stretch of the sidewalk was included in a roped-off area. As we approached it a cop got in the way and commanded, "Cross over and keep moving."

"I came here to look at this," Wolfe told him.

"I know. You and ten thousand more. Cross over."

"I am a friend of the man who was killed. My name is Nero Wolfe."

"Yeah, and mine's General MacArthur. Keep moving."

It might have developed into an interesting conversation if I hadn't caught sight, in one of the spotlights, of a familiar face and figure. I sang out, "Rowcliff!"

He turned and peered, stepped out of the glare and peered some more, and then approached. "Well?" he demanded.

Among all the array of Homicide personnel that Wolfe and I have had dealings with, high and low, Lieutenant Rowcliff is the only one of whom I am dead sure that our feelings are absolutely reciprocal. He would like to see me exactly where I would like to see him. So, having summoned him, I left it to Wolfe, who spoke.

"Good evening, Mr. Rowcliff. Is Mr. Cramer here?"

"No."

"Mr. Stebbins?"

"No."

"I want to see the spot where Mr. Vukcic died."

"You'll be in the way. We're working."

"So am I."

Rowcliff considered. He would have loved to order a couple of the help to take us to the river and dump us in, but the timing would have been bad. Since it was unheard of for Wolfe to leave his house to work as a matter of routine, he knew this was something extraordinary, and there was no telling how his superiors might react if he let his personal inclinations take charge. Of course he also knew that Wolfe and Vukcic had been close friends.

He hated to do it, but he said, "Come this way," and led us along to the front of the house and to the curb. "This is open to correction," he said, "but we think we've got it about right. Vukcic left the building alone. He passed between two parked cars to look west for a taxi. A car that was double-parked about twenty yards to the west—not a hack, a black or dark blue Ford sedan—started and came forward, and when it was about even with him an occupant of the car started shooting. It's not settled whether it was the driver or someone with him. We haven't found anyone that got a good look. He fell right there." Rowcliff pointed. "And stayed there. As you see, we're still at it here. Nothing from inside so far. Vukcic lived alone on the top floor, and there was no one there with him when he left. Of course he ate at his restaurant. Anything else?"

"No, thank you."

"Don't step off the curb. We're going over the pavement again in daylight." He left us.

Wolfe stood a moment, looking down at the spot on the pavement where Marko had dropped, then lifted his head to glance around. A moving spotlight hit his face and he blinked. Since that was the first time to my knowledge that he had ever started investigating a murder by a personal visit to the scene of the crime—not counting the occasions when he had been jerked loose by some other impulse, such as saving my life—I was curious to see how he would proceed. It was a chance he had seldom had.

He hopped on it by turning to me and asking, "Which way to the restaurant?"

I nodded west. "Up Lexington four blocks and around the corner. We can get a taxi—"

"No. We'll walk." He was off.

I went along, more and more impressed. The death of his oldest and closest friend had certainly hit him hard. He would have to cross five street intersections, with wheeled monsters waiting for him at every corner, ready to spring, but he strode on regardless, as if it were a perfectly natural and normal procedure.

2

Things were not natural and normal at Rusterman's. The six-foot, square-jawed doorman opened for us and let us pass through, and then blurted to Wolfe's broad back, "Is it true, Mr. Wolfe?" Wolfe ignored it and went on, but I turned and gave him a nod. Wolfe marched on past the cloakroom, so I did likewise. In the big front room, which you crossed on your way to the dining room, and which Marko had called the lounge but which I called the bar because it had one at its far side, there were only a few customers scattered around at the tables, since it was nearly nine-thirty and by that hour the clientele were inside, busy with *perdrix en casserole* or *tournedos Beauharnais*. The tone of the place, subdued but not stiff, had of course been set by Marko, with the able assistance of Felix, Leo, and Joe, and I had never seen one of them break training by so much as a flicker of an eyelash until that evening. As we entered, Leo, standing at the entrance to the dining room, caught sight of us and started toward us, then wheeled and went back and shouted into the dining room, "Joe!"

There were murmurs from the few scattered customers in the bar. Leo wheeled again, clapped his hand to his mouth, crossed to us, and stood staring at Wolfe. I saw sweat on his brow, another misdemeanor. In restaurants that sell squabs for five bucks or more apiece, captains and headwaiters are not allowed to sweat.

"It's true," Leo hissed, his hand still covering his mouth. He seemed to be shrinking in front of our eyes, and he was none too big anyway—not a shorty, but quite narrow up to his shoulders, where he spread out some. He let the hand fall, but kept his voice down. "Good God, Mr. Wolfe, is it true? It must—"

A hand gripped his shoulder from behind. Joe was there, and Joe was built for gripping. His years with Marko had polished him so that he no longer looked like a professional wrestler, but he had the size and lines.

"Get hold of yourself, damn it," he muttered at Leo. "Did you want a table, Mr. Wolfe? Marko's not here."

"I know he's not. He's dead. I don't—"

"Please not so loud. Please. Then you know he's dead?"

"Yes. I saw him. I don't want a table. Where's Felix?"

"Felix is up in the office with two men. They came and said Marko had been shot and killed. He left the dinner to Leo and me and took them upstairs. No one has been told except Vincent at the door because Felix said Marko would not want the dinner to be spoiled. It makes me want to vomit to see them eating and drinking and laughing, but it may be that Felix is right—and the face he had, it was no time to argue. Do you think he is right? I would myself want to put everybody out and lock the door."

Wolfe shook his head. "No. Felix is right. Let them eat. I'm going upstairs. Archie?" He headed for the elevator.

The third floor of the building had been remodeled a year or so previously to provide an office in front and three private dining rooms to the rear. Wolfe opened the door to the office, without knocking, and entered, and I followed. The three men in chairs over by a table turned to us. Felix Martin, a wiry, compact little guy with quick black eyes and gray hair—in his uniform, of course —got up and started toward us. The other two stayed put. They rated uniforms too, one an inspector's and the other a sergeant's, but didn't wear them to work.

"Mr. Wolfe," Felix said. You didn't expect a voice so deep from one that size, even after you were acquainted with it. "The worst thing on earth! The worst thing! Everything was going so fine!"

Wolfe gave him a nod and went on by to Inspector Cramer. "What have you got?" he demanded.

Cramer controlled himself. His big round face was always a little redder, and his cold gray eyes a little colder, when he was exercising restraint. "I know," he conceded, "that you're interested in this one personally. Sergeant Stebbins was saying to me that we would have to make allowances, and I agreed. Also this is one time when I'll gladly take all the help you'll give, so let's all take it easy. Bring chairs, Goodwin."

For Wolfe I went and got the one at Marko's desk because it was nearer the size desired than any of the others. For myself I wasn't so particular. As I was joining the party Wolfe was demanding, not taking it easy at all, "Have you got anything?"

Cramer tolerated it. "Anything hot, no. The murder was committed just two hours ago."

"I know." Wolfe tried to shift to a more acceptable position in the chair. "Of course you have asked Felix if he can name the murderer." His eyes moved. "Can you, Felix?"

"No, sir. I can't believe it."

"You have no suggestions?"

"No, sir."

"Where have you been since seven o'clock?"

"Me?" The black eyes were steady at Wolfe. "I've been right here."

"All the time?"

"Yes, sir."

"Where has Joe been?"

"Right here too."

"All the time?"

"Yes, sir."

"You're sure of that?"

"Yes, sir."

"Where has Leo been?"

"Here too, all the time. Where else would we be at dinnertime? And when Marko didn't come—"

"If you don't mind," Cramer cut in, "I've already got this. I don't need—"

"I do," Wolfe told him. "I have a double responsibility, Mr. Cramer. If you assume that I intend to see that the murderer of my friend is caught and brought to account with the least possible delay, you are correct. But another onus is on me. Under my friend's will, as you will soon learn officially, I am executor of his estate and trustee ad interim. I am not a legatee. This restaurant is the only substantial asset, and it was left to six of the men who work here, with the biggest shares going to the three men I have just inquired about. They were told of the terms of the will when it was altered a year ago. Mr. Vukcic had no close relatives, and none at all in this country."

Cramer was eying Felix. "What's this place worth?"

Felix shrugged. "I don't know."

"Did you know that if Vukcic died you would be part owner of it?"

"Certainly. You heard what Mr. Wolfe said."

"You hadn't mentioned it."

"Good God!" Felix was out of his chair, on his feet, quivering. He stood a moment, got the quivering stopped, sat down again, and leaned forward at Cramer. "It takes time to mention things, officer. There is nothing about Marko and me, about him and us here, that I will not be glad to mention. He was hard about the work, hard and sometimes rough, and he could roar, but he was a great man. Listen, and I'll tell you how I feel about him. Here I am. Here at my side is Marko." Felix tapped his elbow with a finger. "A man appears and points a gun at him and is going to shoot. I jump to put myself in front of Marko. Because I am a big hero? No. I am no hero at all. Only because that's how I feel about Marko. Ask Mr. Wolfe."

Cramer grunted. "He was just asking you where you've been since seven o'clock. What about Leo and Joe? How do they feel about Marko?"

Felix straightened up. "They will tell you."

"How do you think they feel?"

"Not like me because they are not of my temperament. But to suppose it possible they would try to hurt him—never. Joe would not jump in front of Marko to stop the bullet. He would jump for the man with the gun. Leo—I don't know, but it is my opinion he would yell for help, for the police. I don't sneer at that; it would take more than a coward to yell for help."

"It's too bad one of you wasn't there when it happened," Cramer observed. It seemed to me uncalled-for. Obviously he didn't like Felix. "And you say you have no knowledge whatever of anyone who might have wanted Vukcic dead?"

"No, sir, I haven't." Felix hesitated. "Of course there is one thing—or I should say, more than one. There is women. Marko was a gallant man. Only one thing could ever take him away from his work here: a woman. I will not say that to him a woman was more important than a sauce—he could not be accused of ever neglecting a sauce—but he had a warm eye for women. After all, it was not essential for him to be in the kitchen when everything was planned and ready, and Joe and Leo and I are competent for the tables and service, so if Marko chose to enjoy dinner at his own table with a guest there was no feeling about it among us. But it might have caused feeling among others. I have no personal knowledge. Myself, I am married with four children and have no time, but everybody knows that women can arouse strong feelings."

"So he was a chaser," Sergeant Stebbins growled.

"Pfui!" Wolfe growled back at him. "Gallantry is not always a lackey for lust."

Which was a fine sentiment with company present, but the fact remained that Wolfe had himself asked me about Marko's relations with women. For the next three hours, there in Marko's office, that subject came close to monopolizing the conversation. Felix was dismissed and told to send Joe up. Other Homicide dicks arrived, and an assistant district attorney, and waiters and cooks were brought up for sessions in the private dining rooms; and with each one, after a few personal questions, the emphasis was on the female guests who had eaten at Marko's own table in the past year or so. By the time Wolfe was willing to call it a day and got himself erect and stretched, it was well after midnight and a respectable bulk of data had been collected, including the names of seven women, none of them notorious.

Cramer rasped at Wolfe, "You said you intend to see that the murderer is caught and brought to account with the least possible delay. I don't want to butt in, but I'll just mention that the Police Department will be glad to help."

Wolfe ignored the sarcasm, thanked him politely, and headed for the door.

On the way downtown in the cab I remarked that I had been pleased to note that no one had pronounced the name of Sue Dondero. Wolfe, on the edge of the seat, gripping the strap, set to jump for his life, made no reply.

"Though I must say," I added, "there were enough of them without her. They're not going to like it much. By noon tomorrow there'll be thirty-five dicks, five to a candidate, working on that list. I mention it merely for your consideration, in case you are thinking of telling me to have all seven of them in the office at eleven in the morning."

"Shut up," he muttered.

Usually I react to that command vocally, but that time I thought it just as well to obey. When we rolled to the curb in front of the old brownstone on West Thirty-fifth Street I paid the driver, got out and held the door for Wolfe, mounted the seven steps to the stoop, and opened the door with my key. After Wolfe had crossed the threshold I closed the door and put the chain bolt on, and when I turned Fritz was there and was telling Wolfe, "There's a lady to see you, sir."

It popped into my mind that it would save me a lot of trouble if they were going to drop in without being invited, but Fritz was adding, "It's your daughter, Mrs. Britton."

There was a faint suggestion of reproach in Fritz's tone. For years he had disapproved of Wolfe's attitude toward his adopted daughter. A dark-haired Balkan girl with an accent, she had appeared out of the blue one day long ago and proceeded to get Wolfe involved in an operation that had been no help to the bank account. When it was all over she had announced that she didn't intend to return to her native land, but neither did she intend to take any advantage of the fact that she had in her possession a paper, dated in Zagreb years before, establishing her as the adopted daughter of Nero Wolfe. She had made good on both intentions, having got a job with a Fifth Avenue travel agency, and having, within a year, married its owner, one William R. Britton. No friction had developed between Mr. and Mrs. Britton and Mr. Wolfe, because for friction you must have contact, and there had been none. Twice a year, on her birthday and on New Year's Day, Wolfe sent her a bushel of orchids from his choicest plants, but that was all, except that he had gone to the funeral when Britton died of a heart attack in 1950.

That was what Fritz disapproved of. He thought any man, even Nero Wolfe, should invite his daughter, even an adopted one, to dinner once in a while. When he expressed that opinion to me, as he did occasionally, I told him that he knew damn well that Carla found Wolfe as irritating as he found her, so what was the use?

I followed Wolfe into the office. Carla was in the red leather chair. As we entered she got up to face us and said indignantly, "I've been waiting here over two hours!"

Wolfe went and took her hand and bowed over it. "At least you had a comfortable chair," he said courteously, and went to the one behind his desk, the only one in the world he thoroughly approved of, and sat. Carla offered me a hand with her mind elsewhere, and I took it without bowing.

"Fritz didn't know where you were," she told Wolfe.

"No," he agreed.

"But he said you knew about Marko."

"Yes."

"I heard it on the radio. I was going to go to the restaurant to see Leo, then I thought I would go to the police, and then I decided to come here. I suppose you were surprised, but I wasn't."

She sounded bitter. She looked bitter too, but I had to admit it didn't make her any less attractive. With her dark eyes flashing, she might still have been the young Balkan damsel who had bounded in on me years before.

Wolfe's eyes had narrowed at her. "If you are saying that you came here and waited two hours for me on account of Marko's death, I must ask why. Were you attached to him?"

"Yes."

Wolfe shut his eyes.

"If I know," she said, "what that word means—attached. If you mean attached as a woman to a man, no, of course not. Not like that."

Wolfe opened his eyes. "Then how?"

"We were attached in our devotion to a great and noble cause! The freedom of our people! And your people! And there you sit making faces! Marko has told me—he has asked you to help us with your brains and your money, and you refused!"

"He didn't tell me you were in it. He didn't mention you."

"I suppose not." She was scornful. "He knew that would make you sneer even more. Here you are, rich and fat and happy with your fine home and fine food and your glass rooms on the roof with ten thousand orchids for you to smirk at, and with this Archie Goodwin for a slave to do all the work and take all the danger! What do you care if the people of the land you came from are groaning under the heel of the oppressor, with the light of their liberty smothered and the fruits of their labor snatched from them and their children at the point of the sword? *Stop making faces!*"

Wolfe leaned back and sighed deeply. "Apparently," he said dryly, "I must give you a lecture. I grimaced neither at your impudence nor at your sentiment, but at your diction and style. I contemn clichés, especially those that have been corrupted by fascists and communists. Such phrases as 'great and noble cause' and 'fruits of their labor' have been given an ineradicable stink by Hitler and Stalin and all their vermin brood. Besides, in this century of the overwhelming triumph of science, the appeal of the cause of human freedom is no longer that it is great and noble; it is more or less than that; it is essential. It is no greater or nobler than the cause of edible food or the cause of effective shelter. Man must have freedom or he will cease to exist as man. The despot, whether fascist or communist, is no longer restricted to such puny tools as the heel or the sword or even the machine gun; science has provided weapons that can give him the planet; and only men who are willing to die for freedom have any chance of living for it."

"Like you?" She was disdainful. "No. Like Marko. He died."

Wolfe flapped a hand. "I'll get to Marko. As for me, no one has ordained you as my monitor. I make my contributions to the cause of freedom—they are mostly financial—through those channels and agencies that seem to me most efficient. I shall not submit a list of them for your inspection and judgment. I refused to contribute to Marko's project because I distrusted it. Marko was himself headstrong, gullible, oversanguine, and naïve. He had—"

"For shame! He's dead, and you insult—"

"That will do!" he roared. It stopped her. He went down a few decibels. "You share the common fallacy, but I don't. I do not insult Marko. I pay him the tribute of speaking of him and feeling about him precisely as I did when he lived; the insult would be to smear his corpse with the honey excreted by my fear of death. He had no understanding of the forces he was trying to direct from a great distance, no control of them, and no effective check on their honor or fidelity. For all he knew, some of them may be agents of Tito, or even of Moscow—"

"That isn't true! He knew all about them—anyway, the leaders. He wasn't an idiot, and neither am I. We do check on them, all the time, and I— Where are you going?"

Wolfe had shoved his chair back and was on his feet. "You may not be an idiot," he told her, "but I am. I was letting this become a pointless brawl when I should have known better. I'm hungry. I was in the middle of dinner when the news came of Marko's death. It took my appetite. I tried to finish anyway, but I couldn't swallow. With an empty stomach, I'm a dunce, and I'm going to the kitchen and eat something." He glanced up at the wall clock. "It's nearly two o'clock. Will you join me?"

She shook her head. "I had dinner. I couldn't eat."

"Archie?"

I said I could use a glass of milk and followed him out. In the kitchen Fritz greeted us by putting down his magazine, leaving his chair, telling Wolfe, "Starving the live will not profit the dead," and going to open the refrigerator door.

"The turkey," Wolfe said, "and the cheese and pineapple. I've never heard that before. Montaigne?"

"No, sir." Fritz put the turkey on the table, uncovered it, and got the slicer and handed it to Wolfe. "I made it up. I knew you would have to send for me, or come, and I wished to have an appropriate remark ready for you."

"I congratulate you." Wolfe was wielding the knife. "To be taken for Montaigne is a peak few men can reach."

I had only had milk in mind, but Fritz's personal version of cottage cheese with fresh pineapple soaked in white wine is something that even a Vishinsky wouldn't veto. Also Wolfe offered me a wing and a drumstick, and it would have been unsociable to refuse. Fritz fixed a tasty tray and took it in to Carla, but when Wolfe and I rejoined her, some twenty minutes later, it was still untouched on the table at her elbow. I admit it could have been that she was too upset to eat, but I suspected her. She knew damn well that it irritated Wolfe to see good food turned down.

Back at his desk, he frowned at her. "Let's see if we can avoid contention. You said earlier that you supposed I was surprised, but that you weren't. Surprised at what?"

She was returning the frown. "I don't—oh, of course. Surprised that Marko was murdered."

"And you weren't?"

"No."

"Why not?"

"Because of what he was doing. Do you know what he was doing?"

"Circumstantially, no. Tell me."

"Well, in the past three years he has put nearly sixty thousand dollars of his own money into the cause, and he has collected more than half a million. He has gone seven times to Italy to confer with leaders of the movement who crossed the Adriatic to meet him. He has sent twelve men and two women over from this country to help—three Montenegrins, three Slovenians, two Croats, and six Serbs. He has had things printed and arranged for them to get to the peasants. He has sent over many tons of supplies, many different things—"

"Weapons? Guns?"

She gave it a thought. "I don't know. Of course, that would be against the law—American law. Marko had a high regard for American law."

Wolfe nodded. "Not unmerited. I didn't know he was in so deep. So you are assuming that he was murdered because of these activities. That either Belgrade or Moscow regarded him as a menace, or at least an intolerable nuisance, and arranged for his removal. Is that it?"

"Yes."

"Belgrade or Moscow?"

Carla hesitated. "I don't know. Of course there are those who secretly work with the Russians all over Yugoslavia, but more in Montenegro than other parts, because it is next to Albania, and Albania is ruled by the puppets of the Russians."

"So are Hungary and Rumania and Bulgaria."

"Yes, but you know the border between Montenegro and Albania. You know those mountains."

"I do indeed. Or I did." From the look on Wolfe's face, the emotions aroused by the memory were mixed. "I was nine years old the first time I climbed the Black Mountain." He shrugged it off. "Whether Belgrade or Moscow, you think they had an agent in New York, or sent one, to deal with Marko. Do you?"

"Of course!"

"Not of course if it is merely a surmise. Can you validate it? Have you any facts?"

"I have the fact that they hated him and he was a danger to them."

Wolfe shook his head. "Not that kind. Something specific—a name, an act, a thing said."

"No."

"Very well. I accept your surmise as worthy of inquiry. How many persons are there in and around New York, other than contributors of money, who have been associated with Marko in this?"

"Why, altogether, about two hundred."

"I mean closely associated. In his confidence."

She had to think. "Four or five. Six, counting me."

"Give me their names and addresses and phone numbers. Archie, take them down."

I got my notebook and pen and was ready, but nothing came. I looked at her. She was sitting with her dark Montenegrin eyes focused on Wolfe, her chin up and her lips pressed together.

"Well?" he demanded.

"I don't trust you," she said.

Naturally he would have liked to tell me to bounce her, and I must say I couldn't have blamed him, but she wasn't just a prospective client with a checkbook. She had or might have something he needed for paying a personal debt. So he merely barked at her, "Then why the devil did you come here?"

They glared at each other. It was not a sight to impel me to hurry up and get married and have a daughter, especially not an adopted one.

She broke the tableau. "I came because I had to do something. I knew if I went to the police they would want me to tell everything about us, and I couldn't do that because some of the things some of us do—well, you asked about sending weapons." She fluttered a hand. "But Marko was your good friend, and he thought you were his, and you have a famous reputation for catching murderers, and after all I still have that paper that says I am your daughter, so I came without really thinking. Now I don't know. You refused to give money to the cause. When I speak of freedom and the oppressor you make a face. It is true you have Montenegrin blood, you are of the race that fought back the savage Turks for five hundred years, but so are others, still in those mountains, who are licking the bloody feet of the tyrant. Have I looked into your heart? How do I know who you serve? How do I know if you too get your orders from Belgrade or Moscow?"

"You don't," Wolfe said bluntly.

She stared at him.

"You are not a fool," he assured her. "On the contrary, you would be a fool if you took my probity for granted, as little as you know of me. As far as you know it's quite possible that I'm a blackguard. But you haven't thought it through. To test your surmise about the death of Marko I need some facts from you, but what are they? Names and addresses and dates—things that are already known to the enemy. I have no means of convincing you that I am not verminous, so I offer a suggestion. I will ask you questions. You will assume that I am a Communist, owing allegiance either to Belgrade or Moscow, no matter which. You will also assume—my vanity insists on it—that I am not far from the top in the councils of depravity. So. Each question I put, ask yourself if it isn't extremely likely either that I already know the answer or that it is readily available to me. If yes, tell me. If no, don't. The way I act on the information will show you whether you should trust me, but that's unimportant."

She was concentrating on it. "It's a trick."

He nodded. "And rather ingenious. For the record, I say that your misgiving about me is groundless; but assuming that I am of the enemy, I'll certainly try to pry something out of you that I don't already have, so you must keep your wit sharp. Shall we start and see how it goes?"

She didn't like it. "You might tell the police. We are not criminals, but we have a right to our secrets, and the police could make it very difficult."

"Bosh. You can't have everything. You can't have me both a Communist agent and a police informer; I'm not a chameleon. You're making it a travesty, and you might as well go. I'll manage without you."

She studied him. "All right. Ask me."

"Eat something first. That food is still palatable."

"No, thank you."

"Beer, then? A glass of wine? Whisky?"

"No, thank you. Nothing."

"I'm thirsty. Archie? Beer, please. Two bottles."

I went to the kitchen for it.

3

Three weeks and eight hours later, at eleven in the morning of the second Friday in April, Wolfe descended from the plant rooms in his elevator, entered the office, crossed to the chair at his desk, and sat.

As usual, I had opened the morning mail, gone through it, and put it on his blotter under a paperweight. "That memo on top needs immediate attention," I told him. "Cartright of Consolidated Products is being gypped again, or thinks he is. Last time he paid our bill for twelve grand without a squeak. You're to call him."

He shoved the paperweight off with such enthusiasm that it rolled across the desk and off to the floor. Then he picked up the pile of mail, squeezed it into a ball between his hands, and dropped it into his wastebasket.

Of course it was childish, since he knew darned well I would retrieve it later, but it was a nice gesture, and I fully appreciated it. The humor he was in, it wouldn't have surprised me any if he had taken the other paperweight, a hunk of carved ebony that had once been used by a man named Mortimer to crack his wife's skull, and fired it at me. And the humor I was in, I probably wouldn't have bothered to dodge.

There had been plenty of activity during those 512 hours. Saul Panzer, Fred Durkin, and Orrie Cather had all been summoned the first morning and given errands, and had been paid a total of $3,143.87, including expenses. I had put in a good sixteen hours a day, part in the office and part on the go. Wolfe had worked on thirty-one different people, mostly at his desk, but for five of them who couldn't be wrangled in he had gone outdoors and traveled, something he had never done for a fee. Among the hours he had spent on the phone had been time for six calls to London, five to Paris, and three to Bari in Italy.

Of course all that had been only a dab compared to the capers of the cops. As the days went by and lead after lead petered out, things would have simmered down if it hadn't been for the papers. They kept hot on it for two reasons: first, they had a suspicion there were international complications and wanted to smoke them out; and second, they thought it was the joke of the year that Nero Wolfe's best friend had been croaked, and Wolfe was supposed to be working on it, but apparently no one had even been nominated for a charge, let alone elected. So the papers kept it going, and the law couldn't relax a little even if it wanted to. Cramer had called on Wolfe five times, and Stebbins more than that, and Wolfe had been downtown twice to conferences at the DA's office.

We had dined nine times at Rusterman's, and Wolfe had insisted on paying the check, which probably broke another precedent—for an executor of an estate. Wolfe went early to spend an hour in the kitchen, and twice he raised hell—once about a Mornay sauce and once about a dish which the menu called *Suprêmes de Volaille en Papillote*. I would have suspected he was merely being peevish if the look on the chefs' faces hadn't indicated that he was absolutely right.

Of course Cramer and his army had covered all the routine. The car the shots had been fired from had been hot, stolen an hour earlier from where it had been parked on West Fifty-sixth Street, and abandoned soon after the shooting, on Second Avenue. The scientists, from fingerprint-lifters and bullet-gazers on up, had supplied a lot of dope but no answers, and the same goes for the three or four dozen who went after the woman angle, which after a couple of weeks was spread to include several more, going back four years instead of one, in addition to the original seven. One day Cramer told Wolfe he could go over the whole file if he wanted to, some three hundred reports of sessions with eighty-four people, and Wolfe took him up. He spent eleven hours at it, at the DA's office. The only result was that he made nine suggestions, all of which were followed, and none of which opened a crack.

He left the women and the feelings they had aroused to the cops, and kept Saul and Fred and Orrie, not to mention me, on the international angle. A great deal was accomplished. We learned a lot about the ten organizations listed in the Manhattan phone directory whose names began with "Yugoslav." Also that Serbs don't care much for Bosnians, and less for Croats. Also that the overwhelming majority of the Yugoslavs in New York are anti-Tito, and practically all of them are anti-Russian. Also that eight per cent of the doormen on Park Avenue are Yugoslavs. Also that New Yorkers who are, or whose parents were, from Yugoslavia are fairly cagey about opening up to strangers and are inclined to shut the valves tight if they get the notion that you're being nosy. Also many other things, including a few that seemed to offer a faint hope of starting a trail that could lead to the bird who had put three bullets in Marko Vukcic; but they all blew a fuse.

In the first four days of the three weeks we saw Carla twice more. Saturday noon she came and asked Wolfe if it was true, as announced, that there would be no funeral. He said yes, in accordance with Marko's wish, in writing, that he be cremated and that there should be no services. She objected that there were hundreds of people who wanted to show their respect and love for him, and Wolfe replied that if a man's prejudices were to be humored at all after he was no longer around to impose them, surely he should be allowed to dictate the disposal of his own clay. The best she could get was a promise that the ashes would be delivered to her. Then she had asked about progress in the investigation, and he had said he would report when there was anything worth reporting, which hadn't satisfied her at all.

She came again late Monday afternoon. I had had enough of answering the damn doorbell and left it to Fritz. She came charging in and across to Wolfe's desk, and blurted at him, "You told the police! They've had Leo down there all day, and this afternoon they went to Paul's place and took him too! I knew I shouldn't trust you!"

"Please—" Wolfe tried, but she had pulled the cork and it had to come. He leaned back and shut his eyes. She went on ranting until she had to stop for breath. He opened his eyes and inquired, "Are you through?"

"Yes! I'm *all* through! With you!"

"Then there's no more to say." He jerked his head. "There's the door."

She went to the red leather chair and sat on the edge. "You said you wouldn't tell the police about us!"

"I did not." He was disgusted and tired. "Since you mistrust me you will credit nothing I say, so why should I waste words?"

"I want to hear them!"

"Very well. I have said nothing to the police about you or your associates or your surmise about Marko's death, but they are not donkeys, and I knew they would get onto it. I'm surprised it took them so long. Have they come to you?"

"No."

"They will, and it's just as well. I have only four men, and we are getting nowhere. They have regiments. If you tell them about coming to see me Thursday night they'll resent my withholding it, but that's of no consequence. Tell them or not, as you please. As for giving them the information you gave me, do as you please about that too. It might be better to let them dig it up for themselves, since in the process they might uncover something you don't know about. So much for that. Since you're here I may as well tell you what progress I have made. None." He raised his voice. "None!"

"Nothing at all?"

"Nothing."

"I won't tell the police what I told you, but that doesn't matter. If you haven't, you will." Suddenly she was on her feet with her arms spread out. "Oh, I need you! I need to ask you—I need to tell you what I must do! But I won't! I won't!" She turned and was gone. She moved so fast that when I got to the hall she already had the front door open. By the time I reached it she was out and the door was shut. Through the one-way glass panel I saw her going down the steps, sure and supple, like a fencer or a dancer, which was reasonable, since she had been both.

That was the last we saw of her during the three weeks, but not the last we heard. Word of her came four days later, Friday morning, from an unexpected quarter. Wolfe and I were having a session in the office with Saul and Fred and Orrie, one of a series, trying to think up some more stones to look under, when the doorbell rang and a moment later Fritz entered to announce, "A man to see you, sir. Mr. Stahl of the Federal Bureau of Investigation."

Wolfe's brows went up; he glanced at me, I shook my head, and he told Fritz to bring the man in. The hired help, including me, exchanged glances. An FBI man was no rare spectacle for any of us, but Stahl wasn't just one of the swarm; he had worked up to where he gave more orders than he took, and the word was that by Christmas he would be occupying the big corner room down at 290 Broadway. He didn't often go out to run errands, so it was quite an event for him to drop in, and we all knew it and appreciated it. When he entered and marched across to Wolfe's desk and offered a hand, Wolfe even did him the honor of rising to shake, which showed how desperate the situation was.

"It's been quite a while since I saw you last," Stahl observed. "Three years?"

Wolfe nodded. "I believe so." He indicated the red leather chair, which Fred Durkin had vacated. "Be seated."

"Thank you. May we make this private?"

"If necessary." Wolfe glanced at the trio, and they got up and filed out and shut the door. Stahl went and sat. Medium-sized and beginning to be a little short on hair, he wasn't impressive to look at, except his jaw, which came straight down a good two inches and then jutted forward. He was well designed for ramming. He gave me a look, and Wolfe said, "As you know, Mr. Goodwin is privy to all that I hear and see and do."

Stahl knew no such thing, because it wasn't true. I'd like to have a nickel—or make it a dime, with the dollar where it is—for every item Wolfe has withheld from me just for the hell of it.

Stahl merely nodded. "In a way," he said, "you might consider this a personal matter—personal to you. We want to get in touch with your daughter, Mrs. Carla Britton."

Wolfe's shoulders went up an eighth of an inch and down again. "Then do so. Her address is nine-eighty-four Park Avenue. Her phone number is Poplar three-three-oh-four-three."

"I know. She hasn't been there since Tuesday, three days ago. She left no word with anyone. Nobody knows where she is. Do you?"

"No, sir."

Stahl passed a fingertip across the prow of his chin. "One thing I like about you, you prefer things put plain and straight. I've never seen the room upstairs, right above yours, that you call the South Room, but I've heard about it. You've been known to use it for guests, clients and otherwise, from time to time. Do you mind if I go up and take a look at it?"

Wolfe shrugged again. "It will be wasted energy, Mr. Stahl."

"That's all right, I have some to spare."

"Then go ahead. Archie?"

"Yes, sir." I went and opened the door to the hall and, with Stahl at my heels, went to the stairs and mounted the two flights. At the door to the South Room I stepped aside and told him politely, "You go first. She might shoot." He opened the door and went in, and I crossed the sill. "It's nice and sunny," I said, "and the beds are first-rate." I pointed. "That door's the bathroom, and that's a closet. A girl named Priscilla Eads once rented it for fifty bucks a day, but she's dead. I'm pretty sure Mr. Wolfe would shade that for a prominent public servant like you. . . ."

I saved it because he was moving. He knew he had drawn a blank, but he went and opened the door to the bathroom and looked in, and on his way back detoured to open the door to the closet for a glance. As he retreated to the hall I told his back, "Sorry you don't like it. Would you care to take a look at my room just down the hall? Or the plant rooms, just one flight up?" I kept trying to sell him on the way downstairs. "You might like Mr. Wolfe's own room better—the bed has a black silk coverlet. I'll be glad to show it to you. Or if you want a bargain there's a couch in the front room."

He entered the office, returned to his chair, focused on Wolfe, and inquired, "Where is she?"

Wolfe focused back. "I don't know."

"When did you see her last?"

Wolfe straightened in his chair. "Aren't you being crass, sir? If this inquisition isn't gratuitous, warrant it."

"I told you she has been away from her home for three days and we can't find her."

"That doesn't justify your tramping in here and branding me a liar."

"I didn't."

"Certainly you did. When I said I didn't know where she was you proceeded to search my house for her. When you didn't find her you demanded to know where she is. Pfui."

Stahl smiled like a diplomat. "Well, Goodwin evened it up by riding me. I guess I'd better start over. You know we are aware of your qualities and abilities. We know you don't need to have a thing all spelled out for you. I didn't think I'd have to tell you that my coming here and asking about Mrs. Britton meant that we are interested in some aspects of the investigation into the murder of Marko Vukcic, that we have reason to think he was engaged in activities that are the proper concern of the federal government, that your daughter was associated with him in those activities, and that her disappearance is therefore a matter for inquiry. I might as well add that as yet we have no evidence that you have been connected with those activities in any way, either loyally with Vukcic or subversively."

Wolfe snorted. "I have not applied for a certificate of virtue."

"No. You wouldn't. I might also add that I have discussed this with Inspector Cramer and he knows I'm here. We learned of Mrs. Britton's involvement only last night. To put it all on the table, her disappearance suggests two possibilities: one, that she has been dealt with as Vukcic was, by the same person or persons; and two, that she was double-crossing Vukcic, working for the Communists, and was in on the plan to kill him and helped with it, and it was getting too hot for her here. Is that enough to warrant the question, when did you see her last?"

"The answer won't help you much. In this room four days ago, Monday afternoon, about six-thirty. She was here not more than ten minutes. She gave no hint of an intention to disappear or of any reason for such an intention. Of your two possibilities, I advise you to dismiss the second, but that will not necessarily leave only the first; there are others."

"Why dismiss the second?"

Wolfe cocked his head. "Mr. Stahl. The miasma of distrust that has poisoned the air we breathe is so pervasive that it reduced you to the fatuity of going up to look in my South Room. I would have liked then to tell you to leave, but I couldn't afford the gesture because I'm up a stump. I've been hunting the murderer of Marko Vukcic for eight days now, and am floundering in a bog, and if there is any chance that you can offer a straw I want it. So I'll tell you all I know about Mrs. Britton's connection with this affair."

He did so in full, making no objection to Stahl's getting out his notebook and taking notes. At the end he observed, "You asked why I advised you to dismiss the second of your two possibilities, and that's my answer. You will discount it as your caution may dictate. Now I would appreciate a straw. With your prerogatives and resources, you must have one to toss me."

I had never heard or seen him being abject before, and in spite of the strain he was under I didn't care for it. Stahl didn't either. He smiled, and I would have liked to wipe it off with one hand. He glanced at his wristwatch and rose from the chair. He didn't even bother to say he was late for an appointment. "This is something new," he stated, "Nero Wolfe asking for a straw. We'll think it over. If you hear from your daughter, or of her, we'll appreciate it if you'll let us know."

When I returned to the office after letting him out I told Wolfe, "There are times when I wish I hadn't been taught manners. It would have been a pleasure to kick his ass down the stoop."

"Get them in here," he growled. "We must find her."

But we didn't. We certainly tried. It is true that Stahl and Cramer had it on us in prerogatives and resources, but Fred Durkin knows how to dig, Orrie Cather is no slouch, Saul Panzer is the best operative north of the equator, and I have a good sense of smell. For the next six days we concentrated on picking up a trace of her, but we might as well have stayed up in my room and played pinochle. Not a glimmer. It was during that period that Wolfe made most of his long-distance calls to London and Paris and Bari. At the time I thought he was just expanding the bog to flounder in, and I still think he was merely making some wild stabs, but I have to admit it was Hitchcock in London and Bodin in Paris who finally put him onto Telesio in Bari; and if he hadn't found Telesio we might still be looking for Carla and for the murderer of Marko. I also admit that I regard myself as the one for hunches around this joint, and I resent anyone horning in, even Wolfe. His part is supposed to be brainwork. However, what matters is that if he hadn't got in touch with Telesio and talked with him forty bucks' worth, in Italian, the Tuesday after Stahl's visit, he would never have got the calls from Telesio.

There were three of them. The first one came Thursday afternoon while I was out tracking down a lead that Fred thought might get somewhere. When I got back to the office just before dinner Wolfe snapped at me, "Get them here this evening for new instructions."

"Yes, sir." I went to my desk, sat, and swiveled to face him. "Any for me?"

"We'll see." He was glowering. "I suppose you have to know. I had a call from Bari. It is now past midnight in Italy. Mrs. Britton arrived in Bari at noon and left a few hours later in a small boat to cross the Adriatic."

I goggled. "How the hell did she get to Italy?"

"I don't know. My informant may, but he thinks it necessary to use discretion on the phone. I am taking it that she's there. For the present we shall keep it to ourselves. The new instructions for Saul and Fred and Orrie will be on the ground that it is more urgent to disclose the murderer than to find Mrs. Britton. As for—"

"Saul will smell it. He'll know."

"Let him. He won't know where she is, and even if he did, no matter. Who is more trustworthy, Saul or you?"

"I would say Saul. I have to watch myself pretty close."

"Yes. As for Mr. Cramer and Mr. Stahl, we owe them nothing. If they're still looking for her they may find someone else." He sighed way down, leaned back, and shut his eyes, presumably to try to devise a program for the hired help.

So the first call from Telesio didn't stop operations, it merely changed the strategy. With the second one it was different. It came four days later, at two-thirty a.m. Monday. Of course it was half-past eight in the morning at Bari, but I was in no shape to manage that calculation as I yanked myself enough awake to realize that I hadn't dreamed it—the phone was ringing. I rolled over and reached for it. When I heard that it was a call from Bari, Italy, for Mr. Nero Wolfe I told the operator to hold it, turned on the light, went and flipped the switch controlling the gong that splits the air if anyone steps within ten feet of the door of Wolfe's room at night, and then descended one flight and knocked. His voice came, and I opened the door and entered and pushed the wall switch.

He made a magnificent mound under the electric blanket, lying there blinking at me. "Well?" he demanded.

"Phone call from Italy. Collect."

He refuses to concede the possibility that he will ever be willing to talk on the phone while in bed, so the only instrument in his room is on a table over by a window. I went and switched it on. He pushed the blanket back, maneuvered his bulk around and up, made it over to the table in his bare feet, and took the phone. Even in those circumstances I was impressed by the expanse of his yellow pajamas.

I stood and listened to a lingo that I didn't have in stock, but not for long. He didn't even get his money's worth, for it had been less than three minutes when he cradled the thing, gave me a dirty look, padded back to the bed, lowered himself onto its edge, and pronounced some word that I wouldn't know how to spell.

He went on. "That was Signor Telesio. His discretion has been aggravated into obscurity. He said he had news for me, that was clear enough, but he insisted on coding it. His words, translated: 'The man you seek is within sight of the mountain.' He would not elucidate, and it would have been imprudent to press him."

I said, "I've never known you to seek a man harder or longer than the guy who killed Marko. Does he know that?"

"Yes."

"Then the only question is, which mountain?"

"It may safely be presumed that it is Lovchen—the Black Mountain, from which Montenegro got its name."

"Is this Telesio reliable?"

"Yes."

"Then there's no problem. The guy that killed Marko is in Montenegro."

"Thank you." He twisted around, got his legs onto the bed and under the blanket, and flattened out, if that term may be used about an object with such a contour. Folding the end of the yellow sheet over the edge of the blanket, he pulled it up to his chin, turned on his side, said, "Put the light out," and closed his eyes.

He was probably asleep before I got back upstairs.

That leaves four days of the three weeks to account for, and they were by far the worst of the whole stretch. It was nothing new that Wolfe was pigheaded, but that time he left all previous records way behind. He knew damn well the subject had got beyond his reach and he was absolutely licked, and the only intelligent thing to do was to hand it over to Cramer and Stahl, with a fair chance that it would get to the CIA, and, if they happened to have a tourist taking in the scenery in those parts, they might think it worth the trouble to give him an errand. Not only that, there were at least two VIPs in Washington, one of them in the State Department, whose ears were accessible to Wolfe on request.

But no. Not for that mule. When—on Wednesday evening, I think it was—I submitted suggestions as outlined above, he rejected them and gave three reasons. One, Cramer and Stahl would think he had invented it unless he named his informant in Bari, and he couldn't do that. Two, they would merely nab Mrs. Britton if and when she returned to New York, and charge her with something and make it stick. Three, neither the New York police nor the FBI could reach to Yugoslavia, and the CIA wouldn't be interested unless it tied in with their own plans and projects, and that was extremely unlikely.

Meanwhile—and this was really pathetic—he kept Saul and Fred and Orrie on the payroll and went through the motions of giving them instructions and reading their reports, and I had to go through with my end of the charade. I don't think Fred and Orrie suspected they were just stringing beads, but Saul did, and Wolfe knew it. Thursday morning Wolfe told me it wouldn't be necessary for Saul to report direct to him, that I could take it and relay it.

"No, sir," I said firmly. "I'll quit first. I'll play my own part in the goddam farce if you insist on it, but I'm not going to try to convince Saul Panzer that I'm a halfwit. He knows better."

I have no idea how long it might have gone on. Sooner or later Wolfe would have had to snap out of it, and I prefer to believe it would have been sooner. There were signs that he was beginning to give under the strain—for instance, the scene in the office the next morning, Friday, which I have described. As for me, I was no longer trying to needle him. I was merely offering him a chance to shake loose when I told him the memo from Cartright of Consolidated Products needed immediate attention and reminded him that Cartright had once paid a bill for twelve grand without a squeak, and it looked hopeful when he shoved the paperweight off the desk and dumped the mail in the wastebasket. I was deciding how to follow through and keep him going when the phone rang, and I would have liked to treat it as Wolfe had treated the mail. I turned and got it. A female voice asked me if I would accept a collect call from Bari, Italy, for Mr. Nero Wolfe, and I said yes and told Wolfe. He lifted his instrument.

It was even briefer than it had been Sunday night. I am not equipped to divide Italian into words, but my guess was that Wolfe didn't use more than fifty altogether. From his tone I suspected it was some more unwelcome news, and his expression as he hung up verified it. He tightened his lips, glaring at the phone, and then transferred the glare to me.

"She's dead," he said glumly.

It always irritated him if I talked like that. He had drilled it into me that when giving information I must be specific, especially in identifying objects or persons. But since the call had been from Bari, and there was only one female in that part of the world that we were interested in, I didn't raise the point.

"Where?" I asked. "Bari?"

"No. Montenegro. Word came across."

"What or who killed her?"

"He says he doesn't know, except that she died violently. He wouldn't say she was murdered, but certainly she was. Can you doubt it?"

"I can, but I don't. What else?"

"Nothing. But for the bare fact, nothing. Even if I could have got more out of him, what good would it do me, sitting here?"

He looked down at his thighs, then at the right arm of his chair, then at the left arm, as if to verify the fact that he really was sitting. Abruptly he shoved his chair back, arose, and moved. He went to the television cabinet and stood a while staring at the screen, then turned and crossed to the most conspicuous object in the office, not counting him—the thirty-six-inch globe—twirled it, stopped it, and studied geography a minute or two. He about-faced, went to his desk, picked up a book he was halfway through—*But We Were Born Free* by Elmer Davis—crossed to the bookshelves, and eased the book in between two others. He turned to face me and inquired, "What's the bank balance?"

"A little over twenty-six thousand, after drawing the weekly checks. You put the checks in the wastebasket."

"What's in the safe?"

"A hundred and ninety-four dollars and twelve cents in petty, and thirty-eight hundred in emergency reserve."

"How long does it take a train to get to Washington?"

"Three hours and thirty-five minutes to four hours and fifteen minutes, depending on the train."

He made a face. "How long does it take an airplane?"

"Sixty to a hundred minutes, depending on the wind."

"How often does a plane go?"

"Every thirty minutes—on the hour and the half."

He shot a glance at the wall clock. "Can we make the one that leaves at noon?"

I cocked my head. "Did you say 'we'?"

"Yes. The only way to get passports in a hurry is to go after them in person."

"Where do we want passports for?"

"England and Italy."

"When are we leaving?"

"As soon as we get the passports. Tonight if possible. Can we make the noon plane for Washington?"

I stood up. "Look," I said, "it's quite a shock to see a statue turn into a dynamo without warning. Is this just an act?"

"No."

"You've told me over and over not to be impetuous. Why don't you sit down and count up to a thousand?"

"I am not being impetuous. We should have gone days ago, when we learned he was there. Now it is imperative. Confound it, can we make that plane?"

"No. Nothing doing. God knows what you'll be eating for the next week—or maybe year—and Fritz is working on shad roe mousse Pocahontas for lunch, and if you miss it you'll take it out on me. While I phone the airline and get your naturalization certificate and my birth certificate from the safe, you might go and give Fritz a hand since you're all of a sudden in such a hell of a hurry."

He was going to say something, decided to skip it, and turned and headed for the kitchen.

4

We got back home at nine o'clock that evening, and we had not only the passports but also seats on a plane that would leave Idlewild for London at five the next afternoon, Saturday.

Wolfe was not taking it like a man. I had expected him to quit being eccentric about vehicles, since he had decided to cross an ocean and a good part of a continent, and relax, but there was no visible change in his reactions. In the taxis he sat on the front half of the seat and gripped the strap, and in the planes he kept his muscles tight. Apparently it was so deep in him that the only hope would be for him to get analyzed, and there wasn't time for that. Analyzing him would take more like twenty years than twenty hours.

Washington had been simple. The VIP in the State Department, after keeping us waiting only ten minutes, had tried at first to explain that high-level interference with the Passport Division was against policy, but Wolfe interrupted him, not as diplomatically as he might have under that roof. Wolfe asserted that he wasn't asking for interference, merely for speed; that he had come to Washington instead of handling it through New York because a professional emergency required his presence in London at the earliest possible moment; and that he had assumed that the VIP's professions of gratitude for certain services rendered, and expressions of willingness to reciprocate, could reasonably be expected to bear the strain of a request so moderate and innocent. That did it, but the technicalities took a while anyway.

Saturday was crowded with chores. There was no telling how long we would be away. We might be back in a few days, but Wolfe had to have things arranged for an indefinite absence, so I had my hands full. Fred and Orrie were paid off. Saul was signed up to hold down the office and sleep in the South Room. Nathaniel Parker, the lawyer, was given authority to sign checks, and Fritz was empowered to take charge at Rusterman's. Theodore was given bales of instructions that he didn't need about the orchids. The assistant manager of the Churchill Hotel obliged by cashing a check for ten grand, in tens and twenties and Cs, and I spent a good hour getting them satisfactorily stashed in a belt I bought at Abercrombie's. The only squabble the whole day came at the last minute, as Wolfe stood in the office with his hat and coat on, and I opened a drawer of my desk and got out the Marley .32 and two boxes of cartridges.

"You're not taking that," he stated.

"Sure I am." I slipped the gun into my shoulder holster and dropped the boxes into a pocket. "The registration for it is in my wallet."

"No. It may make trouble at the customs. You can buy one at Bari before we go across. Take it off."

It was a command, and he was boss. "Okay," I said, and took the gun out and returned it to the drawer. Then I sat down in my chair. "I'm not going. As you know, I made a rule years ago never to leave on an errand connected with a murder case without a gun, and this is a super errand. I'm not going to try chasing a killer around a black mountain in a foreign land with nothing but some damn popgun I know nothing about."

"Nonsense." He looked up at the clock. "It's time to go."

"Go ahead."

Silence. I crossed my legs. He surrendered. "Very well. If I hadn't let you grow into a habit I could have done this without you. Come on."

I retrieved the Marley and put it where it belonged, and we departed. Fritz and Theodore escorted us to the sidewalk and the curb, where Saul sat at the wheel of the sedan. The luggage was in the trunk, leaving all the back seat for Wolfe. From the woebegone look on Fritz's and Theodore's faces we might have been off for the wars, and in fact they didn't know. Only Saul and Parker had been shown the program.

At Idlewild we got through the formalities and into our seats on the plane without a hitch. Thinking it wouldn't hurt Wolfe to have a little comic relief to take his mind off the perils of the takeoff, I told him of an amusing remark I had overheard from someone behind us as we had ascended the gangway. "My God," a voice had said, "they soak me thirty dollars for overweight baggage, and look at him." Seeing it didn't produce the desired effect, I fastened my seat belt and left him to his misery.

I admit he didn't make a show of it. For the first couple of hours I hardly saw his face as he sat staring through the window at the ocean horizon or the clouds. We voted to have our meal on trays, and when it came, fricassee and salad with trimmings, he did all right with it, and no snide remarks or even looks. Afterward I brought him two bottles of beer and was properly thanked, which was darned plucky of him, considering that he held that all moving parts of all machinery are subject to unpredictable whim, and if the wrong whim had seized our propellers we would have dropped smack into the middle of the big drink in the dead of night.

On that thought I went to sleep, sound. When I woke up my watch said half-past two, but it was broad daylight and I smelled fried bacon, and Wolfe's voice was muttering at my ear, "I'm hungry. We're ahead of time, and we'll be there in an hour."

"Did you sleep?"

"Some. I want breakfast."

He ate four eggs, ten slices of bacon, three rolls, and three cups of coffee.

I still haven't seen London, because the airport is not in London and Geoffrey Hitchcock was there at the gate waiting for us. We hadn't seen him since he had last been in New York, three years before, and he greeted us cordially for an Englishman and took us to a corner table in a restaurant, and ordered muffins and marmalade and tea. I was going to pass, but then I thought what the hell, I might as well start here as anywhere getting used to strange foreign food, and accepted my share.

Hitchcock took an envelope from his pocket. "Here are your tickets for the Rome plane. It leaves in forty minutes, at twenty after nine, and arrives at three o'clock, Rome time. Since your luggage is being transferred directly to it, the customs chaps here don't want you. We have half an hour. Will that be enough?"

"Ample." Wolfe dabbed marmalade on a muffin. "Mostly I want to know about Telesio. Thirty years ago, as a boy, I could trust him with my life. Can I now?"

"I don't know."

"I need to know," Wolfe snapped.

"Of course you do." Hitchcock used his napkin on his thin, pale lips. "But nowadays a man you can trust farther than you can see is a rare bird. I can only say I've been dealing with him for eight years and am satisfied, and Bodin has known him much longer, from back in the Mussolini days, and he vouches for him. If you have—"

A crackling metallic voice, probably female, from a loudspeaker split the air. It sounded urgent. When it stopped I asked Hitchcock what she had said, and he replied that she was announcing that the nine-o'clock plane for Cairo was ready at Gate Seven.

"Yeah." I nodded. "I thought I heard Cairo. What language was she talking?"

"English."

"I *beg* your pardon," I said politely and sipped some tea.

"I was saying," he went on to Wolfe, "that if you have to trust someone on that coast I doubt if you could do better than Telesio. From me that's rather strong, for I'm a wary man."

Wolfe grunted. "It's better than I hoped for. One other thing—a plane at Rome for Bari."

"Yes." Hitchcock cleared his throat. "One has been chartered and should be in readiness." He took a worn old leather case from his pocket, fingered in it, and extracted a slip of paper. "You should be met on arrival, but if there's a hitch here's the name and phone number." He handed it over. "Eighty dollars, and you may pay in dollars. The agent I deal with in Rome, Giuseppe Drogo, is a good man by Roman standards, but he is quite capable of seeking some trivial personal advantage from his contact with his famous American fellow. Of course he had to have your name. If it is now all over Rome, I must disclaim responsibility."

Wolfe did not look pleased, which showed how concentrated he was on his mission. Any man only one-tenth as conceited as he was couldn't help but glow at being told that his name was worth scattering all over Rome. As for Hitchcock, the British might be getting short on empire, but apparently they still had their share of applesauce.

A little later the loudspeaker announced in what I guess was English that the plane for Rome was ready, and our host convoyed us out to the gate and stood by to watch us take the air. As we taxied to the runway Wolfe actually waved to him from the window.

With Wolfe next to the window, I had to stretch my neck for my first look at Europe, but it was a nice sunny day and I kept a map open on my knee, and it was very interesting, after crossing the Strait of Dover, to look toward Brussels on the left and Paris on the right, and Zurich on the left and Geneva on the right, and Milan on the left and Genoa on the right. I recognized the Alps without any trouble, and I actually saw Bern. Unfortunately I missed looking toward Florence. Passing over the Apennines a little to the north, we hit an air pocket and dropped a mile or so before we caught again, which is never much fun, and some of the passengers made noises. Wolfe didn't. He merely shut his eyes and set his jaw. When we had leveled off I thought it only civil to remark, "That wasn't so bad. That time I flew to the Coast, going over the Rockies we—"

"Shut up," he growled.

So I missed looking toward Florence. We touched concrete at the Rome airport right on the nose, at three o'clock of a fine warm Sunday afternoon, and the minute we descended the gangway and started to walk across to the architecture my association with Wolfe, and his with me, changed for the worse. All my life, needing a steer in new surroundings, all I had had to do was look at signs and, if that failed, ask a native. Now I was sunk. The signs were not my kind. I stopped and looked at Wolfe.

"This way," he informed me. "The customs."

The basic setup between him and me was upset, and I didn't like it. I stood beside him at a table and listened to the noises he exchanged with a blond basso, my only contribution being to pro-

duce my passport when told to do so in English. I stood beside
him at a counter in another room and listened to similar noises,
exchanged this time with a black-haired tenor, though I concede
that there I played a more important part, being permitted to open
the bags and close them again after they had been inspected. More
noises to a redcap with a mustache who took over the bags—only
his cap was blue. Still more, out in the sunshine, with a chunky
signor in a green suit with a red carnation in his lapel. Wolfe kindly
let me in on that enough to tell me that his name was Drogo and
that the chartered plane for Bari was waiting for us. I was about
to express my appreciation for being noticed when a distinguished-
looking college boy, dressed for a wedding or a funeral, stepped up
and said in plain American, "Mr. Nero Wolfe?"

Wolfe glared at him. "May I ask your name, sir?"

He smiled amiably. "I'm Richard Courtney from the embassy.
We thought you might require something, and we would be glad to
be of service. Can we help you in any way?"

"No, thank you."

"Will you be in Rome long?"

"I don't know. Must you know?"

"No, no." He perished the thought. "We don't want to intrude
on your affairs—just let us know if you need any information, any
assistance at all."

"I shall, Mr. Courtney."

"Please do. And I hope you won't mind—" From the inside
breast pocket of his dark gray tailored coat that had not come from
stock he produced a little black book and a pen. "I would like very
much to have your autograph." He opened the book and proffered
it. "If you will?"

Wolfe took the book and pen, wrote, and handed them back.
The well-dressed college boy thanked him, urged him not to fail to
call on them for any needed service, included Drogo and me in a
well-bred smile, and left us.

"Checking on you?" I asked Wolfe.

"I doubt it. What for?" He said something to Drogo and then
to the bluecap, and we started off, with Drogo in the lead and the
bluecap with the bags in the rear. After a stretch on concrete and
a longer one on gravel of a color I had never seen, we came to a

hangar, in front of which a small blue plane was parked. After the one we had crossed Europe in it looked like a toy. Wolfe stood and scowled at it a while and then turned to Drogo and resumed the noises. They got louder and hotter, then simmered down a little, and finally ended by Wolfe telling me to give him ninety dollars.

"Hitchcock said eighty," I objected.

"He demanded a hundred and ten. As for paying in advance, I don't blame him. When we leave that contraption we may be in no condition to pay. Give him ninety dollars."

I shelled it out, was instructed to give the bluecap a buck and did so after he had handed the luggage up to the pilot, and steadied the portable stile while Wolfe engineered himself up and in. Then I embarked. There was space for four passengers, but not for four Wolfes. He took one seat and I the other, and the pilot stepped on it, and we rolled toward the runway. I would have preferred not to wave to Drogo on account of the extra sawbuck he had chiseled, but for the sake of public relations I flapped a mitt at him.

Flying low over the Volscian hills—see map—in a pint-sized plane was not an ideal situation for a chat with my fellow passenger, but it was only ninety minutes to Bari, and something had to get settled without delay. So I leaned across and yelled to him above the racket, "I want to raise a point!"

His face came around to me. It was grim. I got closer to his ear. "About the babble. How many languages do you speak?"

He had to jerk his mind onto it. "Eight."

"I speak one. Also I understand one. This is going to be too much for me. What I see ahead will be absolutely impossible except on one condition. When you're talking with people, I can't expect you to translate as you go along, but you will afterward, the first chance we get. I'll try to be reasonable about it, but when I ask for it I want it. Otherwise I might as well ride this thing back to Rome."

His teeth were clenched. "This is a choice spot for an ultimatum."

"Nuts. You might as well have brought a dummy. I said I'll be reasonable, but I've been reporting to you for a good many years and it won't hurt you to report to me for a change."

"Very well. I submit."

"I want to be kept posted in full."

"I said I submit."

"Then we can start now. What did Drogo say about the arrangements for meeting Telesio?"

"Nothing. Drogo was told only that I wanted a plane for Bari."

"Is Telesio meeting us at the airport?"

"No. He doesn't know we're coming. I wanted to ask Mr. Hitchcock about him first. In nineteen twenty-one he killed two Fascisti who had me cornered."

"What with?"

"A knife."

"In Bari?"

"Yes."

"I thought you were Montenegrin. What were you doing in Italy?"

"In those days I was mobile. I have submitted to your ultimatum, as you framed it, but I'm not going to give you an account of my youthful gestes—certainly not here and now."

"What's the program for Bari?"

"I don't know. There was no airport then, and I don't know where it is. We'll see." He turned away to look through the window. In a moment he turned back. "I think we're over Benevento. Ask the pilot."

"I can't, damn it! I can't ask anybody anything. You ask him."

He ignored the suggestion. "It must be Benevento. Glance at it. The Romans finished the Samnites there in three hundred and twelve B.C."

He was showing off, and I approved. Only two days earlier I would have given ten to one that up in an airplane he wouldn't have been able to remember the date of anything whatever, and here he was rattling off one twenty-two centuries back. I went back to my window for a look down at Benevento. Before long I saw water ahead and to the left, my introduction to the Adriatic, and watched it spread and glisten in the sun as we sailed toward it; and then there was Bari floating toward us. Part of it was a jumble on a neck stretched into the sea, apparently with no streets, and the other part, south of the neck along the shore, had streets as straight and regular as midtown Manhattan, with no Broadway slicing through.

The plane nosed down.

5

From here on, please have in mind the warning I put at the front of this. As I said, I have had to do some filling in, but everything important is reported as Wolfe gave it to me.

Sure, it was five o'clock of a fine April Sunday afternoon, Palm Sunday, and our plane was unscheduled, and Bari is no metropolis, but even so you might have expected to see some sign of activity around the airport. None. It was dead. Of course there was some-one in the control tower, and also presumably someone in the small building which the pilot entered, presumably to report, but that was all except for three boys throwing things at a cat. From them Wolfe learned where a phone was and entered a building to use it. I stood guard over the bags and watched the communist boys. I assumed they were communists because they were throwing things at a cat on Palm Sunday. Then I remembered where I was, so they could have been fascists.

Wolfe came back and reported. "I reached Telesio. He says the guard on duty at the front of this building knows him and should not see him get us. I phoned a number he gave me and arranged for a car to come and take us to a rendezvous."

"Yes, sir. It'll take me a while to get used to this. Maybe a year will do it. Let's get in out of the sun."

The wooden bench in the waiting room was not too comfortable, but that wasn't why Wolfe left it after a few minutes and went out-side to the front. With three airplanes and four thousand miles be-hind him, he was simply full of get-up-and-go. It was incredible, but there it was: I was inside sitting down, and he was outside standing up. I considered the possibility that the scene of his youthful gestes had suddenly brought on his second childhood, and decided no. He was suffering too much. When he finally reap-peared and beckoned to me, I lifted the bags and went.

The car was a shiny long black Lancia, and the driver wore a neat gray uniform trimmed in green. There was plenty of room for the bags and us too. As we started off, Wolfe reached for the strap and got a good hold on it, so he was still fundamentally normal. We swung out of the airport plaza onto a smooth black-top road, and without a murmur the Lancia stretched its neck and sailed, with the speedometer showing eighty, ninety, and on up over a hundred—when I realized it was kilometers, not miles. Even so, it was no jalopy. Before long there were more houses, and the road became a street, then a winding avenue. We left it, turning right, got into some traffic, made two more turns, and pulled up at the curb in front of what looked like a railroad station. After speaking with the driver Wolfe told me, "He says four thousand lire. Give him eight dollars."

I audited it mentally as I got my wallet, certified it, and handed it over. The tip was apparently acceptable, since he held the door for Wolfe and helped me get the bags out. Then he got in and rolled off. I wanted to ask Wolfe if it was a railroad station, but there was a limit. His eyes were following something, and, taking direction, I saw that he was watching the Lancia on its way. When it turned a corner and disappeared he spoke.

"We have to walk five hundred yards."

I picked up the bags. "*Andiamo*."

"Where the devil did you get that?"

"Lily Rowan, at the opera. The chorus can't get off the stage without singing it."

We set out abreast, but soon the sidewalk was just wide enough for me and the bags, so I let him lead. I don't know whether one of his youthful gestes had been to pace off that particular route, which included three straightaways and three turns, but if so his memory was faulty. It was more like half a mile, and if it had been much farther the bags would have begun to get heavy. A little beyond the third turn, in a street narrower than any of the others, a car was parked, with a man standing alongside. As we approached he stared rudely at Wolfe. Wolfe stopped practically against him and said, "Paolo."

"No." The man couldn't believe it. "Yes, by God, it is. Get in." He opened the car door.

It was a little two-door Fiat that would have done for a tender for the Lancia, but we made it—me with the bags in the back, and Wolfe with Telesio in front. As the car went along the narrow street, with Telesio jerking his head sidewise every second to look at Wolfe, I took him in. I had seen dozens of him around New York—coarse, thick hair, mostly gray; dark, tough skin; quick black eyes; a wide mouth that had done a lot of laughing. He began firing questions, but Wolfe wasn't talking, and I couldn't blame him. I was willing to keep my mind open on whether Telesio was to be trusted as a brother, but in less than a mile it was already closed about trusting him as a chauffeur. Apparently he had some secret assurance that all obstructions ahead, animate or inanimate, would disappear before he got there, and when one didn't and he was about to make contact, his split-second reaction was very gay. When we got to our destination and I was out of it on my feet, I circled the Fiat for a look at the fenders. Not a sign of a scratch, let alone a dent. I thought to myself, a man in a million, thank God.

The destination was a sort of courtyard back of a small white two-story stuccoed house, with flowers and a little pool and high walls on three sides. "Not mine," Telesio said. "A friend of mine who is away. At my place in the old city you would be seen by too many people before I know your plans."

Actually it was two hours later that I learned he had said that, but I'm going to put things in approximately where people said them. That's the only way I can keep it straight.

Telesio insisted on carrying the bags in, though he had to put them down to use a key on the door. In a small square hall he took our hats and coats and hung them up, and ushered us through into a good-sized living room. It was mostly pink, and one glance at the furniture and accessories settled it as to the sex of his friend—at least I hoped so. Wolfe looked around, saw no chair that even approached his specifications, crossed to a couch, and sat. Telesio disappeared and came back in a couple of minutes with a tray holding a bottle of wine, glasses, and a bowl of almonds. He filled the glasses nearly to the brim, gave us ours, and raised his.

"To Ivo and Garibaldi!" he cried.

We drank. They left some, so I did. Wolfe raised his glass again. "There is only one response. To Garibaldi and Ivo!"

We emptied the glasses. I found a comfortable chair. For an hour they talked and drank and ate almonds. When Wolfe reported to me later he said that the first hour had been reminiscent, personal and irrelevant, and their tone and manner certainly indi-

cated it. A second bottle of wine was needed, and another bowl
of almonds. What brought them down to business was Telesio's
raising his glass and proposing, "To your little daughter Carla! A
woman as brave as she was beautiful!"

They drank. By then I was merely a spectator. Wolfe put his
glass down and spoke in a new tone. "Tell me about her. You saw
her dead?"

Telesio shook his head. "No, I saw her alive. She came to me
one day and wanted to go across. I knew about her from Marko,
on his trips to meet them from over there, and of course she knew
all about me. I tried to tell her it was no job for a woman, but she
wouldn't listen. She said that with Marko dead she must see them
and arrange what to do. So I brought Guido to her, and she paid
him too much to take her across, and she went that day. I tried—"

"Do you know how she got here from New York?"

"Yes, she told me—as a stewardess on a ship to Naples, which
was mere routine with certain connections, and from Naples by
car. I tried to phone you before she got away, but there were difficulties, and by the time I got you she had gone with Guido. That
was all I could tell you. Guido returned four days later. He came
to my place early in the morning, and with him was one of them
—Josip Pasic. Do you know of him?"

"No."

"Anyway he is too young for you to remember. He brought a
message from Danilo Vukcic, who is a nephew of Marko. The
message was that I was to phone to you and say these words: 'The
man you seek is within sight of the mountain.' I knew you would
want more and I tried to get more, but that was all Josip would say.
He hasn't known me for many years as the older ones have. So
that was all I could tell you. Naturally I thought it meant that the
man who had killed Marko was there, and was known. Did you?"

"Yes."

"Then why didn't you come?"

"I wanted something better than a cryptogram."

"Not as I remember you—but then, you are older, and so am
I. You are also much heavier and have more to move, but that is
no surprise, since Marko told me about you and even brought me
a picture of you. Anyway, now you are here, but your daughter is
dead. I can't believe how you got here. It was only Friday, forty-

eight hours ago, that I phoned you. Josip came again, not with Guido this time, in another boat, with another message from Danilo. I was to inform you that your daughter had died a violent death within sight of the mountain. Again that was all he would say. If I had known you were coming I would have tried to keep him here for you, but he has gone back. In any case, you will want to see Danilo himself, and for him we will have to send Guido. Danilo will trust only Guido. He could be here—let's see—Tuesday night. Early Wednesday morning. You can await him here. Marko used this place. I believe, in fact, he paid for this wine, and he wouldn't want us to spare it, and the bottle is empty. That won't do."

He left the room and soon was back with another bottle, un-corked. After filling Wolfe's glass he came to me. I would have preferred to pass, but his lifted brows at my prior refusal had indicated that a man who went easy on wine would bear watching, so I took it and got another handful of almonds.

"This place isn't bad," he told Wolfe, "even for you who live in luxury. Marko liked to do his own cooking, but I can get a woman in tomorrow."

"It won't be necessary," Wolfe said. "I'm going over."

Telesio stared. "No. You must not."

"On the contrary. I must. Where do we find this Guido?"

Telesio sat down. "You mean this?"

"Yes. I'm going."

"In what form and what capacity?"

"My own. To find the man who killed Marko. I can't enter Yugoslavia legally, but among those rocks and ravines what's the difference?"

"That's not the problem. The worst Belgrade would do to Nero Wolfe would be to ship him out, but the rocks and ravines are not Belgrade. Nor are they what you remember. Precisely there, around that mountain, are the lairs of the Tito cutthroats and the Albanian thugs from across the border who are the tools of Russia. They reached to kill Marko in far-off America. They killed your daughter within hours after she stepped ashore. She may have exposed herself by carelessness, but what you propose—to appear among them as yourself—would be greatly worse. If you are so eager to commit suicide, I will favor you by providing a knife or a gun, as you may prefer, and there will be no need for you to undertake the journey across our beautiful sea, which is often rough, as you know. I would like to ask a question. Am I a coward?"

"No. You were not."

"I am not. I am a very brave man. Sometimes I am astonished at the extent of my courage. But nothing could persuade me, known as I am, to show myself between Cetinje and Scutari day or night—much less to the east, where the border crosses the mountains. Was Marko a coward?"

"No."

"That is correct. But he never even considered risking himself in that hive of traitors." Telesio shrugged. "That's all I have to say. Unfortunately you will not be alive for me to say I told you so." He picked up his glass and drained it.

Wolfe looked at me to see how I was taking it, realized that I would have nothing to take until he got a chance to report, and heaved a deep sigh. "That's all very well," he told Telesio, "but I can't hunt a murderer from across the Adriatic with the kind of communications available, and now that I've got this far I am not going to turn around and go home. I'll have to consider it and discuss it with Mr. Goodwin. In any event, I'll need this Guido. What's his name?"

"Guido Battista."

"He is the best?"

"Yes. That is not to say he is a saint. The list of saints to be found today in this neighborhood would leave room here." He passed a fingertip over the nail of his little finger.

"Can you bring him here?"

"Yes, but it may take hours. This is Palm Sunday." Telesio stood up. "If you are hungry, the kitchen is equipped and there are some items in the cupboard. There is wine but no beer. Marko told me of your addiction to beer, which I deplore. If the phone rings you may lift it, and if it is me I will speak. If I do not speak you should not. No one is expected here. Draw the curtains properly before you turn lights on. Your presence in Bari may not be known, but they reached to Marko in New York. My friend would not like blood on this pretty pink rug." Suddenly he laughed. He roared with laughter. "Especially not in such a quantity! I will find Guido."

He was gone. The sound came of the outer door closing, and then of the Fiat's engine as it turned in the courtyard and headed for the street.

I looked at Wolfe. "This is fascinating," I said bitterly.

He didn't hear me. His eyes were closed. He couldn't lean back comfortably on the couch, so as a makeshift he was hunched forward.

"I know you're chewing on something," I told him, "but I'm along and I have nothing to chew on. I would appreciate a hint. You've spent years training me to report verbatim, and I would like you to give a demonstration."

His head lifted and his eyes opened. "We're in a pickle."

"We have been for nearly a month. I need to know what Telesio said from the beginning."

"Nonsense. For an hour we merely prattled."

"Okay, that can wait. Then begin where he toasted Carla."

He did so. Once or twice I suspected him of skipping and stopped him, but on the whole I was willing to accept it as an adequate job. When he was through he reached for his glass and drank. I let my head back to rest on my clasped hands, and so was looking down my nose at him.

"On account of the wine," I said, "I may be a little vague, but it looks as if we have three choices. One, stay here and get nowhere. Two, go home and forget it. Three, go to Montenegro and get killed. I have never seen a less attractive batch to pick from."

"Neither have I." He put his glass down and took his watch from his vest pocket. "It's half-past seven, and I'm empty. I'll see what's in the kitchen." He arose and went for the door through which Telesio had gone for the wine and almonds. I followed. It certainly would not have qualified as a kitchen with the *Woman's Home Companion* or *Good Housekeeping,* but there was an electric stove with four units, and the pots and pans on hooks were clean and bright. Wolfe was opening cupboard doors and muttering something to himself about tin cans and civilization. I asked if I could help, and he said no, so I went and got my bag and opened it, got the necessary articles for a personal hour in a bathroom, and then realized that I hadn't seen one. However, there was one, upstairs. There was no hot water. An apparatus in the corner was probably a water heater, but the instructions riveted to it needed a lot of words, and rather than call Wolfe to come up and decode,

I made out without it. The cord of my electric shaver wouldn't plug into the outlet, and even if it had fitted there was no telling what it might do to the circuit, so I used my scraper.

When I went back downstairs the living room was dark, but I made it to the windows and got the curtains over them before turning on the lights. In the kitchen I found Wolfe concentrated on cuisine, with his shirt sleeves rolled up, under a bright light from a ceiling fixture, and the window bare. I had to mount a chair to arrange the curtain so there were no cracks, after making a suitable remark.

We ate at a little table in the kitchen. Of course there was no milk, and Wolfe said he wouldn't recommend the water from the faucet, but I took a chance on it. He stuck to wine. There was just one item on the menu, dished by him out of a pot. After three mouthfuls I asked him what it was. A pasta called *tagliarini,* he said, with anchovies, tomato, garlic, olive oil, salt and pepper from the cupboard, sweet basil and parsley from the garden, and Romano cheese from a hole in the ground. I wanted to know how he had found a hole in the ground, and he said—offhand, as if it were nothing—by his memory of local custom. Actually he was boiling with pride, and by the time I got up to dish my third helping I was willing to grant him all rights to it.

While I washed up and put away, Wolfe went upstairs with his bag. When he came down again to the living room he stood and looked around to see if someone had brought a chair his size during his absence, discovered none, went to the couch and sat, and drew in air clear down to the *tagliarini* he had swallowed.

"Have we made up our mind?" I inquired.

"Yes."

"That's good. Which of the three did we pick?"

"None. I'm going to Montenegro, but not as myself. My name is Toné Stara, and I'm from Galichnik. You have never heard of Galichnik."

"Right."

"It is a village hanging to a mountain near the top, just over the border from Albania in Serbia, which is a part of Yugoslavia. It is forty miles southeast of Cetinje and the Black Mountain, and it is famous. For eleven months of each year only women live there—no men but a few in their dotage—and young boys. It has been that way for centuries. When the Turks seized Serbia more than five hundred years ago, groups of artisans in the lowlands fled to the mountains with their families, thinking the Turks would soon be driven out. But the Turks stayed, and as the years passed, the refugees, who had established a village on a crag and named it Galichnik, realized the hopelessness of wresting a living from the barren rocks. Some of the men, skilled craftsmen, started the practice of going to other lands, working for most of a year, and returning each July to spend a month at home with their women and children. The practice became universal with the men of Galichnik, and they have followed it for five centuries. Masons and stonecutters from Galichnik worked on the Escorial in Spain and the palaces at Versailles. They have worked on the Mormon Temple in Utah, the Château Frontenac in Quebec, the Empire State Building in New York, the Dnieperstroi in Russia."

He joined his fingertips. "So I am Toné Stara of Galichnik. I am one of the few who one July did not return—many years ago. I have been many places, including the United States. Finally I became homesick and curious. What was happening to my birthplace, Galichnik, perched on the border between Tito's Yugoslavia and Russia's puppet Albania? I was eaten by a desire to see and to know, and I returned. The answer was not in Galichnik. There were no men there, and the women suspected me and feared me and wouldn't even tell me where the men were. I wanted to learn and to judge, as between Tito and the Russians, and between them both and certain persons of whom I had vaguely heard, persons who were calling themselves champions of freedom. So I made my way north through the mountains, a hard rocky way, and here I am in Montenegro, determined to find out where the truth is and who deserves my hand. I assert my right to ask questions so I may choose my side."

He turned his palms up. "And I ask questions."

"Uh-huh." I wasn't enthusiastic. "I don't. I can't."

"I know you can't. Your name is Alex."

"Oh. It is."

"It is if you go with me. There are good reasons why it would be better for you to stay here, but confound it, you've been too close to me too long. I'm too dependent on you. However, the decision is yours. I don't claim the right to drag you into a predicament of mortal hazard and doubtful outcome."

"Yeah. I'm not very crazy about the name Alex. Why Alex?"

"We can choose another. It might not increase the risk of exposure for you to keep Archie, and that would make one less demand on our vigilance. You are my son, born in the United States. I must ask you to suffer that presumption because no lesser tie would justify my hauling you back to Galichnik with me. You are an only child and your mother died in your infancy. That will reduce the temptation for you to indulge your invention if we meet someone who speaks English. Until recently I repressed all sentiment about my homeland, so I have taught you no Serbo-Croat and no Serbian lore. At one point, while I was cooking, I decided you should be a deaf-mute, but changed my mind. It would create more difficulties than it would solve."

"It's an idea," I declared. "Why not? I practically am anyway."

"No. You would be overheard talking with me."

"I suppose so," I conceded reluctantly. "I'd like to take a crack at it, but I guess you're right. Are we going to Galichnik?"

"Good heavens, no. There was a time when sixty kilometers through those hills was only a frolic for me, but not now. We'll go across to a spot I used to know, or, if time has changed that too, to one that Paolo—"

The phone rang. I was up automatically, realized I was disqualified, and stood while Wolfe crossed to it and lifted it to his ear. In a moment he spoke, so it was Telesio. After a brief exchange he hung up and turned to me.

"Paolo. He has been waiting for Guido to return from an excursion on his boat. He said he might have to wait until midnight or later. I told him we have decided on a plan and would like to have him come and discuss it. He's coming."

I sat down. "Now about my name . . ."

6

There are boats and boats. The *Queen Elizabeth* is a boat. So was the thing I rowed one August afternoon on the lake in Central

Park, with Lily Rowan lolling in the stern, to win a bet. Guido Battista's craft, which took us across the Adriatic, was in between those two but was a much closer relative of the latter than of the former. It was twelve meters long, thirty-nine feet. It had not been thoroughly cleaned since the days when the Romans had used it to hijack spices from Levantine bootleggers, but had been modernized by installing an engine and propeller. One of my occupations en route was trying to figure out exactly where the galley slaves had sat, but it was too much for me.

We shoved off at three p.m. Monday, the idea being to land on the opposite shore at midnight or not long after. That seemed feasible until I saw the *Cispadana,* which was her name. To expect that affair to navigate 170 miles of open water in nine hours was so damn fantastic that I could make no adequate remark and so didn't try. It took her nine hours and twenty minutes.

Wolfe and I had stuck to the stuccoed hideout, but it had been a busy night and day for Telesio. After listening to Wolfe's plan, opposing it on various grounds, and finally giving in because Wolfe wouldn't, he had gone again for Guido and brought him, and Wolfe and Guido had reached an understanding. Telesio had left with Guido, and I suppose he got a nap somewhere, but before noon Monday he was back with a carload. For me to choose from he had four pairs of pants, three sweaters, four jackets, an assortment of shirts, and five pairs of shoes; and about the same for Wolfe. They weren't new, except the shoes, but they were clean and whole. I picked them more for fit than looks, and ended up with a blue shirt, maroon sweater, dark green jacket, and light gray pants. Wolfe was tastier, with yellow, brown, and dark blue.

The knapsacks weren't new either, and none too clean, but we wiped them out and went ahead and packed. At the first try I was too generous with socks and underwear and had to back up and start over. In between roars of laughter, Telesio gave me sound advice: to ditch the underwear entirely, make it two pairs of socks, and cram in all the chocolate it would hold. Wolfe interpreted the advice for me, approved it, and followed it himself. I had expected another squabble about armament, but quite the contrary. In addition to being permitted to wear the Marley in the holster, I was provided with a Colt .38 that looked like new, and fifty rounds for it. I tried it in my jacket pocket, but it was too heavy, so I shifted it to my hip. I was also offered an eight-inch pointed knife, shiny and sharp, but turned it down. Telesio and Wolfe both insisted, saying there might be a situation where a knife would be much more useful than a gun, and I said not for me because I would be more apt to stick myself than the foe. "If a knife is so useful," I challenged Wolfe, "why don't you take one yourself?"

"I'm taking two," he replied; and he did. He put one in a sheath on his belt, and strapped a shorter one to his left leg just below his knee. That gave me a better idea of the kind of party we were going to, since in all the years I had known him he had never borne any weapon but a little gold penknife. The idea was made even clearer when Telesio took two small plastic tubes from his pocket and handed one to Wolfe and one to me. Wolfe frowned at it and asked him something, and they talked.

Wolfe turned to me. "He says the capsule inside the tube is a lullaby—a jocose term, I take it, for cyanide. He said for an emergency. I said we didn't want them. He said that last month some Albanians, Russian agents, had a Montenegrin in a cave on the border for three days and left him there. When his friends found him the joints of all his fingers and toes had been broken, and his eyes had been removed, but he was still breathing. Paolo says he can furnish details of other incidents if we want them. Do you know what to do with a cyanide capsule?"

"Certainly. Everybody does."

"Where are you going to carry it?"

"My God, give me a chance. I never had one before. Sew it inside my sweater?"

"Your sweater might be gone."

"Tape it under my armpit."

"Too obvious. It would be found and taken."

"Okay, it's your turn. Where will you carry yours?"

"In my handiest pocket. Threatened with seizure and search, in my hand. Threatened more imminently, the capsule out of the tube and into my mouth. It can be kept in the mouth indefinitely if it is not crushed with the teeth. The case against carrying it is the risk of being stampeded into using it prematurely."

"I'll take the chance." I put the tube in my pocket. "Anyway, if you did that you'd never know it, so why worry?"

The lullabies completed our equipment.

It was considered undesirable for Telesio to be seen delivering us at the waterfront, so we said good-by there, with the help of a bottle of wine, and then he took us in the Fiat to the center of town, let us out, and drove away. We walked a block to a cab stand. I guess we weren't half as conspicuous as I thought we were, but the people of Bari didn't have the basis for comparison that I had. To think of Wolfe as I knew him best, seated in his custom-built chair behind his desk, prying the cap from a bottle of beer, a *Laeliocattleya Jaquetta* sporting four flowers to his left and a spray of *Dendrobium nobilius* to his right; and then to look at him tramping along in blue pants, yellow shirt, and brown jacket, with a blue sweater hanging over his arm and a bulging old knapsack on his back—I couldn't help being surprised that nobody turned to stare at him. Also, in that getup, I regarded myself as worth a glance, but none came our way. The hackie showed no sign of interest when we climbed into his cab and Wolfe told him where to go. His attitude toward obstacles was somewhat similar to Telesio's, but he got us into the old city and through its narrow winding streets to the edge of a wharf without making contact. I paid him and followed Wolfe out, and had my first view of the *Cispadana* sitting alongside the wharf.

Guido, standing there, left a man he was talking to and came to Wolfe. Here where he belonged he looked more probable than in the pink living room. He was tall, thin except his shoulders, and stooped some, and moved like a cat. He had told Wolfe he was sixty years old, but his long hair was jet black. The hair on his face was gray and raised questions. It was half an inch long. If he never shaved why wasn't it longer? If he did shave, when? I would have liked to ask him after we got acquainted, but we weren't communicating.

Telesio had said that with the three hundred bucks I had forked over he would take care of everything—our equipment, Guido, and a certain waterfront party—and apparently he had. I don't know what kind of voyage it was supposed to be officially, but no one around seemed to be interested. A couple of characters stood on the wharf and watched as we climbed aboard, and two others untied us and shoved the bow off when Guido had the engine going and gave the sign, and we slid away. I supposed one or both of them would jump on as we cleared, but they didn't. Wolfe and I were seated in the cockpit.

"Where's the crew?" I asked him.

He said Guido was the crew.

"Just him?"

"Yes."

"Good God. I'm not a mariner. When the engine quits or something else, who steers?"

"I do."

"Oh. You *are* a mariner."

"I have crossed this sea eighty times." He was working at the buckle of a knapsack strap. "Help me get this thing off."

My tongue was ready with a remark about a man of action who had to have help to doff his knapsack, but I thought I'd better save it. If the engine did quit, and a squall hit us, and he saved our lives with a display of masterly seamanship, I'd have to eat it.

Nothing happened at all the whole way. The engine was noisy, but that was all right; the point was, it never stopped being noisy. No squall. Late in the afternoon clouds began coming over from the east, and a light wind started up, but not enough to curl the water. I even took a nap, stretched out on a cockpit seat. A couple of times, when Guido went forward on errands, Wolfe took the wheel, but there was no call for seamanship. The third time was an hour before sundown, and Wolfe went and propped himself on the narrow board, put a hand on the wheel, and was motionless, looking ahead. Looking that way, the water was blue, but looking back, toward the low sun over Italy, it was gray except where the sun's rays bounced out of it at us. Guido was gone so long that I stepped down into the cabin to see what was up, and found him stirring something in an old black pot on an alcohol stove. I couldn't ask him what, but a little later I found out, when he appeared with a pair of battered old plates heaped with steaming spaghetti smothered with sauce. I had been wondering, just to myself, about grub. He also brought wine, naturally, and a tin pail filled with green salad. It wasn't quite up to Wolfe's production the day before, but Fritz himself wouldn't have been ashamed of the salad dressing, and it was absolutely a meal. Guido took the wheel while Wolfe and I ate, and then Wolfe went back to it and Guido went to the cabin to eat. He told us he didn't like to eat in the open air. Having smelled the inside of the cabin, I could have made a comment but didn't. By the time he came out it was getting dark, and he lighted the running lights before he went back to the wheel. The clouds had scattered around, so there were spaces with stars, and Guido began to sing and kept it up. With all the jolts I had had the past two days, I wouldn't have been surprised if Wolfe had joined in, but he didn't.

It had got pretty chilly, and I took off my jacket, put on the sweater, and put the jacket back on. I asked Wolfe if he didn't want to do the same, and he said no, he would soon be warming up with exercise. A little later he asked what time it was, my wristwatch having a luminous dial, and I told him ten past eleven. Suddenly the engine changed its tune, slowing down, and I thought uh-huh, I knew it, but it kept going, so evidently Guido had merely throttled down. Soon after that he spoke to Wolfe, and Wolfe went to the wheel while Guido went to douse the lights and then returned to his post. There wasn't a glimmer anywhere on the boat. I stood up to look ahead, and I have damn good eyes, but I had just decided that if there should be anything ahead I wouldn't see it anyway, when I saw something pop up to shut off a star.

I turned to Wolfe. "This is Guido's boat, and he's running it, but we're headed straight for something big."

"Certainly we are. Montenegro."

I looked at my watch. "Five after twelve. Then we're on time?"

"Yes." He didn't sound enthusiastic. "Will you please help me with this thing?"

I went and helped him on with his knapsack and then got mine on. After a little the engine changed tune again, slower and much quieter. The thing ahead was a lot higher and had spread out at the sides, and it kept going up. When it was nearly on top of us Guido left the wheel, ran in and killed the engine, came out and glided around the cabin to the bow, and in a moment there was a big splash. He came gliding back and untied the ropes that lashed the dinghy to the stern. I helped him turn the dinghy over, and we slid it into the water and pulled it alongside. This maneuver had been discussed on the way over, and Wolfe had informed me of the decision. On account of the displacement of Wolfe's weight, it would be safer for Guido to take him ashore first and come back for me, but that would take an extra twenty minutes and there was an outside chance that one of Tito's coast-guard boats would happen along, and if it did, not only would Guido lose his boat but also he would probably never see Italy again. So we were to make it in one trip. Guido held the dinghy in, and I took Wolfe's arm to steady him as he climbed over the side, but he shook me off, made it fairly neatly, and lowered himself in the stern. I followed and perched in the bow. Guido stepped down in the middle, light as a feather, shipped the oars, and rowed. He muttered something, and Wolfe spoke to me in an undertone.

"We have twelve centimeters above water amidships—about five inches. Don't bounce."

"Aye, aye, sir."

Guido's oars were as smooth as velvet, making no sound at all in the water and only a faint squeak in the rowlocks, which were just notches in the gunwale. As I was riding backward in the bow—and not caring to twist around for a look, under the circumstances—the news that we had made it came to me from Wolfe, not much above a whisper.

"Your left hand, Archie. The rock."

I saw no rock, but in a second there it was at my elbow, a level slab a foot above the gunwale. Flattening my palm on its surface, I held us in and eased us along until Guido could reach it too. Following the briefing I had been given, I climbed out, stretched out on the rock on my belly, extended a hand for Guido to moor to, and learned that he had a healthy grip. As we kept the dinghy snug to the rock, Wolfe engineered himself up and over and was lowering above me. Guido released his grip and shoved off, and the dinghy disappeared into the night. I scrambled to my feet.

I had been told not to talk, so I whispered, "I'm turning on my flashlight."

"No."

"We'll tumble in sure as hell."

"Keep close behind me. I know every inch of this. Here, tie this to my sack."

I took his sweater, passed a sleeve under the straps, and knotted it with the other sleeve. He moved across the slab of rock, taking it easy, and I followed. Since I was three inches taller I could keep straight behind and still have a view ahead, though it wasn't much of a view, with the only light from some scattered stars. We stepped off the level slab onto another that sloped up, and then onto one that sloped down. Then we started up again, with loose coarse gravel underfoot instead of solid rock. When it got steeper Wolfe slowed up, and stopped now and then to get his breath. I wanted to warn him that he could be heard breathing for half a mile and therefore we might as well avoid a lot of stumbles by using a light, but decided it would be bad timing.

The idea was to get as far inland as possible before daylight, because we were supposed to have come north through the mountains from Galichnik, and then west toward Cetinje, and therefore it was undesirable to be seen near the coast. Also there was a particular spot about ten miles in, southeast of Cetinje, where we wanted to get something done before dawn. Ten miles in four hours was only a lazy stroll, but not in the dark across mountains, with Wolfe for a pacemaker.

He developed several annoying habits. Realizing that we were at the crest of a climb before I did, he would stop so abruptly that I had to brake fast not to bump into him. He would stumble going uphill but not down, which was unconventional, and I decided he did it just to be eccentric. He would stand still, with his head tilted back and swiveling from side to side, for minutes at a time, and when we were well away from the coast and undertones were permitted and I asked him what for, he muttered, "Stars. My memory has withered." The implication was that he was steering by them, and I didn't believe it. However, there were signs that he knew where he was; for instance, once at the bottom of a slope, after we had traveled at least eight miles, he turned sharply right, passed between two huge boulders where there was barely room for him, picked a way among a jungle of jagged rocks, stopped against a wall of rock that went straight up, extended his hands to it, and bent his head. Sound more than sight told me what he was doing; he had his hands cupped under a trickle of water coming down, and was drinking. I took a turn at it too and found it a lot better than what came from the faucet in Bari. After that I quit wondering if we were lost and just roaming around for the exercise.

No hint of dawn had shown when, on a fairly level stretch, he decelerated until he was barely moving, finally stopped, and turned and asked what time it was. I looked at my wrist and said a quarter past four.

"Your flashlight," he said. I drew it from a loop on my belt and switched it on, and he did the same with his. "You may have to find this spot without me," he said, "so you'd better take it in." He aimed his light to the left down a slope. "That one stone should do it—curled like the tail of a rooster. Put your light on it. There's no other like it between Budva and Podgorica. Get it indelibly."

It was thirty yards away, and I approached over rough ground for a better look. Jutting up to three times my height, one corner swept up in an arc, and it did resemble a rooster's tail if you wanted to use your fancy. I moved my light up and down and across, and, using the light to return to Wolfe, saw that we were on a winding trail.

"Okay," I told him. "Where?"

"This way." He left the trail in the other direction and soon was scrambling up a steep slope. Fifty yards from the trail he stopped and aimed his light up at a sharp angle. "Can you make it up to that ledge?"

It looked nearly perpendicular, twenty feet above our heads. "I can try," I said rashly, "if you stand where you'll cushion me when I fall."

"Start at the right." He pointed. "There. Kneeling on the ledge, the crevice will be about at your eye level, running horizontally. As a boy I used to crawl inside it, but you can't. It slopes down a little from twelve inches in. Put it in as far as you can reach, and poke it farther back with your flashlight. When you come to retrieve it you'll have to have a stick to fork it out with. You must bring the stick along because you won't find one anywhere near here."

As he talked I was opening my pants and pulling up my sweater and shirt to get at the money belt. Preparations for this performance had been made at Bari, wrapping the bills, eight thousand dollars of them, in five tight little packages of oilskin, and putting rubber bands around them. I stuffed them into my jacket pockets and took off my knapsack.

"Call me Tensing," I said, and went to the point indicated and started up. Wolfe changed position to get a better angle for me with his light. I hooked my fingertips onto an inch-wide rim as high as I could reach, got the edge of my sole on another rim two feet up, and pulled, and there was ten per cent of it already done. The next place for a foot was a projecting knob, which I made with no trouble, but then my foot slipped off and I was back at the bottom.

Wolfe spoke. "Take off your shoes."

"I am," I said coldly. "And socks."

It wasn't too bad that way, just plenty bad enough. The ledge, when I finally made it, was at least ten inches wide. I called down to him, "You said to kneel. You come up and kneel. I'd like to see you."

"Not so loud," he said.

By clinging to a crack with one hand I managed to get the packages from my pockets with the other and push them into the crevice as far as my arm would go, and to slip the flashlight from its loop and shove them back. Getting the flashlight back into the loop with one hand was impossible, and I put it in a jacket pocket. I twisted my head to look at the way back and spoke again.

"I'll never make it down. Go get a ladder."

"Hug it," he said, "and use your toes."

Of course it was worse than going up—it always is—but I made it. When I was on his level again he growled, "Satisfactory." Not bothering to reply, I sat down on a rock and played the flashlight over my feet. They weren't cut to the bone anywhere, just some bruises and scratches, and no real flow of blood. There was still some skin left on most of the toes. Putting my socks and shoes on, I became aware that my face was covered with sweat and reached for my handkerchief.

"Come on," Wolfe said.

"Listen," I told him. "You wanted to get that lettuce cached before dawn, and it's there. But if there's any chance that I'll be sent to get it alone, we'd better not go on until daylight. I'll recognize the rooster's tail, that's all right, but how will I find it if I've traveled both approaches in the dark?"

"You'll find it," he declared. "It's only two miles to Rijeka, and a trail all the way. I should have said *very* satisfactory. Come on."

He moved. I got up and followed. It was still pitch dark. In half a mile I realized that we were hitting no more upgrades; it was all down. In another half a mile it was practically level. A dog barked, not far off. There was space around us—my eyes had accommodated to the limit, but I felt it rather than saw it—and underfoot wasn't rock or gravel, more like packed earth.

A little farther on Wolfe stopped, turned, and spoke. "We've entered the valley of the Moracha." He turned on his flashlight and aimed it ahead. "See that fork in the trail? Left joins the road to Rijeka. We'll take it later; now we'll find a place to rest." He turned the light off and moved. At the fork he went right.

This was according to plan as disclosed to me. There was no inn at Rijeka, which was only a village, and we were looking for a haystack. Ten minutes earlier we would have had to use the flashlights to find one, but now, as the trail became a road, there was suddenly light enough to see cart ruts, and in another hundred paces Wolfe turned left into a field, and I followed. The dim outline of the haystack was the wrong shape, but it was no time to be fussy, and I circled to the side away from the road, knelt, and started pulling out handfuls. Soon I had a niche deep enough for Wolfe. I asked him, "Do you wish to eat before going to your room?"

"No." He was grim. "I'm too far gone."

"A bite of chocolate would make a new man of you."

"No. I need help."

I got erect and helped him off with his knapsack. He removed his jacket, got into his sweater, put the jacket back on, and down he went—first to one knee, then both, then out flat. Getting into the niche was more than a simple rolling operation, since its mattress of hay was a good eight inches above ground level, but he made it.

"I'll take your shoes off," I offered.

"Confound it, no! I'd never get them on again!"

"Okay. If you get hungry ask for room service." I knelt to go to work on another niche, and made it long enough to stow the knapsacks at my head. When I was in and had myself arranged, facing outward, I called to Wolfe, "There's a faint pink glow in the east across the valley, ten miles away, above the Albanian Alps. Swell scenery."

No reply. I shut my eyes. Birds were singing.

7

My first daylight view of Montenegro, some eight hours later, when I rolled out of the niche and stepped to the corner of the haystack, had various points of interest. Some ten miles off my port bow as I stood, a sharp peak rose high above the others. It had to be Mount Lovchen, the Black Mountain, so that was northwest, and the sun agreed. To the east was the wide green valley, and beyond it more mountains, in Albania. To the south, some two hundred yards off, was a clump of trees with a house partly showing. To the southwest was Nero Wolfe. He was in his niche, motionless, his eyes wide open, glaring at me.

"Good morning," I told him.

"What time is it?" he demanded. He sounded hoarse.

I looked at my wrist. "I should have said afternoon. Twenty to two. I'm hungry and thirsty."

"No doubt." He closed his eyes and in a moment opened them again. "Archie."

"Yes, sir."

"It is not a question of muscles. My legs ache, of course, and my back; indeed, I ache all over; but that was to be expected and can be borne. What concerns me is my feet. They carry nearly a hundredweight more than yours; they have been pampered for years; and I may have abused them beyond tolerance. They must be rubbed, but I dare not take off my shoes. They are dead. My legs end at my knees. I doubt if I can stand, and I couldn't possibly walk. Do you know anything about gangrene?"

"No, sir."

"It occurs in the extremities when there is interference with both arterial and venous circulation, but I suppose the interference must be prolonged."

"Sure. Eight hours wouldn't do it. I'm hungry."

He shut his eyes. "I awoke to a dull misery, but it is no longer dull. It is overwhelming. I have been trying to move my toes, but

I can't get the slightest sensation of having toes. The idea of squirming out of here and trying to stand up is wholly unacceptable. In fact, no idea whatever is acceptable other than asking you to pull my feet out and take off my shoes and socks; and that would be disastrous because I would never get them back on."

"Yeah. You said that before." I moved nearer. "Look, you might as well face it. This time stalling won't help. For years you've been talking yourself out of pinches, but it won't work on sore feet. If you can't walk there's no use trying. Tomorrow or next day maybe, to prevent gangrene. Meanwhile there's a house in sight and I'll go make a call. How do you say in Serbo-Croat, 'Will you kindly sell me twenty pork chops, a peck of potatoes, four loaves of bread, a gallon of milk, a dozen oranges, five pounds—' "

Unquestionably it was hearing words like pork and bread that made him desperate enough to move. He did it with care. First he eased his head and shoulders out until he had his elbows on the ground, and then worked on back until his feet slid out. Stretched out on his back, he bent his right knee and then his left, slowly and cautiously. Nothing snapped, and he started to pump, at first about ten strokes a minute, then gradually faster. I had moved only enough to give him room, thinking it advisable to be at hand when he tried standing up, but I never had to touch him because he rolled over to the haystack and used it for a prop on his way up. Upright, he leaned against it and growled, "Heaven help me."

"It's you, O Lord. Amen. Is that the Black Mountain?"

He turned his head. "Yes. I never thought to see it again." He turned his back on it and was facing in the direction of the house in the clump of trees. "Why the devil weren't we disturbed long ago? I suppose old Vidin is no longer alive, but someone owns this haystack. We'll go and see. The knapsacks?"

I got them from my niche, and we started for the road, which was only a cart track. Wolfe's gait could not have been called a stride, but he didn't actually totter. The track took us to the edge of the clump of trees, and there was the house, of gray rock, low and long, with a thatched roof and only two small windows and a door in the stretch of stone. Off to the right was a smaller stone building with no windows at all. It looked a little grim, but not grimy. There was no sign of life, human or otherwise. A path of flat stones led to the door, and Wolfe took it. His first knock got no response, but after the second one the door opened about two inches and a female voice came through. After Wolfe exchanged a few noises with the voice the door closed.

"She says her husband is in the barn," he told me. "This is preposterous. I heard a rooster and goats." He started across the yard toward the door of the other building, and when we were halfway there it opened and a man appeared. He shut the door, stood with his back against it, and asked what we wanted. Wolfe told him we wanted food and drink and would pay for it. He said he had no food and only water to drink. Wolfe said all right, we would start with water, told me to come, and led the way over to a well near a corner of the house. It had a rope on a pulley, with a bucket at each end of the rope. One bucket, half full, was on the curb. I poured it into the trough, hauled up a fresh bucket, filled a cup that was there on a flat stone, and handed it to Wolfe. We each drank three cupfuls, and he reported on his talk with our host.

"It's worse than preposterous," he declared, "it's grotesque. Look at him. He resembles old Vidin some and may be a relative. In any case, he is certainly Montenegrin. Look at him. Six feet tall, a jaw like a rock, an eagle's beak for a nose, a brow to take any storm. In ten centuries the Turks could never make him whine. Even under the despotism of Black George he kept his head up as a man. But Communist despotism has done for him. Twenty years ago two strangers who had damaged his haystack would have been called to account; today, having espied us in trespass on his property, he tells his wife to stay indoors and shuts himself in the barn with his goats and chickens. Do you know how Tennyson addressed Tsernagora—the Black Mountain?"

"No."

"The last three lines of a sonnet:

> *"Great Tsernagora, never since thine own*
> *Black ridges drew the cloud and broke the storm*
> *Has breathed a race of mightier mountaineers."*

He scowled in the direction of the mighty mountaineer standing at the barn door. "Pfui! Give me a thousand dinars."

While I was getting the roll from my pocket—procured for us by Telesio in Bari—I didn't need to figure how much I was shelling out because I already had it filed that a thousand dinars was $3.33. Wolfe took it and approached our host. His line as later reported:

"We pay you for the damage to your haystack, which you can repair in five minutes. We also pay you for food. Have you any oranges?"

He looked startled, suspicious, wary, and sullen, all at once. He shook his head. "No."

"Any coffee?"

"No."

"Bacon or ham?"

"No. I have nothing at all."

"Bosh. If you think we are spies from Podgorica, or even Belgrade, you are wrong. We are—"

The man cut in. "You must not say Podgorica. You must say Titograd."

Wolfe nodded. "I am aware that the change has been made, but I haven't made up my mind whether to accept it. We have returned recently from the world outside, we are politically unattached, and we are starving. If necessary, my son, who is armed, can engage you while I enter the barn and get chickens—we would need two. It would be simpler and more agreeable for you to take this money and have your wife feed us. Have you any bacon or ham?"

"No."

"Something left of a kid?"

"No."

Wolfe roared, "Then what the devil have you?"

"Some sausage, of a sort." He hated to admit it. "A few eggs perhaps. Bread, and possibly a little lard."

Wolfe turned to me. "Another thousand dinars." I produced it, and he proffered it, with its twin, to our host. "Here, take it. We're at your mercy—but no lard. I overate of lard in my youth, and the smell sickens me. Your wife might conceivably find a little butter somewhere."

"No." He had the dough. "Butter is out of the question."

"Very well. That would pay for two good meals in the best hotel in Belgrade. Please bring us a pan, a piece of soap, and a towel."

He moved, in no hurry, to the house door and inside. When he came out again he had the articles requested. Wolfe put the metal pan, which was old and dented but clean, on the stone curb of the well, poured it half full of water, took off his jacket and sweater, rolled up his sleeves, and washed. I followed suit. The water was so cold it numbed my fingers, but I was getting used to extreme hardship. The gray linen towel, brought ironed and folded, was two feet wide and four feet long when opened up. After I had got our combs and brushes from the knapsacks, and they had been used and repacked, I poured fresh water in the pan, placed it on the ground, sat on the edge of the well curb, took off my shoes and socks, and put a foot in the water. Stings and tingles shot through every nerve I had. Wolfe stood gazing down at the pan.

"Are you going to use soap?" he asked wistfully.

"I don't know. I haven't decided."

"You should have rubbed them first."

"No." I was emphatic. "My problem is different from yours. I lost hide."

He sat on the curb beside me and watched while I paddled in the pan, one foot and then the other, dried them with gentle pats of the towel, put on clean socks and my shoes, washed the dirty socks, and stretched them on a bush in the sun. When I started to wash the pan out he suddenly blurted, "Wait a minute. I think I'll risk it."

"Okay. I guess you could probably make it to Rijeka barefooted."

The test was never made because our host appeared and spoke, and Wolfe got up and headed for the door of the house, and I followed. The ceiling of the room we entered wasn't as low as I had expected. The wallpaper was patterned in green and yellow, but you couldn't see much of it on account of the dozens of pictures, all about the same size. There were rugs on the floor, carved chests and chairs with painted decorations, a big iron stove, and one small window. By the window was a table with a red cloth, with two places set—knives and forks and spoons and napkins. Wolfe and I went and sat, and two women came through an arched doorway. One of them, middle-aged, in a garment apparently made of old gray canvas, aimed sharp black eyes straight at us as she approached, bearing a loaded tray. The other one, following, made me forget how hungry I was for a full ten seconds. I didn't get a good view of her eyes because she kept them lowered, but the rest of her boosted my rating of the scenery of Montenegro more than the Black Mountain had.

When they had delivered the food and left I asked Wolfe, "Do you suppose the daughter wears that white blouse and embroidered green vest all the time?"

He snorted. "Certainly not. She heard us speaking a foreign tongue, and we paid extravagantly for food. Would a Montenegrin girl miss such a chance?" He snorted again. "Would any girl? So she changed her clothes."

"That's a hell of an attitude," I protested. "We should appreciate her taking the trouble. If you want to take off your shoes, go ahead, and we can rent the haystack by the week until the swelling goes down."

He didn't bother to reply. Ten minutes later I asked him, "Why do they put gasoline in the sausage?"

At that, it wasn't a bad meal, and it certainly was needed. The eggs were okay, the dark bread was a little sour but edible, and the cherry jam, out of a half-gallon crock, would have been good anywhere. Someone told Wolfe later that in Belgrade fresh eggs were forty dinars apiece, and we each ate five, so we weren't such suckers. After one sip I gave the tea a miss, but there was nothing wrong with the water. As I was spreading jam on another slice of bread our host entered and said something and departed. I asked Wolfe what. He said the cart was ready. I asked, what cart? He said to take us to Rijeka.

I complained. "This is the first I've heard about a cart. The understanding was that you report all conversations in full. You have always maintained that if I left out anything at all you would never know whether you had the kernel or not. Now that the shoe's on the other foot, if you'll excuse my choice of metaphor, I feel the same way."

I don't think he heard me. His belly was full, but he was going to have to stand up again and walk, and he was too busy dreading it to debate with me. As we pushed back our chairs and got up, the daughter appeared in the arch and spoke, and I asked Wolfe, "What did she say?"

"*Sretan put.*"

"Please spell it."

He did so.

"What does it mean?"

"Happy going."

"How do I say, 'The going will be happier if you come along'?"

"You don't." He was on his way to the door. Not wanting to be rude, I crossed to the daughter and offered a hand, and she took it. Hers was nice and firm. For one little flash she raised her eyes to mine and then dropped them again. "Roses are red," I said distinctly, "violets are blue, sugar is sweet, and so are you." I gave her hand a gentle squeeze and tore myself away.

Out in the yard I found Wolfe standing with his arms folded and his lips compressed, glaring at a vehicle that deserved it. The horse wasn't so bad—undersized, nearer a pony than a horse, but in good shape—but the cart it was hitched to was nothing but a big wooden box on two iron-rimmed wheels. Wolfe turned to me.

"He says," he said bitterly, "that he put hay in it to sit on."

I nodded. "You'd never reach Rijeka alive." I went and got the knapsacks and our sweaters and jackets, and my socks from the bush. "It's only a little over a mile, isn't it? Let's go."

8

To build Rijeka all they had to do was knock off chunks of rock, roll them down to the edge of the valley, stack them in rectangles, and top the rectangles with thatched roofs; and that was all they had done, about the time Columbus started across the Atlantic to find India. Mud from the April rains was a foot deep in the one street, but there was a raised sidewalk of flat stones on either side. As we proceeded along it, single file, Wolfe in the lead, I got an impression that we were not welcome. I caught glimpses of human forms ahead, one or two on the sidewalk, a couple of children running along the top of a low stone wall, a woman in a yard with a broom; but they all disappeared before we reached them. There weren't even any faces at windows as we went by. I asked Wolfe's back, "What have we got, fleas?"

He stopped and turned. "No. They have. The sap has been sucked out of their spines. Pfui."

He went on. A little beyond the center of the village he left the walk to turn right through a gap in a stone wall into a yard. The house was set back a little farther than most of them, and was a little wider and higher. The door was arched at the top, with fancy carvings up the sides. Wolfe raised a fist to knock, but before his knuckles touched, the door swung open and a man confronted us.

Wolfe asked him, "Are you George Bilic?"

"I am." He was a low bass. "And you?"

"My name is unimportant, but you may have it. I am Toné Stara, and this is my son Alex. You own an automobile, and we wish to be driven to Podgorica. We will pay a proper amount."

Bilic's eyes narrowed. "I know of no place called Podgorica."

"You call it Titograd. I am not yet satisfied with the change, though I may be. My son and I are preparing to commit our sympathy and our resources. Of you we require merely a service for pay. I am willing to call it Titograd as a special favor to you."

"Where are you from and how did you get here?"

"That's our affair. You need merely to know that we will pay two thousand dinars to be driven twenty-three kilometers—or six American dollars, if you prefer them."

Bilic's narrow eyes in his round puffy face got narrower. "I do not prefer American dollars and I don't like such an ugly suggestion. How do you know I own an automobile?"

"That is known to everyone. Do you deny it?"

"No. But there's something wrong with it. A thing on the engine is broken, and it won't go."

"My son Alex will make it go. He's an expert."

Bilic shook his head. "I couldn't allow that. He might damage it permanently."

"You're quite right." Wolfe was sympathetic. "We are strangers to you. But I also know that you have a telephone, and you have kept us standing too long outside your door. We will enter and go with you to the telephone, and you will make a call to Belgrade, for which we will pay. You will get the Ministry of the Interior, Room Nineteen, and you will ask if it is desirable for you to co-operate with a man who calls himself Toné Stara—describing me, of course. And you will do this at once, for I am beginning to get a little impatient."

Wolfe's bluff wasn't as screwy as it sounds. From what Telesio had told him, he knew that Bilic would take no risk either of offending a stranger who might be connected with the secret police, or of calling himself to the attention of headquarters in Belgrade by phoning to ask a dumb question. The bluff not only worked; it produced an effect which seemed to me entirely out of proportion when Wolfe told me later what he had said. Bilic suddenly went as pale as if all his blood had squirted out under his toenails. Simultaneously he tried to smile, and the combination wasn't attractive. "I beg your pardon, sir," he said in a different tone, backing up a step and bowing. "I'm sure you'll understand that it is necessary to be careful. Come in and sit down, and we'll have some wine."

"We haven't time." Wolfe was curt. "You will telephone at once."

"It would be ridiculous to telephone." Bilic was doing his best to smile. "After all, you merely wish to be driven to Titograd, which is natural and proper. Won't you come in?"

"No. We're in a hurry."

"Very well. I know what it is to be in a hurry, I assure you." He turned and shouted, "Jubé!"

He might just as well have whispered it, since Jubé had obviously been lurking not more than ten feet away. He came through a curtained arch—a tall and bony youth, maybe eighteen, in a blue shirt with open collar, and blue jeans he could have got from Sears Roebuck.

"My son is on vacation from the university," Bilic informed us. "He returns tomorrow to learn how to do his part in perfecting the Socialist Alliance of the Working People of Yugoslavia under the leadership of our great and beloved President. Jubé, this is Mr. Toné Stara and his son Alex. They wish to be driven to Titograd, and you will—"

"I heard what was said. I think you should telephone the Ministry in Belgrade."

Jubé was a complication that Telesio hadn't mentioned. I didn't like him. To get his contribution verbatim I would have to wait until Wolfe reported, but his tone was nasty, and I caught the Yugoslav sounds for "telephone" and "Belgrade," so I had the idea. It seemed to me that Jubé could do with a little guidance from an elder, and luckily his father felt the same way about it.

"As I have told you, my son," Bilic said sternly, "the day may have come for you to do your own thinking, but not mine. I think these gentlemen should be conveyed to Titograd in my automobile, and, since I have other things to do, I think you should drive them. If you regard yourself as sufficiently mature to ignore what I think, we can discuss the matter later in private, but I hereby instruct you to drive Mr. Stara and his son to Titograd. Do you intend to follow my instruction?"

They exchanged gazes. Bilic won. Jubé's eyes fell, and he muttered, "Yes."

"That is not a proper reply to your father."

"Yes, sir."

"Good. Go and start the engine."

The boy went. I shelled out some Yugoslav currency.

Bilic explained that the car would have to leave the village by way of the lane in the rear, on higher ground than the street, which the mud made impassable, and conducted us through the house and out the back door. If he had more family than Jubé, it kept out of sight. The grounds back of the house were neat, with thick grass and flowerbeds. A walk of flat stones took us to a stone building, and as we approached, a car backed out of it to the right, with Jubé at the wheel. I stared at it in astonishment. It was a 1953 Ford sedan. Then I remembered an item of the briefing Wolfe had given me on Yugoslavia: we had lent them, through the World Bank, a total of fifty-eight million bucks. How Bilic had managed to promote a Ford for himself out of it was to some extent my business, since I paid income tax, but I decided to table it. As we climbed in, Wolfe asked Bilic to inform his son that the trip had been fully paid for—two thousand dinars—and Bilic did so.

The road was level most of the way to Titograd, across the valley and up the Moracha River, but it took us more than an hour to cover the twenty-three kilometers—fourteen miles to you— chiefly on account of mud. I started in the back seat with Wolfe, but after the springs had hit in a couple of chuckholes I moved up front with Jubé. On the smooth stretches Wolfe posted me some on Titograd—but, since Jubé might have got some English at the university, he was Toné Stara telling his American-born son. As Podgorica, it had long been the commercial capital of Montenegro. Its name had been changed to Titograd in 1950. Its population was around twelve thousand. It had a fine old Turkish bridge across the Moracha. A tributary of the Moracha separated the old Turkish town, which had been inhabited by Albanians thirty years ago and probably still was, from the new Montenegrin town, which had been built in the latter half of the nineteenth century.

Twisted around in the front seat, I tried to deduce from Jubé's profile whether he knew more English than I did Serbo-Croat, but there was no sign one way or the other.

The commercial capital of Montenegro was a letdown. I hadn't expected a burg of twelve thousand to be one of the world's wonders, and Wolfe had told me that, under the Communists, Montenegro was still a backwater—but hadn't they changed the name to Titograd, and wasn't Tito the Number One? So, as we jolted and bumped over holes in the pavement and I took in the old gray two-story buildings that didn't even have thatched roofs to give them a tone, I felt cheated. I decided that if and when I became a dictator I would damn well clean a town up and widen some of its streets and have a little painting done before I changed its name to Goodwingrad. I had just made that decision when the car rolled to the curb and stopped in front of a stone edifice a lot bigger and some dirtier than most of those we had been passing.

Wolfe said something with an edge on his voice. Jubé turned in the seat to face him and made a little speech. For me the words were just a noise, but I didn't like his tone or his expression, so I slipped my hand inside my jacket to scratch myself in the neighborhood of my left armpit, bringing my fingers in contact with the butt of the Marley.

"No trouble, Alex," Wolfe assured me. "As you know, I asked him to leave us at the north end of the square, but he is being thoughtful. He says it is required that on arriving at a place travelers must have their identification papers inspected, and he thought it would be more convenient for us if he brought us here, to the local headquarters of the national police. Will you bring the knapsacks?"

He opened the door and was climbing out. Since the only papers we had with us were engraved dollars and dinars, I had a suspicion that his foot condition had affected his central nervous system and paralyzed his brain, but I was helpless. I couldn't even stop a passer-by and ask the way to the nearest hospital, and I had never felt so useless and so goddam silly as, with a knapsack under each arm, I followed Jubé and Wolfe across to the entrance and into the stone edifice. Inside, Jubé led us along a dim and dingy corridor, up a flight of stairs, and into a room where two men were perched on stools behind a counter. The men greeted him by name, not with any visible enthusiasm.

"Here are two travelers," Jubé said, "who wish to show their papers. I just drove them from Rijeka. I can't tell you how they got to Rijeka. The big fat one says his name is Toné Stara, and the other is his son Alex."

"In one respect," Wolfe objected, "that statement is not accurate. We do not wish to show papers, for an excellent reason. We have no papers to show."

"Hah!" Jubé cried in triumph.

One of the men said reasonably, "Merely the usual papers, nothing special. You can't live without papers."

"We have none."

"I don't believe it. Then where are they?"

"This is not a matter for clerks," Jubé declared. "Tell Gospo Stritar, and I'll take them in to him."

Either they didn't like being called clerks, or they didn't like Jubé, or both. They gave him dirty looks and exchanged mutterings, and one of them disappeared through an inner door, closing it behind him. Soon it opened again, and he stood holding it. I got the impression that Jubé was not specifically included in the invitation to pass through, but he came along, bringing up the rear.

This room was bigger but just as dingy. The glass in the high narrow windows had apparently last been washed the day the name had been changed from Podgorica to Titograd, four years ago. Of the two big old desks, one was unoccupied, and behind the other sat a lantern-jawed husky with bulging shoulders, who needed a haircut. Evidently he had been in conference with an individual in a chair at the end of the desk—one younger and a lot uglier, with a flat nose and a forehead that slanted back at a sharp angle from just above the eyebrows. The husky behind the desk, after a quick glance at Wolfe and me, focused on Jubé with no sign of cordiality.

"Where did you get these men?" he demanded.

Jubé told him. "They appeared at my father's house, from nowhere, and asked to be driven to Podgorica. The big fat one said Podgorica. He said he would pay two thousand dinars or six American dollars. He knew we have an automobile and a telephone. When his request was refused he told my father to telephone the Ministry of the Interior in Belgrade, Room Nineteen, and ask if he should cooperate with a man calling himself Toné Stara. My father thought it unnecessary to telephone, and commanded me to drive them to Titograd. On the way they talked together in a foreign tongue which I don't know but which I think was English. The big fat one told me to let them out at the north end of the square, but I brought them here instead, and now I am fully justified. They admit they have no papers. It will be interesting to hear them explain."

Jubé pulled a chair around and sat down. The husky eyed him. "Did I tell you to be seated?"

"No, you didn't."

"Then get up. I said get up! That's better, little man. You go to the university in Zagreb, that is true, and you have even spent three days in Belgrade, but I have not heard that you have been designated a hero of the people. You did right to bring these men here, and I congratulate you on behalf of our great People's Republic, but if you try to assert yourself beyond your years and your position you will undoubtedly get your throat cut. Now go back home and study to improve yourself, and give my regards to your worthy father."

"You are being arbitrary, Gospo Stritar. It would be better for me to stay and hear—"

"Get out!"

I thought for a second the college boy was going to balk, and he did too, but the final vote was no. He turned and marched out. When the door had closed behind him, the one seated at the end of the desk got up, evidently meaning to leave, but Stritar said something to him, and he went to another chair and sat. Wolfe went and took the one at the end of the desk, and I took the one that Jubé had vacated.

Stritar looked at Wolfe, at me, and back at Wolfe. He spoke. "What's this talk about your having no papers?"

"Not talk," Wolfe told him. "A fact. We have none."

"Where are they? What's your story? Who stole them?"

"Nobody. We had no papers. You will find our story somewhat unusual."

"I already find it unusual. You had better talk."

"I intend to, Mr. Stritar. My name is Toné Stara. I was born in Galichnik, and at the age of sixteen I began to follow the well-known custom of spending eleven months of the year elsewhere to earn a living. For seven years I returned to Galichnik each July, but the eighth year I did not return because I had got married in a foreign land. My wife bore a son and died, but still I did not return. I had abandoned my father's craft and tried other activities, and I prospered. My son Alex grew up and joined in my activities, and we prospered more. I thought I had cut all bonds with my native land, shed all memories, but when Yugoslavia was expelled from the Cominform six years ago my interest was aroused, and so was my son's, and we followed developments more and more closely. Last July, when Yugoslavia resumed relations with Soviet Russia and Marshal Tito made his famous statement, my curiosity became intense. I became involved in arguments, not so much with others as with myself. I tried to get enough reliable information to make a final and just decision about the right and the wrong and the true interest and welfare of the people of my birthland."

He nodded sidewise at me. "My son's curiosity was as great as mine, and we finally concluded that it was impossible to judge from so great a distance. We couldn't get satisfactory information, and we couldn't test what we did get. I determined to come and find out for myself. I thought it best for me to come alone, since my son couldn't speak the language, but he insisted on accompanying me, and in the end I consented. Naturally there was some difficulty, since we could not get passports for either Albania or Yugoslavia, and we chose to go by ship to Naples and fly to Bari. Leaving our luggage—and papers and certain other articles—at Bari, we arranged, through an agent who had been recommended to me, for a boat to take us across to the Albanian coast. Landing at night near Drin, we made our way across Albania to Galichnik, but we discovered

in a few hours that nothing was to be learned there and crossed
the border back into Albania."

"At what spot?" Stritar asked.

Wolfe shook his head. "I don't intend to cause trouble for anyone who has helped us. I had been somewhat inclined to think that
Russian leadership offered the best hope for the people of my
native land, but after a few days in Albania I was not so sure.
People didn't want to talk with a stranger, but I heard enough to
give me a suspicion that conditions might be better under Tito in
Yugoslavia. Also I heard something of a feeling that the most
promising future was with neither the Russians nor Marshal Tito,
but with an underground movement that condemned both of them,
so I was more confused than when I had left my adopted country
in search of the truth. All the time, you understand, we were ourselves underground in a way, because we had no papers. I had,
of course, intended all along to visit Yugoslavia, and now I was
resolved also to learn more of the movement which I was told
was called the Spirit of the Black Mountain. I suppose you have
heard of it?"

Stritar smiled, not with amusement. "Oh yes, I've heard of it."

"I understand it is usually called simply the Spirit. No one would
tell me the names of its leaders, but from certain hints I gathered
that one of them was to be found near Mount Lovchen, which
would seem logical. So we came north through the mountains and
managed to get over the border into Yugoslavia, and across the
valley and the river as far as Rijeka, but then we felt it was useless
to go on to Cetinje without better information. In my boyhood I
had once been to Podgorica to visit a friend named Grudo Balar."
Wolfe turned abruptly in his chair to look at the flat-nosed young
man with a slanting forehead, seated over toward the wall. "I
noticed when I came in that you look like him, and thought you
might be his son. May I ask, is your name Balar?"

"No, it isn't," Flat-nose replied in a low smooth voice that was
barely audible. "My name is Peter Zov, if that concerns you."

"Not at all, if it isn't Balar." Wolfe went back to Stritar. "So we
decided to come to Podgorica—which I shall probably learn to call
Titograd if we stay in this country—first to try to find my old friend,
and second to see what it is like here. Someone had mentioned
George Bilic of Rijeka, with his automobile and telephone, and

we were footsore, so we sought him out and offered him two thousand dinars to drive us here. You will want to know why, when Bilic didn't want to oblige us, I told him to telephone the Ministry of the Interior in Belgrade. It was merely a maneuver—not very subtle, I admit—which I used once or twice in Albania, to test the atmosphere. If he had telephoned, it would have broadened the test considerably."

"If he had telephoned," Stritar said, "you would now be in jail and someone would be on his way from Belgrade to deal with you."

"All the better. That would tell me much."

"Perhaps more than you want to know. You told Bilic to ask for Room Nineteen. Why?"

"To impress him."

"Since you just arrived in Yugoslavia, how did you know about Room Nineteen?"

"It was mentioned to me several times in Albania."

"In what way?"

"As the lair of the panther who heads the secret police, and therefore the center of power." Wolfe flipped a hand. "Let me finish. I told Jubé Bilic to take us to the north corner of the square, but when he brought us here instead I thought it just as well. You would soon have learned of our presence, from someone else if not from him, and it would be better to see you and tell you about us."

"It would be better still to tell me the truth."

"I have told you the truth."

"Bah. Why did you offer to pay Bilic in American dollars?"

"Because we have some."

"How many?"

"Oh, more than a thousand."

"Where did you get them?"

"In the United States. That is a wonderful country to make money, and my son and I have made our full share, but it does not know how to arrange for a proper concentration of power, and therefore there is too much loose talk. That's why we came here to find out. Who can best concentrate the power of the Yugoslavs—the Russians, or Tito, or the Spirit of the Black Mountain?"

Stritar cocked his head and narrowed his eyes. "This is all very interesting, and extremely silly. It occurs to me that of the many millions lent to Yugoslavia by the World Bank—that is to say, by the United States—only one little million is being spent in Montenegro, for a dam and power plant just above Titograd, not three kilometers from here. If the World Bank wanted to know if the money is being spent for the agreed purpose, might it not send some such man as you to look?"

"It might," Wolfe conceded. "But not me. I am not technically qualified, and neither is my son."

"You can't possibly expect me," Stritar asserted, "to believe your fantastic story. I admit that I have no idea what you do expect. You must know that, having no papers, you are subject to arrest and a thorough examination, which you would find uncomfortable. You may be Russian agents. You may, as I said, be agents of the World Bank. You may be foreign spies from God knows where. You may be American friends of the Spirit of the Black Mountain. You may even have been sent from Room Nineteen in Belgrade, to test the loyalty and vigilance of Montenegrins. But I ask myself, if you are any of those, why in the name of God are you not provided with papers? It's ridiculous."

"Exactly." Wolfe nodded approvingly. "It is a pleasure to meet with an intelligent man, Mr. Stritar. You can account for our having no papers only by assuming that my fantastic story is true, as indeed it is. As for arresting us, I don't pretend that we would be delighted to spend a year or two in jail, but it would certainly answer some of the questions we have been asking. As for what we expect, why not allow us a reasonable amount of time, say a month, to get the information we came for? I would know better than to make such a suggestion in Belgrade, but this is Montenegro, where the Turks clawed at the crags for centuries to no purpose, and it seems unlikely that my son and I will topple them. To show that I am being completely frank with you, I said that we have more than a thousand American dollars, but I carry very little of it and my son only a fraction. We have cached most of it, a considerable amount, in the mountains, and it is significant that the spot we chose is not in Albania but in Montenegro. That would seem to imply that we lean to Tito instead of the Russians—did you say something, Mr. Zov?"

Peter Zov, who had made a noise that could have been only a grunt, shook his head. "No, but I could."

"Then say it," Stritar told him.

"American dollars in the mountains must not go to the Spirit."

"There is that risk," Wolfe admitted, "but I doubt if they'll be found, and what I have heard of that movement makes it even more doubtful that we will favor it. You're a man of action, are you, Mr. Zov?"

"I can do things, yes." The low, smooth voice was silky.

"Peter has earned a reputation," Stritar said.

"A good thing to have." Wolfe came back to Stritar. "But if he has in mind prying out of us where the dollars are, it doesn't seem advisable. We are American citizens, and serious violence to us would be indiscreet; and besides, the bulk of our fortune is in the United States, beyond your reach unless you enlist our sympathy and support."

"What place in the United States?"

"That's unimportant."

"Is Toné Stara your name there?"

"It may be, or maybe not. I can tell you, I understand the kind of power that is typified by Room Nineteen, and it attracts me, but I prefer not to call its attention to my friends and associates in America. It might be inconvenient in case I decide to return and stay."

"You may not be permitted to return."

"True. We take that risk."

"You're a pair of fools."

"Then don't waste your time on us. All a fool can do in Montenegro is fall off a mountain and break his neck, as you should know. If I came back here to fulfill my destiny, and brought my son along, why make a fuss about it?"

Stritar laughed. It seemed to me a plain, honest laugh, as if he were really amused, and I wondered what Wolfe had said, but I had to wait until later to find out. Peter Zov didn't join in. When Stritar was through being amused he looked at his wristwatch, gave me a glance—the eighth or ninth he had shot at me—and then frowned at Wolfe. "You are aware," he said, "that everywhere you go in Titograd, and everything you say and do, will get to me. This is not London or Washington, or even Belgrade. I don't need to have you followed. If I want you in an hour, or five hours, or forty, I can get you—alive or dead. You say you understand the kind of power that is typified by Room Nineteen. If you don't, you will. I am now permitting you to go, but if I change my mind you'll know it."

He sounded severe, so it came as a surprise to see Wolfe leave his chair, tell me to come, and head for the door. I picked up the knapsacks and followed. In the outer room only one of the clerks was left, and he merely gave us a brief look as we passed through. Not being posted on our status, I was half expecting a squad to stop us downstairs and collar us, but the corridor was empty. On the sidewalk we got a few curious glances from passers-by as we stood a moment. I noted that Bilic's 1953 Ford was gone.

"This way," Wolfe said, turning right.

The next incident gave me a lot of satisfaction, and God knows I needed it. In New York, where I belong and know my way around and can read the signs, I no longer get any great kick out of it when a hunch comes through for me, but there in Titograd it gave me a lift to find that my nervous system was on the job in spite of all the handicaps. We had covered perhaps a quarter of a mile on the narrow sidewalks, dodging foreigners of various shapes and sizes, turning several corners, when I got the feeling that we had a tail and made a quick stop and wheel.

After one sharp glance I turned and caught up with Wolfe and told him, "Jubé is coming along behind. Not accidentally, because when I turned he dived into a doorway. The sooner you bring me up to date, the better."

"Not standing here in the street, being jostled. I wish you were a linguist."

"I don't. Do we shake Jubé?"

"No. Let him play. I want to sit down."

He went on, and I tagged along. Every fifty paces or so I looked back, but got no further glimpse of our college-boy tail until we had reached a strip of park along the river bank. That time he sidestepped behind a tree that was too thin to hide him. He badly needed some kindergarten coaching. Wolfe led the way to a wooden bench at the edge of a graveled path, sat, and compressed his lips as he straightened his legs to let his feet rest on the heels. I sat beside him and did likewise.

"I would have supposed," he said peevishly, "that yours would be hardier."

"Yeah. Did you climb a precipice barefooted?"

He closed his eyes and sat and breathed. After a little his eyes opened, and he spoke. "The river is at its highest now. This is the Zeta; you see where it joins the Moracha. Over there is the old Turkish town. In my boyhood only Albanians lived there, and according to Telesio only a few of them have left since Tito broke with Moscow."

"Thanks. When you finish telling me about the Albanians, tell me about us. I thought people without papers in Communist countries were given the full treatment. How did you horse him? From the beginning, please, straight through."

He reported. It was a nice enough spot, with the trees sporting new green leaves, and fresh green grass that needed mowing, and patches of red and yellow and blue flowers; and with enough noise from the river for him to disregard the people passing by along the path.

When he had finished I looked it over a little and asked a few questions, and then remarked, "Okay. All I could do was watch to see if you reached in your pocket for the lullaby. Did Stritar sick Jubé on us?"

"I don't know."

"If he did he needs some new personnel." I looked at my wrist. "It's after six o'clock. What's next—look for a good haystack while it's daylight?"

"You know what we came to Podgorica for."

I crossed my legs jauntily to show that I could. "I would like to make a suggestion. Extreme stubbornness is all very well when you're safe at home with the chain-bolt on the door, and if and when we're back there, call it Podgorica if you insist. But here it wouldn't bust a vein for you to call it Titograd."

"These vulgar barbarians have no right to degrade a history and deform a culture."

"No, and they have no right to give two American citizens the works, but they can and probably will. You can snarl 'Podgorica' at them while they're making you over. Are we waiting here for something?"

"No."

"Shall I go tie Jubé to a tree?"

"No. Ignore him."

"Then why don't we go?"

"Confound it, my feet!"

"What they need," I said sympathetically, "is exercise, to stimulate circulation. After a couple of weeks of steady walking and climbing you won't even notice you have feet."

"Shut up."

"Yes, sir."

He closed his eyes. In a minute he opened them again, slowly bent his left knee, and got his left foot flat on the ground, then his right.

"Very well," he said grimly, and stood up.

9

It was a two-story stone house on a narrow cobbled street, back some three hundred yards from the river, with a tiny yard in front behind a wooden fence that had never been painted. If I had been Yugoslavia I would have spent a fair fraction of the fifty-eight million from the World Bank on paint. We had covered considerably more than three hundred yards getting there because of a detour to ask about Grudo Balar at the house where he had lived years before in his youth—a detour, Wolfe explained, which we bothered to make only because he had mentioned Balar to Gospo Stritar. The man who answered the door to Wolfe's knock said he had lived there only three years and had never heard of anyone named Balar, so we crossed him off.

When the door was opened to us at the two-story house on the narrow cobbled street I stared in surprise. It was the daughter of the owner of the haystack who had changed her clothes in our honor. Then a double take showed me that this one was several years older and a little plumper, but otherwise she could have been a duplicate. Wolfe said something, and she replied and turned her head to call within, and in a moment a man appeared, replaced her on the threshold, and spoke in Serbo-Croat.

"I'm Danilo Vukcic. Who are you?"

I won't say I would have spotted him in a crowd, for he didn't resemble his Uncle Marko much superficially, but he was the same family all right. He was a little taller than Marko had been, and not so burly, and his eyes were set deeper, but his head sat exactly the same and he had the same wide mouth with full lips—though it wasn't Marko's mouth, because Marko had spent a lot of time laughing, and this nephew didn't look as if he had laughed much.

"If you would step outside?" Wolfe suggested.

"What for? What do you want?"

"I want to say something not for other ears."

"There are no ears in my house that I don't trust."

"I congratulate you. But I haven't tested them as you have, so if you'll oblige me?"

"Who are you?"

"One who gets messages by telephone. Eight days ago I received one saying, 'The man you seek is within sight of the mountain.' Four days ago I received another saying that a person I knew had died a violent death within sight of the mountain. For speedy communication at a distance the telephone is supreme."

Danilo was staring at him, frowning, not believing. "It's impossible." Then he shifted the stare and frown to me. "Who is this?"

"My associate who came with me."

"Come in." He sidestepped to make room. "Come in quickly." We passed through, and he shut the door. "No one is here but my family. This way." He took us through an arch into an inner room, raising his voice to call as he went, "All right, Meta! Go ahead and feed them!" He stopped and faced Wolfe. "We have two small children."

"I know. Marko was concerned about them. He thought you and your wife were competent to calculate your risks, but they were not. He wanted you to send them to him in New York. Ivan is five years old and Zosha three. It is not a question of trusting ears; they are old enough to babble, as you should know."

"Of course." Danilo went and shut a door and returned. "They can't hear us. Who are you?"

"Nero Wolfe. This is Archie Goodwin. Marko may have spoken of him."

"Yes. But I can't believe it."

Wolfe nodded. "That comes first, naturally, for you to believe. It shouldn't be too difficult." He looked around. "If we could sit?"

None of the chairs in sight met his specifications, but there were several that would serve his main purpose, to get his weight off his feet. I wouldn't have known that the big tiled object in the corner was a stove if I hadn't had the habit of spending an hour or so each month looking at the pictures in the *National Geographic,* and I had also seen most of the other articles of furniture, with the exception of the rug. It was a beaut, with red and yellow roses as big as my head on a blue background. Only a vulgar barbarian would have dragged a chair across it, so I lifted one to place it so as to be in the group after Wolfe had lowered himself onto the widest one available.

"It should help," Wolfe began, "to tell you how we got here." He proceeded to do so, in full, going back to the day, nearly a month earlier, when the news had come that Marko had been killed. From first to last Danilo kept a steady gaze at him, ignoring me completely, making no interruptions. He was a good listener. When Wolfe got to the end and stopped, Danilo gave me a long hard look and then went back to Wolfe.

"It is true," he said, "that through my Uncle Marko I have heard of Nero Wolfe and Archie Goodwin. But why should you go to such trouble and expense to get here, and why do you come to me?"

Wolfe grunted. "So you're not satisfied. I understand the necessity for prudence, but surely this is excessive. If I am an impostor I already know enough to destroy you—Marko's associates in New York, the messages to me through Paolo Telesio, the house in Bari where you have met Marko, a dozen other details which I included. Either I am already equipped as the agent of your doom, or I am Nero Wolfe. I don't understand your incredulity. Why the devil did you send those messages if you didn't expect me to act?"

"I sent only one. The first one, that Carla was here, was only from Telesio. The second, that the man you sought was here, was sent because Carla said to. The last, that she had been killed, I sent because she would have wanted you to know. From what Marko had told me of you, I had no idea that you would come. When he was alive you had refused to give any support to the

Spirit of the Black Mountain, so why should we have expected help from you when he was dead? Am I supposed to believe you have come to help?"

Wolfe shook his head. "No," he said bluntly. "To help your movement on its merits, no. No blow for freedom should be discouraged or scorned, but in this remote mountain corner the best you can do is tickle the tyrant's toes and die for your pains. If by any chance you should succeed in destroying Tito, the Russians would swarm in from all sides and finish you. I came to get a murderer. For years I have made a living catching wrongdoers, murderers in particular, and I don't intend to let the one who killed Marko escape. I expect you to help me."

"The one who killed Marko is only a tool. We have larger plans."

"No doubt. So have I, but this is personal, and at least it rides in your direction. It may be useful to make it clear that your friends in distant places cannot be slaughtered with impunity. I offer no bribe, but when I get back to America I shall probably feel, as the executor of Marko's estate, that his associates in a project dear to him deserve sympathetic consideration."

"I don't believe you'll ever get back. This isn't America, and you don't know how to operate here. Already you have made five bad mistakes. For one thing, you have exposed yourselves to that baby rat, Jubé Bilic, and let him follow you here."

"But," Wolfe objected, "I was told by Telesio that it would place you in no danger if we were seen coming here. He said you are being paid by both Belgrade and the Russians, and you are trusted by neither, and neither is ready to remove you."

"Nobody trusts anyone," Danilo said harshly. He left his chair. "But this Jubé Bilic, for a Montenegrin, has at his age a fatal disease of the bones. Even Montenegrins like Gospo Stritar, who work for Tito and have his picture on their walls if not in their hearts, have only contempt for such as Jubé Bilic, who spies on his own father. Contempt is all right, that's healthy enough, but sometimes it turns into fear, and that's too much. Do I understand that Jubé followed you to this house?"

Wolfe turned to me. "He wants to know if Jubé followed us here."

"He did," I declared, "unless he stumbled and fell in the last two hundred yards. I saw him turn the corner into this street."

Wolfe relayed it. "In that case," Danilo said, "you must excuse me while I arrange something." He left the room through the door toward the back of the house, closing it behind him.

"What's up?" I asked Wolfe. "Has he gone to phone Room Nineteen?"

"Possibly." He was peevish. "Ostensibly he intends to do something about Jubé."

"Where are we?"

He told me. It didn't take long, since most of the long conversation had been Wolfe's explanation of our presence. I asked him what the odds were that Danilo was double-crossing the Spirit and actually earning his pay from either Belgrade or the Russians, and he said he didn't know but that Marko had trusted his nephew without reservation. I said that was jolly, since if Danilo was a louse it would be interesting to see which side he sold us to, and I could hardly wait to find out. Wolfe only growled, whether in Serbo-Croat or English I couldn't tell.

It was quite a wait. I got up and inspected various articles in the room, asking Wolfe some questions about them, and concluded that if I lived to marry and settle down, which at the moment looked like a bad bet, our apartment would be furnished with domestic products, with possibly a few imports to give it tone, like for instance the tasseled blue scarf that covered a table. I was looking at pictures on the wall when the door opened behind me, and I admit that as I about-faced my hand went automatically to my hip, where I still had the Colt .38. It was only Meta Vukcic. She came in a couple of steps and said something, and Wolfe replied, and after a brief exchange she went back out. He reported, without being asked, that she had said that the lamb stew would be ready in about an hour, and meanwhile did we want some goat milk, or vodka with or without water, and he had said no. I protested that I was thirsty, and he said all right, then call her, though he knew damn well I didn't know how to say "Mrs."

I asked him. "How do you say 'Mrs. Vukcic'?" He made a two-syllabled noise without any vowels. I said, "To hell with it," went to the door at the rear, pulled it open, passed through, saw our hostess arranging things on a table, caught her eye, curved my fingers as if holding a glass, raised the glass to my mouth, and drank. She said something that ended with a question mark, and I nodded. While she got a pitcher from a shelf and poured white liquid from it into a glass, I glanced around, saw a stove with a covered pot on it, a bank of cupboards with flowers painted on the doors, a table set for four, a line of shiny pots and pans hanging, and other items. When she gave me the glass I asked myself if it would be appropriate to kiss her hand, which was well shaped but a little red and rough, decided against it, and returned to the other room.

"I had a little chat with Mrs. Vukcic," I told Wolfe. "The stew smells good, and the table is set for four, but there are no place cards, so keep your fingers crossed."

Lily Rowan had once paid a Park Avenue medicine man fifty bucks to tell her that goat milk would be good for her nerves, and while she was giving it a whirl I had sampled it a few times, so the liquid Meta Vukcic had served me was no great shock. By the time I had finished it the room was dark, and I went and turned the switch on a lamp that stood on the tasseled blue table cover, and it worked.

The door opened, and Danilo was back with us, alone. He crossed to the chair facing Wolfe and sat.

"You must excuse me," he said, "for being away so long, but there was a little difficulty. Now. You said you expect me to help you. What kind of help?"

"That depends," Wolfe told him, "on the situation. If you can tell me the name of the man who killed Marko, and where he is, that may be all I'll need from you. Can you?"

"No."

"Don't you know?"

"No."

Wolfe's tone sharpened. "I must remind you that last Friday, four days ago, Josip Pasic took Telesio a message from you to the effect that he was to telephone me that the man I sought was within sight of the mountain. You sent that message?"

"Yes, but, as I told you, I sent it because Carla said to."

"She told you to send that message without telling you who the man was, and you didn't ask her? Pfui."

"I had no chance to ask her. You don't know the circumstances."

"I have come four thousand miles to learn them. I confidently expected you to name the man."

"I can't." Danilo was resentful. "I am accustomed to being regarded with suspicion by nearly everyone here, I invite it and I welcome it, but from you, my uncle's oldest and closest friend, who denied us your help, I would not expect it. Carla came eleven days ago—no, twelve, a week ago Friday. She did not come here to Titograd—like you, she had no papers, and, unlike you, she took precautions. She went to a place she knew of near the Albanian border, in the mountains, and sent me word, and I went to her. I had certain urgent affairs here and could stay there only one day. Her purpose was to arrange matters that Marko, being dead, could no longer attend to, but she shouldn't have crossed the sea. She should have sent for me from Bari. That place in the mountains is at the center of danger. I tried to persuade her to return to Bari, but she wouldn't. You knew her."

"Yes, I knew her."

"She was too headstrong. I had to leave her there. Two days later, on Sunday, word came from her that I was to send you that message, and I sent—"

"Who brought it?"

"Josip Pasic. At the moment there was no one else to send across to Telesio in Bari, and I sent him. Affairs still kept me here, and I couldn't get away until Tuesday—that was a week ago today. I went to the mountains that night—it is always best to go at night—and Carla was not there. We found her body the next morning at the foot of a cliff. She had been stabbed in several places, but on account of the bruises from the fall down the cliff it was impossible to tell to what extent she had been mistreated. Anyway, she was dead. Because she had had no papers, and for other reasons, it would have been difficult to arrange Christian burial for her, but the body was decently disposed of. It would be a pleasure to tell you that we tracked those who had killed her and dealt with them, but it is not that simple in the mountains, and besides, there was another urgent concern—to take precautions regarding materials that must be guarded. It was possible that before killing her they had forced her to reveal the cache. We attended to that Wednesday night; and Thursday, Josip Pasic and I came back to Titograd; and that night he went to the coast and crossed to Bari, to send word to New York about Carla. I thought it proper also to tell Telesio to get word to you, since she was your daughter."

Danilo made a gesture. "So there it is. I had no chance to ask her who killed Marko."

Wolfe regarded him glumly. "You had a chance to ask Josip Pasic."

"He doesn't know."

"He was in the mountains with her."

"Not precisely with her. She was trying to do something alone, against all reason."

"I want to see him. Where is he?"

"In the mountains. He returned there Saturday night."

"You can send for him."

"I can, of course, but I'm not going to." Danilo was emphatic. "The situation there is difficult, and he must stay. Besides, I won't expose Josip to the hazard of a meeting with you in Titograd, not after the way you have performed and made yourself conspicuous. Marching into the headquarters of the secret police! Walking the streets, anywhere you please, in daylight! It is true that Titograd is no metropolis, it is only a poor little town in this little valley surrounded by mountains, but there are a few people here who have been over the mountains and across the seas, and what if one of them saw you? Do you think I am such a fool as to believe you are Nero Wolfe just because you come to my house and say so? I would have been dead long ago. Once—last winter, it was—my uncle showed me a picture of you that had been printed in an American newspaper, and I recognized you as soon as I saw you at my door. There are others in Titograd who might also recognize you, but you march right in and tell Gospo Stritar you are Toné Stara of Galichnik!"

"I apologize," Wolfe said stiffly, "if I have imperiled you."

Danilo waved it away. "That's not it. The Russians know I take money from Belgrade, and Belgrade knows I take money from the Russians, and they both know I am involved with the Spirit of the Black Mountain, so no one can imperil me. I slip through everybody's fingers like quicksilver—or like mud, as they think. But not Josip Pasic. If I had him meet you in Titograd, and by some mischance— No. Anyway, he can't leave. Also, what can he tell you? If he knew— Yes, Meta?"

The door had opened, and Mrs. Vukcic had appeared. She came in a step and said something. Danilo, replying, arose, and so did Wolfe and I as she came toward us.

"I have told my wife who you are," Danilo said. "Meta, this is Mr. Wolfe and Mr. Goodwin. There is no reason why you shouldn't shake hands with them." She did so, with a firm, friendly clasp. Danilo went on, "I know, gentlemen, that, like my uncle, you are accustomed to the finest dishes and delicacies, but a man can only share what he has, and at least we'll have bread."

We certainly had bread. It was a very nice party. At the table in the kitchen an electric lamp with a big pink shade was between Wolfe and me so I couldn't see him without stretching my neck, but that was no great hardship. Mrs. Vukcic was a wonderful hostess. It never occurred to Wolfe or Danilo to give a damn whether I had any notion of what they were talking about, which I hadn't, but Meta couldn't stand a guest at her table feeling out of it, so about once a minute she turned her black eyes to me just to include me in. I was reminded of a dinner party Lily Rowan had once thrown at Rusterman's where one of the guests was an Eskimo, and I tried to remember whether she had been as gracious to him as Meta Vukcic was being to me, but I couldn't, probably because I had completely ignored him myself. I resolved that if I ever got back to New York and was invited to a meal where someone like an Eskimo was present, I would smile at him or her at least every fifth bite.

There was nothing wrong with the lamb stew, and the radishes were young and crisp, but the big treat was the bread, baked by Mrs. Vukcic in a loaf about as big around as my arm and fully as long. We finished two of them, and I did my part. There was no butter, but sopping in the gravy was taken for granted, and, when that gave out, the bread was even better with a gob of apple butter on each bite. It was really an advantage not being able to follow the conversation, since it kept me busy catering for myself and at the same time making sure I met Meta's glances to show proper appreciation; and anyway, when Wolfe reported later, he said the table talk was immaterial.

There was even coffee—at least, when I asked Wolfe about it, he said it was supposed to be. I won't dwell on it. We were all sipping away at it, out of squatty yellow cups, when suddenly

Danilo left his chair, crossed to a door—not the one to the living room—opened it enough to slip through, and did so, closing the door behind him. In view of what followed, there must have been some kind of signal, though I hadn't heard or seen any. Danilo wasn't gone more than five minutes. When he re-entered he opened the door wider, and a breath of outdoor air came in, enough to get to us at the table. He came back to his chair, sat, put a wad of crumpled brown paper on the table, picked up his coffee cup, and emptied it. Wolfe asked him something in a polite tone. He put the cup down, picked up the wad of paper, unfolded it, got it straightened out, and placed it on the table between him and Wolfe. I stared at the object he had unwrapped, resting there on the paper. Though my eyes are good, at the first glance I didn't believe them, but when they checked it I had to. The object was a human finger that had been chopped off at the base, no question about it.

"Not for dessert, I hope," Wolfe said dryly.

"It would be poison," Danilo declared. "It belonged to that baby rat, Jubé Bilic. Meta dear, could I have some hot coffee?"

She got up and went to the stove for the pot.

10

Meta did not seem to be shocked by the display of an unattached human finger on her dining table, but she was. The proof is that she filled her husband's cup with steaming so-called coffee and returned the pot to the stove without asking her guests if they wanted some, which was not like her. When she was back in her chair Wolfe spoke.

"An impressive exhibit, Danilo, no doubt of that. Naturally you expect a question, and I supply it. Where's the rest of him?"

"Where it won't be found." Danilo sipped. "This method of confirming a removal is not a Montenegrin custom, as you know. It was introduced to us by the Russians a few years ago, and we have indulged them by adopting it."

"It seems extreme—not the finger, the removal. I assume that when you left us you went to tell someone that he was lurking in this neighborhood, and to give instructions that he be found and removed."

"That's right."

Wolfe grunted. "Only because he had followed us to your house?"

"No." Danilo picked up the exhibit, wadded the paper around it, got up and went to the stove, opened the door, tossed the thing in, closed the door, and returned to his chair. "It will smell a little," he said, "but no more than a morsel of lamb. Jubé has been a nuisance ever since he started going to the university. For a year now he has made things harder for me by trying to persuade Gospo Stritar that my true loyalty is to the Spirit of the Black Mountain— and also, I have reason to believe, trying to persuade Belgrade. He was already condemned, and by following you here he merely presented an opportunity."

Wolfe lifted his shoulders an eighth of an inch and let them down. "Then it was no disservice to lead him here. I don't pretend that I'm not impressed by the dispatch and boldness with which you grasped the opportunity." His eyes moved to Meta. "And I assure you, Mrs. Vukcic, that the grotesque table decoration served with the coffee has not diminished our gratitude for an excellent meal. I speak for Mr. Goodwin too, because he has none of your words." He returned to Danilo and sharpened his tone. "If I may return to my affair? I must see Josip Pasic."

"He can't come," Danilo said bluntly.

"I ask you to reconsider."

"No."

"Then I'll have to go to him. Where is he?"

"That's impossible. I can't tell you."

Wolfe was patient. "You can't? Or you won't?"

"I'm not going to." Danilo put his hands flat on the table. "For the sake of my uncle, Mr. Nero Wolfe, I have shaken your hand and so has my wife, and we have shared bread with you. But for the sake of what he believed in and supported, I will not run the risk of betraying one of our most carefully guarded secrets. It is not necessary to question your good faith; your rashness is enough. You may already have been recognized."

Wolfe snorted. "In this outlandish getup? Nonsense. Besides, I have arranged for a diversion. Paolo Telesio communicates with you by mail, using this address, and those communications are intercepted by the secret police and inspected before they are delivered to you; and you and Telesio, knowing that, have occasionally taken advantage of it. Is that true?"

Danilo was frowning. "Apparently Paolo has higher regard for your discretion than I have."

"He knew me before you were born. Does the interception delay delivery to you considerably?"

"No. They work it fairly well."

"Did you get a letter from Telesio today?"

"No."

"Then tomorrow, I suppose. He mailed it in Bari yesterday afternoon. In it he tells you that he had just received a cablegram from New York, signed Nero Wolfe, reading as follows: 'Inform proper persons across Adriatic I am handling Vukcic's affairs and assuming obligations. Two hundred thousand dollars available soon. Will send agent conference Bari next month.' Telesio's letter will say that it came in English and he has put it in Italian. As I say, it is a diversion for the police. For you it has no validity. I promised Telesio I would make that plain. To the interceptors it should be plain that Nero Wolfe is in New York and has no intention of crossing an ocean."

Danilo, still frowning, objected, "Belgrade has people in New York. They'll learn you're not there."

"I doubt it. I rarely leave my house, and the man in my office, answering my telephone, named Saul Panzer, could flummox Tito and Molotov put together. There's another purpose the cablegram may possibly serve, but that's an off-chance. Now for Josip Pasic. I intend to see him. You spoke of the risk of betraying a carefully guarded secret, but if it's what I assume it is, I already know it. Marko never told me explicitly that weapons and ammunition were being smuggled in to you, but he might as well have. He said that certain costly and essential supplies were being stored at a spot in the mountains less than three kilometers from the place where I was born, and he identified the spot. We both knew it well in boyhood. It must have been near there that Carla was killed. It must be there, or nearby, that this Josip Pasic is so importantly engaged that you refuse to call him away. So my course is simple. I don't fancy spending another night cruising the mountains, and we'll stay the night in Titograd, heaven knows where, and go tomorrow. We shall betray no secrets heedlessly, but we have to find Pasic."

He pushed back his chair and stood up. "Thank you again, Mrs. Vukcic, for your hospitality. And you, Danilo, thank you for whatever you consider to deserve thanks." He switched to English. "If you'll get the knapsacks, Archie? We're leaving. What time is it?"

I looked at my wrist as I arose. "Quarter to ten."

"Sit down, you fools," Danilo growled.

Wolfe ignored it. "You can do us one more favor," he suggested. "Tell me, is there a hotel in town with good beds?"

"By God," Danilo growled. In Serbo-Croat "by God" is *"Boga ti"*—good for growling. Danilo repeated it. "By God, without papers, with nothing but money, you would go to a hotel! You'd get a good bed all right! Gospo Stritar is a man who is capable of a thought, or you would be in jail now, and not in bed either! He merely decided you would be more interesting loose, and by God he was correct! You tell me to my face you know where our cache is, and tomorrow in the sunshine, like going to a picnic, you will go there, doubtless to the very spot, and shout for Josip Pasic!"

He calmed down a little. "Only," he said, "you would be dead before you got there, and that would be nothing to regret. You may be fit to live in America, but not here. There are only twenty-two men in Montenegro who know where that cache is, and you two are not with us, so obviously you must die. Damn it, sit down!"

"We're going, Danilo."

"You can't go. While I was out I made other arrangements besides Jubé. There are men out front and out back, and if you leave and I don't go to the door with you and give a signal, you won't get far. Sit down."

Wolfe told me, "There's a snag, Archie," and sat, and I followed suit.

"I would like to say something, Danilo," Mrs. Vukcic said quietly.

He frowned at her. "Well?" he demanded.

She looked at Wolfe, at me, and back at her husband. "These

men are not crazy like you and me," she told him. "They are not doomed like us. We try to pretend there is hope, but our hearts are dead, and we can only pray that someday there will be real life for Ivan and Zosha, but we know there can be none for us. Oh, I don't complain! You know I love you for fighting instead of giving in like the others, and I'm proud of you—I am, Danilo—but I don't want to be afraid of you. It is too easy for you to say these men must die, and it makes me afraid, because they are the only hope for Ivan and Zosha, men like them. I know you had to kill Jubé Bilic, I can understand that; but these men are our friends, or anyway they are the friends of our children. Do you love anybody?"

"Yes. I love you."

"And the children, I know. Do you love anybody else?"

"Who else would I love?"

She nodded, her black eyes flashing. "That's what I mean, you see? These men can still love people! They came so far, so many thousands of miles into danger, because they loved your Uncle Marko and they want to find the man who killed him. What else did they come for? All I want—I want you to understand that, and I know it isn't easy because it wasn't easy for me—we can't have that kind of love, but we can understand it, and we can hope for Ivan and Zosha to grow up to have it someday. You can't just say these men must die."

"I can say whatever is necessary."

"But it isn't. And anyway, you didn't mean it. I know how you say a thing when you mean it. You must forgive me, Danilo, for speaking, but I was afraid you would go on like that until you couldn't back down. It made my heart stop beating to hear you say these men must die, because that is exactly wrong. The real truth is that these men must *not* die."

"Bah." He was scowling at her. "You talk like a woman."

"I talk like a mother, and if you think that is something no fine, brave man should listen to, I ask you, who made me a mother? You can't wipe it out now."

All I knew was that it was no longer a very nice party, and all I could do was watch their faces, including Wolfe's, and listen to their voices, and try to guess what was up. Also I had to keep an eye on Wolfe's left hand, because we had arranged that he would close his left fist and open it again if a conversation reached a point where I should be ready to join in with the Marley or the Colt. It was damned unsatisfactory. As far as I knew, Danilo might be scowling at his wife because she was begging him to stick a knife in me so she could have my green jacket to make over for Ivan and Zosha. I heard their names three times.

Wolfe put in. "You're in a fix, Danilo," he said sympathetically. "If you let us go we might unwittingly endanger your plans, I admit it. If you have us removed, you will affront the memory of Marko and all he did for you, and also, if you listen to your wife, you will forfeit your claim on the future. I suggest a compromise. You say it is always best to go there at night. Take us there now. If it is impossible for you to leave, get someone to take us. We will be as circumspect as occasion will permit."

"Yes, Danilo!" Meta cried. "That would be the best—"

"Be quiet," he commanded her. He leveled his deepset eyes at Wolfe. "It would be unheard of, to take strangers there."

"Pfui. A stranger to my own birthplace?"

"I'll take you to the coast instead, tonight, and arrange for you to cross to Bari. You can wait there for word from me. I promise to do all I can to find the man who killed Marko, and to deal with him."

"No. I have made a promise to myself that has priority, and I will not delegate it. Besides, if you failed I would have to come back; and anyway, if you sent me a finger how would I know who it had belonged to? No, Danilo. I will not be diverted."

Danilo got up, went to the stove, opened the door, and looked in at the fire. I suppose Wolfe's mention of a finger had reminded him that he had a cremation under way and he wanted to check. Apparently he thought it needed stoking, for he got some sticks of wood from a box and poked them in before he closed the door. Then he came and stood directly behind my chair. Since Wolfe's last words had sounded like an ultimatum, and since I didn't care for the idea of a knife in my back without even catching sight of it, I twisted around enough to get a glimpse of it on its way. His hands were buried in his pockets.

"You're barely able to stand up," he told Wolfe. "What about your feet?"

"I'll manage," Wolfe said without a quaver. "Must we walk the whole way?"

"No. We'll ride twenty kilometers along the Cijevna, as far as the road goes. From there it's rough and steep."

"I know it is. I herded goats there. Do we leave now?"

"No. Around midnight. I must go and make arrangements for a car and driver. Don't step outside while I'm gone."

He went. I must say for him that once he had accepted a situation he didn't waste any time bellyaching. As soon as the door had closed behind him I went at Wolfe.

"Now what? Has he gone for another finger?"

He said something to Meta, and she replied, and he pushed back his chair and stood up, flinching only a little. "We'll go in the other room," he told me, and moved, and I followed, leaving the door open, not to be rude to our hostess. He lowered himself onto his former chair, put his palms on his knees, and sighed as far down as it would go. "We're in for another night of it," he said glumly, and proceeded to report. First he sketched it, and then, when I insisted, filled it in. He was in no humor to oblige me or anyone else, but I was in no humor to settle for a skeleton.

When he had finished I sat a minute and turned it over. I had certainly seen sweeter prospects. "Is there such a thing," I asked, "as a metal dinar any more? A coin?"

"I doubt it. Why?"

"I'd like to have one to toss, to decide which side Danilo is really on. I admit his wife thinks she knows, but does she? As it stands now, I could name at least fourteen people I would rather have take me for a ride than Marko's nephew."

"I am committed," he said grumpily. "You are not."

"Phooey. I want to see your birthplace and put a plaque on it."

No comment. He sighed again, arose from his chair, crossed to a sofa with a high back that was against the far wall, placed a cushion to suit him, and stretched out. He tried it first on his back, but protruded over the edge, and turned on his side. It was a pathetic sight, and to take my mind off it I went to another wall and looked at pictures some more.

I think he got a nap in. Some time later, when Danilo returned, I had to go to the sofa and touch Wolfe's arm before he would open his eyes. He gave me a dirty look, and one just as dirty to Danilo, swung his legs around, sat, and ran his fingers through his hair.

"We can go now," Danilo announced. He had on a leather jacket.

"Very well." Wolfe made it to his feet. "The knapsacks, Archie?"

As I bent to lift them Meta's voice came from the doorway. Her husband answered her, and Wolfe said something and then spoke to me. "Archie, Mrs. Vukcic asks if we would like to look at the children, and I said yes."

I kept my face straight. The day that Wolfe would like to climb steps to look at children will be the day I would like to climb Mount Everest barefooted to make a snowman. However, it was good public relations, and I don't deny he might have felt that we should show some appreciation for her contribution to the discussion of our future. I know I did, so I dropped the knapsacks and gave her a cordial smile. She led the way through the arch and up a flight of narrow wooden stairs, uncarpeted, with Wolfe and me following and Danilo bringing up the rear. On the top landing she murmured something to Wolfe, and we waited there while she disappeared through a doorway and in a moment rejoined us, carrying a lighted candle. After going to another door that was closed, she opened it gently and crossed the sill. With the heavy shoes we were wearing it wasn't easy to step quietly, and with the condition Wolfe's feet were in it wasn't easy for him to tiptoe, but by gum he tried, and made, on the bare floor, quite a little less noise than a team of horses.

They were in beds, not cribs, with high wooden posts, against opposite walls. Zosha, who was on her back, with one of her long black curls across her nose, had kicked the cover off, and Meta pulled it up. Wolfe, looking down at her, muttered something, but I can't say what because he has always refused to tell me. Ivan, who was on his side with an arm stretched out, had a smudge on his cheek, but you have to make allowance for the fact that when Meta put them to bed unexpected guests had arrived and she had been under pressure. When Meta turned away with the candle, and Wolfe and I followed, Danilo stayed by Ivan's bed, and we waited for him at the foot of the stairs, with Meta holding the candle high to light him.

In the living room Danilo spoke to Wolfe, and Wolfe relayed

it to me. "We'll go first, by a route I know, not far, and Danilo will follow. We won't want the knapsacks on our backs in the car, so if you'll carry them?"

We shook hands with Meta. I picked up the luggage. Danilo escorted us to the front door and let us out, and we were loose again. It was past midnight and the houses were all dark, and so was the street, except for one dim excuse for a light at the corner a hundred yards away. We headed in the other direction. When we had gone some fifty paces I stopped and wheeled to look back, and Wolfe grumbled, "That's futile."

"Okay," I conceded, "but I trust Danilo as far as I can see him, and now I can't see him."

"Then why look? Come on."

I obeyed, with my arms full of knapsacks. There were some stars, and soon my eyes were adjusted enough for objects thirty feet off and for movements much farther. Before long we came to a dead end and turned left. At the next intersection we turned right, and in a few minutes went left again and were on a dirt road with ruts. There were no more houses, but ahead in the distance was a big black outline against the sky, and I asked Wolfe what it was.

"Sawmill. The car's there."

He sounded more confident than I felt, but he was right. When we approached the outline it became a building surrounded by other outlines, and closer up they became stacks of lumber. I saw the car first, off the road, in between the second and third stacks, which were twice as high as my head. We went up to it. It was a car all right, an old Chevvy sedan, and the hood was warm to my hand, but it was empty.

"What the hell," I said. "No driver? I have no road map."

"He'll come." Wolfe opened the rear door and was climbing in. "There'll be four of us, so you'll have to ride with me."

I put the knapsacks in, taking care not to drop them on his feet, but stayed out on the ground. With my hands free, I had a strong impulse to get the Marley in one and the Colt in the other, and I had to explain to myself why it would be a waste of energy. If someone not Danilo arrived I certainly wasn't going to shoot on sight, and I wouldn't even know what his viewpoint was until Wolfe interpreted for me. I compromised by transferring the Colt from my hip to my side pocket.

It was Danilo who arrived. Hearing footsteps, I looked around the corner of the lumber pile and saw him coming down the road. When he was close enough to recognize I took my hand out of my pocket, which shows the state of mind I was in. According to me, he was as likely to saw off our limb as anyone. He turned in, brushing past me, went to the car and spoke to Wolfe, turned, and pronounced a word that sounded something like Steven. Immediately a man appeared beside him, coming from above. He had jumped down from the lumber pile, where he had been perched, probably peeking down at me, while I had been talking myself out of drawing my guns.

"This is Stefan Protic," Danilo told Wolfe. "I have told him about you and your son Alex. Seen anything, Stefan?"

"No. Nothing."

"All right, we'll go."

Danilo got in with Wolfe, so I circled the car and climbed in beside Stefan. He gave me a long, hard, deliberate look, and I returned it as well as I could in the darkness. About all I could tell was that he was some shorter than me, with a long narrow face that certainly wasn't pale, and broad shoulders. He started the engine, which sounded as if it would appreciate a valve job, rolled into the road, and turned right, without turning his lights on.

I can't tell you anything about the first three miles, or five kilometers, of that ride, because I saw nothing. I had already suspected that European drivers had kinks that nothing could be done about, and now concluded that Stefan's was an antipathy for lights, when suddenly he flashed them on, and I saw why we had been bumping so much. You couldn't have driven that road without bumping if it had been lined on both sides with continuous neons. I remarked over my shoulder, "If you'll tell this bird to stop I'd rather get out and run along behind."

I expected no reply but got one. Wolfe's voice came, punctuated by bumps. "The main routes from Podgorica are north and south. This is merely a lane to nowhere."

Podgorica again. Also he wasn't going to have me casting slurs at Montenegro, which was pretty generous of him, considering the kind of reception Montenegro was giving us.

In another mile or so the road smoothed off a little and started up and began to wind. Wolfe informed me that we were now along the Cijevna, and on our right, quite close, I caught glimpses of the white of a rushing stream, but the engine was too noisy for me to hear it. I remembered that one evening after dinner I had heard Wolfe and Marko discussing the trout they had caught in their early days, Marko claiming he had once landed one forty centimeters long, and I had translated it into inches—sixteen. I swiveled my head to ask Wolfe if it was in the Cijevna that he and Marko had got trout, and he said yes, but in a tone of voice that did not invite conversation, so I let it lay.

The road got narrower and steeper, and after a while there was no more Cijevna, anyhow not visible. Stefan shifted to second to negotiate a couple of hairpin turns, tried to get going in high again, couldn't make it, and settled for second. The air coming in my open window was colder and fresher, and in the range of our lights ahead there were no longer any leaves or grass, or anything growing; nothing but rock. I had seen no sign of a habitation for more than a mile, and was thinking that Wolfe must have been hatched in an eagle's nest, when suddenly space widened out in front of us, and right ahead, not fifty feet away, was a stone house, and the car stopped with a jerk. I was making sure it was really a house and not just more of the rock, when Stefan switched off the lights and everything was black.

Danilo said something, and we all piled out. I got the knapsacks. Stefan went toward the house, came back in a moment with a can, lifted the hood and removed the radiator cap, and poured water in. When that chore was finished he got in behind the wheel, got turned around with a lot of noisy backing and tacking, and was gone. Soon I was relieved to see, down below, his lights flash on.

Wolfe spoke. "My knapsack, Archie, if you please?"

11

We got to Josip Pasic, according to the luminous dial on my wrist, at eighteen minutes past three in the morning. I did not, and still don't, understand how Wolfe ever made it. We didn't actually scale any cliffs—it was supposed to be a trail all the way except the last three hundred yards—but it was all up, and at least fifty times my hands had to help my feet. I must admit that Danilo was very decent about it. Even in the dark he could probably have romped along like a goat, but he would always wait like a gentleman for Wolfe to catch up. I had no choice. I was behind, and if Wolfe had toppled he would have taken me with him.

There was no taboo on talking, and during the halts Danilo did some briefing, and Wolfe passed it on to me when he had a little breath to spare. Our destination was not the cache but a decoy. The costly and essential supplies had been moved. There were guards at the new cache, but Pasic and five others were at the old one, now empty, expecting and awaiting an invasion. It sounded goofy to me, six guys sitting in a cave asking for it, but I understood it better when we got there.

The last three hundred yards, after we left the trail, were not the hardest but they were the most interesting. Danilo, saying that at one point we would have to walk a ledge less than a meter wide with a five-hundred-meter drop, had suggested that he bring Pasic to us at the trail, but Wolfe had vetoed it. When we got to the ledge, which was nearly level, apparently it meant nothing to him. As for me, I didn't spend my boyhood herding goats around cliffs and chasms, and I would have preferred to be walking down Fifth Avenue, or even Sixth. There was enough light from the stars to see the edge, and then nothing. Wide open spaces are okay fairly horizontal, but not straight down.

We were still on the ledge, at least I was, when Danilo stopped and uttered a word, raising his voice a little, and at once an answering voice came from up ahead. Our guide replied, "Danilo. Two men are with me, but I'll come on alone. You can use the light."

We had to stand there and wait on the damn ledge. When the beam of a spotlight hit us, after taking in Danilo, it was worse. The light left us and went back to Danilo, and then was turned off. In a moment voices came, not loud, and kept on, and my feeling for the Spirit of the Black Mountain took a dive. I admit it was in order for Danilo to explain us to his pals, but that ledge was one hell of an anteroom. Finally the light came at us again, and Danilo called to us to come. When we moved, the light didn't attend us but stayed

focused on the ledge. In a few steps we left it. I would have had
to grope, but Wolfe didn't, and I realized it wasn't so much his
eyes he steered by as his memory.

Two figures were standing in front of a black blotch on the dim
face of perpendicular rock—the entrance to the cave. As we
reached them Danilo gave us the name of Josip Pasic, and gave
him ours—Nero Wolfe and Archie Goodwin. That had been
accepted as unavoidable, since Danilo couldn't have justified bringing Toné Stara and his son Alex in to his friends, nor account for
their interest in Carla. Pasic didn't offer a hand, and neither did
Wolfe, who is allergic to handshaking anyhow. Danilo said he had
told Pasic who we were and why we wanted to see him. Wolfe
said he wanted to sit down. Danilo said there were blankets in the
cave, but men were sleeping on them. I thought if it was me I
would be under them. It was cold as the devil.

Pasic said, "Montenegrins sit on rocks."

We did so, after Pasic had turned off the spotlight, Wolfe and
Danilo side by side on one, and Pasic and me facing them on
another.

"What I want is simple," Wolfe said. "I want to know who killed
Marko Vukcic. He was my oldest friend. As boys we often explored this cave. Danilo says you don't know who killed him."

"That's right. I don't."

"But nine days ago you took a message from Carla to Danilo
that the man who killed him was here."

"That wasn't the message."

"That's what it meant. Please understand, Mr. Pasic, I have
no desire or intention to try to badger you. I merely want all the
information you can give me about that message and the events
behind it. Danilo will tell you I can be trusted with it."

"Carla was his daughter," Danilo said. "He has a certain right
to know."

"I knew a man who had a daughter." Pasic was scornful. "So
did you. She betrayed him to the police."

"That's another matter. I brought him here, Josip. I don't think
the time has come for you to question your trust in me."

I was wishing I could have a good look at Pasic. He was just
a blur, a big one, taller than me, with a tight, bitter voice. At first,

sitting next to him, I had noticed that he smelled, and then had realized that it was me, after the sweat of the climb.

"All right," he said, "this is what happened. Carla came to the house—that's the house at the end of the road, where the car brought you. You saw the house?"

"Yes," Wolfe said. "I was born there."

"That's right, you were, I have been told. We didn't know she was coming, and it was a big surprise. She wanted to see Danilo, and I went and brought him. They talked a whole day. I don't know what they said because it was not thought desirable for me to be present."

"That's foolish," Danilo declared. "I told you what was said. Many things were said, but the main one was that Carla knew from Marko that we had reason to think there was a spy among us, and she wanted to know who. There are spies in the Spirit, of course, that is to be expected, but this one seemed to be close to our most secret affairs. Coming from a distance, Carla was right to exclude no one, not even you or me. She had to talk with someone, and she chose me. And as I told you, I didn't satisfy her."

"I know you didn't. Neither did I, when she talked with me after you left. She trusted none of us, and she died for it." Pasic moved his head, to Wolfe. "She decided to find the spy herself. Since you were born here, you know that it is only two kilometers from this spot to Albania, and that just across the border is an old Roman fort."

"Certainly. I've killed bats in it."

"There are no bats in it now. The Albanians, under the whip of the Russians, have cleaned it up some, and they like to stand in the tower and look across the border. For a while they kept a squad there, but now not so many. I had told Carla that if there was a spy among us working for the Russians it would surely be known to the Albanians at the fort, and they would be in touch with him, and I'm sorry I told her that because it gave her the idea. She decided to go herself to the fort, go straight to them, and offer her services as a spy. I told her it was not only dangerous, it was absurd, but she wouldn't listen. If you think I should have kept her from going, you will please remember that in her mind it was possible that I was myself the spy. Besides, I would have had to restrain her physically. She had decided on it."

Wolfe grunted. "So she went."

"Yes. She went early Sunday morning. I couldn't keep her, but I persuaded her to make an arrangement with me. I knew how things were in the fort. There are places to sleep and a place to cook, but there is no plumbing. For private necessities there is only one place to go, a little room on the lower side that is more like a cell, with no light when the door is closed, because there is no window."

"I know that room."

"You seem to know everything. When you knew it, it was not furnished with a bench to sit on with holes in it."

"No."

"It is now. I figured that if Carla were left free to move at all, she would be allowed to go to that room. A few meters from it, on the other side of the corridor, is another room whose outer wall has crumbled, not used for anything—but of course you know that too. The arrangement was that I would be in that other room at nine o'clock that evening, and Carla would walk past it to the cell. That was all we arranged. We left it to circumstances whether she would enter the room to speak to me, or I would join her in the cell, or what. But she was to walk past the room unless it was absolutely impossible, as near nine o'clock as she could, for if she didn't I was going to find out why."

Pasic turned his head to cock an ear in the direction of the ledge, heard nothing whatever if my ears are any good, and turned back. He went on, "There is a thing I would like to mention, since you too are from America, where there is plenty of good food. There are still a few men in Montenegro with some pride, and I am one of them. On Saturday, after Carla arrived, I sent a man down to a farm in the valley and he brought back eight eggs and a piece of bacon. So Sunday morning before she left Carla had for breakfast three of the eggs and some slices of bacon, and she said it was better than American bacon. I want you to know that her last meal in Montenegro was a good one."

"Thank you," Wolfe said courteously.

"You are welcome. Soon after she left—in fact, nearly on her heels—I sent a man, one named Stan Kosor, with a binocular. It is a very fine binocular with a long range, one of the many fine things we have received from America through Marko Vukcic. It has a name engraved on it, 'E. B. Meyrowitz,' which certainly does not seem to be an American name, but it came from America. Stan Kosor went to a high spot near the border, from which the fort is in plain view with the binocular, and stayed there all day. He is now in the cave asleep, and you can speak with him in the morning if you wish. He saw nothing out of the ordinary. No one arrived from the south—and, particularly, no one departed. Naturally I wanted to know if they took Carla toward Tirana, which is only a hundred and fifty kilometers away. I am trying to accommodate you. You said you wanted all the information I can give you about that message and the events behind it."

"Yes. Go ahead."

"There were four men here with me besides Stan Kosor. A little after dark Sunday evening we took the trail to the border, and Stan Kosor joined us there. He said he was sure that Carla was still at the fort. We took off our shoes before we went on, not so much on account of the men in the fort, who are merely Albanians, but because of the dog, which liked to lie after dark on a certain rock that is raised a little, at the corner nearest the trail. I left the men at a certain spot and approached alone, and had to climb and circle clear around the fort in order to come at the dog from the other direction, against the wind. That way I got to his rock and sank my knife in him before he moved or made a sound. I pulled his carcass out of the way behind a boulder, and stood a while to listen. I had seen lights at four windows, and I could hear voices, very faint, and I thought one of them was Carla's."

He stopped again to turn his ears toward the ledge, and, after ten seconds of the deadest silence I had ever listened to, turned back and resumed. "With the dog out of the way it was simple. I went around to where the wall had crumbled and climbed through a hole into the room where I was to wait. The door into the corridor was open a little, and I stood so I could see through. It wasn't nine o'clock yet. My plan was to wait until ten o'clock, and then, if she hadn't come, I was going to go and bring the men, and we would find her. Of course we would first have to deal with the Albanians, but that wouldn't take long because there wouldn't be more than four of them, and probably only two or three."

His hand moved in a quick little gesture. "You will permit me to confess something. I was hoping she would not come, and the

Albanians would try to fight and would have to be killed, and we would find her locked in a room, unharmed. That way she would be back with us, and also some enemies would be dead. Of course we could go there and kill them any time, but I admit that would be useless, because, as Danilo says, others would come to take their place, who would give us more trouble than they do now. However, that is what I was hoping. It is not what happened. It was barely nine o'clock when I heard footsteps that sounded like Carla's, and then I saw her in the corridor, carrying a little lantern. I started to stick a hand through the opening for her to see, but pulled it back for fear she was being watched from the end of the corridor. She stopped right at the opening and turned to face the way she had come, and said my name in a whisper, and I answered. She said she was all right and she might come back tomorrow, and then she gave me that message, and—"

"If you don't mind," Wolfe put in, "try to remember the exact words."

"I don't have to try. She said, 'I'm all right, don't worry, I may come back tomorrow. Tell Danilo to send word to Nero Wolfe that the man he seeks is within sight of the mountain. Did you hear that?' I said, 'Yes.' She said, 'Do it at once, tonight. That's all, I must hurry.' She crossed the corridor and went in the little room and shut the door. Naturally I wanted to ask her things, but it was impossible to go and join her in the little room, both for reasons of decency and because it might have placed her in danger. I waited until I saw her come out and return down the corridor and turn a corner, and then I left. I returned to the others and put on my shoes, and we came back to the cave, and I went at once to Podgorica and told Danilo. Is that the information you wanted from me?"

"Yes. Thank you. You didn't see her again?"

"Not alive. Wednesday morning Danilo and I found her body. I would like to ask you something."

"Go ahead."

"I have been told that you are an expert detective, with a great reputation for understanding things. In your opinion, am I responsible for Carla's death? Were they moved to kill her because I killed the dog?"

"That's silly, Josip," Danilo said gruffly. "I was in a temper when I said that. Can't you forget it?"

"He wants my opinion," Wolfe said. "It is this. Many men are responsible for Carla's death, but if I were to name one it would be Georgi Malenkov. He is the foremost champion of the doctrine that men and women must be subjected to the mandates of despotic power. No, Mr. Pasic, you cannot be held accountable, either for Carla's death or for the fact that your information forces me to undertake a distasteful errand. There's nothing else for it; I must go to that fort—that is, if I can walk in the morning." He started to rise, dropped back on the rock, and groaned as if he meant it. "By heaven, if I can stand up! Can you spare me a blanket, Danilo?"

He tried again and made it to his feet.

12

I nearly froze.

There were no extra blankets. I suppose there would have been if the costly and essential supplies had not been moved to another cache, but that didn't keep me warm. Pasic gave Wolfe his blanket, and, being a proud Montenegrin with guests, offered to get one from one of the sleeping men for me, but I said oh no, I wouldn't think of it, through my interpreter. I spent the rest of the night—what was left—thinking of it. Wolfe had told me the elevation there was five thousand feet, but he must have meant meters. The pile of hay Pasic assigned me to was damp, and pulling some of it over me only made things worse. I guess I must have slept some, because I know I dreamed, something about a lot of dogs with cold noses.

I heard voices and opened my eyes and saw bright sunshine outside the cave entrance. My watch said ten past eight, so I had been refrigerating for more than four hours. I lay and figured it out: if I was frozen I couldn't move, so if I could move I wasn't frozen. I bent the legs and raised the torso, scrambled to my feet, and tottered to the entrance.

The sun wasn't there yet. To get it on me I would have had to go to the ledge and out on it a way, and I was all through with that ledge if there was any other possible route out of there. Then I remembered; we weren't going back, but forward; we were going to cross the border to the old Roman fort to visit Albanians. Wolfe had explained it all to me before we had entered the cave to hit the hay, including Pasic's strategy with the dog. No doubt that had influenced my dream.

"Good morning," Wolfe said. He was sitting on a rock, looking exactly the way I felt.

If I reported all the details of the next hour you would think I was piling on the misery just for the hell of it, so I'll mention only a few to give you a notion. The sun stuck to a crazy slant so as not to touch us. There was water in a can to drink, but none to wash in. I was told that to wash all I had to do was go over the ledge to the trail and down it less than a kilometer to a brook. I didn't wash. For breakfast we had bread, nothing like Meta's, cold slices of mush that had been fried in lard, and canned beans from the United States of America. When I asked Wolfe why they didn't at least start a fire and make some tea, he said because there was nothing to burn, and, looking around, I had to admit he was right. There wasn't a single stick, alive or dead, anywhere in sight. Just rock. And of course I couldn't talk, which might have helped to get the blood started. There wasn't even anything to listen to, except the goddam jabber as usual. The five men whom I hadn't met formally kept off in a group, with their jabber pitched low, evidently, judging from their sidelong glances, discussing Wolfe and me. Wolfe and Danilo and Pasic had a long argument, won by Wolfe, though I didn't know that until later, when he told me they had opposed his announced plan so strongly they had even threatened to set up a trail block.

Then he started an argument with me and lost it. His idea was that he would stand a better chance with the Albanians if he went alone, because they would be much more reluctant to talk if there were two of us, and they would be particularly suspicious of one who couldn't speak Albanian, which was a different language from Serbo-Croat. Actually it wasn't an argument, because I didn't argue.

I merely said flatly nothing doing, on the ground that there would be nothing at the cave for lunch but cold mush, and Pasic had said there was a place at the fort for cooking.

It wasn't until the knapsacks were strapped on and we were ready to go that I realized we would have to return to the trail by way of the ledge. Numb and dumb with cold, I had been supposing that we would go on to the border without any backtracking. With seven pairs of eyes on me, not counting Wolfe's, it was up to me to sustain the honor of American manhood, and I set my jaw and did my best. It helped that my back was to them. An interesting question about walking a narrow ledge over a fifteen-hundred-foot drop is whether it's better to do it at night or in the daytime. My answer is that it's better not to do it at all.

After we got to the trail it wasn't bad. The sun and the exercise were thawing me out, and there was no hard going. When we came to a rivulet crossing the trail we stopped and drank, and ate some chocolate. I told Wolfe it would take me only five minutes to rinse off my feet and put on fresh socks, and he said there was no great hurry, so I took off my knapsack and went to it. The water was like ice, but you can't have everything. Wolfe sat on a rock and chewed chocolate. He informed me that Albania was just ahead, about three hundred meters, but was unmarked because a debate had been going on for centuries as to the exact line of the water-parting in this section of the mountains. Also he pointed to a niche in a crag towering above us and said that was where Stan Kosor had perched with the binocular to watch the fort the day Carla had gone there. He added that almost certainly Kosor would be back in the niche today, to watch again. It was a perfect spot for it, since he could aim his glass at the fort through a crack.

I asked Wolfe how his feet were. "It is no longer merely my feet," he declared. "It is every muscle and nerve in my body. No words would serve, so I won't waste any."

It was warming up, so we took off our sweaters before going on. We crossed into Albania without knowing precisely when, and in another three minutes rounded a corner, and there was the fort. It was against a perpendicular wall of rock so high there was no point in straining my neck to find the top, and was of course a perfect match. Where the trail passed it there was a level space twenty yards wide and twice as long, and at its farther end a little brook splashed across the trail. There were slits in the walls, and in the one facing the trail the rock had crumbled to leave a big hole, presumably Pasic's point of entry for his appointment with Carla.

There was no sign of life, not even a dog. The idea was just to walk in and introduce ourselves, announcing, I suppose, that we had about decided to hook up with the Kremlin and wanted to discuss matters, so we headed for the only visible door, a big wooden one, standing wide open. We were about twenty paces short of it when somebody inside screamed, a long scream and a real one. A man's scream has more body to it than a woman's. We stopped dead and looked at each other.

The scream came again, longer.

Wolfe jerked his head to the left and moved that way, toward the hole in the wall, on his toes, though it must have killed him. I was right behind. Climbing through the hole would have been a cinch, even for him, if noise hadn't been a factor, but crawling over the rubble silently was complicated. He managed it, and in a moment I was in beside him. We crossed to a door in the inner wall, which was open a crack, probably just as Pasic had left it ten days before, stood to listen, and heard a voice, and then another, from a distance. Then came another scream, a bad one, and while it was still in the air Wolfe opened the door more and stuck his head out. A voice came faintly. Wolfe pulled his head back in and murmured, "They're down below. Let's see."

If there had been a movie camera that would register in that dark corridor, and if I had had it with me, a film of Wolfe trying to navigate that stone floor without making any noise would be something I wouldn't part with. I didn't fully enjoy it at the time, being too busy myself with the problem of moving quietly in the heavy shoes, but it's wonderful to look back at it. At the end was another corridor to the right, narrower and even darker, and ten feet along that took us to the head of a flight of steps going down. The voices were down there. Wolfe started down, going sidewise with his palms flat against the wall, and it was a good thing the steps were stone, since wooden treads would certainly have had something to say to his seventh of a ton. I took the other side right behind him, using the wall too. A thing like that distorts time out of all proportion. It seemed like a good ten minutes on those steps,

but afterward I figured it. There were fifteen steps. Say we aver-
aged ten seconds to a step—and it wasn't that much—that would
make only two and a half minutes.

At the bottom it was darker still. We turned left, in the
direction of the voices, and saw a little spot of light in the left wall
twenty feet away. Inching along, we got to it. There was the dim
outline of a closed door, and the light was coming through a hole
in it, eight inches square, with its center at eye level for a man a
little shorter than me. Wolfe started to slide an eye past the edge
of the hole, thought better of it, moved an arm's length away from
the wall, and looked through the hole. Inside, a man was talking,
loud. Wolfe moved closer to the hole, then sidestepped and put
his face almost against the door, with his left eye at the right edge
of the hole. Taking it as an invitation, I moved beside him and got
my right eye at the left edge of the hole. Our ears rubbed.

There were four men in the room. One of them was sitting on
a chair with his back to us. Another one was neither sitting nor
standing nor lying down. He was hanging. He was over by the far
wall, with his arms stretched up and his wrists bound with a cord,
and the cord was fastened to a chain suspended from the ceiling.
His feet were six inches above the floor. Tied to each ankle was
the end of a rope a few feet long, and the other end of each rope
was held by a man, one standing off to the right and the other to
the left. They were holding the ropes tight enough to keep the subject's feet spread apart a yard or more. The face of the subject
was so puffed and contorted that it was half a minute before I realized I had seen him before, and that long again before I placed
him. It was Peter Zov, the man with the flat nose, slanting forehead, and low, smooth voice who had been in Gospo Stritar's office,
and who had told Wolfe he was a man of action. He was getting
action, no question about that, but his voice wouldn't be so low
and smooth after the screams he had let loose.

The man in the chair with his back to us, who had been talking,
stopped. The two men standing started to pull on the ropes, slow
but sure. The gap between the subject's feet widened to four feet,
four and a half, five—more, and then no one looking at Peter Zov's
face would have recognized him. An inch more, two, and he
screamed. I shut my right eye. I must have made some other movement too, for Wolfe gripped my arm. The scream stopped, with a

gurgle that was just as bad, and when my eye opened the ropes were slack.

"That won't do, Peter," the man in the chair said. "You are reducing it to a routine. With your keen mind you have calculated that all you have to do is scream, and that time you screamed prematurely. Your scream is not musical, and we may be forced to muffle it. Would you prefer that?"

No answer.

"I repeat," the man in the chair said, "that you are wrong to think you are finished. It is not impossible that we can still find you useful, but not unless you play fair with us. Much of the information you have brought us has been of no account because we already had it. Some of it has been false. You failed completely in the one important operation we have entrusted to you, and your excuses are not acceptable."

"They're not excuses," Peter Zov mumbled. He was choking.

"No? What are they?"

"They're facts. I had to be away."

"You said that before. Perhaps I didn't explain fully enough, so I'll do it more patiently. I am a patient man. I admit that you must make sure to keep your employers convinced that you are to be trusted, since if you don't you are of no value whatever, either to them or to us. I am quite realistic about it. You're being discourteous, Peter; you're not listening to me. Let him down, Bua."

The man on the left dropped the rope, turned to the wall, unfastened a chain from a peg, and played it out through a pully on the ceiling. Peter Zov's feet got to the floor, and his arms were lowered, but only until his hands were even with his shoulders. He swayed from side to side as if he were keeping time to slow music.

"That should improve your manners temporarily," the man in the chair told him. "I was saying that I realize you must satisfy that fool, Gospo Stritar, that you serve him well, but you must also satisfy me, which is more difficult because I am not a fool. You could have carried out that operation without the slightest risk of arousing his suspicion, but instead you went to America on a mission for him, and now you have the impudence to come here and expect to be welcomed—even to be paid! So I am paying you. If you answer my questions properly the payment may be more to your taste."

"I had to go," Peter Zov gasped. "I thought you would approve."

"That's a lie. You're not such a blockhead. Those enemies of progress who call themselves the Spirit of the Black Mountain —you know their chief target is the Tito regime, not us, and it suits our purpose for them to make things as difficult as possible for Belgrade. There is little chance, perhaps none, that they will be able to overthrow the regime, but if they do that will suit us even better. We would march in and take over in a matter of hours. Our hostility to the Spirit of the Black Mountain is only a pretense, and you understood that perfectly. The more help they got from America the better. If that lackey of a cook, that Marko Vukcic who made himself rich pandering to the morbid appetites of the bloated American imperialists—if he had increased his help tenfold it would have been a great favor to us. You knew that, and what did you do? At the command of Belgrade you went to America and killed him."

He made a gesture. "If you thought we wouldn't know, you are so big a fool that you would be better dead. The night of March fourth you entered Italy at Gorizia, with papers under the name of Vito Rizzo, and went on to Genoa. You sailed from Genoa as a steward on the *Amilia* on March sixth. She docked at New York on March eighteenth, and you went ashore that night and killed Marko Vukcic and were back on the *Amilia* before nine o'clock. I don't know who briefed you in New York, or whether you had help in such details as stealing the car, but that's of no importance. You stayed aboard the *Amilia* until she sailed on March twenty-first, left her at Genoa on April second, and returned to Titograd that night. I tell you all this so you may know that you can hide nothing from us. Nothing."

He gestured again. "And on Sunday, April fourth, you came here to explain to these men that you had been unable to carry out our operation because you had been sent abroad on a mission. You found a woman here, drinking vodka with them, which was a surprise to you, but a greater surprise was to find that they already knew where you had been and what your mission was. Mistakes were made, I admit it; I only learned of them when I returned to Tirana yesterday from Moscow. They told you that they knew about your mission, and that alarmed you and you fled, and not only that, after you left they told the woman about you.

They blame the vodka, but they will learn that it is not a function of vodka to drown a duty. Later they corrected their blunder by disposing of the woman—that is in their favor—but they will have to be taught a lesson."

His tone sharpened. "That can wait, but you can't. Up with him, Bua."

Peter Zov sputtered something, but Bua ignored it. He had it on Peter in bulk, so when he pulled the chain not only Peter's arms went up but also the rest of him. When the feet were well off the floor Bua hooked the chain on the peg and picked up the end of the rope and was ready to resume. So was his colleague.

"Of course," the man in the chair said, "you had to come when you got my message yesterday, since you knew what to expect if you didn't, so that's no credit to you. You can get credit only by earning it. First, once more, how many boats patrol out of Dubrovnik, and what are their schedules?"

"Damn it, I don't know!" Peter was choky again.

"Bah. My patience can't last forever. Split him."

As the men tightened the ropes Wolfe lowered himself to a squat, pulling at my sleeve, and I went down to him. He had the long knife in his right hand. I had been so intent with my eye at the hole that I hadn't seen him take it from his belt. His left hand was fumbling at a pocket. He whispered in my ear, "We're going in when he screams. You open the door, and I go first. Gun in one hand and capsule in the other."

I whispered back, "Me first. No argument. Rescue him?" He nodded. As we straightened up he was still fumbling in his pocket, and I was reaching to the holster for the Marley. It didn't carry the punch of the Colt, but I knew it better. I admit I felt in my pocket to touch the capsule, but I didn't take it out, wanting the hand free. The door should be no problem. On our side was a hasp with a padlock hanging on a chain.

He started to scream. A glance showed me that Wolfe's left hand had left his pocket, and he nodded at me. As I pushed the door open and stepped through, what was at the front of my mind was light. Its source hadn't been visible through the hole. If it was a lamp, as it must be, and if one of them killed it, knives would have it on guns. The only insurance against it would be to plug the three of them in the first three seconds.

I didn't do that, I don't know why—probably because I had never shot a man unless there was nothing else left. The scream drowned the sound of our entry, but Bua saw us and dropped the rope and goggled, and then the other one; and the man in the chair jumped up and whirled to face us. He was closest, and I put the Marley on him. Wolfe, beside me, with the hand that held the knife at his belt level, started to say something but was interrupted. The closest man's hand went for his hip. Either he was a damn fool or a hero, or because I didn't say anything he thought I wasn't serious. I didn't try anything fancy like going for his arm or shoulder, but took him smack in the chest at nine feet. As I moved the gun back to level, the hand of the man on the right darted back and then forward, and how I knew a knife was coming and jerked myself sidewise the Lord only knows. It went by, but he was coming too, pulling something from his belt, and I pressed the trigger and stopped him.

I wheeled left and saw a sight. Bua was at the wall with his knife raised, holding it by the tip, and Wolfe, with his knife still at belt level, was advancing on him step by step, leaning forward in a crouch. When I asked him later why Bua hadn't let fly, he explained elementary knife tactics, saying that you never throw a knife against another knife at less than five meters, because if you don't drop your man in his tracks, which is unlikely if he's in a crouch, you'll be at his mercy. If I had known that I might have tried for Bua's shoulder, but I didn't, and all I wanted was to get a bullet to him before his knife started for Wolfe. I fired, and he leaned against the wall, with his hand still raised. I fired again, and he went down.

This is funny, or call it dumb. Before Bua even hit the floor I turned around to look for the light. I had entered the room with the light on top of my mind, and apparently it had stayed there and I had to get it off. It was a letdown to see that it came from three spots: two lanterns on a shelf to the right of the door, and one on the floor at the left. I had worried about nothing.

Wolfe walked past me to the chair, sat, and said, "Better look at them."

Peter Zov, still hanging, croaked something. Wolfe said, "He wants down. Look at them first. One of them may be shamming."

They weren't. I took my time and made sure. I suspected Bua

when I put a piece of fuzz from my jacket on his nostrils, holding his lips shut, and it floated off, but two more tries showed that it had been only a current in the air. "No shamming," I reported. "It was close quarters. If you wanted any—"

"This is what I wanted. Let him down."

I went and took the chain off the peg and eased it up. I suppose I should have been more careful, but my nerves were a little ragged, and when I saw his feet were on the floor I loosened my grip, and his weight jerked the chain out of my hands as he collapsed on the stone. I went to him and got out my pocket knife to cut the cord from his wrists, but Wolfe spoke.

"Wait a minute. Is he alive?"

I inspected him. "Sure he's alive. He just passed out, and I don't blame him."

"Will he die?"

"Of what? Did you bring smelling salts?"

"By heaven," he blurted with sudden ferocity, "you'll clown at your funeral! Tie his ankles and we'll go upstairs. I doubt if the shots could have been heard outside even if there were anyone to hear them, but I want to get out of here."

I obeyed. There was a choice of ropes to tie his ankles with, and it didn't take long. When I finished, Wolfe was at the door with a lantern in his hand, and I got one from the shelf and followed him out and up the fifteen steps. We went up faster than we had come down. He said we had better make sure there was no one else in the fort, and I agreed. He knew his way around as well as if he had built it himself, and we covered it all. He even had me climb the ladder to the tower, while he stood at the foot with my Colt in his hand, talking Albanian—I suppose warning anyone in the tower that if I were attacked he would pump them. When I rejoined him intact we went back to ground level and on outdoors, and he sat down on a flat rock at the corner nearest the trail. On its surface beside him was a big dark blotch.

"That's where Pasic killed the dog," I remarked.

"Yes. Sit down. As you know, I look at people when I talk to them, and I don't like to stretch my neck."

I sat on the blotch. "Oh, you want to talk?"

"I don't want to, I have to. Peter Zov is the man who murdered Marko."

I stared at him. "What is this, a hunch?"

"No. A certainty."

"How come?"

He told me what the man in the chair had said.

13

I sat for a minute and chewed on it, squinting at the sun. "If you had told me before we walked in," I said, "it would have taken just one more bullet."

"Pfui. Could you have shot him hanging there?"

"No."

"Then don't try to saddle me with it."

I chewed on it some more. "It's cockeyed. He killed Marko. I killed the birds that killed Carla."

"In a fight. You had no choice. With him we have."

"Name it. You go down and knife him. Or I go and shoot him. Or one of us challenges him to a duel. Or we shove him off a cliff. Or we leave him there to starve." I had an idea. "You wouldn't buy any of those, and neither would I, but what's wrong with this? We turn him over to Danilo and his pals and tell them what you heard. That ought to do it."

"No."

"Okay, it's your turn. We may not have all day because company may come."

"We must take him back to New York."

I guess I gaped. "And you scold me for clowning."

"I'm not clowning. I said with him we have a choice, but we haven't. We are constrained."

"By what?"

"By the obligation that brought us here. What Danilo's wife told him was cogent but not strictly accurate. If personal vengeance were the only factor I could, as you suggested, go and stick a knife in him and finish it, but that would be accepting the intolerable doctrine that man's sole responsibility is to his ego. That was the doctrine of Hitler, as it is now of Malenkov and Tito and Franco and Senator McCarthy; masquerading as a basis of freedom, it is the oldest and toughest of the enemies of freedom. I reject it and contemn it. You look skeptical. I suppose you're thinking that I have sometimes been high-handed in dealing with the hired protectors of freedom in my adopted land—the officers of the law."

"Not more than a thousand times," I protested.

"You exaggerate. But I have never flouted their rightful authority or tried to usurp their lawful powers, and being temporarily in the domain of dictatorial barbarians gives me no warrant to embrace their doctrines and use their methods. Marko was murdered in New York. His murderer is accountable to the People of the State of New York, not to me. Our part is to get him there."

"Hooray for us. The only way to get him there legally is to have him extradited."

"That isn't true. You're careless with your terms. Extradition is the only way to get him there *by action of law,* but that's quite different and of course impossible. The point is to get him under the jurisdiction of civilized law without violating it ourselves."

"I see the point all right. How?"

"That's it. Can he walk?"

"I should think so. I heard no bones crack. Shall I go and find out?"

"No." He got to his feet with only a couple of grunts during the operation. "I must speak with that man—Stan Kosor. I don't want to leave you here alone, because if someone should come you couldn't talk except with the gun, so I'll try this first."

He faced in the direction of Montenegro and beckoned, using the whole length of his arm, again and again. I booked it as a one-to-ten shot, because first, Kosor might not be up in the niche at all, and second, if he was there I doubted if he trusted Wolfe enough to cross the border to him. I lost the bet. I don't know how the man got down from the crag so quickly unless he just let go and slid, but I hadn't even begun to look for him in earnest when my eye was attracted by movement, and there he was on the bend in the trail where it emerged from a defile. He strode along until he reached the spot where the trail began to widen for the space in front of the fort, stopped abruptly, and called something. By then I had seen that it wasn't Kosor but Danilo Vukcic. We had been honored. Wolfe answered him, and he came on.

They jabbered. Danilo sounded and looked as if he didn't believe what he heard, got persuaded apparently, and looked at me with a different expression from any he had had for me before. Deducing that I was being admired for my prowess with small arms, I yawned to show that it was nothing out of the ordinary. Then they got into a hot argument. After that was settled, Wolfe did most of the talking, and there was no more arguing. Evidently everything was rosy, for they shook hands as if they meant it, and Danilo offered me a hand and I took it. He was absolutely cordial. When he went he turned twice, once at the far edge of the wide space and once just before he disappeared into the defile, to wave at us.

"He's a different man," I told Wolfe. "Report, please?"

"There isn't time. I must talk with that man, and we must get away. I told Danilo what happened. He insisted on going down to look at them, but I said no. If he had gone alone he might have come back with a collection of fingers, including Zov's, and if we had gone along and Zov had been conscious he would have seen us together on friendly terms, which wouldn't do. We're going to take Zov out the way we came, and Danilo is going to try to stop us and fail."

"I'm not going to shoot Danilo."

"You won't have to, if he does as agreed, and he will. I would prefer not to go back down there. Will you go? If he can move, bring him here."

"Leave his wrists tied?"

"No. Free him."

I entered the fort by the door, crossed to the entrance to a narrow passage, and after a couple of turns was in the long corridor. At the top of the fifteen steps I turned on my flashlight. Why I got a gun in my hand as I approached the door of the room I don't exactly know, but I did. The lantern on the shelf was still burning. I made the rounds of the three casualties, checked that they still weren't shamming, and then went to Zov. He was stretched out, in a different position from when we left him, with his eyes shut, motionless. I took my knife and cut the rope on his ankles, and then the cord on his wrists, which were red and bruised and swollen, and when I let go of them he tried to let them fall dead to the floor but botched it.

I stood and looked down at him, thinking how much I could simplify matters if I forgot doctrines for just two seconds. Another thought followed it. Was it possible that Wolfe had had that in mind when he sent me down alone, on the chance that I would come back up and report that Zov had kicked off? Let Archie do it? I decided no. I had known him to pull some raw ones, but no.

"Nuts," I told Zov. "Open your eyes."

No sign. I kicked his shoulder, just gently, but the shoulder had had a hard day, and he winced. I stooped and grabbed an ear and started to lift him by it, and his eyes opened and focused on me. I let the ear go, hooked my fingers in his armpits from behind, raised his torso, and hauled him on up. He clutched at my sleeve and said something, and I took hold of his belt in the rear and started him for the door, and he did fine. I was afraid I might have to carry him up the steps, but he made it on his own, though I kept a good hold on the belt for fear he might tumble and break his neck and Wolfe would think I had pushed him. After that there was nothing to it. Halfway down the corridor I shifted from his belt to his elbow, and when we got to the door, in sight of Wolfe, I broke contact. I had some vague feeling that I preferred to have him go on to Wolfe without my touching him. He went to the rock and sat down, and Wolfe moved over a little.

"Well, Mr. Zov," Wolfe said, "I'm glad you can walk."

"Comrade Zov," he said.

"If you like, certainly. Comrade Zov. We'd better be moving. Someone might come, and my son has done enough for one day."

Zov looked at his wrists. It was just as well he didn't have a mirror to look at his face. The flat nose and slanting forehead would never have been a treat, but with the sun on them, and still twitching from spasms, they were something special.

He looked at Wolfe. "You were in Titograd yesterday afternoon. How did you get here?"

"Surely that can wait. We must get away."

"I want to know."

"You heard me mention the Spirit of the Black Mountain. I had been told that one of its leaders could be found here near the border, and we came to find him. We did so, and talked with him, and we were disappointed. We decided to cross into Albania, and saw this fort, and were about to enter, when we heard a scream.

We went in to investigate, and you know what we found. We interfered because we disapprove of torture. Violence is often unavoidable, as it was on your mission to New York, but not torture. If that's how—"

"How do you know of my mission to New York?"

"We heard that Russian talking to you. If that's how the Russians do things, we are not their friends. We intend to return to Titograd and see Gospo Stritar. He impressed us." Wolfe stood up without grunting. "Let's go. But did they take anything from you? Weren't you armed?"

"We can't go through the mountains in the daytime. We'll have to hole up—I know a place—until dark."

"No. We're going now."

"That's crazy. We'll never reach the valley alive. It's risky enough at night."

Wolfe tapped him on the shoulder. "It's your nerves, Comrade Zov, and no wonder. But I'm in charge momentarily, and I insist. You have seen my son in action, and you may rely on him to get us through, as I do. I will not undertake that trail again at night, and I refuse to leave you here in your present condition. Were you armed?"

"Yes."

"With a gun?"

"A gun and a knife. They put them in a table drawer." He put his hands on the rock to push himself up. "I'll go get them."

Wolfe halted him with a hand on his shoulder. "You have no energy to waste. My son will go. Alex, a gun and a knife they took from Comrade Zov are in a drawer in a table. Bring them."

"What kind of a gun?"

He asked him and didn't have to relay it. The word "Luger" is neither Serbo-Croat nor Albanian, and I had heard it before. After entering the fort, I went to the first room on the right, which seemed the most likely because I had seen a big table there, and hit it at the first try. At the front of the drawer, with a Luger and a big clasp knife, were a stainless steel wristwatch and a leather fold containing papers, one of them with a red seal and a picture of Peter Zov. He was not photogenic. I went back out with them.

As I approached, Wolfe spoke. "Keep the gun. Give him the knife."

"There's a watch and a fold with papers."

"Give him those." He turned to Zov. "My son will keep the gun for the time being. If an attempt is made to stop us you might be overhasty with it after what you've just gone through."

Zov took the other things and said, "I want the gun."

"You'll get it. Is it an old friend?"

"Yes. I took it from a dead German in the war."

"No wonder you value it. I suppose you had it on your mission to New York."

"I did, and other missions. I want it."

"Later. I assume the responsibility for our safe passage through the mountains, and I don't know you well, though I hope to. You're about my son's age, and it's a pity you can't communicate. Do you know any English at all?"

"I know a few words, like 'okay' and 'dollar' and 'cigarette.' "

"I'm sorry I didn't teach him Serbo-Croat. We've been here long enough. I'll lead, and my son will bring up the rear. Come on."

If Zov had had his gun he might have balked, and we would have had either to go on without him or find a place to spend the day. He did try to argue, but Wolfe got emphatic, and I had the gun, so he came. We went to the brook for a drink and then hit the trail, with Zov in between us. His gait was more of a shuffle than a walk, but he didn't seem to be in any great pain. It could have been as much from lack of enthusiasm as from the condition of his legs. When we had passed through the defile and topped a rise, and Wolfe stopped for breath, I asked him, "Where will the charade be? You didn't tell me."

"It isn't necessary. We'll keep colloquy at a minimum. Statements about linguistic proficiency may be equivocal. I'll tell you when to draw a gun."

"You might tell me now about the colloquy you just had."

He did so, and then turned and proceeded. As I padded along behind I was thinking that we certainly had the bacon—not only the murderer but the weapon, and I knew the rest of the evidence was on file because I had seen the assistant medical examiner getting it from Marko's corpse. I remembered the first sentences of a book I had read on criminology. *In criminal investigation,* it said, *the investigator must always have in mind the simple basic re-*

*quirements. Once he gains possession of the person of the crimi-
nal and of evidence adequate for conviction, the job is done.* It is,
like hell, I thought. If I had that book here, and the author, I'd
make him eat it.

I was supposed to forget about being stopped and leave it to
Wolfe, but as we approached the point where one left the trail if
one was ass enough to want to walk the ledge to the cave, I kept
close behind Zov and had my eyes peeled. We went on by without
sight or sound of anyone. If you wonder why Wolfe didn't let me
know, which he could have done in ten words, I can tell you. I
would have had to put on an act for Zov's benefit until I reached
the spot that had been agreed on, and he thought I might overdo
it or underdo it, I don't know which. He thought that, not knowing,
I would just act natural. You may also wonder why I didn't resent
it. I did. I had been resenting it for years, but that was my first
crack at resenting it in the mountains of Montenegro.

With the sun nearly straight above us, blazing down, I wouldn't
have recognized the trail as the one we had climbed the night before with Danilo. We went down rock faces on our rumps, skirted
the edges of cliffs, slithered down stretches of loose shale, and at
one place crossed a crevice ten feet wide, on a narrow plank bridge
with no rails, which I didn't remember at all. My watch said ten
minutes past one when we stopped at a brook for a drink and a
meal of chocolate. Comrade Zov ate as much chocolate as Wolfe
and me together.

Half an hour later the trail suddenly spilled us out at the edge of
a wide level space, and there was the house Wolfe had been born
in. I stopped for a look. Apparently its back wall was the side of a
cliff. It had two stories, with a roof that sloped four ways from the
center, and eight windows on the side I was looking at, four below and four above. The glass in three windows was broken. The
door was wooden.

I was just starting to turn to tell Wolfe I was going to step inside for a glance around when his voice snapped at my back, "Gun,
Alex!"

I whirled, drawing the Colt from my hip. Danilo, Josip Pasic,
and two other men were grouped at the far edge of the space, evidently having come from behind a massive boulder. Danilo had a
gun, but the others were empty-handed.

"Don't shoot," Danilo said. "You can go wherever you're going. We only want Peter Zov."

Wolfe had put himself in front of Zov. "He's with us, and he's going with us."

"No, he's not. We're taking him."

Wolfe's attitude was perfect for saying "Over my dead body," but he didn't say it. My own attitude was no slouch, with my feet planted apart and my Colt steady at Danilo's belly. Wolfe said, "He's under our protection, and you can't have him. We're American citizens, and if you harm us you'll regret it."

"We don't want to harm you. Zov is a traitor to his country. He crossed the border to the Albanians. We have a right to him."

"What do you intend to do with him?"

"I'm going to find out what he told the Albanians."

They must have been ad libbing, for there hadn't been time to write a script during their brief talk at the fort.

"I don't believe it," Wolfe said. "After the hours I spent with you, I don't believe anything you say. Heaven only knows where your allegiance lies, if anywhere. If you are a true son of Yugoslavia, come with us—you alone, not the others. If Zov has betrayed his country the proper person to deal with him is Gospo Stritar in Titograd, and that's where we're taking him. If you want to come, drop your gun and start down the road. You others stay where you are."

"We'll deal with him here."

"You will not. Are you coming?"

"No."

"Then touch us at your peril. Comrade Zov, I'm going to turn around. You turn also, to face the road entrance. Keep against me, away from them, and we'll make the road slowly, and on down. Alex, cover us. You'll have to back out, steering by my voice."

He turned and had his back to the enemy. Zov turned likewise, and Wolfe put his hands on Zov's shoulders. I sidestepped and was directly behind Wolfe, back to back, with the Colt still focused on the group. As Wolfe and Zov moved forward, and I backward, Wolfe gave me his voice to guide by.

" 'Preamble. We, the People of the United States, in order to form a more perfect Union, establish justice, insure domestic tranquility, provide for the common defense, promote the general welfare, and secure the blessings of liberty to ourselves and our posterity, do ordain and establish this Constitution for the United States of America.'"

We had left the open space and started down the road. Since Zov couldn't possibly see me, I had a strong impulse to grin at Danilo and to wave to him as he had waved to us when he left the fort. I had to bite my lip to control it. He might misunderstand and ruin everything.

Wolfe was guiding me. "I skip to the ten original amendments, the Bill of Rights. 'Article One. Congress shall make no law respecting an establishment of religion, or prohibiting the free exercise thereof; or abridging the freedom of speech or of the press; or the right of the people peaceably to assemble and to petition the Government for a redress of grievances. Article Two. A well-regulated militia being necessary to the security of a free State, the right of the people to keep and bear arms shall not be infringed. Article Three. No soldier shall, in time of peace, be quartered in any house without the consent of the owner, nor in time of war but in a manner to be prescribed by law. Article Four. The right—'"

"Hold it," I cut in. "I'm not going to back clear to Titograd."

"I'll finish Article Four. It's Article Four that has us in this mess. 'The right of the people to be secure in their persons, houses, papers, and effects, against unreasonable searches and seizures, shall not be violated, and no warrants shall issue but upon probable cause, supported by oath or affirmation, and particularly describing the place to be searched, and the persons or things to be seized.'"

"Is that all?"

"That will do."

I turned around.

14

We arrived in Titograd in style, in an old Ford truck that Zov requisitioned at the first farm we came to that had one, and pulled up in front of police headquarters at twenty minutes past three, just twenty-two hours after Jubé Bilic had delivered us there the day before. As we piled out, Wolfe told me to give the driver three thousand dinars, and I obeyed. I was stuck again with the knapsacks, which we had taken off when we boarded the truck, and with the sweaters. We followed Zov into the big old stone edifice, along the dingy corridor, up the stairs, and into the room where the two clerks sat on stools. Zov spoke to Wolfe, and Wolfe told me we were to wait there and went to a chair and sat. Zov didn't go on in. He sent one of the clerks, who entered the inner room, returned in a moment, and motioned Zov to come. I put the luggage on a chair beside Wolfe and myself on another one.

It was a long wait, so long that I began to nurse the possibility that Gospo Stritar was going to relieve us of our problem. Evidently Zov had been completely confident that his loyalty would not be questioned, but Stritar might not see it that way. The idea had its attractions, but it led to another, that if a visit to the Albanians was enough to do for Zov, what about Toné Stara and his son Alex? That wasn't so attractive. I would have liked to ask Wolfe a couple of pertinent questions, but his head had fallen forward until his chin touched, his eyes were closed, and he was breathing as if he were a week behind on oxygen, so I let him alone.

I became aware that someone was yelling at somebody named Alex, and wished Alex would answer. Also someone had hold of my shoulder. I opened my eyes, saw Wolfe, and jerked upright.

"You were sound asleep," he said testily.

"So were you. First."

"We're wanted. Bring the knapsacks."

I gathered them up and followed him between the counters and across to the inner room. Zov, holding the door for us, shut it and went to a chair at the end of Stritar's desk and sat. Stritar waved us to chairs without getting up. He hadn't got a haircut. His underhung jaw didn't seem quite as impressive as it had the day before, but I had seen a lot of underhung rocks in the meantime. After giving Wolfe a sharp glance, he concentrated on me as I went to the chair, and after I sat he looked me up and down. Not knowing what our line was going to be, or his either, I neither grinned nor glowered at him but merely looked self-reliant.

He turned to Wolfe. "It's too bad your son doesn't speak our language. I'd like to talk with him."

Wolfe nodded. "I was wrong not to teach him. I would be glad to interpret for you."

"That's not the same. Comrade Zov has told me what happened today. You and your son have acted boldly and bravely. It is appreciated by me and will be appreciated by my superiors. You can add to that appreciation by giving me a full account of your movements since you left here yesterday."

Wolfe raised his brows. "I'm surprised that you ask. You said everything would get to you."

"Perhaps it has. I would like to hear it from you."

"You may. We went first to the house where I visited my friend Grudo Balar many years ago. A stranger was there who had never heard of him. We went next to an address that someone in Albania had given me. I had been told that a man named Danilo Vukcic could give me much information if he would, particularly about the Spirit of the Black Mountain."

"Who in Albania told you about him?"

Wolfe shook his head. "I told you yesterday that I will not cause trouble for anyone who has helped us. We found Danilo Vukcic at that address, and he did indeed have information. It seemed to me that he was overready to impart it to strangers, but later, thinking it over, I realized that it was only such matters as were probably common knowledge—or merely current rumors. I was quite candid with him. You may remember I told you that we had cached a considerable sum in American dollars somewhere in the mountains, and I told him about it too. I now think that was a mistake. I now think it was my telling him about that cache that caused him to offer to take us to a place in the mountains where we could meet one of the leaders of the Spirit of the Black Mountain. Anyway, we accepted the offer, and he took us. After a difficult journey we arrived—"

"One moment. Did you see Jubé Bilic anywhere? The boy who brought you here yesterday?"

Wolfe was surprised and puzzled. "Him? Where? In the mountains?"

"Did you see him anywhere after you left here?"

"I did not. Why?"

Stritar waved it away. "Go on."

"We arrived at a cave—near the Albanian border, I was told— in the middle of the night. There were five men there, and Vukcic said that one of them was a leader of the Spirit, but he didn't impress me as a leader of men or of a movement. By that—"

"What was his name?"

"I was given no names. By that time I was suspicious of the whole business. They insisted on knowing where our dollars were cached, and at one time I thought they were going to try to force us to tell by methods that I consider barbarous. Also I distrusted Vukcic. I have had many dealings with men, mostly in America, and I concluded that Vukcic was not honest or sincere, and that I would have nothing to do with a movement in which he was prominent or influential. I didn't tell him that, of course. If I had we might not have left the mountains alive, in spite of the fact that they would rather not lay a hand on American citizens. The question was, how to get away from them without serious trouble, and I think I managed it pretty well. In the morning I said we would like to have a look at the border, at Albania, and Vukcic went with us to show us where the border is, since it isn't marked. When we got there we simply kept on going. Vukcic wanted to stop us, but we paid no attention to him. He stuck to us for a distance, protesting, but stopped when we emerged from a defile. We soon knew why, when we saw the fort. We went to it and were about to enter, when we heard a scream, and we went in to investigate. You have heard the rest from Comrade Zov."

"I want to hear it from you. All of it—if you can, every word."

When Wolfe reported to me later, I liked that. Up to that point the indications were that Stritar really trusted Zov, which would have been silly. The one rule everybody in Yugoslavia stuck to was: never trust anybody, anywhere, any time.

I don't need to report the rest of it to you, as Wolfe didn't to me. He gave it to Stritar just as it had happened, omitting only his conversations with me and Danilo's visit to the fort. I will, however, include something that he tacked on at the end, after he had got us into the truck on our way to Titograd. "My son and I," he said, "claim no special credit for what we did, but you expressed appreciation for it. If you would like us to have a token of your appreciation, one little favor would be welcome. For some time my son has wanted a Luger pistol, and he says that Comrade Zov's is in excellent condition. He would like to trade his Colt for it if Comrade Zov is willing."

Of course I didn't know then what he had said, but I saw he had made a mistake. Zov's reaction, which was prompt, was merely a loud and emphatic protest, but Stritar narrowed his eyes and tightened his lips. Later, when I learned what Wolfe had said, I thanked God Stritar hadn't been quite keen enough. He had suspected there was something phony about it, but he hadn't gone a step further and realized that Toné Stara was from America and that Zov's gun had been used to commit a murder in America. If he had, good-by. I'm not blaming Wolfe for making the try. He wanted me to hang on to that Luger if I possibly could, and he took the chance. He saw at once that it wouldn't work and he had nearly gummed it, and was quick to repair the damage.

He raised a hand to stop Zov's protest. "No, Comrade Zov, not if you feel so strongly about it. It was just a suggestion, of no importance. I thought you might welcome it. Alex, give Comrade Zov his gun."

I took it from my pocket, went over and handed it to him, and returned to my chair.

Stritar's eyes were back to normal. "You will be glad to know that your account agrees in every respect with Peter Zov's. Of course you could have arranged for that, there was plenty of time, but I have at present no reason to suppose that you did. You can tell your son that the man he killed was Dmitri Shuvalov, one of the three top Russians in Albania."

Wolfe told me, and I said that was interesting.

"So," Stritar said, "I'm glad I let you go yesterday, to see what you would get into. I certainly didn't anticipate your performance at the fort. Zov, who speaks Russian, has been in contact with Shuvalov for some time, and was doing well, he thought; but evidently he was wrong. It was lucky for him you came along, and I tell you frankly, you have earned some consideration. What are you going to do now? Would you like to go to Belgrade? It is not out of the question for you to meet the marshal."

"We have no papers, as you know."

"That will be no difficulty, under the circumstances."

"I don't know." Wolfe looked doubtful. "My son and I feel that we have accomplished what we came for. It doesn't take us a year to tell an apple from a wart. We are satisfied that the true interests of the people of my native land will be best served by the present regime. We were particularly impressed by your treatment of us yesterday, because it could only have come from the confidence of a secure and just authority. We want to help as far as our modest resources will permit, but we can do more good in America than we could here. Our property is there, and our—oh, by the way, speaking of property, I told you of our cache in the mountains."

"Yes."

"It's eight thousand dollars in American currency, and we wish to contribute it as a token of our belief in the regime and our desire to support it. I'll tell my son what I have said so he may indicate his concurrence." He turned to me. "Alex, I'm telling them that we donate our cache of eight thousand dollars to the regime. If you agree, please nod at them."

I did so, first at Stritar and then at Zov. But if I know anything about men's faces, having seen the look they exchanged as Wolfe spoke, all the regime would ever see of that eight grand wouldn't get the windows washed in that one room. I took in their expressions as Wolfe proceeded to furnish in careful detail the location of the cache, and I'll bet I had them right. Zov was thinking: It ought to be an even split. I brought them here. Stritar was thinking: Ten per cent is enough for Zov. He's lucky to be in on it at all.

Wolfe went on, "Of course that amount is nothing, it's merely a gesture, but we wish to make it. When we get back to America we'll see what we can do. You suggested our going to Belgrade, but that doesn't appeal to us. Our interest centers in the people of these mountains, and even under the present progressive regime they seem to be a little neglected. Also I like to deal with men I have met, men I know. From America I would rather be in touch with you than with names in Belgrade that mean nothing to me personally. I suppose you regard that as a bourgeois sentiment."

"Well." Stritar considered it. "It's human."

Wolfe looked apologetic. "I admit I have acquired some bourgeois habits of thought during my years in America, and that is regrettable. I am of peasant origin. The peasant is out of date, and the bourgeois is doomed. You and your kind represent the future, and my son wants to be a part of the future. I intend to teach him Serbo-Croat, and in time, when our affairs in America have been properly arranged, he hopes to return here for good. Meanwhile I shall communicate with you, and you can tell me now if you have any suggestions how we can be of use."

"We need friends in America," Stritar said.

"Naturally. You need friends everywhere. We will do what we can in that direction. Would you advise us to join the Communist Party of the United States and try to influence them in your favor?"

"Good God, no." Stritar was contemptuous. "They belong to Moscow, body and soul, and they're a nest of slimy vermin. Where do you live in America?"

"In Philadelphia."

"Where is that?"

"It's a city with two million people, ninety miles southwest of New York."

"Two million! That's incredible. Is your name there Toné Stara?"

"No." Wolfe hesitated. "It is not a question of being frank with you, Comrade Stritar. It is merely that I would not want any inquiries made among my friends or associates until I return. As soon as I arrive I'll let you know, and of course give you my American name and address. One thing you should tell me now; in case I have money to send, which is very probable, I would want to be sure it reaches you safely. How would I send dollars?"

Stritar pursed his lips. "I'll think it over and let you know. You're right, it should be properly arranged. When are you leaving, and how?"

"We have no papers."

"I know."

"Also, I'll be frank, we want to get away as soon as possible. You must forgive us if we feel that we are in danger. I know that the police here are under you and are therefore extremely efficient, but today we heard that Russian tell Comrade Zov that he had to come to the fort when he got his message, because he knew what to expect if he didn't. So not only can they get messages to Titograd, but also if the messages are not heeded they can do something about it. They will certainly not let the death of that Dmitri Shuvalov go unavenged, not to mention the other two. We are not comfortable in Titograd."

"No one saw you. No one knows you were there."

"Danilo Vukcic knows, and his friends. My suspicions of Vukcic may be unfounded, but I have them. He may be in Albania now, to report about us. And that suggests another matter, though it is not our concern."

"What other matter?"

Wolfe glanced at Zov and back at Stritar. "Regarding Comrade Zov. I presume his danger is greater than ours. If Shuvalov was confident that he could reach him in Titograd to punish him for ignoring a message, surely they can reach him when the motive is so much stronger. That is his concern, and yours, but, having rescued him from torture and perhaps death, naturally we feel an interest in him. I am willing to propose something if it is not impertinent."

"You couldn't be more impertinent than to march into my office and announce you had no papers. What do you propose?"

"That you send Zov to America for a while. He could either go with us or come to us after he arrives, and we would see to his needs and his safety. It offers several advantages: it would remove him temporarily from peril here, if there is any; it would give us someone in America who is familiar with conditions here, to advise us; it would give you an agent there whom you trust, to report on us and our associates; and it would give me a messenger I could rely on if I had something confidential or valuable to send to you." Wolfe flipped a hand. "Of course, for some reason unknown to me, it may be quite impractical."

Stritar and Zov had exchanged not one glance, but several. Stritar said, "It is worth considering. It may not be entirely impractical."

"I thought it might not be," Wolfe said, "since Zov returned only recently from a trip to America. That was what suggested it to me. I even thought it possible you might have another mission for him there. If so, he might need help, and what we did today, especially my son, may have demonstrated that we could be capable of supplying it."

Stritar looked at Zov. Then he studied Wolfe. Then he transferred to me. I was aware, from tones and expressions and the atmosphere, that we were at a crisis, but I didn't know what kind, so all I could do was meet his eyes and look loyal and confident and absolutely intrepid. After he had analyzed me clear through to my spine he returned to Wolfe.

"Did you ever," he asked, "hear of a man named Nero Wolfe?"

I claim a medal for handling not only my face but all my nerves and muscles. His pronunciation was fuzzy, but not too fuzzy for me to get it. I knew they were at a crisis, and suddenly that bozo snaps out the name Nero Wolfe. How I kept my hand from starting for my holster I don't know. Wolfe showed no sign of panic, but that was no help. He wouldn't panic if you paid him.

"Of course," he said. "If you mean the well-known detective in New York. Everyone in America has heard of him."

"Do you know him?"

"I haven't met him, no. I know a man who has. He says I look like him, but I've seen a picture of him, and the only resemblance is that we're both big and fat."

"Did you know a man named Marko Vukcic?"

"No, but I heard his name today, as I told you, when Shuvalov was speaking to Zov. Was he any relation to Danilo Vukcic?"

"His uncle. He owned a de luxe restaurant. This detective, Nero Wolfe, was his friend, and there is reason to believe that he intends to take Vukcic's place and send money and other help to the Spirit of the Black Mountain. In large amounts."

Wolfe grunted. "Then it did no good to kill Vukcic."

"I don't agree. We couldn't know that a friend of his would take over so promptly and effectively. But he has. I got the news only today."

"And now you propose to kill Nero Wolfe."

Stritar snapped, "I didn't say so."

"No, but you might as well. I haven't got a quick mind, but it didn't have to be quick for that. I suggested that you might have another mission for Zov in America, and you asked me if I had ever heard of this Nero Wolfe. That's just adding two and two, or rather one and one. So you propose to kill him."

"What if I do?"

"It may be necessary. I don't know."

"You told Zov that you disapprove of torture but that violence is often unavoidable, as it was on his mission to New York."

"That's true. I meant that. But I don't think a man should be killed merely on suspicion. Have you any evidence that this Nero Wolfe will really help your enemies as Vukcic did?"

"I have." Stritar opened a drawer of his desk and took out a paper. "Day before yesterday a man in Bari received a telegram from Nero Wolfe which read as follows: 'Inform proper persons across Adriatic I am handling Vukcic's affairs and assuming obligations. Two hundred thousand dollars available soon. Will send agent conference Bari next month.'" Stritar put the paper back and shut the drawer. "Is that evidence?"

"It sounds like it. Who is the man in Bari that got the telegram?"

"That's not important. You want to know too much."

"I don't think so, Comrade Stritar—if I am to call you Comrade. If I am to trust you on vital matters, as I am prepared to do, you will trust me to some extent. My son and I will have to go through Bari on our way back, to get our papers and effects, and we might possibly encounter him. His name?"

Stritar shrugged his bulging shoulders. "Paolo Telesio."

Wolfe's eyes widened. "What!"

Stritar stared. "What's the matter?"

"Enough." Wolfe was grim. "Paolo Telesio has our papers and belongings. We left them in his care. A man in Philadelphia gave me his name, as one trustworthy and capable, who would arrange for getting us across the Adriatic. And he serves the Spirit of the Black— No, wait! After all, you have that telegram." He shook his head. "No, it is just as well we're going back. Here it's impossible to tell who you're dealing with. My brain is not equipped for it."

"Not many brains are," Stritar declared. "Don't make any assumptions about Telesio. I didn't say he sent me the telegram. You are not to tell him I have seen it. You understand that?"

"Certainly. We're not a pair of fools, though yesterday you called us that. Do you still think so?"

"I think it is possible I was wrong. I agree with you that you can do more good in America than you can here. It is in your favor that you are inclined to be skeptical, as for instance about Nero Wolfe. You asked for evidence that he intends to send major assistance to our subversive underground, and I furnished it. I regard it as conclusive. Do you?"

Wolfe hesitated. "Conclusive is a strong word. But I—yes. I will say yes."

"Then he must be dealt with. Will you help?"

"That depends. If you mean will I or my son engage to kill him, no. Killing a man in America is not the same as killing a man here. Circumstances might develop that would lead us to undertake it, but I won't commit myself, and neither will he."

"I didn't ask you to. I asked if you'll help. Peter Zov will need it. The preparations and arrangements will have to be made for him, and provision for his safety afterward. You say Philadelphia is ninety miles from New York—that's a hundred and fifty kilometers—and that is well, for New York would be dangerous for him. That's the kind of help he'll need. Will you give it?"

Wolfe considered. "There's a difficulty. No matter how well it is arranged, it's conceivable that Zov will be caught. If he is, under pressure he might betray us."

"You saw him under pressure today. Will the American police use greater pressure than that?"

"No." Wolfe looked at me. "Alex, it is suggested that Comrade Zov shall go to America, and we shall provide for his necessities and also help him with the preparations to kill a man named Nero Wolfe. I am willing to undertake it if you are."

I looked serious. I would have given eight thousand cents to be able to reply that I had been wanting to kill a man named Nero Wolfe for years, but I wasn't sure that Stritar and Zov understood no English. I had to skip it. I said earnestly, "I am willing, Father, to help with anything you approve of."

He looked at Stritar. "My son says he is willing. We want to leave here as soon as possible. Can you get us to Bari tonight?"

"Yes. But Zov will have to go by another route." Stritar looked at his watch. "There is much to arrange." He raised his voice to call, "Jin!"

The door opened, and one of the clerks came in. Stritar spoke to him. "Find Trumbic and Levstik and get them here. I'll be busy for an hour or more. No interruptions unless it's urgent."

Zov had his Luger out, rubbing it with his palm.

15

We got arrested for having no papers after all, and it damn near bollixed everything.

Not in Montenegro. Stritar took no chances on our changing our minds and deciding to go to Belgrade, where we would probably mention the eight thousand dollars and the promise of more to come. He fed us there in his office, on meat and cheese and bread and raisins that he had brought in, and a little after dark took us down to the street himself and put us in a 1953 Ford, a different color from Jubé Bilic's. Our destination was Budva, a coast village which Wolfe said was five miles north of the spot where we had been landed by Guido Battista two nights before. During the hour and a half that it took to cover the thirty miles, the driver had no more than a dozen words for Wolfe, and none at all for me. As he delivered us at the edge of a slip and exchanged noises with a man waiting there, it started to rain.

It rained all the way across the Adriatic, but the boat was a few centuries newer than Guido's, with a cabin where I could lie down. Wolfe tried it too, but the bench was so narrow he had to grip a bracket to keep from rolling off, and finally he gave up and stretched out on the floor. The boat, with a crew of two besides the skipper, was fast, noisy, was rated 500 v.p.m., which means vibrations per minute, and was a steeplechaser. It loved to jump waves. No wonder it beat Guido's time by nearly three hours. It was still raining, and dark as pitch, when it anchored in choppy water and we were herded into a dinghy some bigger than Guido's. The skipper rowed us into the wall of night until he hit bottom, dumped us on the beach, shoved the nose of the dinghy off, hopped in, and was gone.

Wolfe called to him, "Confound it, where are we?"

He called back, "Where you're supposed to be!"

"The genial sonofabitch," I remarked.

With the sweaters draped over our heads, and flashlights, we headed inland. A road going to Molfetta, a fishing village two miles away if we had been landed in the right place, was supposed to be only two hundred yards from the shore, and we found it, turned left, and trudged along in the rain. It was 3:28 a.m. when we hit the road. I was thinking that when we got to the stucco house in Bari I would have Wolfe translate the directions on the water heater in the bathroom.

We made it to Molfetta, knocked at the door of a white house with trees in front, and Wolfe spoke through a crack to the man who unlocked it, and handed him a slip of paper. He was about as genial as the skipper had been, but he agreed to drive us to Bari, twenty-five kilometers down the coast, for five thousand lire. We weren't invited in out of the rain. We waited under a tree, a European species called a dripping tree, while he put on some clothes, and when he appeared on the driveway in a little Fiat we climbed in the back and sat on wet fannies and were off.

I took my mind off the wet by thinking. Wolfe had reported in full on the boat. There were some aspects that seemed to me a little sour, such as donating the eight grand to that character, but I had to admit he was justified in making his proposal as tempting to Stritar as he possibly could. The only bad flaw was that we didn't have Zov, and no guarantee that we would get him again. He was to sneak into Italy at Gorizia, as he had before, I don't know how often, and meet us at Genoa. Wolfe explained that even if Stritar had been willing to send him with us through Bari, having him along would have made matters very difficult.

I was going over it when suddenly the car stopped, the left front door opened, and a beam of light focused on the driver. A man in a raincoat was there. He asked the driver some questions and got answered, and then opened the rear door, aimed the light at us, and spoke. Wolfe replied. It developed into quite a chat, with the man insisting on something and Wolfe insisting back. Finally the man shut the door, circled around the hood to the right front door, got in beside the driver, spoke to him, and twisted in the seat to face us. His hand, resting on the back of the seat, had a gun in it.

I asked Wolfe, "Am I supposed to do something?"

"No. He wanted to see our papers."

"Where are we going?"

"Jail."

"But my God, aren't we in Bari?"

"Entering it, yes."

"Then tell him to take us to that house and we'll show him the damn papers."

"No. At the risk of having it get across the Adriatic tomorrow that I am here? Impossible."

"What did you tell him?"

"That I wish to see the American consul. Naturally he refuses to disturb him at this hour."

I am thinking of starting a movement to push for a law requiring two consuls in every city, a day consul and a night consul, and you would join it if you had ever spent a night, or part of one, in the hoosegow at Bari. We were questioned—or Wolfe was—first by a handsome baritone in a slick uniform and then by a fat animal in a soiled seersucker. Our guns and knives didn't make them any more cordial. Then we were locked in a cell with two cots which were already occupied by fifty thousand others. Twenty thousand of the others were fleas, and another twenty thousand were bedbugs, but I never found out what the other ten thousand were. After a night in a haystack and one in a deep-freeze cave, it would have been reasonable to suppose that anything different would be an improvement, but it wasn't. I got a lot of walking done, back and forth the full length of the cell, a good ten feet, being careful not to step on Wolfe, who was sitting on the concrete floor. All I will say about the breakfast is that we didn't eat it. The chocolate, what was left of it, was in the knapsacks, and they had been taken.

Another section of that law will provide that day consuls will get to work at eight o'clock. It was after ten when the door of the cell opened and a man appeared and said something. Wolfe told me to come, and we were conducted down a corridor and some stairs and into a sunny room where two men sat talking. One of them spoke; and then the other, a lanky, tired-looking specimen with ears as big as saucers, said in American, "I'm Thomas Arnold, the American consul. I'm told you want to see me."

"I have to see you"—Wolfe glanced at the other man—"in private."

"This is Signor Angelo Bizzaro, the warden."

"Thank you. All the same, privacy is essential. We are not armed."

"I'm told that you were." Arnold turned and spoke to the warden, and after a little exchange Bizzaro got up and left the room. "Now what is it?" Arnold demanded. "Are you American citizens?"

"We are. The quickest way to dispose of this, Mr. Arnold, would be for you to telephone the embassy in Rome and ask for Mr. Richard Courtney."

"Not until you tell me who you are and why you were out on the road at night, armed, with no papers."

"You'll have to know who we are, of course," Wolfe agreed. "And so will the police, but I hope through you to arrange that our presence here will not be published. I thought a talk with Mr. Courtney would help, but it's not essential. My name is Nero Wolfe. I am a licensed private detective with an office in New York. This is my assistant, Archie Goodwin."

The consul was smiling. "I don't believe it."

"Then telephone Mr. Courtney. Or, perhaps better, do you know a man in Bari, a broker and agent, named Paolo Telesio?"

"Yes. I've met him."

"If you'll phone him and let me speak to him, he'll bring our passports, properly stamped at Rome when we arrived there on Sunday, four days ago. Also he'll identify us."

"I'll be damned. You *are* Nero Wolfe?"

"I am."

"Why the hell were you wandering around at night with guns and knives and no papers?"

"That was indiscreet but necessary. We are here on an important and confidential matter, and our presence must not be known."

I thought he was doing fine. His asking Arnold to phone the embassy would make the consul suspect that we were on a secret job for the State Department, and if he phoned and Courtney told him we weren't, that would only make him think the job was super-secret. He didn't get the embassy, at least not from there. He got Telesio, let Wolfe talk to him, and then sat and chewed the fat with us until Telesio arrived with the passports. Wolfe had pressed it on him that as few people as possible should know we were there, so he didn't tell even the warden our names. He made another phone call, and another signor came, who looked and acted more important than a warden, and he looked at our passports and made it legal for us to breathe. When we left with Telesio they shook hands with us, perfectly friendly, but I noticed they avoided any close contact, which was understandable. They knew where we had been for five hours, that we hadn't been alone, and that some of our companions were leaving with us.

Telesio knew it too. When he stopped the car in the courtyard of the stuccoed house, and we got out and followed the path to the door, he spoke to Wolfe and Wolfe turned to me. "We'll undress in the hall and throw these things outdoors."

We did so. Telesio brought a chair for Wolfe, but I said I didn't need one. Our first donning of those duds was in that house, and so was our first doffing. I won't go into detail except for Wolfe's shoes and socks. He was afraid to take them off. When he finally set his jaw and pitched in, he gazed at his feet in astonishment. I think he had expected to see nothing but a shapeless mass of raw red flesh, and it wasn't bad at all, only a couple of heel blisters and a rosy glow, and the toes ridged and twisted some.

"They'll be back to normal in a year easy," I told him. I didn't have to ask him for help with the water heater because Telesio had already gone up and turned it on.

Two hours later, at a quarter past one, we were in the kitchen with Telesio, eating mushroom soup and spaghetti and cheese, and drinking wine, clean and dressed and sleepy. Wolfe had phoned to Rome and had an appointment with Richard Courtney at the embassy at five o'clock. Telesio had arranged for a plane to be ready for us at the Bari airport at two-thirty. I never asked Wolfe for a full report of his conversation with Telesio that day, and probably wouldn't have got it if I had, but I did want to know about two points, and he told me. First, what did Telesio think of letting Stritar cop the eight grand? He had thought it was unnecessary, immoral, and outrageous. Second, what did Telesio think of what Wolfe had said to Stritar about Danilo Vukcic? Did he agree with me that Wolfe may have put Danilo on a spot? No. He said Danilo was a very smooth customer, and for three years Stritar had been trying to decide whether he was coming or going, and in what direction, and nothing Wolfe had said would hurt him any. That relieved my mind. I had hated to think that we might have helped to deprive Meta of her provider of flour to make bread with. I was telling Fritz only yesterday he should go to a certain address in Titograd and learn how to make bread.

There had been a three-way argument in two languages, which made it complicated. Wolfe's initials were not on his bag, but they were on his made-to-order shirts and pajamas. How much of a risk was there that Zov would snoop around and see them, and get suspicious, and also maybe get a bright idea? Wolfe thought it was slight, but we ganged up on him and he gave in. The shirts and pajamas were left behind, to be shipped by Telesio, and Telesio went out and bought replacements, which were pretty classy but not big enough. My bag had my initials on it, but we agreed that AG wasn't as risky as NW—that is, they agreed, and I said I did, not caring to start another argument.

Telesio drove us to the airport in the Fiat, which still didn't have a dent, though he hadn't changed his attitude on obstructions. There were more people and activity at the airport than there had been on Palm Sunday, but apparently word had been passed along by the signor who had legalized us, for Telesio merely popped into a room with our passports and popped right out again, and took us out to a plane that was waiting on the apron. With tears in his eyes—which didn't mean he was suffering, because I had noticed that they came when he laughed—he kissed Wolfe on both cheeks and me on one, and stood and watched us take off.

Since on our way in we hadn't left the airport, I couldn't say I had been in Rome, but now I can. A taxi took us through the city to the American embassy, and later another one took us back to the airport, so I know Rome like a book. It has a population of 1,695,477, and has many fine old buildings.

When we entered one of the buildings, the embassy, we were ten minutes early for our appointment, but we didn't have to wait. A young woman who was fair enough at the moment but would have two chins in a few years if she didn't take steps was obviously interested in us, which was natural, since Wolfe declined to give our names, saying only that we were expected by Mr. Courtney; and she had been briefed, for after a quick survey trying to guess whether we were CIA or just a couple of congressmen trying to be cagey, she used a phone, and before long Richard Courtney appeared, greeted us diplomatically without pronouncing names, and escorted us within, to a little room halfway down a long, wide corridor. Three chairs were about all it had room for without crowding. He invited us to take two of them and went to the third, which was behind a desk stacked with papers.

He eyed us. Superficially he was still a distinguished-looking college boy, but a lot more reserved than four days earlier. From the way he looked at us, he wasn't exactly suspicious, but he intended to find out whether he ought to be.

"You said on the phone," he told Wolfe, "that you wanted to ask a favor."

"Two favors," Wolfe corrected him. "One was to let us get to you without mention of names."

"That has been done. I've mentioned your name, since you phoned, only to Mr. Teague, the Secretary. What's the other one?"

"I'll make it as brief as possible. Mr. Goodwin and I came to Italy on an important and confidential matter, a private matter. During our stay on Italian soil we have violated no law and committed no offense, except the minor one of being abroad without our papers. Our errand is satisfactorily completed and we're ready to go home, but there is a small difficulty. We wish to sail tomorrow from Genoa on the *Basilia,* but incognito. The success of our errand will be compromised if it is known that we are sailing on that ship. From Bari I telephoned the Rome office of the steamship company and was able to reserve a double cabin in the names of Carl Gunther and Alex Gunther. I want to go there now and get the tickets. I ask you to telephone them and tell them it's all right to let me have them."

"You mean to guarantee that you'll pay for them when you get to New York?"

"No, I'll pay for them in cash."

"Then what's the favor?"

"To establish our *bona fides.* To approve our being listed under different names than those on our passports."

"Just that?"

"Yes."

"But my dear sir"—Courtney was relieved and amused—"that's nothing. Thousands of people travel incognito. You don't need the sanction of the embassy for that!"

"That may be. But," Wolfe persisted, "I thought it desirable to take this precaution. With all the restrictions imposed nowadays on people who wish to move around, or need to, I wanted to preclude any possibility of a snag. Also I prefer not to undertake lengthy explanations to a clerk in a steamship office. Will you phone them?"

Courtney smiled. "This is a pleasant surprise, Mr. Wolfe. Certainly I'll phone them. I wish all the favors our fellow citizens ask for were as simple. And now I hope you won't mind if I ask for a favor from you. After I told Mr. Teague, the Secretary, that you were coming here this afternoon, he must have spoken of it to the Ambassador, because he told me later that the Ambassador would like to meet you. So if you can spare a few minutes, after I phone?"

Wolfe was frowning. "She's a woman."

"Yes, indeed."

"I must ask your forbearance. I'm tired clear to my bones, and I must catch a seven-o'clock plane to Genoa. Unless—will you take it ill and change your mind about phoning?"

"My God, no!" Courtney laughed. He threw his head back and roared. It struck me as pretty boisterous for a diplomat.

16

At noon the next day, Friday, we sat in our cabin on B deck on the *Basilia*. She was to sail at one. Everything was under control except one thing. At the Forelli Hotel in Genoa we had had eleven hours sleep on good mattresses, and a good breakfast. Wolfe could walk without shuffling or staggering, and my bruises weren't quite as raw. We were listed as Carl Gunther and Alex Gunther, had paid for the tickets, and had a little over six hundred bucks in our jeans. It was an outside cabin, twice as big as our cell in the Bari can, with two beds and two chairs, and one of the chairs was upholstered and Wolfe could squeeze into it.

But what about Peter Zov?

All Wolfe had been told was that he would enter Italy at Gorizia Wednesday night, cross to Genoa by way of Padua and Milan, and be on the *Basilia* as a cabin steward by Thursday night. Wolfe had wanted to know what his name would be, but Stritar had said that would be decided after he got to Genoa. Of course we knew nothing about where Zov would get his name or his papers, or from whom, or how the fix was set up for him to replace a steward. We didn't know how good the fix was, or whether it always worked or only sometimes. As we sat there in the cabin, we didn't give a damn about any of that; all that was eating us was, was he on board or not? If he wasn't, did we want to sail anyhow and hope he would come later? Didn't we have to? If we abandoned ship just because Zov didn't show up, wouldn't that be a giveaway?

"There's an hour left," I said. "I'll go and look around some more. Stewards are popping in and out everywhere."

"Confound it." Wolfe hit the chair arm with his fist. "We should have kept him with us."

"Stritar would have smelled a rat if you had insisted on it, and anyway he wouldn't buy it."

"Pfui. What is ingenuity for? I should have managed it. I'm a dunce. I should have foreseen this and prevented it. By heaven, I won't start back without him!"

There was a knock at the door, I said, "Come in," it opened, and Peter Zov entered with our bags.

"Oh, it's you," he said in Serbo-Croat. He put the bags down and turned to go.

"Wait a minute," Wolfe said. "There is something to say."

"You can say it later. This is a busy time."

"Just one word, then. Don't go to any pains to keep us from hearing you speak English. Of course you do—some, at least—or you couldn't be a cabin steward on this boat."

"You're smart," he said in Serbo-Croat. "Okay," he said in American, and went.

Wolfe told me to shut the door, and I did. When I turned back he had his eyes closed and was sighing, deep, and then again, deeper. He opened his eyes, looked at the bags and then at me, and told me what had been said.

"We ought to know his name," I suggested.

"We will. Go on deck and watch the gangway. He might take it into his head to skedaddle."

"Why should he?"

"He shouldn't. But a man with his frontal lobes pushed back like that is unpredictable. Go."

So I was on deck, at the rail, when we shoved off, and had a good look at the city stretching along the strip at the edge of the water and climbing the hills. The hills might have impressed me more if I hadn't just returned from a jaunt in Montenegro. By the time we had cleared the outer harbor and were in open water most of my fellow passengers had gone below for lunch, and I decided that now was as good a time as any for getting a certain point settled.

I went back down to the cabin and told Wolfe, "It's lunchtime. You've decided to stay put in this cabin all the way across, and you may be right. It's not likely that there's anyone on board who would recognize you, but it's possible, and if it happened and it got around, as it would, the best that could result would be that you'd have to write another script. But we're going to see a lot of each other in the next twelve days, not to mention the last six, and I think it would be bad policy for us to eat all our meals together in this nook."

"So do I."

"I'll eat in the dining room."

"By all means. I've already given Peter Zov my order for lunch."

"What?" I stared. "Zov?"

"Certainly. He's our steward."

"Good God. He'll bring all your meals and you'll eat them?"

"Yes. It will be trying, and it won't help my digestion, but it will have its advantages. I'll have plenty of opportunities to discuss our plans."

"And if he gets ideas and mixes in some arsenic?"

"Nonsense. Why should he?"

"He shouldn't. But a man with his frontal lobes pushed back like that is unpredictable."

"Go get your lunch."

I went, and found that though eating in the dining room would provide a change, it would offer nothing spectacular in companionship. Table Seventeen seated six. One chair was empty and would be all the way, and the other four were occupied by a German who thought he could speak English but was mistaken, a woman from

Maryland who spoke it too much, and a mother and daughter, Italian or something, who didn't even know "dollar" and "okay" and "cigarette." The daughter was seventeen, attractive, and almost certainly a smoldering volcano of Latin passion, but even if I had been in the humor to try stirring up a young volcano, which I wasn't, mamma stayed glued to her all the way over.

During the twelve days there was plenty of time, of course, to mosey around and make acquaintances and chin at random, but by the third day I had learned that the only three likely prospects, not counting the volcano, were out. One, a black-eyed damsel with a lisp, was on her way to Pittsburgh to get married. Another, a tall slender Nordic who needed no makeup and used none, loved to play chess, and that was all. The third, a neat little blonde, started drinking Gibsons an hour before lunch and didn't stop. One morning I decided to do some research in physiology and keep up with her, but late in the afternoon I saw that she was cheating. There were two of her, and they could both float around in the air. So I called it off, fought my way down to the cabin, and flopped on the bed. Wolfe shot me a glance but had no comment. In Genoa he had bought a few dozen books, all in Italian, and apparently had bet himself he would clean them up by the time we sighted Sandy Hook.

He and I did converse now and then during the voyage, but not too cordially, because of a basic difference of opinion. I completely disapproved of the plan which he wanted opportunity to discuss with Peter Zov. The argument had started in the hotel at Genoa and had continued, off and on, ever since. My first position had been that the way to handle it was to wait until we were well at sea, the second or third day, and then see the captain and tell him Zov had committed a murder in New York and had the weapon with him, and ask him to lock Zov up, and find his gun and take it, and radio Inspector Cramer of the New York Police Department to meet the boat at Quarantine. Wolfe had rejected it on the ground that the New York police had never heard of Zov and would probably radio the captain to that effect, and with nothing but our word, unsupported by evidence, the captain would refuse to act; and not only that, but also the captain, or someone he told about it, might warn Zov and even arrange somehow to get him off the ship before we reached American waters. On the high seas there was no jurisdiction but the captain's. If not the captain himself, someone on board with some authority must be a Communist, or at least a friend of the Tito regime, or how could it be arranged to get Zov on as a steward whenever they wanted to?

So I took a new position. As soon as we entered the North River everyone on board, including the captain, would be under the jurisdiction of the New York police, and Wolfe could call Cramer on the ship-to-shore phone, give him the picture, and tell him to meet the boat at the pier. That way there couldn't possibly be any slip. Even if the whole damn crew and half the officers were Commies, there was nothing they could do if Sergeant Stebbins once got his paws on Zov and the Luger.

Wolfe didn't try to talk me out of that one; he just vetoed it, and that was the argument. It wasn't only that he was pigheaded. It was his bloated conceit. He wanted to sit in his own chair at his desk in his office, with a bottle of beer and a glass in front of him, tell me to get Cramer on the phone, pick up his instrument, and say in a casual tone, "Mr. Cramer? I've just got home from a little trip. I have the murderer of Marko Vukcic here, and the weapon, and I can tell you where to get witnesses to testify that he was in New York on March eighteenth. Will you please send someone to get him? Oh, you'll come yourself? At your convenience. Mr. Goodwin, who was with me on the trip, has him safely in charge."

That was his plan. The *Basilia* was scheduled to dock at noon on Wednesday. We would disembark and go home. That evening after dark Zov would come ashore and meet me at a waterfront bar, to go with me to the house of a friend of ours who would lend us his car to drive to Philadelphia. The house would be on West Thirty-fifth Street. I would take Zov in and introduce him to Nero Wolfe, taking adequate precautions that he didn't execute his mission then and there. Possibly Wolfe would have to get Cramer on the phone himself instead of telling me to.

Wolfe wouldn't budge. That was the plan, no matter what I said, or how often I said it, about the risks involved or the defects in Wolfe's character that made him hatch it. I admit that my remarks about the defects got fairly pointed by the twelfth day, and that morning as we packed, him with his bag on his bed and me with mine on mine, our relations were so strained that when he had prolonged trouble with his zipper he didn't call for help and I didn't offer any. When I had my bag closed and labeled I told him, "See you in the dining room with the immigration officers," and left him. Out in the passage there was Zov, coming along. He asked, "Okay?" and I told him, "Yep, okay." He entered our cabin. Being good and sore, I told my legs to go on to the dining room, but they said no. They kept me standing there until Zov came out again with our bags, and headed for the stairs. I wanted to stop him and make sure he knew where we were going to meet that evening, but Wolfe had said it was all arranged in Serbo-Croat, and the few times I had tried exchanging English with Zov it hadn't worked too well, so I skipped it.

When we had finished immigrating, Wolfe went back to the cabin and I went on deck to take in the harbor and the Statue of Liberty and the skyline. The neat little blonde came and joined me at the rail, and if you had guessed her Gibson intake from the way she looked you would have been way off. She was just a happy and healthy little doll with nice clear eyes and a clear, smooth skin, so much so that a news photographer, who had taken a dozen shots of the only notable on board, an orchestra conductor, and was looking around for something that might appeal to his public, came and asked her to pose. She said all right, but refused to sit on the rail with her skirt up, and I thought it might have been worth the trouble to try to reform her. There was nothing wrong with her legs, so it wasn't that.

It was a bright, sunny day. As we passed the Battery and slid up the river I was thinking that now would be the time to telephone Cramer if that big baboon had listened to reason. It would be a crime if something happened now to spoil it—as, for instance, Zov deciding he liked some other contact in New York better than us. I had a notion to go down to the cabin and have one more try at talking sense into Wolfe, and was debating it as we were being nosed into the slip, when his voice sounded behind me and I turned. He was looking placid and pleased. He glanced left and right at the line of waving passengers and then down at the group of waving welcomers on the pier. He nodded at somebody, and I stretched my neck to see who it was, and there was Zov with three or four other stewards, back against the bulkhead.

"Satisfactory," Wolfe said.

"Yeah," I agreed. "So far."

Somebody yelled, "Nero Wolfe!"

I jerked around. It was the news photographer. He was headed for us down the deck, beaming, jostling passengers. "Mr. Wolfe! Look this way! Just a second!" He advanced and got set to focus.

It may have been partly me. If I hadn't looked at Zov and started my hand inside my jacket he might have hesitated long enough for Wolfe to get behind something or somebody. He was fast. I never saw a faster hand. Mine had just touched the butt of the Marley when he pulled the trigger. Wolfe took one step toward him and went down. I had the Marley out but couldn't shoot because the other stewards were all over Zov. I jumped over Wolfe's body and was there to help, but they had Zov flat on the deck, and one of them had his gun. I went back to Wolfe, who was on his side, propping himself with an elbow. People were crowding in and jabbering.

"Lie down," I commanded him. "Where did he get you?"

"Leg. Left leg."

I squatted and looked. The hole was in the left leg of his pants, ten inches above the knee. I wanted to laugh, and I don't know why I didn't. Maybe I was afraid the photographer would shoot it and it would look silly.

"Probably in the bone," I said. "What did I tell you?"

"Have they got him?"

"Yes."

"The gun?"

"Yes."

"Was it the Luger?"

"Yes."

"Satisfactory. Find a phone and get Mr. Cramer."

He flattened out and closed his eyes. The ham.

If Death Ever Slept

1

It would not be strictly true to say that Wolfe and I were not speaking that Monday morning in May.

We had certainly spoken the night before. Getting home—home being the old brownstone on West 35th Street owned by Wolfe, and occupied by him and Fritz and Theodore and me—around two a.m., I had been surprised to find him still up, at his desk in the office, reading a book. From the look he gave me as I entered, it was plain that something was eating him, but as I crossed to the safe to check that it was locked for the night I was supposing that he had been riled by the book, when he snapped at my back, "Where have you been?"

I turned. "Now really," I said. "On what ground?"

He was glaring. "I should have asked, where have you *not* been. Miss Rowan has telephoned five times, first shortly after eight o'clock, last half an hour ago. If I had gone to bed she wouldn't have let me sleep. As you know, Fritz was out for the evening."

"Hasn't he come home?"

"Yes, but he must be up to get breakfast and I didn't want him pestered. You said you were going to the Flamingo Club with Miss Rowan. You didn't. She telephoned five times. So I, not you, have spent the evening with her, and I haven't enjoyed it. Is that sufficient ground?"

"No, sir." I was at his desk, looking down at him. "Not for demanding to know where I've been. Shall we try it over? I'll go out and come in again, and you'll say you don't like to be interrupted when you're reading and you wish I had let you know I intended to teach Miss Rowan a lesson but no doubt I have a good explanation, and I'll say I'm sorry but when I left here I didn't know she would need a lesson. I only knew it when I took the elevator up to her penthouse and found that there were people there whom she knows I don't like. So I beat it. Where I went is irrelevant, but if you insist I can give you a number to call and ask for Mrs. Schrebenwelder. If her husband answers, disguise your voice and say—"

"Pfui. You could have phoned."

Of course that left him wide open. He was merely being childish, since my phoning to tell him I had changed my program for the evening wouldn't have kept Lily Rowan from interrupting his reading. I admit it isn't noble to jab a man when his arms are hanging, but having just taught Lily a lesson I thought I might as well teach him one too, and did so. I may have been a little too enthusiastic. Anyway, when I left to go up to bed we didn't say good night.

But it wouldn't be true to say that we were not speaking Monday morning. When he came down from the plant rooms at eleven o'clock I said good morning distinctly, and he muttered it as he crossed to his desk. By the time Otis Jarrell arrived at noon, by appointment, we had exchanged at least twenty words, maybe more. I remember that at one point he asked what the bank balance was and I told him. But the air was frosty, and when I answered the doorbell and ushered Otis Jarrell into the office, and to the red leather chair at the end of Wolfe's desk, Wolfe practically beamed at him as he inquired, "Well, sir, what is your problem?"

For him that was gushing. It was for my benefit. The idea was to show me that he was actually in the best of humor, nothing wrong with him at all, that if his manner with me was somewhat reserved it was only because I had been very difficult, and it was a pleasure, by contrast, to make contact with a fellow being who would appreciate amenities.

He was aware that the fellow being, Otis Jarrell, had at least one point in his favor: he was rated upwards of thirty million dollars. Checking on him, as I do when it's feasible on everyone who makes an appointment to see Nero Wolfe, I had learned, in addition to that important item, that he listed himself in *Who's Who* as "capitalist," which seemed a little vague; that he maintained no office outside of his home, on Fifth Avenue in the Seventies; that he was fifty-three years old; that (this through a phone call to Lon Cohen of the *Gazette*) he had a reputation as a tough operator who could smell a chance for a squeeze play in his sleep; and that he had never been in jail.

He didn't look tough, he looked flabby, but of course that's no sign. The toughest guy I ever ran into had cheeks that needed a brassière. Jarrell's weren't that bad, but they were starting to sag. And although the tailor who had been paid three hundred bucks, or maybe four hundred, for making his brown shadow-striped suit had done his best, the pants had a problem with a ridge of surplus flesh when he sat.

But that wasn't the problem that had brought the capitalist to Nero Wolfe. With his sharp brown eyes leveled at Wolfe's big face, he said, "I want to hire you on a confidential matter. Absolutely confidential. I know your reputation or I wouldn't be here, and your man's, Goodwin's, too. Before I tell you what it is I want your word that you'll take it on and keep it to yourselves, both of you."

"My dear sir." Wolfe, still needing to show me that he was perfectly willing to have sociable intercourse with one who deserved it, was indulgent. "You can't expect me to commit myself to a job without knowing what it is. You say you know my reputation; then you are satisfied of my discretion or you wouldn't have come. Short of complicity in a felony, I can keep a secret even if I'm not working on it. So can Mr. Goodwin."

Jarrell's eyes moved, darted, and met mine. I looked discreet.

He went back to Wolfe. "This may help." His hand went to a pocket and came out again with a brown envelope. From it he extracted a bundle of engravings held by a paper band. He tossed the bundle onto Wolfe's desk, looked around for a wastebasket, saw none, and dropped the envelope on the floor. "There's ten thousand dollars for a retainer. If I gave you a check it might be known, possibly by someone I don't want to know it. It will be charged to expense without your name appearing. I don't need a receipt."

It was a little raw, but there is always human nature, and net without taxes instead of net after taxes certainly has its attractions. I thought I saw two of Wolfe's fingers twitch a little, but the state of our relations may have influenced me.

"I prefer," he said dryly, "to give a receipt for anything I accept. What do you want me to do?"

Jarrell opened his mouth, closed it, made a decision, and spoke. "I want you to get a snake out of my house. Out of my family." He made fists. "My daughter-in-law. My son's wife. It must be absolutely confidential. I want you to get evidence of things she has done, things I know damn well she has done, and she will have to go!" He defisted to gesture. "You get the proof and I'll know what to do with it! My son will divorce her. He'll have to. All I need—"

Wolfe stopped him. "If you please, Mr. Jarrell. You'll have to go elsewhere. I don't deal with marital afflictions."

"It's not marital. She's my daughter-in-law."

"You spoke of divorce. Divorce is assuredly marital. You want evidence that will effect divorce." Wolfe straightened a finger to point at the bundle of bills. "With that inducement you should get it, if it exists—or even if it doesn't."

Jarrell shook his head. "You've got it wrong. Wait till I tell you about her. She's a snake. She's not a good wife, I'm sure she's two-timing my son, that's true, but that's only part of it. She's cheating me too. I'll have to explain how I operate. My office is at my home; I keep a secretary and a stenographer there. They live there. Also my wife, and my son and his wife, and my daughter, and my wife's brother. I buy and sell. I buy and sell anything from a barn full of horses to a corporation full of red ink. What I have is cash on hand, plenty of it, and everybody knows it from Rome to Honolulu, so I don't need much of an office. If you know anyone who needs money and has something that is worth money, refer him to me."

"I shall." Wolfe was still demonstrating, to me, so he was patient. "About your daughter-in-law?"

"This is about her. Three times in the past year I've had deals ruined by people who must have had information of my plans. I think they got that information through her. I don't know exactly how she got it—that's part of the job I want you to do—but on one of the deals the man who got in ahead of me, a man named Brigham, Corey Brigham—I'm sure she's playing with him, but I can't prove it. I want to prove it. If you want to call that a marital affliction, all right, but it's not my marital affliction. My marital affliction is named Trella, and I can handle her myself. Another thing, my daughter-in-law is turning my home into a madhouse, or trying to. She wants to take over. She's damned slick about it, but that's what she's after. I want her out of there."

"Then eject her. Isn't it your house?"

"It's not a house, it's an apartment. Penthouse. Duplex. Twenty rooms. I own it. If I eject her my son will go too, and I want him with me. That's another thing, she's getting between him and me, and I can't stop it. I tell you she's a snake. You said with that inducement"—he gestured at the bundle of bills—"I should get evidence for a divorce, but you don't know her. She's as slick as grease. The kind of man you were suggesting—one of that kind would never get her. It will take a man of your quality, your ability." He shot a glance at me. "And Archie Goodwin's. As I said, I know Goodwin's reputation too. As a matter of fact, I had a specific suggestion about Goodwin in my mind when I came here. Do you want to hear it?"

"I doubt if it's worth the trouble. What you're after is divorce evidence."

"I told you what I'm after, a snake. About Goodwin, I said I have a secretary, but I haven't. I fired him a week ago. One of those deals I got hooked on, the most recent one, I suspected him of leaking information on it to a certain party, and I fired him. So that—"

"I thought you suspected your daughter-in-law."

"I did. I do. You can't say a man can't suspect two different people at once, not you. So that job is vacant. What was in my mind, why can't Goodwin take it? He would be right there, living under the same roof with her. He can size her up, there'll be plenty of opportunities—she'll see to that if he doesn't. My secretary had his meals with us, so of course Goodwin will. It occurred to me that that would be the best and quickest way, at least to start. If you're not tied up with something he could come today. Right now."

I didn't like him, but I was feeling sorry for him. A man of my broad sympathies must make allowances. If she was as slick a snake as he thought she was, and he should have been a good judge of slickness, he was out of luck. Of course the idea that Wolfe would consider getting along without me at hand, to be called on for anything from typing a letter to repelling an invasion in force, was ludicrous. It was hard enough to get away for week ends. Add to that Wolfe's rule against spouse-snooping, and where was he?

So I was feeling sorry for him when I heard Wolfe say, "You realize, Mr. Jarrell, that there could be no commitment as to how long he would stay there. I might need him."

"Yes, certainly. I realize that."

"And the job itself, the nominal job. Isn't there a danger that it would be apparent that he isn't qualified for it?"

"No, none whatever. Not even to Miss Kent, my stenographer. No secretary I hired would know how I operate until I broke him in. But there's a detail to consider, the name. Of course his name is not as widely known as yours, but it is known. He'll have to use another name."

I had recovered enough to risk my voice. Unquestionably Wolfe had figured that, taken by surprise, I would raise a squawk, giving him an out, and equally unquestionably he was damned well going to be disappointed. I admit that after the jolt he had given me I was relieved when my voice came out perfectly okay. "About the name, Mr. Jarrell." I was talking to him, not to Wolfe. "Of course I'll have to take some luggage, quite a lot since I may stay indefinitely, and mine has my initials on it. The usual problem. A.G. Let's see. How about Abe Goldstein?"

Jarrell, regarding me, screwed his lips. "I don't think so. No. I've got nothing against Jews, especially when they need money, but you don't look it. No."

"Well, I'll try again. I suppose you're right, I ought to look it. How about Adonis Guilfoyle?"

He laughed. It started with a cackle, then he threw his head back and roared. It tapered off to another cackle before he spoke.

"One thing about me, I've got a sense of humor. I could appreciate you, Goodwin, don't think I couldn't. We'll get along. You'd better let me try. A. Alan? That's all right. G. Green? Why not? Alan Green."

"Okay." I arose. "It hasn't got much flavor, but it'll do. It will take me a little while to pack, fifteen or twenty minutes." I moved.

"Archie! Sit down."

The round was mine, against big odds. He owned the house and everything in it except the furniture in my bedroom. He was the boss and paid my salary. He weighed nearly a hundred pounds more than my 178. The chair I had just got up from had cost $139.95; the one he was sitting in, oversized and custom-made of Brazilian Mauro, had come to $650.00. We were both licensed private detectives, but he was a genius and I was merely an operative. He, with or without Fritz to help, could turn out a dish of *Couronne de Canard au Riz à la Normande* without batting an eye; I had to concentrate to poach an egg. He had ten thousand orchids in his plant rooms on the roof; I had one African violet on my windowsill, and it wasn't feeling well. Etc.

But he was yelling uncle. He had counted on getting a squawk out of me, and now he was stuck, and he would have to eat crow instead of *Couronne de Canard au Riz à la Normande* if he wanted to get unstuck.

I faced him and inquired pleasantly, "Why, don't you like Alan Green?"

"Pfui. I haven't instructed you to comply with Mr. Jarrell's suggestion."

"No, but you indicated plainly that you intended to. Very plainly."

"I intended to confer with you."

"Yes, sir. We're conferring. Points to consider: would you like to improve on Alan Green, and would it be better for me to get a thorough briefing here, and get it in my notebook, before going up there? I think maybe it would."

"Then—" He swallowed it. What had started for his tongue was probably, "Then you persist in this pigheaded perversity," or something stronger, but he knew darned well he had asked for it, and there was company present. You may be thinking that the bundle of bills was also present, but I doubt if that was a factor. I have heard him turn down more than a few husbands, and more than a few wives, who had offered bigger bundles than that one if he would get them out of bliss that had gone sour. No. He knew he had lost the round, and knew that I knew it, but he wasn't going to admit it in front of a stranger.

"Very well," he said. He pushed his chair back, got up, and told Jarrell, "You will excuse me. Mr. Goodwin will know what information he needs." He circled around the red leather chair and marched out.

I sat at my desk, got notebook and pen, and swiveled to the client. "First," I said, "all the names, please."

2

I can't undertake to make you feel at home in that Fifth Avenue duplex penthouse because I never completely got the hang of it myself. By the third day I decided that two different architects had worked on it simultaneously and hadn't been on speaking terms. Jarrell had said it had twenty rooms, but I think it had seventeen or nineteen or twenty-one or twenty-three. I never made it twenty. And it wasn't duplex, it was triplex. The butler, Steck, the housekeeper, Mrs. Latham, and the two maids, Rose and Freda, slept on the floor below, which didn't count. The cook and the chauffeur slept out.

Having got it in my notebook, along with ten pages of other items, that Wyman, the son, and Lois, the daughter, were Jarrell's children by his first wife, who had died long ago, I had supposed that there were so many variations in taste among the rooms because Jarrell and the first wife and the current marital affliction, Trella, had all had a hand at it, but was set right on that the second day by Roger Foote, Trella's brother. It was decorators. At least eight decorators had been involved. Whenever Jarrell decided he didn't like the way a room looked he called in a decorator, never one he had used before, to try something else. That added to the confusion the architects had contributed. The living room, about the right size for badminton, which they called the lounge because some decorator had told them to, was blacksmith modern—black iron frames for chairs and sofas and mirrors, black iron and white tile around the fireplace, black iron and glass tables; and the dining room, on the other side of an arch, was Moorish or something. The arch itself was in a hell of a fix, a very bad case of split personality. The side terrace outside the dining room was also Moorish, I guess, with mosaic tubs and boxes and table tops. It was on the first floor, which was ten stories up. The big front terrace, with access from both the reception hall and the lounge, was Dupont frontier. The tables were redwood slabs and the chairs were chromium with webbed plastic seats. A dozen pink dogwoods in bloom, in big wooden tubs, were scattered around on Monday, the day I arrived, but when I went to the lounge at cocktail time on Wednesday they had disappeared and been replaced by rhododendrons covered with buds. I was reminded of the crack George Kaufman made once to Moss Hart—"That just shows what God could do if only he had money."

Jarrell's office, which was called the library, was also on the first floor, in the rear. When I arrived, with him, Monday afternoon, he had taken me straight there after turning my luggage over to Steck, the butler. It was a big square room with windows in only one wall, and no decorator had had a go at it. There were three desks, big, medium, and small. The big desk had four phones, red, yellow, white, and black; the medium one had three, red, white, and black; and the small one had two, white and black. All of one wall was occupied by a battery of steel filing cabinets as tall as me. Another was covered by shelves to the ceiling, crammed with books and magazines; I found later that they were all strictly business, everything from *Profits in Oysters* to *North American Corporation Directory* for the past twenty years. The other wall had three doors, two big safes, a table with current magazines—also business—and a refrigerator.

Jarrell had led me across to the small desk, which was the size of mine at home, and said, "Nora, this is Alan Green, my secretary. You'll have to help me show him the ropes."

Nora Kent, seated at the desk, tilted her head back to aim a pair of gray eyes at me. Her age, forty-seven, was recorded in my notebook, but she didn't look it, even with the gray showing in her soft brown hair. But the notebook also said that she was competent, trustworthy, and nobody's fool, and she looked that. She had been with Jarrell twenty-two years. There was something about the way she offered a hand that gave me the feeling it would be more appropriate to kiss it than to grip it, but she reciprocated the clasp firmly though briefly.

She spoke. "Consider me at your service, Mr. Green." The gray eyes went to Jarrell. "Mr. Clay has called three times. Toledo operator seven-nineteen wants you, a Mr. William R. Bowen. From Mrs. Jarrell, there will be three guests at dinner; the names are on your desk, also a telegram. Where do you want me to start with Mr. Green?"

"There's no hurry. Let him get his breath." Jarrell pointed to the medium-sized desk, off to the right. "That's yours, Green. Now you know your way here, and I'll be busy with Nora for a while. I told Steck—here he is." The door had opened and the butler was there. "Steck, before you show Mr. Green to his room take him around. We don't want him getting lost. Have you told Mrs. Jarrell he's here?"

"Yes, sir."

Jarrell was at his desk. "Don't come back, Green. I'll be busy. Get your bearings. Cocktails in the lounge at six-thirty."

Steck moved aside for me to pass, pulled the door shut as he backed out, said, "This way, sir," and started down the corridor a mile a minute.

I called to him, "Hold it, Steck," and he braked and turned.

"You look harassed," I told him. He did. He was an inch taller than me, but thinner. His pale sad face was so long and narrow that he looked taller than he was. His black tie was a little crooked. I added, "You must have things to do."

"Yes, sir, certainly, I have duties."

"Sure. Just show me my room."

"Mr. Jarrell said to take you around, sir."

"You can do that later, if you can work it in. At the moment I need a room. I want to gargle."

"Yes, sir. This way, sir."

I followed him down the corridor and around a corner to an elevator. I asked if there were stairs and was told that there were three, one off the lounge, one in the corridor, and one for service in the rear. Also three elevators. The one we were in was gold-plated, or possibly solid. On the upper floor we went left, then right, and near the end of the hall he opened a door and bowed me in. He followed, to tell me about the phones. A ring would be for the green one, from the outside world. A buzz would be for the black one, from somewhere inside, for instance from Mr. Jarrell. I would use that one to get Steck when I was ready to be taken around. I thanked him out.

The room was twelve by sixteen, two windows with venetians, a little frilly but not bad, mostly blue and lemon-yellow except the rugs, which were tan with dark brown stripes. The bed was okay, and so was the bathroom. Under ordinary circumstances I would have used the green phone to ring Wolfe and report arrival, but I skipped it, not wanting to rub it in. After unpacking, taking my time, deciding not to shave, washing my hands, and straightening my tie, I got out my notebook, sat by a window, and turned to the list of names:

Mrs. Otis Jarrell (Trella)
Lois Jarrell, daughter by first wife
Wyman Jarrell, son by ditto
Mrs. Wyman Jarrell (Susan)
Roger Foote, Trella's brother
Nora Kent, stenographer
James L. Eber, ex-secretary
Corey Brigham, friend of family who queered deal

The last two didn't live there, but it seemed likely that they would need attention if I was going to get anywhere, which was doubtful. If Susan was really a snake, and if the only way to earn a fee was to get her bounced out of the house and the family, leaving her husband behind, it would take a lot of doing. My wrist watch said there was still forty minutes before cocktail time. I returned the notebook to my bag, the small one, which contained a few personal items not appropriate for Alan Green, locked the bag, left the room, found the stairs, and descended to the lower floor.

It would be inaccurate to say I got lost five times in the next quarter of an hour, since you can't get lost when you have no destination, but I certainly got confused. Neither of the architects had had any use for a straightaway, but they had had conflicting ideas on how to handle turns and corners. When I found myself passing an open door for the third time, recognizing it by the view it gave of a corner of a grand piano, and the blah of a radio or TV, with no notion of how I got there, I decided to call it off and make for the front terrace, but a voice came through to my back. "Is that you, Wy?"

I backtracked and stepped through into what, as I learned later, they called the studio.

"I'm Alan Green," I said. "Finding my way around."

She was on a couch, stretched out from the waist down, with

her upper half propped against cushions. Since she was too old for either Lois or Susan, though by no means aged, she must be Trella, the marital affliction. There was a shade too much of her around the middle and above the neck—say six or eight pounds. She was a blue-eyed blonde, and her face had probably been worthy of notice before she had buried the bones too deep by thickening the stucco. What showed below the skirt hem of her blue dress—from the knees on down—was still worthy of notice. While I noticed it she was reaching for a remote-control gadget, which was there beside her, to turn off the TV.

She took me in. "Secretary," she said.

"Yes, ma'am," I acknowledged. "Just hired by your husband—if you're Mrs. Otis Jarrell."

"You don't look like a secretary."

"I know, it's a handicap." I smiled at her. She invited smiles. "I try to act like one."

She put up a hand to pat a yawn—a soft little hand. "Damn it, I'm still half asleep. Television is better than a pill, don't you think so?" She patted the couch. "Come and sit down. What made you think I'm Mrs. Otis Jarrell?"

I stayed put. "To begin with, you're here. You couldn't be Miss Lois Jarrell because you must be married. You couldn't be Mrs. Wyman Jarrell because I've got the impression that my employer feels a little cool about his daughter-in-law and it seemed unlikely he would feel cool about you."

"Where did you get the impression?"

"From him. When he told me not to discuss his business affairs with anyone, including members of the family, I thought he put some emphasis on his daughter-in-law."

"Why must I be married?"

I smiled again. "You'll have to pardon me because you asked. Seeing you, and knowing what men like, I couldn't believe that you were still at large."

"Very nice." She was smiling back. "*Very* nice. My God, I don't have to pardon you for that. You don't talk like a secretary, either." She pushed the remote-control gadget aside. "Sit down. Do you like leg of lamb?"

I felt that a little braking was required. It was all very well to get on a friendly basis with the mistress of the house as soon as possible, since that might be useful in trapping the snake, and the smiling and sit-downing was very nice, but her concern about feeding the new secretary right after only three minutes with him was going too far too quick. Since I didn't look like a secretary or talk like one, I thought I had better at least act like one, and I was facing up to it when help came.

There were footsteps in the corridor and a man entered. Three steps in he stopped short, at sight of me. He turned to her. "Oh. I don't need to wake you."

"Not today, Wy. This is your father's new secretary. Green. Alan Green. We were getting acquainted."

"Oh." He went to her, leaned over, and kissed her on the lips. It didn't strike me as a typical filial operation, but of course she wasn't his mother. He straightened up. "You don't look as sleepy as usual. Your eyes don't look sleepy. You've had a drink."

"No, I haven't." She was smiling at him. She gestured at me. "He woke me up. We're going to like him."

"Are we?" He turned, moved, and extended a hand. "I'm Wyman Jarrell."

He was two inches shorter than me and two inches narrower across the shoulders. He had his father's brown eyes, but the rest of him came from somebody else, particularly his tight little ears and thin straight nose. There were three deep creases down the middle of his brow, which at his age, twenty-seven, seemed precocious. He was going on. "I'll be talking with you, I suppose, but that's up to my father. I'll be seeing you." He turned his back on me.

I headed for the door, was told by Mrs. Jarrell there would be cocktails in the lounge at six-thirty, halted to thank her, and left. As I moved down the corridor toward the front a female in uniform came around a corner and leered at me as she approached. Taken by surprise, I leered back. Evidently, I thought, this gang doesn't stand on formality. I was told later by somebody that Freda had been born with a leer, but I never went into it with Freda.

I had stepped out to the front terrace for a moment during my tour, so had already met the dogwoods and glanced around the layout of redwood slabs and chrome and plastic, and now I crossed to the parapet for a look down at Fifth Avenue and across to the park. The sun was smack in my eyes, and I put a hand up to shade them for a view of a squirrel perched on a limb high in a tree, and was in that pose when a voice came from behind.

"Who are you, Sitting Bull?"

I pivoted. A girl all in white with bare tanned arms and a bare tanned throat down to the start of the curves and a tanned face with dimples and greenish brown eyes and a pony tail was coming. If you are thinking that is too much to take in with a quick glance, I am a detective and a trained observer. I had time not only to take her in but also to think, Good Lord, if that's Susan and she's a snake I'm going to take up herpetology, if that's the word, and I can look it up.

She was still five steps off when I spoke. "Me good Indian. Me good friend white man, only you're not a man and you're not white. I was looking at a squirrel. My name is Alan Green. I am the new secretary, hired today. I was told to get my bearings and have been trying to. I have met your husband."

"Not *my* husband, you haven't. I'm a spinster named Lois. Do you like squirrels?"

"It depends. A squirrel with integrity and charm, with no bad habits, a squirrel who votes right, who can be counted on in a pinch, I like *that* squirrel." At close quarters they weren't what I would call dimples, just little cheek dips that caught shadows if the light angle was right. "I hope I don't sound fussy."

"Come here a minute." She led me off to the right, put a hand on the tiled top of the parapet, and with the other pointed across the avenue. "See that tree? See the one I mean?"

"The one that lost an arm."

"That's it. One day in March a squirrel was skipping around on it, up near the top. I was nine years old. My father had given my brother a rifle for his birthday. I went and got the rifle and loaded it, and came out and stood here, right at this spot, and waited until the squirrel stopped to rest, and shot it. It tumbled off. On the way down it bumped against limbs twice. I yelled for Wy, my brother, and he came and I showed it to him, there on the ground not moving, and he—but the rest doesn't matter. With anyone I might possibly fall in love with I like to start off by telling him the worst thing I ever did, and anyway you brought it up by saying you were looking at a squirrel. Now you know the worst, unless you think it's worse that several years later I wrote a poem called 'Requiem for a Rodent.' It was published in my school paper."

"Certainly it's worse. Running it down by calling it a rodent, even though it was one."

She nodded. "I've suspected it myself. Some day I'll get analyzed and find out." She waved it away, into the future. "Where did you ever get the idea of being a secretary?"

"In a dream. Years ago. In the dream I was the secretary of a wealthy pirate. His beautiful daughter was standing on the edge of a cliff shooting at a gopher, which is a rodent, down on the prairie, and when she hit it she felt so sorry for it that she jumped off the cliff. I was down below and caught her, saving her life, and it ended romantically. So I became a secretary."

Her brows were lifted, opening her eyes as wide as they would go. "I can't imagine how a pirate's daughter happened to be standing on a cliff on top of a prairie. You must have been dreaming."

No man could stop a conversation as dead in its tracks as that. It takes a woman. But at least she had the decency to start up another one. With her eyes back to normal, she cocked her head a little to the side and said, "You know, I'm bothered. I'm sure I've seen you before somewhere, and I can't remember where, and I always remember people. Where was it? Have you forgotten too?"

I had known that might come from one or more of them. My picture hadn't been in the papers as often as the president of Egypt's, or even Nero Wolfe's, and the latest had been nearly a year ago, but I had known it might happen. I grinned at her. I hadn't been grinning in any published picture. One thing, it gave me a chance to recover the ball she had taken away from me.

I shook my head. "I wouldn't forget. I only forget faces I don't care to remember. The only way I can account for it, you must have seen me in a dream."

She laughed. "All right, now we're even. I wish I could remember. Of course I may have seen you in a theater or restaurant, but if that's it and I do remember I won't tell you, because it would puff you up. Only you'll need puffing up after you've been here a while. He's my dear father, but he must be terrible to work for. I don't see— Hi, Roger. Have you met Alan Green? Dad's new secretary. Roger Foote."

I had turned. Trella's brother bore as little resemblance to her as Wyman Jarrell did to his father. He was big and broad and brawny, with no stuffing at all between the skin and the bones of his big wide face. If his size and setup hadn't warned me I might have got some knuckles crushed by his big paw; as it was, I gave as good as I got and it was a draw.

"Muscle man," he said. "My congratulations. Trust the filly to arch her neck at you. Ten to one she told you about the squirrel."

"Roger," Lois told me, "is horsy. He nearly went to the Kentucky Derby. He even owned a horse once, but it sprang a leak. No Pimlico today, Roger?"

"No, my angel. I could have got there, but I might never have got back. Your father has told Western Union not to deliver collect telegrams from me. Not to mention collect phone calls." He switched to me. "Do you suppose you're going to stick it?"

"I couldn't say, Mr. Foote. I've only been here two hours. Why, is it rough going?"

"It's worse than rough. Even if you're not a panhandler like me. My brother-in-law is made of iron. They could have used him to make that godawful stuff in the lounge, and I wish they had. Look at the Derby. I was on Iron Liege, or would have been if I had had it. I could have made myself independent for a week or more. You get the connection. You would think a man made of iron would stake me for a go on Iron Liege? No." He lifted a hand to look at it, saw it was empty, and dropped it. "I must have left my drink inside. You're not thirsty?"

"I am," Lois declared. "You, Mr. Green? Or Alan. We make free with the secretary." She moved. "Come along."

I followed them into the lounge, and across to a portable bar where Otis Jarrell, with a stranger at each elbow, a man and a woman, was stirring a pitcher of Martinis. The man was a wiry little specimen, black-eyed and black-haired, very neat in charcoal, with a jacket that flared at the waist. The woman, half a head taller, had red hair that was either natural or not, a milk-white face, and a jaw. Jarrell introduced me, but I didn't get their names until later: Mr. and Mrs. Herman Dietz. They weren't interested in the new secretary. Roger Foote moved to the other side of the bar and produced a Bloody Mary for Lois, a scotch and water for me, and a double bourbon with no accessories for himself.

I took a healthy sip and looked around. Wyman, the son, and

Nora Kent, the stenographer, were standing over near the fireplace, which had no fire, presumably talking business. Not far off
Trella was relaxed in a big soft chair, looking up at a man who was
perched on one of the arms.

Lois' voice came up to my ear. "You've met my stepmother,
haven't you?"

I told her yes, but not the man, and she said he was Corey
Brigham, and was going to add something but decided not to. I
was surprised to see him there, since he was on my list as the guy
who had spoiled a deal, but the guests had been invited by her, not
him. Or maybe not. Possibly Jarrell had suggested it, counting on
bringing me home with him and wanting me to meet him. From a
distance he was no special treat. Leaning over Trella with a well-
trained smile, he had all the earmarks of a middle-aged million-
dollar smoothie who would slip a head waiter twenty bucks and
tip a hackie a dime. I was taking him in, filing him under unfinished
business, when he lifted his head and turned it left, and I turned
mine to see what had got his attention.

The snake had entered the room.

3

Of course it could have been that she planned it that way, that she
waited until everyone else was there to make her entrance, and
then, floating in, deliberately underplayed it. But also it could have
been that she didn't like crowds, even family crowds, and put it off
as long as she could, and then, having to go through with it, made
herself as small and quiet as possible. I reserved my opinion, without prejudice—or rather, with two prejudices striking a balance. The
attraction of the snake theory was that she had to be one if we were
going to fill our client's order. The counterattraction was that I
didn't like the client and wouldn't have minded seeing him stub
his toe. So my mind was open as I watched her move across toward the fireplace, to where her husband was talking with Nora
Kent. There was nothing reptilian about the way she moved. It

might be said that she glided, but she didn't slither. She was slender, not tall, with a small oval face. Her husband kissed her on the cheek, then headed for the bar, presumably to get her a drink.

Trella called my name, Alan, making free with the secretary, and I went over to her and was introduced to Corey Brigham. When she patted the vacant arm of the chair and told me to sit I did so, thinking it safer there than it had been in the studio, and Brigham got up and left. She said I hadn't answered her question about leg of lamb, and she wanted to know. It seemed possible that I had got her wrong, that her idea was merely to function as a help-mate and see to it that the hired help liked the grub—but no. She might have asked it, but she didn't; she cooed it. I may not know as much about women as Wolfe pretends he thinks I do, but I know a coo when I hear it.

While giving her due attention as my hostess and my boss's wife, I was observing a phenomenon from the corner of my eye. When Wyman returned to Susan with her drink, Roger Foote was there. Also Corey Brigham was wandering over to them, and in a couple of minutes there went Herman Dietz. So four of the six males pres-ent were gathered around Susan, but as far as I could see she hadn't bent a finger or slanted an eye to get them there. Jarrell was still at the bar with Dietz's redheaded wife. Lois and Nora Kent had stepped out to the terrace.

Apparently Trella had seen what the corner of my eye was do-ing, for she said, "You have to be closer to appreciate her. She blurs at a distance."

"Her? Who?"

She patted my arm. "Now, now. I don't mind, I'm used to it. Susan. My stepdaughter-in-law. Go and put an oar in."

"She seems to have a full crew. Anyway, I haven't met her."

"You haven't? That won't do." She turned and sang out, "Susan! Come here."

She was obeyed instantly. The circle opened to make room, and Susan crossed to us. "Yes, Trella?"

"I want to present Mr. Green. Alan. He has taken Jim's place. He has met everyone but you, and that didn't seem fair."

I took the offered hand and felt it warm and firm for the fifth of a second she let me have it. Her face *had* blurred at a distance.

Even close up none of her features took your eye; you only saw the whole, the little oval face.

"Welcome to our aerie, Mr. Green," she said. Her voice was low, and was shy or coy or wary or demure, depending on your attitude. I had no attitude, and didn't intend to have one until I could give reasons. All I would have conceded on the spot was that she didn't hiss like a cobra or rattle like a rattler. As for her being the only one of the bunch to bid me welcome, that was sociable and kindhearted, but it would seem that she might have left that to the lady of the house. I thanked her for it anyway. She glanced at Trella, apparently uncertain whether to let it go at that or stay for a chat, murmured something polite, and moved away.

"I think it's in her bones," Trella said. "Or maybe her blood. Anyhow it's nothing you can see or hear. Some kind of hypnotism, but I think she can turn it on and off. Did you feel anything?"

"I'm a secretary, Mrs. Jarrell. Secretaries don't feel."

"The hell they don't. Jim Eber did. Of course you've barely met her and you may be immune."

Trella was telling me about a book on hypnotism she had read when Steck came to tell her dinner was ready.

It was uneven, five women and six men, and I was put between Lois and Roger Foote. There were several features deserving comment. The stenographer not only ate with the family, she sat next to Jarrell. The housekeeper, Mrs. Latham, helped serve. I had always thought a housekeeper was above it. Roger Foote, who had had enough to drink, ate like a truck driver—no, cut that—like a panhandler. The talk was spotty, mostly neighbor-to-neighbor, except when Corey Brigham sounded off about the Eisenhower budget. The leg of lamb was first-rate, not up to Fritz's, but good. I noticed Trella noticing me the second time around. The salad was soggy. I'm not an expert on wine, but I doubted if it deserved the remarks it got from Herman Dietz.

As we were passing through the Moorish arch—half-Moorish, anyway—to return to the lounge for coffee, Trella asked me if I played bridge, and Jarrell heard her.

"Not tonight," he said. "I need him. I won't be here tomorrow. You've got enough."

"Not without Nora. You know Susan doesn't play."

"I don't need Nora. You can have her."

If Susan had played, and if I could have swung it to be at her table, I would have been sorry to miss it. Perhaps you don't know all there is to know about a woman after watching her at an evening of bridge, but you should know more than when you sat down. By the time we were through with coffee they had chosen partners and Steck had the tables ready. I had wondered if Susan would go off to her pit, but apparently not. When Jarrell and I left she was out on the terrace.

He led the way through the reception hall, across a Kirman twice as big as my room at home—I have a Kirman there, paid for by me, 8'4" x 3'2"—down the corridor, and around a couple of corners, to the door of the library. Taking a key fold from a pocket, he selected one, used it, and pushed the door open; and light came at us, so sudden and so strong that it made me blink. I may also have jumped.

He laughed, closing the key fold. "That's my idea." He pointed above the door. "See the clock? Anyone coming in, his picture is taken, and the clock shows the time. Not only that, it goes by closed circuit to the Horland Protective Agency, only three blocks away. A man there saw us come in just now. There's a switch at my desk and when we're in here we turn it off—Nora or I. I've got them at the doors of the apartment too, front and back. By the way, I'll give you keys. With this I don't have to wonder about keys— for instance, Jim Eber could have had duplicates made. I don't give a damn if he did. What do you think of it?"

"Very neat. Expensive, but neat. I ought to mention, if someone at Horland's saw me come in with you, he may know me, by sight anyway. A lot of them do. Does that matter?"

"I doubt it." He had turned on lights and gone to his desk. "I'll call them. Damn it, I could have come in first and switched it off. I'll call them. Sit down. Have a cigar?"

It was the cigar he had lit in the lounge after dinner that had warned me to keep my eyes on the road. I don't smoke them myself, but I admit that the finest tobacco smell you can get is a whiff from the lit end of a fine Havana, and when the box had been passed I had noticed that they were Portanagas. But I had not enjoyed the whiff I had got from the one Jarrell had lit. In fact, I had snorted it out. That was bad. When you can't stand the smell of a Portanaga because a client is smoking it, watch out or you'll be giving him the short end of the stick, which is unethical. Anyway, I saved him three bucks by not taking one.

He leaned back, let smoke float out of his mouth, and inquired, "What impression did you get?"

I looked judicious. "Not much of any. I only spoke a few words with her. Your suggestion that I get the others talking about her, especially your wife and your wife's brother—there has been no opportunity for that, and there won't be while they're playing cards. I think I ought to cultivate Corey Brigham."

He nodded. "You saw how it was there before dinner."

"Sure. Also Foote and Dietz, not to mention your son. Your wife thinks she hypnotizes them."

"You don't know what my wife thinks. You only know what she says she thinks. Then you discussed her with my wife?"

"Not at any length. I don't quite see when I'm going to discuss her at length with any of them. I don't see how this is going to work. As your secretary I should be spending my day in here with you and Miss Kent, and if they spend the evening at bridge?"

"I know." He tapped ash off in a tray. "You won't have to spend tomorrow in here. I'm taking a morning plane to Toledo, and I don't know when I'll be back. Actually my secretary has damn little to do when I'm not here. Nora knows everything, and I'll tell her to forget about you until I return. As I told you this afternoon, I'm certain that everybody here, every damn one of them, knows things about my daughter-in-law that I don't know. Even my daughter. Even Nora." His eyes were leveled at me. "It's up to you. I've told you about my wife, she'll talk your head off, but anything she tells you may or may not be so. Do you dance?"

"Yes."

"Are you a good dancer?"

"Yes."

"Lois likes to dance, but she's particular. Take her out tomorrow evening. Has Roger hit you for a loan yet?"

"No. I haven't been alone with him."

"That wouldn't stop him. When he does, let him have fifty or a hundred. Give him the impression that you stand in well with me —even let him think you have something on me. Buy my wife some flowers—nothing elaborate, as long as it's something she thinks you paid for. She loves to have men buy things for her. You might take her to lunch, to Rusterman's, and tip high. When a man tips high she takes it as a personal compliment."

I wanted to move my chair back a little to get less of his cigar, but vetoed it. "I don't object to the program personally," I said, "but I do professionally. That's a hell of a schedule for a secretary. They're not halfwits."

"That doesn't matter." He flipped it off with the cigar. "Let them all think you have something on me—let them think anything they want to. The point is that the house is mine and the money is mine, and whatever I stand for they'll accept whether they understand it or not. The only exception to that is my daughter-in-law, and that's what you're here for. She's making a horse's ass out of my son, and she's getting him away from me, and she's sticking a finger in my affairs. I'm making you a proposition. The day she's out of here, with my son staying, you get ten thousand dollars in cash, in addition to any fee Nero Wolfe charges. The day a divorce settles it, with my son still staying, you get fifty thousand. You personally. That will be in addition to any expenses you incur, over and above Wolfe's fee and expenses."

I said that no man can stop a conversation the way a woman can, but I must admit that Otis Jarrell had made a darned good stab at it. I also admit I was flattered. Obviously he had gone to Wolfe just to get me, to get me there in his library so he could offer me sixty grand and expenses to frame his daughter-in-law, who probably wasn't a snake at all. If she had been, his itch to get rid of her would have been legitimate, and he could have left it as a job for Wolfe and just let me earn my salary.

It sure was flattering. "That's quite a proposition," I said, "but there's a hitch. I work for Mr. Wolfe. He pays me."

"You'll still be working for him. I only want you to do what I hired him to do. He'll get his fee."

That was an insult to my intelligence. He didn't have to make it so damned plain. It would have been a pleasure to square my shoulders and lift my chin and tell him to take back his gold and go climb a tree, and that would have been the simplest way out, but there were drawbacks. For one thing, it was barely possible that she really was a snake and no framing would be required. For another, if she wasn't a snake, and if he was determined to frame her, she needed to know it and deserved to know it, but he was still

Wolfe's client, and all I had was what he had said to me with no witnesses present. For still another, there was the ten grand in Wolfe's safe, not mine to spurn. For one more if we need it, I have my full share of curiosity.

I tightened my face to look uncomfortable. "I guess," I said, "I'll have to tell Mr. Wolfe about your proposition. I think I will. I've got to protect myself."

"Against what?" he demanded.

"Well . . . for instance, you might talk in your sleep."

He laughed. "I like you, Goodwin. I knew we'd get along. This is just you and me, and you don't need protection any more than I do. You know your way around and so do I. What do you want now for expenses? Five thousand? Ten?"

"Nothing. Let it ride and we'll see." I loosened the face. "I'm not accepting your proposition, Mr. Jarrell. I'm not even considering it. If I ever found myself feeling like accepting it, I'd meet you somewhere that I was sure wasn't wired for sound. After all, Horland's Protective Agency might be listening in right now."

He laughed again. "You *are* cagey."

"Not cagey, I just don't want my hair mussed. Do you want me to go on with the program? As you suggested?"

"Certainly I do. I think we understand each other, Goodwin." He put a fist on the desk. "I'll tell you this, since you probably know it anyway. I'd give a million dollars cash any minute to get rid of that woman for good and call it a bargain. That doesn't mean you can play me for a sucker. I'll pay for what I get, but not for what I don't get. Any arrangements you make, I want to know who with and for exactly what and how much."

"You will. Have you any more suggestions?"

He didn't have, at least nothing specific. Even after proposing, as it looked to me, an out-and-out frame, he still thought, or pretended to, that I might raise some dust by cultivating the inmates. He tried to insist on an advance for expenses, but I said no, I would ask for it if and when needed. I was surprised that he didn't refer again to my notion that I might have to tell Wolfe about his proposition; apparently he was taking it for granted that I would take my bread buttered on both sides if the butter was thick enough. He was sure we understood each other, but I wasn't. I wasn't sure of anything. Before I went he gave me two keys, one

for the front door and one for the library. He said he had to make
a phone call, and I said I was going out for a walk. He said I could
use the phone there, or in my room, and I said that wasn't it, I always took a little walk in the evening. Maybe we understood each
other at that, up to a point.

I went to the front vestibule, took the private elevator down,
nodded at the sentinel in the lobby—not the one who had been
there when I arrived—walked east to Madison, found a phone
booth, and dialed a number.

After one buzz a voice was in my ear. "Nero Wolfe's residence,
Orville Cather speaking."

I was stunned. It took me a full second to recover. Then
I spoke, through my nose. "This is the city mortuary. We have a
body here, a young man with classic Grecian features who jumped
off Brooklyn Bridge. Papers in his wallet identify him as Archie
Goodwin and his address—"

"Toss it back in the river," Orrie said. "What good is it? It never
was much good anyway."

"Okay," I said, not through my nose. "Now I know. May I
please speak to Mr. Wolfe?"

"I'll see. He's reading a book. Hold it."

I did so, and in a moment got a growl. "Yes?"

"I went for a walk and am in a booth. Reporting: the bed is good
and the food is edible. I have met the family and they are not mine,
except possibly the daughter, Lois. She shot a squirrel and wrote
a poem about it. I'm glad you've got Orrie in to answer the phone
and do the chores because that may simplify matters. You can
stop my salary as of now. Jarrell has offered me sixty grand and
expenses, me personally, to get the goods on his daughter-in-law
and bounce her. I think his idea is that the goods are to be hand-
made, by me, but he didn't say so in so many words. If it takes me
twelve weeks that will be five grand a week, so my salary would be
peanuts and you can forget it. I'll get it in cash, no tax to pay, and
then I'll probably marry Lois. Oh yes, you'll get your fee too."

"How much of this is flummery?"

"None of the facts. The facts are straight. I am reporting."

"Then he's either a nincompoop or a scalawag or both."

"Probably but not necessarily. He said he would give a million
dollars to get rid of her and consider it a bargain. So it's just possible he has merely got an itch he can't reach and is temporarily nuts.

I'm giving him the benefit of the doubt because he's your client."

"And yours."

"No, sir. I didn't accept. I declined an advance for expenses. I turned him down, but with a manner and a tone of voice that sort of left it hanging. He thinks I'm just being cagey. What I think, I think he expects me to fix up a stew that will boil her alive, but I have been known to think wrong. I admit it's conceivable that she has it coming to her. One thing, she attracts men without apparently trying to. If a woman gathers them around by working a come-on, that's okay, they have a choice, they can play or not as they please. But when they come just because she's there, with no invitation visible to the naked eye, and I have good eyes, look out. She may not be a snake, in fact she may be an angel, but angels can be more dangerous than snakes and usually are. I can stick around and try to tag her, or you can return the ten grand and cross it off. Which?"

He grunted. "Mr. Jarrell has taken me for a donkey."

"And me for a goop. Our pride is hurt. He ought to pay for the privilege, one way or another. I'll keep you informed of developments, if any."

"Very well."

"Please remind Orrie that the bottom drawer of my desk is personal and there's nothing in it he needs."

He said he would, and even said good night before he hung up. I bought a picture postcard at the rack, and a stamp, addressed the card to Fritz, and wrote on it, "Having wonderful time. Wish you were here. Archie," went and found a mailbox and dropped the card in, and returned to the barracks.

In the tenth-floor vestibule I gave my key a try, found that it worked, and was dazzled by no flash of light as I entered, so the thing hadn't been turned on for the night. As I crossed the reception hall I was thinking that the security setup wasn't as foolproof as Jarrell thought, until I saw that Steck had appeared from around a corner for a look at me. He certainly had his duties.

I went to him and spoke. "Mr. Jarrell gave me a key."

"Yes, sir."

"Is he around?"

"In the library, sir, I think."

"They're playing cards?"

"Yes, sir."

"If you're not tied up I cordially invite you to my room for some gin. I mean gin rummy."

He batted an eye. "Thank you, sir, but I have my duties."

"Some other time. Is Mrs. Wyman Jarrell on the terrace?"

"I think not, sir. I think she is in the studio."

"Is that on this floor?"

"Yes, sir. The main corridor, on the right. Where you were with Mrs. Jarrell this afternoon."

Now how the hell did he know that? Also, was it proper for a butler to let me know he knew it? I suspected not. I suspected that my gin invitation, if it hadn't actually crashed the sound barrier, had made a dent in it. I headed for the corridor and for the rear, and will claim no credit for spotting the door because it was standing open and voices were emerging. Entering, I was in semi-darkness. The only light came from the corridor and the television screen, which showed the emcee and the panel members of "Show Your Slip." The voices were theirs. Turning, I saw her, dimly, in a chair.

"Do you mind if I join you?" I asked.

"Of course not," she said, barely loud enough. That was all she said. I moved to a chair to her left, and sat.

I have no TV favorites, because most of the programs seem to be intended for either the under-brained or the over-brained and I come in between, but if I had, "Show Your Slip" wouldn't be one of them. If it's one of yours, you can assume you have more brains than I have, and what I assume is my own affair. I admit I didn't give it my full attention that evening because I was conscious of Susan there within arm's reach, and was keeping myself receptive for any sinister influences that might be oozing from her, or angelic ones either. I felt none. All that got to me was a faint trace of a perfume that reminded me of the one Lily Rowan uses, but it wasn't quite the same.

When the windup commercial started she reached to the chair on her other side, to the control, and the sound stopped and the picture went. That made it still darker. The pale blur of her face turned to me. "What channel do you want, Mr. Green?"

"None particularly. Mr. Jarrell finished with me, and the others were playing cards, and I heard it going and came in. Whatever you want."

"I was just passing the time. There's nothing I care for at ten-thirty."

"Then let's skip it. Do you mind if we have a little light?"

"Of course not."

I went to the wall switch at the door, flipped it, and returned to the chair, and her little oval face was no longer merely a pale blur. I had the impression that she was trying to produce a smile for me and couldn't quite make it.

"I don't want to intrude," I said. "If I'm in the way—"

"Not at all." Her low voice, shy or coy or wary or demure, made you feel that there should be more of it, and that when there was you would like to be present to hear it. "Since you'll be living here it will be nice to get acquainted with you. I was wondering what you are like, and now you can tell me."

"I doubt it. I've been wondering about it myself and can't decide."

The smile got through. "So to begin with, you're witty. What else? Do you go to church?"

"No. Should I?"

"I don't know because I don't know you yet. I don't go as often as I should. I noticed you didn't eat any salad at dinner. Don't you like salad?"

"Yes."

"Aha!" A tiny flash came and went in her eyes. "So you're frank too. You didn't like *that* salad. I have been wanting to speak to my mother-in-law about it, but I haven't dared. I think I'm doing pretty well. You're witty, and you're frank. What do you think about when you're alone with nothing to do?"

"Let's see. I've got to make it both frank and witty. I think about the best and quickest way to do what I would be doing if I were doing something."

She nodded. "A silly question deserves a silly answer. I guess it was witty too, so that's all right. I would love to be witty—you know, to sparkle. Do you suppose you could teach me how?"

"Now look," I protested, "how could I answer that? It makes three assumptions—that I'm witty, that you're not, and that you have something to learn from me. That's more than I can handle. Try one with only one assumption."

"I'm sorry," she said. "I didn't realize. But I do think you could teach me— Oh!" She looked at her wrist watch. "I forgot!" She got up—floated up—and was looking down at me. "I must make a phone call. I'm sorry if I annoyed you, Mr. Green. Next time, you ask questions." She glided to the door and was gone.

I'll tell you exactly how it was. I wasn't aware that I had moved until I found myself halfway to the door and taking another step. Then I stopped, and told myself, I will be damned, you might think she had me on a chain. I looked back at the chair I had left; I had covered a good ten feet before I had realized I was being pulled.

I went and stood in the doorway and considered the situation. I started with a basic fact: she was a little female squirt. Okay. She hadn't fed me a potion. She hadn't stuck a needle in me. She hadn't used any magic words, far from it. She hadn't touched me. But I had come to that room with the idea of opening her up for inspection, and had ended by springing up automatically to follow her out of the room like a lapdog, and the worst of it was I didn't know why. I am perfectly willing to be attracted by a woman and to enjoy the consequences, but I want to know what's going on. I am not willing to be pulled by a string without seeing the string. Not only that; my interest in this particular specimen was supposed to be strictly professional.

I had an impulse to go to the library and tell Jarrell he was absolutely right, she was a snake. I had another impulse to go find her and tell her something. I didn't know what, but tell her. I had another one, to pack up and go home and tell Wolfe we were up against a witch and what we needed was a stake to burn her at. None of them seemed to be what the situation called for, so I found the stairs and went up to bed.

4

By Wednesday night, forty-eight hours later, various things had happened, but if I had made any progress I didn't know it.

Tuesday I took Trella to lunch at Rusterman's. That was a little

risky, since I was well known there, but I phoned Felix that I was
working on a case incognito and told him to pass the word that I
mustn't be recognized. When we arrived, though, I was sorry I
hadn't picked another restaurant. Evidently everybody, from the
doorman on up to Felix, knew Mrs. Jarrell too, and I couldn't
blame them for being curious when, working on a case incognito, I
turned up with an old and valued customer. They handled it pretty
well, except that when Bruno brought my check he put a pencil
down beside it. A waiter supplies a pencil only when he knows
the check is going to be signed and that your credit is good. I ignored it, hoping that Trella was ignoring it too, and when Bruno
brought the change from my twenty I waved it away, hoping he
wouldn't think I was setting a precedent.

She had said one thing that I thought worth filing. I had
brought Susan's name into the conversation by saying that perhaps I should apologize for being indiscreet the day before, when
I had mentioned the impression I had got that Jarrell felt cool
about his daughter-in-law, and she said that if I wanted to apologize, all right, but not for being indiscreet, for being wrong. She
said her husband wasn't cool about Susan, he was hot. I said okay,
then I would switch from cool to hot and apologize for that. Hot
about what?

"What do you think?" Her blue eyes widened. "About her. She
slapped him. Oh, for God's sake, quit trying to look innocent!
Your first day as his secretary, and spending the morning on the
terrace with Lois and taking me to Rusterman's for lunch!
Secretary!"

"But he's away. He said to mark time."

"He'll get a report from Nora when he comes back, and you
know it. I'm not a fool, Alan, really I'm not. I might be fairly
bright if I wasn't so damn lazy. You probably know more about
my husband than I do. So quit looking innocent."

"I have to look innocent, I'm his secretary. So does Steck, he's
his butler. As for what I know, I didn't know Susan had slapped
him. Were you there?"

"Nobody was there. I don't mean slapped him with her hand,
she wouldn't do that. I don't know how she did it, probably just
by looking at him. She can look a man on or look him off, either
way. I wouldn't have thought any woman could look *him* off, I'd

think she'd need a hatpin or a red-hot poker, but that was before I had met her. Before she moved in. Has she given you a sign yet?"

"No." I didn't know whether I was lying or not. "I'm not sure I'm up with you. If I am, I'm innocent enough to be shocked. Susan is his son's wife."

"Well. What of it?"

"It seems a little undignified. He's not an ape."

She reached to pat the back of my hand. "I must have been wrong about you. Look innocent all you want to. Certainly he's an ape. Everybody knows that. Since I'm in walking distance I might as well do a little shopping. Would you care to come along?"

I declined with thanks.

On my way uptown, walking the thirty blocks to stretch my legs, I had to decide whether to give Wolfe a ring or not. If I did, and reported the development, that Trella said our client had made a pass at his daughter-in-law and had been looked off, and that therefore it seemed possible he had hired Wolfe and tried to suborn me only to cure an acute case of pique, I would certainly be instructed to pack and come home; and I preferred to hang on a while, at least long enough to expose myself to Susan once more and see how it affected my pulse and respiration. And if I rang Wolfe and didn't report the development, I had nothing to say, so I saved a dime.

Mrs. Wyman Jarrell was out, Steck said, and so was Miss Jarrell. He also said that Mr. Foote had asked to be informed when I returned, and I said all right, inform him. Thinking it proper to make an appearance at my desk before nightfall, I left my hat and topcoat in the closet around the corner and went to the library. Nora Kent was at Jarrell's desk, using the red phone, and I moseyed over to the battery of filing cabinets and pulled out a drawer at random. The first folder was marked PAPER PRODUCTION BRAZIL, and I took it out for a look.

I was fingering through it when Nora's voice came at my back. "Did you want something, Mr. Green?"

I turned. "Nothing special. It would be nice to do something useful. If the secretary should be acquainted with these files I think I could manage it in two or three years."

"Oh, it won't take you that long. When Mr. Jarrell gets back he'll get you started."

"That's polite, and I appreciate it. You might have just told me to keep hands off." I replaced the folder and closed the drawer. "Can I help with anything? Like emptying a wastebasket or changing a desk blotter?"

"No, thank you. It would be a little presumptuous of me to tell you to keep hands off since Mr. Jarrell has given you a key."

"So it would. I take it back. Have you heard from him?"

"Yes, he phoned about an hour ago. He'll return tomorrow, probably soon after noon."

There was something about her, her tone and manner, that wasn't just right. Not that it didn't fit a stenographer speaking to a secretary; of course I had caught on that calling her a stenographer was like calling Willie Mays a bat boy. I can't very well tell you what it was, since I didn't know. I only felt that there was something between her and me, one-way, that I wasn't on to. I was thinking a little more conversation might give me an idea, when a phone buzzed.

She lifted the receiver of the black one, spoke and listened briefly, and turned to me. "For you. Mr. Foote."

I went and took it. "Hello, Roger?" I call panhandlers by their first names. "Alan."

"You're a hell of a secretary. Where have you been all day?"

"Out and around. I'm here now."

"So I hear. I understand you're a gin player. Would you care to win a roll? Since Old Ironsides is away and you're not needed."

"Sure, why not? Where?"

"My room. Come on up. From your room turn right, first left, and I'll be at my door."

"Right." I hung up, told Nora I would be glad to run an errand if she had one, was assured that she hadn't, and left. So, I thought, Roger was on pumping terms with the butler. It was unlikely that Steck had volunteered the information that I had invited him to a friendly game.

Foote's room was somewhat larger than mine, with three windows, and it was all his. The chairs were green leather, and the size and shape of one of them, over by a window, would have been approved even by Wolfe. Fastened to the walls with Scotch Tape were pictures of horses, mostly in color, scores of them, all sizes. The biggest one was Native Dancer, from the side, with his head turned to see the camera.

"Not one," Roger said, "that hasn't carried my money. Muscle.

Beautiful. Beautiful! When I open my eyes in the morning there they are. Something to wake up to. That's all any man can expect, something to wake up to. You agree?"

I did.

I had supposed, naturally, that the idea would be something like a quarter a point, maybe more, and that if he won I would pay, and if I won he would owe me. But no, it was purely social, a cent a point. Either he gambled only on the beautiful muscles, or he was stringing me along, or he merely wanted to establish relations for future use. He was a damn good gin player. He could talk about anything, and did, and at the same time remember every discard and every pickup. I won 92 cents, but only because I got most of the breaks.

At one point I took advantage of something he had said. "That reminds me," I told him, "of a remark I overheard today. What do you think of a man who makes a pass at his son's wife?"

He was dealing. His hand stopped for an instant and then flipped me a card. "Who made the remark?"

"I'd rather not say. I wasn't eavesdropping, but I happened to hear it."

"Any names mentioned?"

"Certainly."

He picked up his hand. "Your name's Alfred?"

"Alan."

"I forget names. People's. Not horses'. I'll tell you, Alan. For what I think about my brother-in-law's attitude on money and his wife's brother, come to me any time. Beyond that I'm no authority. Anyone who thinks he ought to be shot, they can shoot him. No flowers. Not from me. Your play."

That didn't tell me much. When, at six o'clock, I said I had to wash and change for a date with Lois, and he totaled the score, fast and accurate, he turned it around for me to check. "At the moment," he said, "I haven't got ninety-two cents, but you can make it ninety-two dollars. More. Peach Fuzz in the fifth at Jamaica Thursday will be eight to one. With sixty dollars I could put forty on his nose. Three hundred and twenty, and half to you. And ninety-two cents."

I told him it sounded very attractive and I'd let him know tomorrow. Since Jarrell had said to let him have fifty or a hundred I could have dished it out then and there, but if I did he probably wouldn't be around tomorrow, and there was an off chance that I would want him for something. He took it like a gentleman, no shoving.

When, that morning on the terrace, I had proposed dinner and dance to Lois, I had mentioned the Flamingo Club, but the experience at Rusterman's with Trella had shown me it wouldn't be advisable. So I asked her if she would mind making it Colonna's in the Village, where there was a good band and no one knew me, at least not by name, and we weren't apt to run into any of my friends. For a second she did mind, but then decided it would be fun to try one she had never been to.

Jarrell had said she was particular about her dancing partners, and she had a right to be. The rhythm was clear through her, not just from her hips down, and she was right with me in everything we tried. To give her as good as she gave I had to put the mind away entirely and let the body take over, and the result was that when midnight came, and time for champagne, I hadn't made a single stab at the project I was supposed to be working on. As the waiter was pouring I was thinking, What the hell, a detective has to get the subject feeling intimate before he can expect her to discuss intimate matters, and three more numbers ought to do it. Actually I never did get it started. It just happened that when we returned to the table again and finished the champagne, she lifted her glass with the last thimbleful, said, "To life and death," and tossed it down. She put the glass on the table and added, "If death ever slept."

"I'm with you," I said, putting my empty glass next to hers, "or I guess I am. What does it mean?"

"I don't know. I ought to, since I wrote it myself. It's from that poem I wrote. The last five lines go:

> "Or a rodent kept
> High and free on the twig of a tree,
> Or a girl who wept
> A bitter tear for the death so near,
> If death ever slept!"

"I'm sorry," I said. "I like the sound of it, but I'm still not sure what it means."

"Neither am I. That's why I'm sure it's a poem. Susan understands it, or says she does. She says there's one thing wrong with it, that instead of 'a bitter tear' it ought to be 'a welcome tear.' I don't like it. Do you?"

"I like 'bitter' better. Is Susan strong on poems?"

"I don't really know. I don't understand her any better than I understand that poem. I think she's strong on Susan, but of course she's my sister-in-law and her bedroom is bigger than mine, and I'm fond of my brother when I'm not fighting with him, so I probably hate her. I'll find out when I get analyzed."

I nodded. "That'll do it. I noticed last evening the males all gathered around except your father. Apparently he didn't even see her."

"He saw her all right. If he doesn't see a woman it's because she's not there. Do you know what a satyr is?"

"More or less."

"Look it up in the dictionary. I did once. I don't believe my father is a satyr because half the time his mind is on something else—making more money. He's just a tomcat. What's that they're starting? 'Mocajuba?'"

It was. I got up and circled the table to pull her chair back.

To be fair to Wednesday, it's true that it was more productive than Tuesday, but that's not saying I got any farther along. It added one more to my circle of acquaintances. That was in the morning, just before noon. Having turned in around two and stayed in bed for my preferred minimum of eight hours, as I went downstairs I was thinking that breakfast would probably be a problem, but headed for the dining room anyway just to see, and in half a minute there was Steck with orange juice. I said that and coffee would hold me until lunch, but no, sir. In ten minutes he brought toast and bacon and three poached eggs and two kinds of jam and a pot of coffee. That attended to, in company with the morning *Times,* I went to the library and spent half an hour not chatting with Nora Kent. She was there, and I was willing to converse, but she either had things to do or made things to do, so after a while I gave up and departed. She did say that Jarrell's plane would be due at La Guardia at 3:05 p.m.

Strolling along the corridor toward the front and seeing that my watch said 11:56, I thought I might as well stop in at the studio

for the twelve-o'clock news. The door was closed, and I opened
it and entered, but two steps in I stopped. It was inhabited. Susan
was in a chair, and standing facing her was a stranger, a man in a
dark gray suit with a jaw that looked determined in profile. Evidently he had been too occupied to hear the door opening, for he
didn't wheel to me until I had taken the two steps.

"Sorry," I said, "I'm just cruising," and was going, but Susan
spoke.

"Don't go, Mr. Green. This is Jim Eber. Jim, this is Alan Green.
You know he— I mentioned him."

My predecessor was still occupied, but not too much to lift a
hand. I took it, and found that his muscles weren't interested. He
spoke, not as if he wanted to. "I dropped in to see Mr. Jarrell, but
he's away. Nothing important, just a little matter. How do you like
the job?"

"I'd like it fine if it were all like the first two days. When Mr.
Jarrell gets back, I don't know. I can try. Maybe you could give
me some pointers."

"Pointers?"

You might have thought it was a word I had just made up. Obviously his mind wasn't on his vocabulary or on me; it was working on something, and not on getting his job back or I would have
been a factor.

"Some other time," I said. "Sorry I interrupted."

"I was just going," he said, and, with his jaw set, marched past
me and on out.

"Oh dear," Susan said.

I looked down at her. "I don't suppose there's anything I can
help with?"

"No, thank you." She shook her head and her little oval face
came up. Then she left the chair. "Do you mind? But of course
you don't—only I don't want to be rude. I want to think something
over."

I said something polite and she went. Eber had closed the door
behind him and I opened it for her. She made for the rear and
turned a corner; and in a moment I heard the elevator. With that
settled, that she hadn't set out after Eber, I turned on the radio
and got the tail end of the newscast.

That was the new acquaintance. The only other contribution

that Wednesday made worth mentioning came six hours later, and though, as I said, it got me no farther along, it did add a new element to the situation. Before reporting it I should also mention my brief exchange with Wyman. I was in the lounge with a magazine when he appeared, stepped out to the terrace, came back in, and approached.

"You're not overworked, are you?" he asked.

There are several possible ways of asking that, running from the sneer to the brotherly smile. His was about in the middle. I might have replied, "Neither are you," but didn't. He was too skinny, and too handicapped by his tight little ears and thin straight nose, to make a good target, and besides, he thought he was trying. He had produced two shows on Broadway, and while one had folded after three days, the other had run nearly a month. Also his father had told me that in spite of the venomous influence of the snake he was still trying to teach him the technique of making money grow.

So I humored him. "No," I said.

The creases in his brow deepened. "You're not very talkative, either."

"You're wrong there. When I get started I can talk your head off. For example. An hour ago I went into the studio to catch the newscast, and a man was there speaking with your wife, and she introduced me to him. It was Jim Eber. I'm wondering if he's trying to get his job back, and if so, whether he'll succeed. I left a good job to come here, and I don't want to find myself out on a limb. I don't want to ask your wife about it, and I'd appreciate it if you would ask her and let me know."

His lips had tightened, and he had become aware of it and had loosened them. "When was this? An hour ago?"

"Right. Just before noon."

"Were they talking about the—uh, about the job?"

"I don't know. I didn't know they were there and I opened the door and went in. I thought he might have said something that would show if he's trying to get it back."

"Maybe he did."

"Will you ask her?"

"Yes. I'll ask her."

"I'll appreciate it a lot."

"I'll ask her." He turned, and turned back. "It's lunch time. You're joining us?"

I said I was.

There were only five of us at the table—Trella, Susan, Wyman, Roger, and Alan. Lois didn't show, and Nora lunched from a tray in the library. When, afterward, Roger invited me up to his room, I thought the two hours before Jarrell arrived might as well be spent with him as with anyone. He won $2.43, and I deducted 92 cents and paid him $1.51. Wanting to save him the trouble of bringing up the Peach Fuzz project, I brought it up myself and told him the sixty bucks would be available that evening after dinner.

I was in the library with Nora when Jarrell returned, shortly after four o'clock. He breezed in, tossed his bag under a table, told Nora, "Get Clay," and went to his desk. Apparently I wasn't there. I sat and listened to his end of three phone conversations which I would have paid closer attention to if my name had been Alan Green. I did attend, with both ears, when I heard Nora, reporting on events during his absence, tell him that Jim Eber had called that morning.

His head jerked to her. "Called? Phoned?"

"No, he came. He got some papers he had left in his desk. He said that was what he came for. That was all. I looked at the papers; they were personal. Then he was with Susan in the studio; I don't know whether it was by appointment or not. Mr. Green was there with them when he left."

Evidently everybody knew everything around there. The fact that Eber had been there had been mentioned at the lunch table, but Nora hadn't been present. Of course any of the others might have told her, including Steck.

Jarrell snapped at me, "You were with them?"

I nodded. "Only briefly. I was going to turn on the radio for the news, and opened the door and went in. Your daughter-in-law introduced me to him and that was about all. He said he was just going, and he went."

He opened his mouth and closed it again. Questions he might have asked Archie Goodwin could not properly be asked Alan Green with the stenographer there. He turned to her. "What else did he want? Besides the papers."

"Nothing. That was all, except that he thought you would be here and wanted to see you. That's what he said."

He licked his lips, shot me a glance, and turned back to her. "All right, hand me the mail."

She got it from a drawer of her desk and took it to him. If you think it would have been natural for it to be on his desk waiting for him you're quite right, but in that case it would have been exposed to the view of the new secretary, and that wouldn't do. After sticking around a while longer I asked Jarrell if I was wanted, was told not until after dinner, and left them and went up to my room.

I can't tell you the exact minute that Jarrell came dashing in, yelling at me, but I can come close. It was a quarter to six when I decided to shower and shave before going down to the lounge for cocktails, and my par for that operation when I'm not pressed is half an hour, and I was pulling on my pants when the door flew open and he was there yapping, "Come on!" Seeing me, he was off down the hall, yapping again, "Come on!" It seemed that the occasion was informal enough not to demand socks and shoes, so I merely got my shirttail in, and fastened my belt and closed my zipper en route. I could hear him bounding down the stairs, and made for them and on down, and turned the corner just as he reached the library door. As I came up he tried the knob and then stood and stared at it.

"It's locked," he said.

"Why not?" I asked. "What's wrong?"

"Horland's phoned. He said the signal flashed and the screen showed the door opening and a blanket or rug coming in. He's sending a man. There's somebody in there. There must be."

"Then open the door."

"Horland's said to wait till his man got here."

"Nuts. I will." Then I realized I couldn't. My key, along with my other belongings, was up on the dresser. "Give me your key."

He got out his key fold and handed it to me, and I picked one and stuck it in the slot. "It's just possible," I said, "that we'll be rushed. Move over." He did so. I got behind the jamb, turned the key and the knob, pushed on the door with my bare toes, and it swung open. Nothing happened. I said, "Stay here," and stepped inside. Nothing and no one. I went and took a look, behind desks, around corners of cabinets and shelves, in the closet, and in the bathroom. I was going to call to him to come on in when the sound came of footsteps pounding down the corridor, and I reached the door in time to see the reinforcement arrive—a middle-aged athlete in a gray uniform. He wasn't one that I knew. He was panting, and he had a gun in his hand.

"At ease," I commanded. "False alarm. Apparently. What's this about a blanket or a rug?"

"It's not a false alarm," Jarrell said. "I turned the switch on myself when I left, and the light didn't flash when you opened the door. Someone went in and turned the switch off. What was it you saw?"

Horland's didn't answer. He was looking at the floor at our feet. "By God, that's it," he said. He pointed. "That's it right there."

"What the hell are you talking about?" Jarrell blurted.

"That rug. That's what came in. The signal flashed and I looked at the screen, and in came that rug, hanging straight down, that was all I could see. Then it was gone, and in about two seconds the screen was dead. You get it? Someone came in holding that rug in front of him, and went and turned the switch off, and when he came out he put the rug back here where he got it. That's how I know he's not still in there; if he was, the rug wouldn't be here." He sounded as pleased as if he had just done a job of brain work that would be hard to match.

Thinking a little pruning wouldn't hurt him, I asked, "How do you know it was this rug?"

"Why, the pattern. The squares, the lines crossing. I saw it."

"It might be one of a pair. He might be in there now, in the closet or the bathroom."

"Oh." He squared his shoulders. "Stand aside."

"Don't bother, I looked. He's gone. He didn't stay long." I turned to Jarrell. "You might try the switch. Go and turn it on and we'll enter."

He did so. After he was in I shut the door, and when he called to us I pushed it open, and the blaze of light came. I swung the door shut, and the light went, and we crossed to his desk.

"After you saw it on the screen, the rug coming in," I asked Horland's, "how long was it before you phoned here?"

"Right away. No time at all. I didn't phone, the other man did, I told him to."

"How long did it take the call to get through?"

"It got through right away. I was putting on my cap and jacket and getting my gun, and I wasn't wasting any time, and he had Mr. Jarrell when I left."

"Then say thirty seconds. Make it a minute, not to skimp. Even two minutes. You answered the phone in your room, Mr. Jarrell?"

"Yes."

"How long were you on the phone?"

"Only long enough for him to tell me what had happened. Not more than a minute."

"And you came on the run immediately? Only stopping at my door on the way?"

"You're damn right I did."

"Then add another minute. That makes four minutes from the time the rug came in to the time we got here, and probably less, and he was gone. So he didn't have time for much more than turning off the switch."

"We ought to find out who it was," Horland's said. "While it's hot."

He certainly worked his brain, that bird. Obviously it had been a member of the household, and how and when to find out who it was was strictly a family affair. Jarrell didn't bother to tell him so. He merely gave him a chore, to unlock and open the door of a metal box that was set in the wall facing the entrance. Its door had a round hole for the lens to see through, and inside was the camera. Horland's took the camera out, extracted the film and put in a new one, returned the camera and locked the door, and departed.

Jarrell regarded me. "You realize it could have been anybody. We may know more when we see the picture. But with that rug in front of her, she could have held it up high with her hands not showing, nothing at all showing, and you couldn't tell."

"Yes," I agreed, "she could. Anybody could. One pronoun is as good as another. As I said, she didn't have time for much more than turning off the switch, but you might look around. Is any little item missing?"

He moved his head from side to side, got up, went and tried the knobs of the safes, crossed to the battery of cabinets and pulled at the handles of the drawers in the two end tiers, which had locks on them, went and opened the top drawer of Nora Kent's desk and took a look, and then came back to his own desk and opened the top drawer of it. His face changed immediately. He pulled the drawer wide open, moved things around, and pushed it shut. He looked at me.

"Don't tell me," I said. "Let me guess."

He took a breath. "I keep a gun in there, a Bowdoin thirty-eight. It's gone. It was there this afternoon."

"Loaded?"

"Yes."

"Whoever got it knew you had it. He—I beg your pardon—she came straight to the desk, turned off the switch, grabbed the gun, and ran. That's all there was time for."

"Yes."

"Horland's was right about one thing. If you want to find out who it was, the sooner the better, while it's hot. The best way would be to get them all in here, now, and go to it."

"What good would that do?" His hands were fists. "I know who it was. So do you."

"I do not." I shook my head. "Look, Mr. Jarrell. Suspecting her of cheating your son and diddling you, without any evidence, that's your privilege. But saying that I know she came in here and took a loaded gun, when I don't, that is not your privilege. Of course you have a permit for it?"

"Certainly."

"The law says when a gun is stolen it must be reported. It's a misdemeanor not to. Do you want to report it?"

"Good God, no." The fists relaxed. "How about this? I'll get her in here, and Wyman too, and I'll keep them here while you go up and search their room. You know how to search a room."

One of two things, I thought. Either he is sure it was her, for some reason or no reason, or he took it himself and planted it in her room. "No good," I declared. "If she took it, the last place she would hide it would be in her room. I could find it, of course, in a couple of days, or much quicker if I got help in, but what if it turned up in one of the tubs on the terrace? You'd have the gun back, that's true, if that's what you want."

"You know damn well what I want."

"Yes, I ought to, but that's not the point now, or not the whole point. Anyone going to all that trouble and risk to get hold of a gun, he must—I beg your pardon—she must intend to use it for something. I doubt if it's to shoot a squirrel. It might even be to shoot you. I would resent that while I'm employed as your secretary. I advise you to get them in here and let me ask questions. Even better, take them all down to Mr. Wolfe and let him ask questions."

"No."

"You won't?"

"No."

"Then what?"

"I don't know. I'll see. I'll have to think." He looked at his wrist. "They're in the lounge." He stood up. "I'll see."

"Okay." I stood up. "I'd rather not appear barefooted. I'll go up and put on my shoes and socks."

As I said before, that added a new element to the situation.

5

When Nero Wolfe came down from the plant rooms at six o'clock Thursday afternoon I was at my desk in the office, waiting for him. Growling a greeting, if you can call it that, as he crossed to his chair, he lowered his bulk and got it properly disposed, rested his elbows on the chair arms, and glared at me.

"Well?"

I had swiveled to him. "To begin with," I said, "as I told you on the phone, I'm not asking you to exert yourself if you'd rather not. I can hang on up there if it takes all summer, and with Orrie here you certainly don't need me. Only I didn't want you to have a client shot from under you with no warning from me. By the way, where is Orrie?"

"He stepped out. Who is going to shoot Mr. Jarrell?"

"I don't know. I don't even know he's going to be the target. Do you care to hear about it?"

"Go ahead."

I did so. Giving him only a sketchy outline of my encounters and experiences up to 6:15 p.m. Wednesday, when Jarrell had opened my door and yelled at me to come on, from there I made it more detailed. I reported verbatim my conversation with Jarrell after Horland's had gone.

Wolfe grunted. "The man's an ass. Every one of those people would profit by his death. They need a demonstration, or one of them does. He should have corralled them and called in the police to find the gun."

"Yeah. He's sure his daughter-in-law took it, or pretends he is. As I said on the phone Monday night, he may have an itch he can't reach and is not accountable. He could have pulled the rug act himself, answered the phone call from Horland's there in the library, raced upstairs to get me, and raced down again. He could have taken the gun earlier. I prefer it that way, since in that case there will probably be no bullets flying, but I admit it's not likely. He is not a nitwit."

"What has been done?"

"Nothing, actually. After dinner we played bridge, two tables— Trella, Lois, Nora, Jarrell, Wyman, Roger Foote, Corey Brigham, me. Incidentally, when I finally got down to the lounge before dinner Brigham was there with them, and I learned from Steck that he had come early, shortly after six o'clock, so I suppose it could have been him that got the gun, provided he had a key to the library. It was around midnight when we quit, and—"

"You didn't include the daughter-in-law."

"Haven't I mentioned that she doesn't play bridge? She doesn't. And we went to bed. Today I saw four of them at breakfast— Jarrell, Wyman, Lois, and Nora—but not much of anybody since, except Susan and Trella at lunch. Jarrell mentioned at lunch that he would be out all afternoon, business appointments. At two-thirty, when I went around looking for company, they were all out. Of course Roger had gone to Jamaica, with the sixty bucks I gave him—by the way, I haven't entered that on the expense account. At three o'clock I went for a walk and phoned you, and when I got back there was still nobody at home except Nora, and she is no—oh, I forgot. The pictures."

"Pictures?"

"Sure, from the camera. A Horland's man brought them while I was out phoning you, and when I got back Nora had them. She wasn't sure whether she should let me look at them, but I was. That woman sure plays them close to her chin; I don't know now whether Jarrell had told her about the rug affair or not. If not, she must have wondered what the pictures were all about. There were three of them; the camera takes one every two seconds until the door is shut. They all showed the rug broadside, coming straight in. He must have kicked the door shut. That rug is seven by three, so it could have been a tall man holding the top edge a little above the top of his head, or it could have been a short woman holding it as high as she could reach. At the bottom the rug was just touching the floor. At the top its edge was turned back, hiding the hands. I was going to bring the pictures along to show you, but would have had to shoot Nora to get away with them. Jarrell wasn't back when I left at five-thirty."

I turned a hand over. "That's it. Any instructions?"

He made a face. "How the devil can I have instructions?"

"You might. For instance, instruct me to take Lois out tonight. Or take Trella to lunch tomorrow. Or stick around until Sunday and take Susan to church."

"Pfui. Give me a plain answer for once. How likely is it that you'll accomplish anything up there?"

"One in a million, if you mean fairly soon. Give me until Thanksgiving and I might show you something. However, there's one little teaser. Its name is Eber, James L. Eber. He was upset about something when I found him in the studio with Susan, and so was she. Wyman was upset when I told him Eber had been there. When it was mentioned at the lunch table Roger was upset, and maybe one or two of the others. Jarrell was upset when Nora told him about it. And it was only an hour or so later that the gun was taken. There might be something to be pried out of Eber. I've been prying for three days without breaking off a splinter, and as a last resort he might have one loose. He just might have something interesting to say to the guy who took his job."

He grunted. "I doubt if any of those people has anything interesting to say to anyone."

I said I did too but that Eber should have a chance and I would go and give him one after dinner.

Orrie Cather dined with us. I went upstairs two flights to tell my room hello, and when I went back down Orrie was there, and we had time to exchange some friendly insults before Fritz announced dinner. The main dish was shad roe with créole sauce. Shad roe is all right, and Fritz's créole sauce is one of his best, but the point is that with that item Fritz always serves bread triangles fried in anchovy butter; and since he had known four hours ago that I would be there, and he was aware of my attitude toward bread triangles fried in anchovy butter, he had proceeded beyond the call of duty. Again I passed up a salad, but only because there wasn't room for it.

Back in the office, with coffee, Orrie, who had been told that I was going on an errand, asked if I needed any help, and I said I hoped not. When he saw me getting a ring of keys from a drawer he said I might need a lookout, and I repeated that I hoped not. When he saw me getting a shoulder holster and a gun from another drawer he said I might need a loader, and I told him he ought to know better, that if six wasn't enough what I would need would be a meat basket to bring me home in.

I had no reason to think there would be any occasion for the gun, but ever since Jarrell had opened the drawer and found his gone I had felt unfurnished. A man who—I beg your pardon—a woman who steals a loaded gun deserves to be treated with respect. As for the keys, they were routine equipment when calling on a stranger who might have useful information and who might or might not be home. There would probably be no occasion for them either, but I dislike waiting in dark halls with nothing to sit on.

The address, which I got from my notebook, on 49th Street between Second and Third Avenues, was above the door of an old five-story building that was long past its glory if it had ever had any. In the vestibule, I found EBER in the middle of the row of names, and pushed the button. No click. I pushed it five times, with waits in between, before giving up. I certainly wasn't going to do my waiting there, if any, and the old Manson lock was no problem, so I got out the keys, selected one, and in less than a minute was inside. If the position of his name in the row was correct he was two flights up, and he was—or his name was, on the jamb of a door in the rear, with a button beside it. When I pushed the button I could hear the ring inside.

I was in the dark hall with nothing to sit on that I don't like to wait in. Since there might be some information inside, in some form or other, that I could get more easily with him not there, I was sorry I hadn't brought Orrie along, because with a lookout there would have been nothing to it, but in three minutes I was glad I hadn't. That was how long it took me to decide to go on in, to get the lock worked, to enter, to see him sprawled on the floor, and to check that he was dead. Then I was glad Orrie hadn't come.

He was backside up, so I didn't have to disturb him in order to see the hole in the back of his head, a little below the center. When I spread the hair it looked about the right size for a .38, but I wasn't under oath. Standing up, I looked around, all the way around. There was no gun in sight, and it couldn't very well be under him. I didn't have to sniff to get the smell of powder, but there were no open windows, so it would take it a while to go.

I stood and considered. Had I been seen by anybody who might identify me later? Possibly, but I doubted it. Certainly by no one inside, or even in the vestibule. Was it worth the risk to give the dump a good going over to see what I could find? Maybe; but I had no gloves, and everything there would be tried for prints; and it would be embarrassing if someone came before I left. Had I touched anything besides his hair? You can touch something without knowing it—the top of a table, for instance, as you cross a room. I decided I hadn't.

It was a pity that I had to wipe the doorknob and the surface around the keyhole outside, since there might be prints there that Homicide could use, but there was no help for it. I did it thoroughly but quickly. I hadn't liked the idea of hanging around the hall before, and I liked it much less now. At the top of the stairs I listened three seconds, and, descending, did the same on the next landing. My luck held, and I was down, out to the sidewalk, and on my way without anyone to notice me. I was thinking that items of routine that become automatic through habit, though they are usually wasted, can be very useful—for instance, my having the taxi drop me at 49th Street and Third Avenue instead of taking me to the address. Now, not caring to have anything at all to do with a taxi on the East Side, I walked crosstown all the way to Ninth Avenue before flagging one. I needed a little walk anyway, to jolt my brain back into place. It had been 8:57 when I had stood up after looking at the hole in Jim Eber's head. It was 9:28 when the taxi pulled up at the curb in front of the old brownstone on West 35th Street.

When I entered the office Orrie was in one of the yellow chairs over by the big globe, with a magazine. I noted that with approval, since it showed that he fully appreciated the fact that my desk was mine. At sight of me Wolfe, behind his desk with a book, dropped his eyes back to the page. I hadn't been gone long enough to get much of a splinter.

I tossed my hat on my desk and sat. "I have a comment to make about the weather," I said, "privately. Orrie hates to hear the weather mentioned. Don't you, Orrie?"

"I sure do." He got up, closing the magazine. "I can't stand it. If you touch on anything you think I'd be interested in, whistle." He went, closing the door behind him.

Wolfe was scowling at me. "What is it now?"

"A vital statistic. Ringing James L. Eber's bell several times and getting no reaction, and finding the door was locked, I used a key and entered. He was on the floor face down in the middle of the room, with a bullet hole in the back of his head which could have been made by a thirty-eight. He was cooling off, but not cold. I would say, not for quotation, that he had been dead from three to seven hours. As you know, that depends. I did no investigating because I didn't care to stay. I don't think I was seen entering or leaving."

Wolfe's lips had tightened until he practically didn't have any. "Preposterous," he said distinctly.

"What is?" I demanded. "It's not preposterous that he's dead, with that hole in his skull."

"This whole affair. You shouldn't have gone there in the first place."

"Maybe not. You suggested it."

"I did not suggest it. I raised difficulties."

I crossed my legs. "If you want to try to settle that now," I said, "okay, but you know how things like that drag on, and I need instructions. I should have called headquarters and told them where to find something interesting, but didn't, because I thought you might possibly have a notion."

"I have no notion and don't intend to have one," Wolfe said.

"Then I'll call. From a booth. They say they can't trace a local dial call, but there might be a miracle. Next, do I get back up there quick, I mean to Jarrell's, and if so what's my line?"

"I said I have no notion. Why should you go back there at all?" I uncrossed my legs. "Look," I said, "you might as well come on down. I could go back just to return his ten grand and tell him we're bowing out, if that's what you want, but it's not quite so simple and you know it. When the cops learn that Eber was Jarrell's secretary and got fired, they'll be there asking questions. If they learn that Jarrell hired you and you sent me to take his place—don't growl at me, they'll think you sent me no matter what you think— you know what will happen, they'll be on our necks. Even if they don't learn that, we have a problem. We know that a thirty-eight revolver was taken from Jarrell's desk yesterday afternoon, and we know that Eber was there yesterday morning and it made a stir, and if and when we also know that the bullet that killed him came from a thirty-eight, what do we do, file it and forget it?"

He grunted. "There is no obligation to report what may be merely a coincidence. If Mr. Jarrell's gun is found and it is established that Eber was killed by a bullet from it, that will be different."

"Meanwhile we ignore the coincidence?"

"We don't proclaim it."

"Then I assume we keep the ten grand and Jarrell is still your client. If he turns out to be a murderer, what the hell, many lawyers' clients are murderers. And I'm back where I started, I need instructions. I'll have to go—"

The phone rang. I swiveled and got it, and I noticed that Wolfe reached for his too, which he rarely does unless I give him a sign.

"Nero Wolfe's residence, Archie Goodwin speaking."

"Where the hell are you? This is Jarrell."

"You know what number you dialed, Mr. Jarrell. I'm with Mr. Wolfe, reporting and getting instructions about your job."

"I've got instructions for you myself. Nora says you left at five-thirty. You've been gone over four hours. How soon can you be here?"

"Oh, say in an hour."

"I'll be in the library."

He hung up. I cradled it and turned.

"He reminds me of you a little," I said—just an interesting fact, nothing personal. "I was about to say, I'll have to go back up there and I need to know what for. Just hang around or try to start something? For instance, it would be a cinch to put the bee on Jarrell. You couldn't ask for a better setup for blackmail. I tell him that if he makes a sizable contribution in cash, say half a million, we'll regard the stolen gun as a coincidence and forget it. If he doesn't, we'll feel that we must report it. Of course I'll have to wait until the news is out about Eber, but if—"

"Shut up."

"Yes, sir."

He eyed me. "You understand the situation. You have expounded it."

"Yes, sir."

"This may or may not affect the job you undertook for Mr. Jarrell—don't interrupt me—very well, that *we* undertook. Murder sometimes creates only ripples, but more frequently high seas. Assuredly you are not going back there to take women to lunch at Rusterman's or to taverns to dance. I offer no complaint for what has been done; I will concede that we blundered into this mess by a collaboration in mulishness; but if it was Mr. Jarrell's gun that was used to kill Eber, and it isn't too fanciful to suppose that it was, we are in it willy-nilly, and we should emerge, if not with profit, at least without discomfiture. That is our joint concern. You ask if you should start something up there. I doubt if you'll need to; something has already started. It is most unlikely that the murder had no connection with that hive of predators and parasites. I can't tell you how to proceed because you'll have to wait on events. You will be guided by your intelligence and experience, and report to me as the occasion dictates. Mr. Jarrell said he has instructions for you. Have you any notion what they'll be?"

"Not a glimmer."

"Then we can't anticipate them. You will call police headquarters?"

"Yes, on my way."

"That will expedite matters. Otherwise there's no telling when the body would be found."

I was on my feet. "If you phone me there," I told him, "keep it decent. He has four phones on his desk, and I suspect two of them."

"I won't phone you. You'll phone me."

"Okay," I said, and went.

6

Passing the gantlet of the steely eyes of the lobby sentinel, mounting in the private elevator, and using my key in the tenth-floor vestibule, I found that the electronic security apparatus hadn't been switched on yet. Steck appeared, of course, and said that Mr. Jarrell would like to see me in the library. The eye I gave him was a different eye from what it had been. It could even have been Steck who had worked the rug trick to get hold of a gun. He had his duties, but he might have managed to squeeze it in.

Hearing voices in the lounge, I crossed the reception hall to glance in, and saw Trella, Nora, and Roger Foote at a card table.

Roger looked up and called to me. "Pinochle! Come and take a hand!"

"Sorry, I can't. Mr. Jarrell wants me."

"Come when you're through! Peach Fuzz ran a beautiful race! Beautiful! Five lengths back at the turn and only a head behind at the finish! Beautiful!"

A really fine loser, I was thinking as I headed for the corridor. You don't often meet that kind of sporting spirit. Beautiful!

The door of the library was standing open. Entering, I closed it. Jarrell, over by the files with one of the drawers open, barked at me, "Be with you in a minute," and I went to the chair at an end of his desk. A Portanaga with an inch of ash intact was there on a tray, and the smell told me it was still alive, so it couldn't have been more than ninety seconds since he left his desk to go to the files. That's the advantage of being a detective with a trained mind; you collect all kinds of useless facts without even trying.

He came and sat, picked up the cigar and tapped the ash off, and took a couple of puffs. He spoke. "Why did you go to see Wolfe?"

"He pays my salary. He likes to know what he's getting for it. Also I had told him on the phone about your gun disappearing, and he wanted to ask me about it."

"Did you have to tell him about that?"

"I thought I'd better. You're his client, and he doesn't like to have his clients shot, and if somebody used the gun to kill you with and I hadn't told him about it he would have been annoyed. Besides, I thought he might want to make a suggestion."

"Did he make one?"

"Not a suggestion exactly. He made a comment. He said you're an ass. He said you should have corralled everybody and got the cops in to find the gun."

"Did you tell him I'm convinced that my daughter-in-law took it?"

"Sure. But even if she did, and if she intends to use it on you, that would still be the best way to handle it. It would get the gun back, and it would notify her that you haven't got a hole in your head and don't intend to have one."

He showed no reaction to my mentioning a hole in the head. "It was you who said we'd probably find it in a tub on the terrace."

"I didn't say probably, but what if I did? We'd have the gun. You said on the phone you've got instructions for me. About looking for it?"

"No, not that." He took a pull on the cigar, removed it, and let the smoke float out. "I don't remember just how much I've told you about Corey Brigham."

"Not much. No details. That he's an old friend of yours—no, you didn't use the word friend—that he got in ahead of you on a deal, and that you think your daughter-in-law was responsible. I've been a little surprised to see him around."

"I want him around. I want him to think I've accepted his explanation and I don't suspect anything. The deal was about a shipping company. I found out about a claim that could be made against it, and I was all set to buy the claim and then put the screws on, and when I was ready to close in I found that Brigham was there ahead of me. He said he had got next to it through somebody else, that he didn't know I was after it, but he's a damn liar. There wasn't anybody else. The only source was mine, and I had it clamped tight. He got it through information that was in this room, and he got it from my daughter-in-law."

"That raises questions," I told him. "I don't have to ask why Susan gave it to him because I already know your answer to that. She gives things to men, including her—uh, favors, because that's what she's like. But how did she get it?"

"She got my gun yesterday, didn't she?"

"I don't know and neither do you. Anyhow, how many times has that rug walked in here?"

"Not any. That was a new one. But she knows how to find a way to get anything she wants. She could have got it from Jim Eber. Or from my son. Or she could have been in here with my son when Nora and I weren't here, and sent him out for something, and got it herself. God only knows what else she got. Most of my operations are based on some kind of inside information, and a lot of it is on paper, it has to be, and I'm afraid to leave anything important in here any more. Goddamn it, she has to go!"

He pulled at the cigar, found it was out, and dropped it in the tray. "There's another aspect. I stood to clear a million on that deal, probably more. So Brigham did instead of me, and she got her share of it. She gives things to men, including her favors if you want to call it that, but all the time her main object is herself. She got her share. That's what I've got instructions about. See if you can find it. She's got it salted away somewhere and maybe you can find it. Maybe you can get a lead to it through Brigham. Get next to him. He's a goddamn snob, but he won't be snooty to my secretary if you handle him right. Another possibility is Jim Eber. Get next to him too. You met him yesterday. I don't know just what your approach will be, but you should be able to work that out yourself. And don't forget our deal—yours and mine. Ten thousand the day she's out of here, with my son staying, and fifty thousand more when the divorce papers are signed."

I had been wondering if he had forgotten about that. I was also wondering if he figured that later, remembering that he had told me Thursday night to get next to Jim Eber, I would regard that as evidence that he hadn't been aware that Eber was no longer approachable.

I reminded him that it takes two to make a deal and that I hadn't accepted his offer, but he waved that away as not worth discussing. His suggestion that I cultivate Eber made it relevant for me to ask questions about him, and I did so, but while some of the answers I got might have been helpful for getting to know him better, none of them shed any light on the most important fact about him, that he was dead. He had been with Jarrell five years, was unmarried, was a Presbyterian but didn't work at it, played golf on Sunday, was fair to good at bridge, and so on. I also collected some data on Corey Brigham.

When Jarrell finished with me and I went, leaving him at his desk, I stood outside for a moment, on the rug that walked like a man, or a woman, debating whether to go and join the pinochle players, to observe them from the new angle I now had on the whole bunch, or to go for a walk and call Wolfe to tell him what Jarrell's instructions had been. It was a draw, so I decided to do neither and went upstairs to bed.

I slept all right, I always sleep, but woke up at seven o'clock. I turned over and shut my eyes again, but nothing doing. I was awake. It was a damn nuisance. I would have liked to get up and dress and go down to the studio and hear the eight-o'clock news. It had been exactly ten-thirty when I had phoned headquarters to tell them, in falsetto, that they had better take a look at a certain apartment at a certain number on 49th Street, and by now the news would be out and I wanted to hear it. But on Tuesday I had appeared for breakfast at 9:25, on Wednesday at 10:15, and on Thursday at 9:20, and if I shattered precedent by showing before eight, making for the radio, and announcing what I had heard to anyone available—and it would be remarkable not to announce it—someone might have wondered how come. So when my eyes wouldn't stay closed no matter which side I tried, I lay on my back and let them stay open, hoping they liked the ceiling. They didn't. They kept turning—up, down, right, left. I got the impression that they were trying to turn clear over to see inside. When I found myself wondering what would happen if they actually made it I decided that had gone far enough, kicked the sheet off, and got up.

I took my time in the shower, and shaving, and putting cuff links in a clean shirt, and other details; and history repeated itself. I was pulling on my pants, getting the second leg through, when there was a knock at the door, and nothing timid about it. I called out, "Who is it?", and for reply the door opened, and Jarrell walked in.

I spoke. "Good morning. Come some time when I've got my shoes on."

He had closed the door. "This can't wait. Jim Eber is dead. They found his body in his apartment. Murdered. Shot."

I stared, not overdoing it. "For God's sake. When?"

"I got it on the radio—the eight-o'clock news. They found him last night. He was shot in the head, in the back. That's all it said. It didn't mention that he worked for me." He went to a chair, the big one by the window, and sat. "I want to discuss it with you."

I had put my shoes and clean socks by that chair, intending to sit there to put them on. Going to get them, taking another chair, pulling my pants leg up, and starting a sock on, I said, "If they don't already know he worked for you they soon will, you realize that."

"Certainly I realize it. They may phone, or come, any minute. That's what I want to discuss."

I picked up the other sock. "All right, discuss. Shoot."

"You know what a murder investigation is like, Goodwin. You know that better than I do."

"Yeah. It's no fun."

"It certainly isn't. Of course they may already have a line on somebody, they may even have the man that did it, there was nothing on the radio about that. But if they haven't, and if they don't get him soon, you know what it will be like. They'll dig everywhere as deep as they can. He was with me five years, and he lived here. They'll want to know everything about him, and it's mostly here they'll expect to get it."

I was tying a shoelace. "Yeah, they have no respect for privacy, when it's murder."

He nodded. "I know they haven't. And I know the best way to handle it is to tell them anything they want to know, within reason. If they think I'm holding out that will only make it worse, I appreciate that. One thing I want to discuss with you, they'll ask why I fired Eber, and what do I say?"

I had my shoes on now and was on equal terms. Conferring in bare feet with a man who is properly shod may not put you at a disadvantage, but it seems to. It may be because he could step on your toes. With mine now protected, I said, "Just tell them why you fired him. That you suspected him of leaking business secrets."

He shook his head. "If I do that they'll want details—what secrets he leaked and who to, all that. That would take them onto ground where I don't want them. I would rather tell them that Eber was getting careless, he seemed to be losing interest, and I decided to let him go. No matter who else they ask, nobody could contradict that, not even Nora, except one person. You. If they ask you, you can simply say that you don't know much about it, that you understand that I was dissatisfied with Eber but you don't know why. Can't you?"

I was frowning at him. "This must have given you quite a jolt, Mr. Jarrell. You'd better snap out of it. Two of Mr. Wolfe's oldest and dearest enemies, and mine, are Inspector Cramer and Sergeant Stebbins of Homicide. The minute they catch sight of me and learn that I'm here under another name in Eber's job, the sparks will start flying. No matter what reason you give them for firing him they won't believe you. They won't believe me. They won't believe anybody. The theory they'll like best will be that you decided that Eber had to be shot and got me in as a technical consultant. That may be stretching it a little, but it gives you an idea."

"Good God." He was stunned. "Of course."

"So I can't simply say I don't know much about it."

"Good God no. My mind wasn't working." He leaned forward at me. "Look, Goodwin. The other thing I was going to ask, I was going to ask you to say nothing about what happened Wednesday —about my gun being taken. I'm not afraid that gun was used to shoot Eber, that's not it, it may not have been that caliber, but when they come here on a murder investigation you know how it will be if they find out that my gun was stolen just the day before. And if it was that caliber it will be a hundred times worse. So I was going to ask you not to mention it. Nobody else knows about it. Horland's man doesn't. He left before I found it was gone."

"I told you I told Mr. Wolfe."

"They don't have to get to Wolfe."

"Maybe they don't have to but they will, as soon as they see me. I'll tell you, Mr. Jarrell, it seems to me you're still jolted.

You're not thinking straight. The way you feel about your daughter-in-law, this may be right in your lap. You want to sink her so bad you can taste it. You hired Mr. Wolfe and gave him ten thousand dollars for a retainer, and then offered me another sixty thousand. If you tell Inspector Cramer all about it—only Cramer, not Stebbins or Rowcliff or any of his gang, and not some squirt of an assistant district attorney—and tell him about the gun, and he starts digging at it and comes up with proof that Susan shot Eber, what better could you ask? You said you knew Susan took the gun, and if so she wanted to use it on someone, and why not Eber? And if you're afraid Cramer might botch it, keep Mr. Wolfe on the job. He loves to see to it that Cramer doesn't botch something."

"No," he said positively.

"Why not? You'll soon know if Eber was shot with a thirty-eight. I can find out about that for you within an hour, as soon as I get some breakfast. Why not?"

"I won't have them— I won't do it. No. You know damn well I won't. I won't tell the police about my personal affairs and have them spread all over. I don't want you or Wolfe telling them, either. I see now that my idea wouldn't work, that if they find out you're here in Eber's place there'll be hell to pay. So they won't find out. You won't be here, and you'd better leave right now because they might come any minute. If they want to know where my new secretary is I'll take care of that. He has only been here four days and knew nothing about Eber. You'd better leave now."

"And go where?"

"Where you belong, damn it!" He gestured, a hand out. "You'll have to make allowances for me, Goodwin. I've had a jolt, certainly I have. If you're not here and if I account for the absence of my new secretary, they'll never get to you or Wolfe either. Tell Wolfe I'm still his client and I'll get in touch with him. He said he was discreet. Tell him there's no limit to what his discretion may be worth to me."

He left the chair. "As for you, no limit with you too. I'm a tough operator, but I pay for what I get. Go on, get your necktie on. Leave your stuff here, that won't matter, you can get it later. We understand each other, don't we?"

"If we don't we will."

"I like you, Goodwin. Get going."

I moved. He stood and watched me while I got my tie and jacket on, gathered a few items and put them in the small bag, and closed the bag. When I glanced back as I turned the corner at the end of the hall, he was standing in front of the door of my room. I was disappointed not to see Steck in the corridor or reception hall; he must have had morning duties somewhere. Outside, I crossed the avenue, flagged a taxi headed downtown, and at a quarter past nine was mounting the stoop of the old brownstone. Wolfe would be up in the plant rooms for his morning session, from nine to eleven, with the orchids.

The chain bolt was on, so I had to ring, and it was Orrie Cather who opened up. He extended a hand. "Take your bag, sir?"

I let him take it, strode down the hall to the kitchen, and pushed the door.

Fritz, at the sink, turned. "Archie! A pleasure! You're back?"

"I'm back for breakfast, anyhow. My God, I'm empty! No orange juice even. One dozen pancakes, please."

I did eat seven.

7

I was in the office, refreshed and refueled, in time to get the ten-o'clock news. It didn't add much to what Jarrell had heard two hours earlier, and nothing that I didn't already know.

Orrie, at ease on the couch, inquired, "Did it help any? I'm ignorant, so I have to ask. What's hot, the budget?"

"Yeah, I'm underwriting it. I'm also writing a book on criminology and researching it. Excuse me, I'm busy."

I dialed a number I didn't have to look up, the *Gazette,* asked for Lon Cohen's extension, and in a minute had him.

"Lon? Archie. I'm col—"

"I'm busy."

"So am I. I'm collecting data for a book. What did you shoot James L. Eber with, an arquebus?"

"No, my arquebus is in hock. I used a flintlock. What is it to you?"

"I'm just curious. If you'll satisfy my curiosity I'll satisfy yours some day. Have they found the bullet?"

Lon is a fine guy and a good poker player, but he has the occupational disease of all journalists: before he'll answer a question he has to ask one. So he did. "Has Wolfe got a thumb in it already?"

"Not a thumb, a foot. No, he hasn't, not for the record. If and when, you first as usual. Have they found the bullet?"

"Yes. It just came in. A thirty-eight, that's all so far. Who is Wolfe's client?"

"J. Edgar Hoover. Have they arrested anybody?"

"No. My God, give 'em time to sweep up and sit down and think. It was only twelve hours ago. I've been thinking ever since I heard your voice just now. What I think, I think it was you who called headquarters last night and told them to go and look, and I'm sore. You should have called me first."

"I should, at that. Next time. Have they or you or anyone got any kind of a lead?"

"To the murderer, no. So far the most interesting item is that up to a couple of weeks ago he was working for a guy named Otis Jarrell, you know who he is—*by God!* It was him you phoned me the other day to get dope on!"

"Sure it was. That's one reason—"

"Is Jarrell Wolfe's client?"

"For the present, as far as you're concerned, Wolfe has no client. I was saying, that's one reason I'm calling now. I thought you might remember I had asked about him, and I wanted to tell you not to trust your memory until further notice. Just go ahead and gather the news and serve the public. You may possibly hear from me some day."

"Come on up here. I'll buy you a lunch."

"I can't make it, Lon. Sorry. Don't use any wooden bullets."

As I pushed the phone back Orrie asked, "What's an arquebus?"

"Figure it out yourself. A combination of an ark and a bus. Amphibian."

"Then don't." He sat up. "If I'm not supposed to be in on whatever you think you're doing, okay, but I have a right to know what an arquebus is. Do you want me out of here?"

I told him no, I could think better with him there for contrast.
But he got bounced when Wolfe came down at eleven o'clock.
From the kitchen I had buzzed the plant rooms on the house phone
to tell him I was there, so he wasn't surprised to see me. He went
to his desk, glanced at the morning mail, which was skimpy,
straightened his desk blotter, and focused on me. "Well?"

"In my opinion," I said, "the time has come for a complete
report."

His eyes went over my shoulder to the couch. "If we need you
on this, Orrie, you will get all the required information. That can
wait."

"Yes, sir." Orrie got up and went.

When the door had closed behind him I spoke. "I called Lon
Cohen. The bullet that killed Eber is a thirty-eight. Jarrell didn't
know that when he entered my room this morning, knocking but
not waiting for an invitation. He only knew what he had heard on
the radio at eight o'clock, and I suppose you heard it too. Even
so, he badly needed a tranquilizer. When I report in full you'll know
what he said. It ended with his telling me to beat it quick before
the cops arrived. He said to tell you he's still your client and he'll
get in touch with you, and there's no limit to what your discretion
may be worth to him. Me too. My discretion is as good as yours.
Now that I know it was a thirty-eight, I have only two alternatives.
Either I go down to Homicide and open the bag, or I give you the
whole works from the beginning, words and music, and you listen,
and then put your mind on it. If I get tossed in the coop for withholding evidence you can't operate anyhow, with me not here to
supervise, so you might as well be with me."

"Pfui. As I said last night, there is no obligation to report what
may be merely a coincidence." He sighed. "However, I concede
that I'll have to listen. As for putting my mind on it, we'll see. Go
ahead."

It took me two hours. I will not say that I gave him every word
that had been pronounced in my hearing since Monday afternoon,
four days back, but I came close to it. I left out some of Tuesday
evening at Colonna's with Lois; things that are said between
dances, when the band is good and your partner is better than good,
are apt to be irrelevant and off key in a working detective's report.
Aside from that I didn't miss much, and nothing of any importance,
and neither did he. If he listens at all, he listens. The only inter-

ruptions were the two bottles of beer he rang for, brought by Fritz —both, of course, for Wolfe. The last half hour he was leaning back in his chair with his eyes closed, but that didn't mean he wasn't getting it.

I stood up and stretched and sat down again. "So what it amounts to is that we are to sit it out, nothing to do but eat and sleep, and name our figure."

"Not an intolerable lot, Archie. The figure you suggested last evening was half a million."

"Yes, sir. I've decided that Billy Graham wouldn't approve. Say that the chance is one in ten that one of them killed Eber. I think it's at least fifty-fifty, but even if it's only one in ten I pass. So do you. You have to. You know darned well it's one of two things. One is to call it off with Jarrell, back clear out, and hand it over to Cramer. He would appreciate it."

He made a face. His eyes opened. "What's the other?"

"You go to work."

"At what? Investigating the murder of Mr. Eber? No one has hired me to."

I grinned at him. "No good. You call it quibbling, I call it dodging. The murder is in only because one of them might have done it, with Jarrell's gun. The question is, do we tell Cramer about the gun? We would rather not. The client would rather not. The only way out, if we're not going to tell Cramer, is to find out if one of them killed Eber—not to satisfy a judge and jury, just to satisfy us. If they didn't, to hell with Cramer. If they did, we go on from there. The only way to find out is for you to go to work, and the only way for you to get to work is for me to phone Jarrell and tell him to have them here, all of them, at six o'clock today. What's wrong with that?"

"You would," he growled.

"Yes, sir. Of course there's a complication: me. To them I'm Alan Green, so I can't be here as Archie Goodwin, but that's easy. Orrie can be Archie Goodwin, at my desk, and I'll be Alan Green. Since I was in on the discovery that the gun was gone, I should be present." I looked up at the wall clock. "Lunch in eight minutes. I should phone Jarrell now."

I made it slow motion, taking ten seconds to swivel, pull the phone over, lift the receiver, and start dialing, to give him plenty of time to stop me. He didn't. How could he, after my invincible logic? Nor did he move to take his phone.

Then a voice was in my ear. "Mr. Otis Jarrell's office."

It wasn't Nora, but a male, and I thought I knew what male. I said I was Alan Green and wanted to speak to Mr. Jarrell, and in a moment had him.

"Yes, Green?"

I kept my voice down. "Is anyone else on?"

"No."

"You're sure?"

"Yes."

"Was that Wyman answering?"

"Yes."

"He's there in the office with you?"

"Yes."

"Then you'd better let me do the talking and stick to yes and no. I'm here with Mr. Wolfe. Do you know that the bullet that killed Eber is a thirty-eight?"

"No."

"Well, it is. Have you had any callers?"

"Yes."

"Anything drastic?"

"No."

"Ring me later and tell me about it if you want to. I'm calling for Mr. Wolfe. Now that we know it was a thirty-eight, he thinks I should tell the police about your gun. It could be a question of withholding evidence. He feels strongly about it, but he is willing to postpone it, on one condition. The condition is that you have everybody in this office at six o'clock today so he can question them. By everybody he means you, your wife, Wyman, Susan, Lois, Nora Kent, Roger Foote, and Corey Brigham. I'll be here as Alan Green, your secretary. Another man will be at my desk as Archie Goodwin."

"I don't see how—"

"Hold it. I know you're biting nails, but hold it. You can tell them that Mr. Wolfe will explain why this conference is necessary, and he will. Have you told any of them about your gun being taken?"

"No."

"Don't. He will. He'll explain that when you learned that Eber had been shot with a thirty-eight—that should be on the air by now, and it will be in the early afternoon papers—you were concerned, naturally, and you hired him to investigate, and he insisted on seeing all of you. I know you've got objections. You'll have to swallow them, but if you want help on it get rid of Wyman and Nora and call me back. If you don't call back we'll be expecting you, all of you, here at six o'clock."

"No. I'll call back."

"Sure, glad to have you."

I hung up, turned, and told Wolfe, "You heard all of it except his noes and yeses. Satisfactory?"

"No," he said, but that was just reflex.

I'll say one thing for Wolfe, he hates to have anyone else's meal interrupted almost as much as his own. One of the standing rules in that house is that when we are at table, and nothing really hot is on, Fritz answers the phone in the kitchen, and if it seems urgent I go and get it. There may be something or somebody Wolfe would leave the table for, but I don't know what or who.

That day Fritz was passing a platter of what Wolfe calls hedgehog omelet, which tastes a lot better than it sounds, when the phone rang, and I told Fritz not to bother and went to the office. It was Jarrell calling back, and he had a lot of words besides yes and no. I permitted him to let off steam until it occurred to me that the omelet would be either cold or shriveled, and then told him firmly that it was either bring them or else. Back at the table, I found that the omelet had had no chance to either cool or shrivel, not with Orrie there to help Wolfe with it. I did get a bite.

We had just started on the avocado, whipped with sugar and lime juice and green chartreuse, when the doorbell rang. During meals Fritz was supposed to get that too, but I thought Jarrell might have rushed down to use more words face to face, so I got up and went to the hall for a look through the one-way glass panel in the front door. Having looked, I returned to the dining room and told Wolfe, "One's here already. The stenographer. Nora Kent."

He swallowed avocado. "Nonsense. You said six o'clock."

"Yes, sir. She must be on her own." The bell rang again. "And she wants in." I aimed a thumb at Orrie. "Archie Goodwin here can take her to the office and shut the door."

"Confound it." He was going to have to work sooner than expected. To Orrie: "You are Archie Goodwin."

"Yes, sir," Orrie said. "It's a comedown, but I'll try. Do I know her?"

"No. You have never seen or heard of her." The bell rang again. "Take her to the office and come and finish your lunch."

He went. He closed the door, but the office was just across the hall, and it might startle her if she heard Alan Green's voice as she went by, so I used my mouth for an avocado depot only. Sounds came faintly, since the walls and doors on that floor are all sound-proofed.

When Orrie entered he shut the door, returned to his place, picked up his spoon, and spoke. "You didn't say to rub it in that I'm Archie Goodwin, and she didn't ask, so I didn't mention it. She said her name was Nora Kent, and she wants to see Mr. Wolfe. How long am I going to be Archie Goodwin?"

I put in. "Mr. Wolfe never talks business at the table, you know that, Orrie. You haven't been told yet, but you were going to be me at a party later on, and now you can practice. Just sit at my desk and look astute. I'll have my eye on you. I'll be at the hole —unless Mr. Wolfe has other plans."

"No," Wolfe muttered. "I have no plans."

The hole, ten inches square, was at eye level in the wall twelve feet to the right of Wolfe's desk. On the office side it was covered by what appeared to be just a pretty picture of a waterfall. On the other side, in a wing of the hall across from the kitchen, it was covered by nothing, and you could not only see through but also hear through. My longest stretch there was one night when we had four people in the front room waiting for Wolfe to show up (he was in the kitchen chinning with Fritz), and we were expecting and hoping that one of them would sneak into the office to get something from a drawer of Wolfe's desk, and we wanted to know which one. That time I stood there at that hole more than three hours, and the door from the front room never opened.

This time it was much less than three hours. Orrie waited to open the door to the office until I was around the corner to the wing, so I saw his performance when they went in. As Goodwin he was barely adequate introducing Wolfe to her, hamming it, I thought; and crossing to my desk and sitting, he was entirely out of character, no grace or flair at all. I would have to rehearse him before six o'clock came. I had a good view of him and Nora, but could get Wolfe, in profile, only by sticking my nose into the hole and pressing my forehead against the upper edge.

WOLFE: I'm sorry you had to wait, Miss Kent. It is *Miss* Kent?

NORA: Yes. I am employed by Mr. Otis Jarrell. His stenographer. I believe you know him.

WOLFE: There is no taboo on beliefs, or shouldn't be. The right to believe will be the last to go. Proceed.

NORA: You do know Mr. Jarrell?

WOLFE: My dear madam. I have rights too—for instance, the right to decline inquisition by a stranger. You are not here by appointment.

(That was meant to cut. If it did, no blood showed.)

NORA: There wasn't time to make one. I had to see you at once. I had to ask you why you sent your confidential assistant, Archie Goodwin, to take a job with Mr. Jarrell as his secretary.

WOLFE: I wasn't aware that I had done so. Archie, did I send you to take a job as Mr. Jarrell's secretary?

ORRIE: No, sir, not that I remember.

NORA (with no glance at Orrie): He's not Archie Goodwin. I knew Archie Goodwin the minute I saw him, Monday afternoon. I keep a scrapbook, Mr. Wolfe, a personal scrapbook. Among the things I put in it are pictures of people who have done things that I admire. There are three pictures of you, two from newspapers and one from a magazine, put in at different times, and one of Archie Goodwin. It was in the *Gazette* last year when you caught that murderer—you remember—Patrick Degan. I knew him the minute I saw him, and after I looked in my scrapbook there was no question about it.

(Orrie was looking straight at the pretty picture of the waterfall, at me though he couldn't see me, with blood in his eye, and I couldn't blame him. He had been given to understand that the part was a cinch, that he wouldn't have to do or say anything to avert suspicion because she wouldn't have any. And there he was, a monkey. I couldn't blame him.)

WOLFE (not visibly fazed, but also a monkey): I am flattered,

Miss Kent, to be in your scrapbook. No doubt Mr. Goodwin is also flattered, though he might challenge your taste in having three pictures of me and only one of him. It will save—

NORA: Why did you send him there?

WOLFE: If you please. It will save time, and also breath, to proceed on an assumption, without prejudice. Obviously you're convinced that Mr. Goodwin took a job as Mr. Jarrell's secretary, and that I sent him, and it would be futile to try to talk you out of it. So we'll assume you're right. I don't concede it, but I'm willing to assume it for the sake of discussion. What about it?

NORA: I *am* right! You know it!

WOLFE: No. You may have it as an assumption, but not as a fact. What difference does it make? Let's get on. Did Mr. Goodwin take the job under his own name?

NORA: Certainly not. You know he didn't. Mr. Jarrell introduced him to me as Alan Green.

WOLFE: Did you tell Mr. Jarrell that that wasn't his real name? That you recognized him as Archie Goodwin?

NORA: No.

WOLFE: Why not?

NORA: Because I wasn't sure what the situation was. I thought that Mr. Jarrell might have hired you to do something and he knew who Green was, but he didn't want me to know or anyone else. I thought in that case I had better keep it to myself. But now it's different. Now I think that someone else may have hired you, someone who wanted to know something about Mr. Jarrell's affairs, and you arranged somehow for Goodwin to take that job, and Mr. Jarrell doesn't know who he is.

WOLFE: You didn't have to come to me to settle that. Ask Mr. Jarrell. Have you?

NORA: No. I told you why. And then—there are reasons . . .

WOLFE: There often are. If none are at hand we contrive some. A moment ago you said, "But now it's different." What changed it?

NORA: You know what changed it. Murder. The murder of Jim Eber. Archie Goodwin has told you all about it.

WOLFE: I'm willing to include that in the assumption. I think, madam, you had better tell me why you came here and what you want—still, of course, on our assumption.

(I said Monday afternoon that she didn't look her age, forty-seven. She did now. Her gray eyes were just as sharp and competent, and she kept her shoulders just as straight, but she seemed to have creases and wrinkles I hadn't observed before. Of course it could have been the light angle, or possibly it was looking through the waterfall.)

NORA: If we're assuming that I'm right, that man (indicating Orrie) can't be Archie Goodwin, and I don't know who he is. I haven't got *his* picture in my scrapbook. I'll tell *you* why I came.

WOLFE: That's reasonable, certainly. Archie, I'm afraid you'll have to leave us.

(Poor Orrie. As Orrie Cather he had been chased twice, and now he was chased as Archie Goodwin. His only hope now was to be cast as Nero Wolfe. When he was out and the door shut Nora spoke.)

NORA: All right, I'll tell you. Right after lunch today I went on an errand, and when I got back Mr. Jarrell told me that the bullet that killed Jim Eber was a thirty-eight. That was all he told me, just that. But I knew why he told me, it was because his own gun is a thirty-eight. He has always kept it in a drawer of his desk. I saw it there Wednesday afternoon. But it wasn't there Thursday morning, yesterday, and it hasn't been there since. Mr. Jarrell hasn't asked me about it, he hasn't mentioned it. I don't know—

WOLFE: Haven't you mentioned it?

(Orrie was at my elbow.)

NORA: No. If I mentioned it, and he had taken it himself, he would think I was prying into matters that don't concern me. I don't know whether he took it himself or not. But yesterday afternoon a man from Horland's Protective Agency delivered some pictures that must have been taken by the camera that works automatically when the door of the library is opened. The clock above the door said sixteen minutes past six. The pictures showed the door opening and a rug coming in—just the rug, flat, held up perpendicular, hanging straight down. Of course there was someone behind it. Archie Goodwin looked at the pictures, and of course he has told you all about it.

WOLFE: On our assumption, yes.

NORA: The camera must have taken them the day before, at sixteen minutes past six Wednesday afternoon. At that hour I am always up in my room, washing and changing, getting ready to go to the lounge for cocktails. So is everyone else, nearly always. So there it is, take it altogether. On Monday Archie Goodwin comes as the new secretary under another name. Thursday morning Mr. Jarrell's gun is gone. Thursday afternoon the pictures come, taken at a time when I was up in my room alone. Friday morning, today, the news comes that Jim Eber has been murdered, shot. Also this morning Archie Goodwin isn't there, and Mr. Jarrell says he has sent him on a trip. And this afternoon Mr. Jarrell tells me that Jim was shot with a thirty-eight.

(The gray eyes were steady and cold. I had the feeling that if they aimed my way they would see me right through the picture, though I knew they couldn't.)

NORA: I'm not frightened, Mr. Wolfe. I don't scare easily. And I know you wouldn't deliberately conspire to have me accused of murder, and neither would Archie Goodwin. But all those things together, I wasn't going to just wait and see what happened. It wouldn't have helped any to say all this to Mr. Jarrell. I know all about his business affairs, but this is his personal life, his family, and I don't count. I'd rather not have him know I came to you, but I don't really care. I've worked long enough anyhow. Was Archie Goodwin there because Mr. Jarrell hired you, or was it someone else?

WOLFE: Even granting the assumption, I can't tell you that.

NORA: I suppose not. But he's not there today, so you may be through. In the twenty-two years I have been with Mr. Jarrell I have had many opportunities, especially the past ten years, and my net worth today, personally, is something over a million dollars. I know you charge high fees, but I could afford it. I said I'm not frightened, and I'm not, but something is going to happen to somebody, I'm sure of that, and I don't want it to happen to me. I want you to see that it doesn't. I'll pay you a retainer, of course, whatever you say. I believe the phrase is "to protect my interests."

WOLFE: I'm sorry, Miss Kent, but I must decline.

NORA: Why?

WOLFE: I've undertaken a job for Mr. Jarrell. He has—

NORA: Then he did hire you! Then he knew it was Archie Goodwin!

WOLFE: No. That remains only an assumption. He has engaged me to conduct a conference for him. On the telephone today. He feels that the situation calls for an experienced investigator, and at six o'clock, three hours from now, he will come here and bring seven people with him—his family, and a man named Brigham, and you. That is, if you care to come. Evidently you are in no mood to trot when he whistles.

NORA: He phoned you today?

WOLFE: Yes.

NORA: You were already working for him. You sent Archie Goodwin up there.

WOLFE: You have a right, madam, to your beliefs, but I beg you not to be tiresome with them. If you join us at six o'clock, and I advise you to, you should know that the Mr. Goodwin who scurried from this room at your behest will be here, at his desk, and Alan Green, Mr. Jarrell's secretary, will also be present. The others, the members of Mr. Jarrell's family, unlike you, will probably be satisfied that those two men know who they are. Will you gain anything by raising the question?

NORA: No. I see. No. But I don't—then Mr. Jarrell doesn't know either?

WOLFE: Don't get tangled in your own assumption. If you wish to revise it after the conference by all means do so. And now I ask you to reciprocate. I have an assumption too. We have accepted yours as a basis for discussion; now let us accept mine. Mine is that none of the people who will be present at the conference fired the shot that killed Mr. Eber. What do you think of it?

(The gray eyes narrowed.)

NORA: You can't expect me to discuss that. I am employed by Mr. Jarrell.

WOLFE: Then we'll turn it around. We'll assume the contrary and take them in turn. Start with Mr. Jarrell himself. He took his own gun, with that hocus-pocus, and shot Eber with it. What do you say to that?

NORA: I don't say anything.

(She stood up.)

NORA: I know you're a clever man, Mr. Wolfe. That's why your picture is in my scrapbook. I may not be as clever as you are, but I'm not an utter fool.

(She started off, and, halfway to the door, turned.)

NORA: I'll be here at six o'clock if Mr. Jarrell tells me to.

She went. I whispered to Orrie, "Go let her out, Archie." He whispered back, "Let her out yourself, Alan." The result was that she let herself out. When I heard the front door close I left the wing and made it to the front in time to see her, through the one-way glass panel, going down the stoop. When she had reached the sidewalk safely I went to the office.

Wolfe was forward in his chair, his palms on his desk. Orrie was at my desk, in my chair, at ease. I stood and looked down at Wolfe.

"First," I said, "who is whom?"

He grunted. "Confound that woman. When you were introduced to her Monday afternoon I suppose you were looking at her. And you saw no sign that she had recognized you?"

"No, sir. A woman who has it in her to collar a million bucks knows how to hide her feelings. Besides, I thought it was only women under thirty who put my picture in scrapbooks. Then the program will be as scheduled?"

"Yes. Have you a reason for changing it?"

"No, sir. You're in for it. Please excuse me a minute." I pivoted to Orrie. "You'll be me at six o'clock, I can't help that, but you're not me now."

Down went my hands, like twin snakes striking, and I had his ankles. With a healthy jerk he was out of my chair, and I kept him coming, and going, until he was flat on his back on the rug, six feet away. By the time he had bounced up I was sitting. I may or may not know how to deal with a murderer, but I know how to handle an impostor.

8

I made a crack, I remember, about Susan's entrance in the lounge Monday evening, after everyone else was there, as to whether or not she had planned it that way. My own entrance in Wolfe's office that Friday afternoon, after everyone else was there, was planned

that way all right. There were two reasons: first, I didn't want to
have to chat with the first arrivals, whoever they would be, while
waiting for the others; and second, I didn't want to see Orrie being
Archie Goodwin as he let them in and escorted them to the office.
So at five-forty, leaving the furnishing of the refreshment table to
Fritz and Orrie, I left the house and went across the street to the
tailor shop, from where there was a good view of our stoop.

The first to show were Lois and Nora Kent and Roger Foote,
in a taxi. Nora paid the hackie, which was only fair since she could
afford it, and anyway, she probably put it on the expense account.
Transportation to and from a conference to discuss whether anyone present is a murderer is probably tax deductible. The next
customer was also in a taxi—Corey Brigham, alone. Then came
Wyman and Susan in a yellow Jaguar, with him driving. He had
to go nearly to Tenth Avenue to find a place to park, and they
walked back. Then came a wait. It was 6:10 when a black Rolls
Royce town car rolled to the curb and Jarrell and Trella got out.
I hadn't grown impatient, having myself waited for Trella twenty-
five minutes on Tuesday, bound for lunch at Rusterman's. As soon
as they were inside I crossed the street and pushed the button.
Archie Goodwin let me in and steered me to the office. He was
passable.

He had followed instructions on seating. The bad thing about
it was that I had four of them in profile and couldn't see the others'
faces at all, but we couldn't very well give the secretary a seat of
honor confronting the audience. Of course Jarrell had the red
leather chair, and in the front row of yellow chairs were Lois,
Trella, Wyman, and Susan. The family. Behind them were Alan
Green, Roger Foote, Nora Kent, and Corey Brigham. At least I
had Lois right in front of me. She wasn't as eye-catching from the
back as from the front, but it was pleasant.

When Wolfe entered he accepted Jarrell's offer of a hand, got
behind his desk, stood while Jarrell pronounced our names, inclined his head an eighth of an inch, and sat.

Jarrell spoke. "They all know that this is about Eber, and I've
hired you, and that's all. I've told them it's a conference, a family
conference, and it's off the record."

"Then I should clarify it." Wolfe cleared his throat. "It by 'off
the record' you mean that I am pledged to divulge nothing that is

said, I must dissent. I'm not a lawyer and cannot receive a privileged communication. If you mean that this proceeding is confidential and none of it will be disclosed except under constraint
of law, if it ever applies, that's correct."

"Don't shuffle, Wolfe. I'm your client."

"Only if we understand each other." Wolfe's eyes went left to
right and back again. "Then that's understood. I believe none of
you know about the disappearance of Mr. Jarrell's gun. You have
to know that. Since his secretary, Mr. Green, was present when its
absence was discovered, I'll ask him to tell you. Mr. Green?"

I had known that would come, but not that he would pick on
me first. Their heads were turned to me. Lois twisted clear around
in her chair, and her face was only arm's length away. I reported.
Not as I had reported to Wolfe, no dialogue, but all the main
action, from the time Jarrell had dashed into my room until we
left the library. I had their faces.

The face that left me first was Trella's. She turned it to her
husband and protested. "You might have told us, Otis!"

Corey Brigham asked me, "Has the gun been found?" Then he
went to Jarrell too. "Has it?"

Wolfe took over. "No, it has not been found. It has not been
looked for. In my opinion Mr. Jarrell should have had a search
made at once, calling in the police if necessary, but it must be allowed that it was a difficult situation for him. By the way, Mr.
Green, did you get the impression that Mr. Jarrell suspected anyone in particular?"

I hoped I got him right. Since he had asked it he wanted it
answered, but he hadn't asked what Jarrell had said, only if I had
got an impression. I gave him what I thought he wanted. "Yes, I
did. I might have been wrong, but I had the feeling that he
thought he knew who had taken it. It was—"

"Goddamn it," Jarrell blurted, "you knew what I thought! I
didn't think, I knew! If it's out let it come all the way out!" He
aimed a finger at Susan. "You took it!"

Dead silence. They didn't look at Susan, they looked at him,
all except Roger Foote, next to me. He kept his eyes on Wolfe,
possibly deciding whether to place a bet on him.

The silence was broken by Wyman. He didn't blurt, he merely
said, "That won't get you anywhere, Dad, not unless you've got

proof. Have you got any?" He turned, feeling Susan's hand on his arm, and told her, "Take it easy, Sue." He was adding something, but Wolfe's voice drowned it.

"That point should be settled, Mr. Jarrell. Do you have proof?"

"No. Proof for you, no. I don't need any."

"Then you'd better confine your charge to the family circle. Broadcast, it would be actionable." His head turned to the others. "We'll ignore Mr. Jarrell's specification of the culprit, since he has no proof. Ignoring that, this is the situation: When Mr. Jarrell learned this afternoon that Mr. Eber had been killed with a gun of the same caliber as his, which had been taken from a drawer of his desk, he was concerned, and no wonder, since Eber had been in his employ five years, had lived in his house, had recently been discharged, had visited his house on Wednesday, the day the gun was taken, and had been killed the next day. He decided to consult me. I told him that his position was precarious and possibly perilous; that his safest course was to report the disappearance of his gun, with all the circumstances, to the police; that, with a murder investigation under way, it was sure to transpire eventually, unless the murderer was soon discovered elsewhere; and that, now that I knew about it, I would myself have to report it, for my own protection, if the possibility that his gun had been used became a probability. Obviously, the best way out would be to establish that it was not his gun that killed Eber, and that can easily be done."

"How?" Brigham demanded.

"With an if, Mr. Brigham, or two of them. It can be established if it is true, and if the gun is available. Barring the servants, one of you took Mr. Jarrell's gun. Surrender it. Tell me where to find it. I'll fire a bullet from it, and I'll arrange for that bullet to be compared with the one that killed Eber. That will settle it. If the markings on the bullets don't match, the gun is innocent and I have no information for the police. Per contra, if they do match, I must inform the police immediately, and give them the gun, and all of you are in a pickle." He upturned both palms. "It's that simple."

Jarrell snapped at his daughter-in-law, "Where is it, Susan?"

"No," Wolfe snapped back at him, "that won't do. You have admitted you have no proof. I am conducting this conference at your request, and I won't have you bungling it. These people, including you, are jointly in jeopardy, at least of severe harassment, and I insist on making the appeal to them jointly." His eyes went right and left. "I appeal to all of you. Mrs. Wyman Jarrell." Pause. "Mr. Wyman Jarrell." Pause. "Mrs. Otis Jarrell." Pause. "Miss Jarrell." Pause. "Mr. Green." Pause. "Mr. Foote." Pause. "Miss Kent." Pause. "Mr. Brigham."

Lois twisted around in her chair to face me. "He's good at remembering names, isn't he?" she asked. Then she made two words, four syllables, with her lips, without sound. I am not an accomplished lip reader, but there was no mistaking that. The words were "Archie Goodwin."

I was arranging my face to indicate that I hadn't caught it when Corey Brigham spoke. "I don't quite see why I have been included." His well-trained smile was on display. "It's an honor, naturally, to be considered in the Jarrell family circle, but as a candidate for taking Jarrell's gun I'm afraid I don't qualify."

"You were there, Mr. Brigham. Perhaps I haven't made it clear, or Mr. Green didn't. The photograph, taken automatically when the door opened, showed the clock above the door at sixteen minutes past six. You were a dinner guest that evening, Wednesday, and you arrived shortly after six and were in the lounge."

"I see." The smile stayed on. "And I rushed back to the library and worked the great rug trick. How did I get in?"

"Presumably, with a key. The door was intact."

"I have no key to the library."

Wolfe nodded. "Possession of a key to that room would be one of the many points to be explored in a laborious and prolonged inquiry, if it should come to that. Meanwhile you cannot be slighted. You're all on equal terms, if we ignore Mr. Jarrell's specification without evidence, and I do."

Roger Foote's voice boomed suddenly, louder than necessary. "I've got a question." There were little spots of color beneath the cheekbones of his big wide face—at least there was one on the side I could see. "What about this new secretary, this Alan Green? We don't know anything about him, anyway I don't. Do you? Did he know Eber?"

My pal. My pet panhandler. I had lent the big bum sixty bucks, my money as far as he knew, and this was what I got for it. Of course, Peach Fuzz hadn't won. He added a footnote. "He had a key to the library, didn't he?"

"Yes, Mr. Foote, he did," Wolfe conceded. "I don't know much about him and may have to know more before this matter is settled. One thing I do know, he says he was in his room alone at a quarter past six Wednesday afternoon, when the gun was taken. So was Mr. Jarrell, by his account. Mr. Green has told you of Mr. Jarrell's coming for him, and what followed. Mr. Brigham was in the lounge. Where were you, Mr. Foote?"

"Where was I when?"

"I thought I had made it plain. At a quarter past six Wednesday afternoon."

"I was on my way back from Jamaica, and I got home—no. No, that was yesterday, Thursday. I must have been in my room, shaving. I always shave around then."

"You say 'must have been.' Were you?"

"Yes."

"Was anyone with you?"

"No. I'm not Louis the Fourteenth. I don't get an audience in to watch me shave."

Wolfe nodded. "That's out of fashion." His eyes went to Trella. "Mrs. Jarrell, we might as well get this covered. Do you remember where you were at that hour on Wednesday?"

"I know where I am at that hour every day—nearly every day, except week ends." I could see one of her ears, but not her face. "I was in the studio looking at television. At half past six I went to the lounge."

"You're sure you were there on Wednesday?"

"I certainly am."

"What time did you go to the studio?"

"A little before six. Five or ten minutes before."

"You remained there continuously until six-thirty?"

"Yes."

"I believe the studio is on the main corridor. Did you see anyone passing by in either direction?"

"No, the door was closed. And what do you take me for? Would I tell you if I had?"

"I don't know, madam; but unless we find that gun you may meet importunity that will make me a model of amenity by comparison." His eyes went past Wyman to Susan. "Mrs. Jarrell? If you please."

She replied at once, her voice down as usual, but firm and distinct. "I was in my room with my husband. We were there together, from about a quarter to six, for about an hour. Then we went down to the lounge together."

"You confirm that, Mr. Jarrell?"

"I do." Wyman was emphatic.

"You're sure it was Wednesday?"

"I am."

Wolfe's eyes went left and were apparently straight at me, but I was on a line with Lois, who was just in front. "Miss Jarrell?"

"I think I'm it," she said. "I don't know exactly where I was at a quarter past six. I was out, and I got home about six o'clock, and I wanted to ask my father something and went to the library, but the door was locked. Then I went to the kitchen to look for Mrs. Latham, but she wasn't there, and I found her in the dining room and asked her to iron a dress for me. I was tired and I started for the lounge to get a quick one, but I saw Mr. Brigham in there and I didn't feel like company, so I skipped it and went up to my room to change. If I had had a key to the library, and if I had thought of the rug stunt, I might have gone there in between and got the gun, but I didn't. Anyway, I hate guns. I think the rug stunt was absolutely dreamy." She twisted around. "Don't you, Ar—Al—Alan?"

A marvelous girl. So playful. If I ever got her on a dance floor again I'd walk on her toes. She twisted back again when Wolfe asked a question.

"What time was it when you saw Mr. Brigham in the lounge? As near as you can make it."

She shook her head. "Not a chance. If it were someone I'm rather warm on, for instance Mr. Green, I'd say it was exactly sixteen minutes after six, and he would say he saw me looking in and he looked at his watch, and we'd both be out of it, but I'm not warm on Mr. Brigham. So I won't even try to guess."

"This isn't a parlor game, Lois," her father snapped. "This may be serious."

"It already is, Dad. It sounds darned serious to me. You notice I told him all I could. Didn't I, Mr. Wolfe?"

"Yes, Miss Jarrell. Thank you. Will you oblige us, Miss Kent?"

I was wondering if Nora would rip it. Not that it would have been fatal, but if she had announced that the new secretary was Archie Goodwin, that Wolfe was a damn liar when he gave them to understand that he had had no finger in the Jarrell pie until that afternoon, and that therefore they had better start the questions going the other way, it would have made things a little complicated.

She didn't. Speaking as a competent and loyal stenographer, she merely said, "On Wednesday Mr. Jarrell and I left the library together at six o'clock, as usual, locking the door. We took the elevator upstairs together and parted in the hall. I went to my room to wash and change, and stayed there until half past six, or a minute or two before that, perhaps twenty-eight minutes after six, and then I went down to the lounge."

Wolfe leaned back, clasped his fingers at the highest point of his central mound, took in a bushel of air and let it out, and grumbled, "I may have gone about this wrong. Of course one of you has lied."

"You're damn right," Jarrell said, "and I know which one."

"If Susan lied," Roger objected, "so did Wyman. What about this Green?"

I would walk on his toes too, some day when I could get around to it.

"It was a mistake," Wolfe declared, "to get you all on record regarding your whereabouts at that hour. Now you are all committed, including the one who took the gun, and he will be more reluctant than ever to speak. It would be pointless to hammer at you now; indeed, I doubt if hammering would have helped in any case. The time for hammering was Wednesday afternoon, the moment Mr. Jarrell found that the gun was gone. Then there had been no murder, with its menace of an inexorable inquisition."

He looked them over. "So here we are. You know how it stands. I said that I shall have to inform the police if the possibility that Mr. Jarrell's gun was used to kill Mr. Eber becomes a probability. It is nearer a probability, in my mind, now than it was an hour ago —now that all of you have denied taking the gun, for one of you did take it."

His eyes went over them again. "When I speak to a man, or a woman, I like to look at him, but I speak now to the one who took the gun, and I can't look at him because I don't know who he is.

So, speaking to him, I close my eyes." He closed them. "If you know where the gun is, and it is innocent, all you have to do is let it reappear. You need not expose yourself. Merely put it somewhere in sight, where it will soon be seen. If it does not appear soon I shall be compelled to make one of two assumptions."

He raised a finger, his eyes still closed. "One. That it is no longer in your possession and is not accessible. If it left your possession before Eber was killed it may have been used to kill him, and the police will have to be informed. If it left your possession after he was killed and you know it wasn't used to kill him—and, as I said, that can be demonstrated—you will then have to expose yourself, but that will be a trifle since it will establish the innocence of the gun. I don't suppose Mr. Jarrell will prosecute for theft."

Another finger went up. "Two. My alternative assumption will be that you killed Eber. In that case you certainly will not produce the gun even if it is still available to you; and every hour that I delay telling the police what I know is a disservice to the law you and I live under."

He opened his eyes. "There it is, ladies and gentlemen. As you see, it is exigent. There is nothing more to say at the moment. I shall await notice that the gun has been found, the sooner the better. The conference is ended, except for one of you. Mr. Foote has suggested that the record of the man who took Mr. Eber's place, Mr. Alan Green, should be looked into, and I agree. Mr. Green, you will please remain. For the rest of you, that is all for the present. I should apologize for a default in hospitality. That refreshment table is equipped and I should have invited you. I do so now. Archie?"

Orrie Archie Cather Goodwin said, "I asked them, Mr. Wolfe," and got up and headed for the table. Roger Foote was there as soon as he was, so the bourbon would get a ride. Thinking it might be expected that my nerves needed a bracer, since my record was going to be probed, I went and asked Mr. Goodwin for some scotch and water. The others had left their chairs, but apparently not for refreshment. Jarrell and Trella were standing at Wolfe's desk, conversing with him, and Corey Brigham stood behind them, kibitzing. Nora Kent stood at the end of the couch, sending her sharp gray eyes around. Seeing that Wyman and Susan were going, I caught Orrie's eye and he made for the hall to let them out.

I took a sip of refreshment, stepped over to Roger Foote, and told him, "Many thanks for the plug."

"Nothing personal. It just occurred to me. What do I know about you? Nothing. Neither does anybody else." He went to the table and reached for the bourbon bottle.

I had been considering whether I should tackle Lois or let bad enough alone, and was saved the trouble when she called to me and I went to her, over by the big globe.

"We pretend we're looking at the globe," she said. "That's called covering. I just wanted to tell you that the minute I saw that character, when he let us in, I remembered. One thing I've got to ask, does my father know who you are?"

She was pointing at Venezuela on the globe, and I was looking at her hand, which I knew was nice to hold to music. Obviously there was no chance of bulling it; she knew; and there wasn't time to take Wolfe's line with Nora and set it up as an assumption. So I turned the globe and pointed to Madagascar.

"Yes," I said, "he knows."

"Because," she said, "he may not be the flower of knighthood, but he's my father, and besides, he pays my bills. You wouldn't string me, would you?"

"I'd love to string you, but not on this. Your father knew I was Archie Goodwin when he took me to his place Monday afternoon. When he wants you and the others to know I suppose he'll tell you."

"He never tells me anything." She pointed to Ceylon. "If there was anything I wanted to blackmail you for, this would be wonderful, but if I ever do yearn for anything from you I would want it to pour out, just gush out from an uncontrollable passion. I wouldn't meet you halfway, because that wouldn't be maidenly, but I wouldn't run. It's too bad—"

"You coming, Lois?"

It was Roger Foote, with Nora beside him. Lois said the globe was the biggest one she had ever seen and she hated to leave it, and Roger said he would buy her one, what with I don't know, and they went. I stayed with the globe. Jarrell and Trella were still with Wolfe, but Corey Brigham had gone. Then they left too, ignoring me, and while Orrie was in the hall seeing them out I went and sat on one of the yellow chairs, the one Susan had occupied.

I cringed. "Very well, sir," I said, "you want my record. I was born in the maternity ward of the Ohio State Penitentiary on Christmas Eve, eighteen sixty-five. After they branded me I was taken—"

"Shut up."

"Yes, sir." I got up and went to my own chair as Orrie appeared. "Do you want my opinion?"

"No."

"You're quite welcome. One will get you twenty that the gun will not be found."

He grunted.

I replied, "Lois has remembered who I am, and I had to tell her that her father knows. She won't spread it. One will get you thirty that the gun will not be found."

He grunted.

I replied, "To be practical about it, the only real question is how soon we call Cramer, and I'm involved in that as much as you are. More. One will get you fifty that the gun will not be found."

He grunted.

9

At nine-thirty Saturday morning, having breakfasted with Lois and Susan and Wyman, more or less—more or less, because we hadn't synchronized—I made a tour of the lower floor of the duplex, all except the library and the kitchen. It wasn't a search; I didn't look under cushions or in drawers. Wolfe's suggestion had been to put the gun at some spot where it would soon be seen, so I just covered the territory and used my eyes. I certainly didn't expect to see it, having offered odds of fifty to one, and so wasn't disappointed.

There was no good reason why I shouldn't have slept in my own bed Friday night, but Wolfe had told Jarrell (with Trella there) that he would send his secretary back to him as soon as he was through asking him about his past. I hadn't really minded, since even a fifty-to-one shot has been known to deliver, and if one of them sneaked the gun out into the open that very evening it would be a pleasure to be the one to discover it, or even to be there when someone else discovered it. So I made a tour before I went up to bed.

My second tour, Saturday morning, was more thorough, and when, having completed it, I entered the reception hall on my way to the front door, Steck was there.

He spoke. "Could I help you, sir? Were you looking for something?"

I regarded him. What if he was a loyal and devoted old retainer? What if he had been afraid his master was in a state of mind where he might plug somebody, and had pinched the gun to remove temptation? Should I take him up to my room for a confidential talk? Should I take him down to Wolfe? It would make a horse laugh if we unloaded to Cramer, and our client and his family were put through the wringer, and it turned out that the gun had been under Steck's mattress all the time. I regarded him, decided it would have to be referred to a genius like Wolfe, and told him that I was beyond help, I was just fidgety, but thanked him all the same. When he saw I was going out he opened the door for me, trying not to look relieved.

Whenever possible I go out every morning, some time between nine and eleven, when Wolfe is up in the plant rooms, to loosen up my legs and get a lungful of exhaust fumes, but it wasn't just through force of habit that I was headed outdoors. An assistant district attorney, probably accompanied by a dick, was coming to see Jarrell at eleven o'clock, to get more facts about James L. Eber, deceased, and Jarrell and I had agreed that it was just as well for me to be off the premises.

Walking the thirty blocks to the *Gazette* building, I dropped in to ask Lon Cohen if the Giants were going to move to San Francisco. I also asked him for the latest dope on the Eber murder, and he asked me who Wolfe's client was. Neither of us got much satisfaction. As far as he knew, the cops were making a strenuous effort to turn up a lead and serve the cause of justice, and as far as I knew, Wolfe was fresh out of clients but if and when I had anything good enough for the front page I would let him know. From there, having loosened up my legs, I took a taxi to 35th Street.

Wolfe had came down from the plant rooms and was at his desk, dictating to Orrie, at my desk. They took time out to greet me, which I appreciated, from two busy men with important matters to attend to like writing to Lewis Hewitt to tell him that a cross of Cochlioda noezliana with Odontoglossum armainvillierense was going to bloom and inviting him to come and look at it. Not having had my usual forty minutes with the morning *Times* at breakfast, I got it from the rack and went to the couch, and had finished the front-page headlines and the sports pages when the doorbell rang. The man seated at my desk should have answered it, but he was being told by Wolfe how to spell a word which should have been no problem, so I went.

One glance through the panel, at a husky specimen in a gray suit, a pair of broad shoulders, and a big red face, was sufficient. I went and put the chain bolt on, opened the door to the two inches allowed by the chain, and spoke through the crack. "Good morning. I haven't seen you for months. You're looking fine."

"Come on, Goodwin, open up."

"I'd like to, but you know how it is. Mr. Wolfe is engaged, teaching a man how to spell. What do I tell him?"

"Tell him I want to know why he changed your name to Alan Green and got you a job as secretary to Otis Jarrell."

"I've been wondering about that myself. Make yourself comfortable while I go ask him. Of course if he doesn't know, there's no point in your bothering to come in."

Leaving the door open to the chain, not to be rude, I went to the office and crossed to Wolfe's desk. "Sorry to interrupt, but Inspector Cramer wants to know why you changed my name to Alan Green and got me a job as secretary to Otis Jarrell. Shall I tell him?"

He scowled at me. "How did he find out? That Jarrell girl?"

"No. I don't know. If you have to blame it on a woman, take Nora Kent, but I doubt it."

"Confound it. Bring him in."

I returned to the front, removed the chain, and swung the door open. "He's delighted that you've come. So am I."

He may not have caught the last three words, as he had tossed his hat on the bench and was halfway down the hall. By the time I had closed the door and made it back to the office he was at the red leather chair. Orrie wasn't visible. He hadn't come to the hall, so Wolfe must have sent him to the front room. That door was closed. I went to my chair and was myself again.

Cramer, seated, was speaking. "Do you want me to repeat it? What I told Goodwin?"

"That shouldn't be necessary." Wolfe, having swiveled to face him, was civil but not soapy. "But I am curious, naturally, as to how you got the information. Has Mr. Goodwin been under surveillance?"

"No, but a certain address on Fifth Avenue has been, since eight o'clock this morning. When Goodwin was seen coming out, at a quarter to ten, and recognized, and it was learned from the man in the lobby that the man who had just gone out was named Alan Green and he was Otis Jarrell's secretary, and it was reported to me, I wasn't just curious. If I had just been curious I would have had Sergeant Stebbins phone you. I've come myself."

"I commend your zeal, Mr. Cramer. And it's pleasant to see you again, but I'm afraid my wits are a little dull this morning. You must bear with me. I didn't know that taking a job under an alias is an offense against society and therefore a proper subject for police inquiry. And by you? The head of the Homicide Squad?"

"I ought to be able to bear with you, I've had enough practice. But by God, it's just about all I—" He stopped abruptly, got a cigar from a pocket, rolled it between his palms, stuck it in his mouth, and clamped his teeth on it. He never lit one. The mere sight of Wolfe, and the sound of his voice, with the memories they recalled, had stirred his blood, and it needed calming down.

He took the cigar from his mouth. "You're bad enough," he said, under control, "when you're not sarcastic. When you are, you're the hardest man to take in my jurisdiction. Do you know that a man named Eber was shot, murdered, in his apartment on Forty-ninth Street Thursday afternoon? Day before yesterday?"

"Yes, I know that."

"Do you know that for five years he had been Otis Jarrell's secretary and had recently been fired?"

"Yes, I know that too. Permit me to comment that this seems a little silly. I read newspapers."

"Okay, but it's in the picture, and you want the picture.

According to information received, Goodwin's first appearance at Jarrell's place was on Monday afternoon, three days before Eber was killed. Jarrell told the man in the lobby that his name was Alan Green and that he was going to live there. And he has been. Living there." His head jerked to me. "That right, Goodwin?"

"Right," I admitted.

"You've been there since Monday, under an assumed name, as Jarrell's secretary?"

"Right—with time out for errands. I'm not there now."

"You're damn right you're not. You're not there now because you knew someone was coming from the DA's office to see Jarrell and you didn't want to be around. Right?"

"Fifth Amendment."

"Nuts. That's for Reds and racketeers, not for clowns like you." He jerked back to Wolfe, decided his blood needed calming again, stuck the cigar in his mouth, and chewed on it.

He removed it. "That's the picture, Wolfe," he said. "We've got no lead that's worth a damn on who killed Eber. Naturally our best source on his background and his associates has been Jarrell and the others at his place. Eber not only worked there, he lived there. We've got a lot of facts about him, but nothing with a motive for murder good enough to fasten on. We're just about ready to decide we're not going to get anywhere with Jarrell and that bunch and we'd better concentrate on other possibilities, and then this. Goodwin. Goodwin and you."

His eyes narrowed, then he realized that was the wrong attitude and opened them. "Now it's different. If a man like Otis Jarrell hires you for something so important that you're even willing to get along without Goodwin so he can go and stay there under an assumed name, with a job as Jarrell's secretary, and if the man who formerly had the job gets murdered three days later, do you expect me to believe there's no connection?"

"I'm not sure I follow you, Mr. Cramer. Connection between what?"

"Like hell you don't follow me! Between whatever Jarrell hired you for and the murder!"

Wolfe nodded. "I assumed you meant that, but I am wary of assumptions. You should be too. You are assuming that Mr.

Jarrell hired me. Have you grounds for that? Isn't it possible that someone else hired me, and I imposed Mr. Goodwin on Mr. Jarrell's household to get information for my client?"

That settled it. Ever since I had opened the door a crack and got Cramer's message for Wolfe, I had been thinking that Wolfe would probably decide that the cat was too scratchy to hang onto, and would let Cramer take it, but not now. Jarrell's gun would not be mentioned. The temptation to teach Cramer to be wary of assumptions had been irresistible.

Cramer was staring. "By God," he said. "Who's your client? No. I'd never pry that out of you. But you can tell me this: was Eber your client?"

"No, sir."

"Then is it Jarrell or isn't it? Is Jarrell your client?"

Wolfe was having a picnic. "Mr. Cramer. I am aware that if I have information relevant to the crime you're investigating I am bound to give it to you; but its relevance may be established, not by your whim or conjecture, but by an acceptable process of reason. Since you don't know what information I have, and I do, you can't apply that process and it must be left to me. My conclusion is that I have nothing to tell you. I have answered your one question that was clearly relevant, whether Mr. Eber was my client. You will of course ask Mr. Jarrell if he is my client, telling him his secretary is my confidential assistant, Archie Goodwin; I can't prevent that. I'm sorry you gave yourself the trouble of coming, but your time hasn't been entirely wasted; you have learned that I wasn't working for Mr. Eber."

Cramer looked at me, probably because, for one thing, if he had gone on looking at Wolfe he would have had to get his hands on him; and for another, there was the question whether I might possibly disagree with the conclusion Wolfe had reached through an acceptable process of reason. I met his look with a friendly grin which I hoped wouldn't strike him as sarcastic.

He put the cigar in his mouth and closed his teeth on it, got up, risked another look at Wolfe, not prolonged, turned, and tramped out. I stayed put long enough for him to make it down the hall, then went to see if he had been sore enough to try the old Finnegan on us. He hadn't; he was out, pulling the door shut as he went.

As I stepped back into the office Wolfe snapped at me, "Get Mr. Jarrell."

"The assistant DA is probably still with him."

"No matter, get him."

I went to my desk, dialed, got Nora Kent, and told her that Mr. Wolfe wished to speak to Mr. Jarrell. She said he was engaged and would call back, and I said the sooner the better because it was urgent. Say two minutes. It wasn't much more than that before the ring came, and Jarrell was on, and Wolfe got at his phone. I stayed at mine.

Jarrell said he had gone to another phone because two men from the district attorney's office were with him, and Wolfe asked, "Have they mentioned Mr. Goodwin or me?"

"No, why should they?"

"They might have. Inspector Cramer of the Homicide Squad was here and just left. The entrance to your address is under surveillance and Mr. Goodwin was recognized when he came out this morning, and it has been learned that he has been there as your secretary since Monday, with Alan Green as his name. Mr. Goodwin told you what would happen if that were disclosed, and it has happened. I gave Mr. Cramer no information whatever except that Mr. Eber was not my client. Of course you—"

"Did you tell him what I hired you for?"

"You're not listening. I said I gave him no information whatever. I didn't even tell him that you hired me, let alone what for. Of course they'll be at you immediately, since they know about Mr. Goodwin. I suggest that you reflect on the situation with care. Whatever you tell them, do not fail to inform me at once. If you admit that you hired me—"

"What the hell, I've got to admit it! You say they know about Goodwin!"

"So they do. But I mentioned to Mr. Cramer the possibility that someone else hired me to send Goodwin there to spy on you. Merely as a possibility. Please understand that I told him nothing."

"I see." Silence. "I'll be damned." Silence. "I'll have to think it over and decide what to say."

"You will indeed. It will probably be best for you to tell them that you hired me on a personal and confidential matter, and leave it at that. But on one point, between you and me, there must be no ambiguity. I am free to disclose what I know about your gun, and its disappearance, at any moment that I think it necessary or desirable. You understand that."

"That's not the way you put it. You said you'd have to report it if the possibility that my gun was used to kill Eber became a probability."

"Yes, but the decision rests with me. I am risking embarrassment and so is Mr. Goodwin. We don't want to lose our licenses. It would have been prudent to tell Mr. Cramer when he was here, but he provoked me."

He hung up and glared at me as if I had done the provoking. I hung up and glared back. "License my eye," I told him. "We're risking eating on the State of New York for one to ten years with time off for good behavior."

"Do you challenge me?" he demanded. "You were present. You have a tongue, heaven knows. Would you have loosened it if I hadn't been here?"

"No," I admitted. "He goes against the grain. He has bad manners. He lacks polish. Look at you for contrast. You are courteous, gracious, tactful, eager to please. What now? I left up there to be out of the way when company came, but now they're on to me. Do I go back?"

He said no, not until we heard further from Jarrell, and I went to the front room to tell Orrie to come and get on with the day's work, and then returned to the couch and the *Times*.

10

The other day I looked up "moot" in the dictionary. The murderer of James L. Eber had just been convicted, and, discussing it, Wolfe and I had got onto the question of whether or not a life would have been saved if he had told Cramer that Saturday morning about Jarrell's gun, and he had said it was moot, and, though I thought I knew the word well enough, I went to the dictionary to check. In spite of the fact that I had taken a position just to give the discussion some spirit, I had to agree with him on that. It was moot all right, and it still is.

The thirty hours from noon Saturday until six o'clock Sunday afternoon were not without events, since even a yawn is an event, but nobody seemed to be getting anywhere, least of all me. Soon after lunch Saturday, at Wolfe's table with him and Orrie, Jarrell phoned to tell us the score. Cramer had gone straight there from our place to join the gathering in the library. Presumably he hadn't started barking, since even an inspector doesn't bark at an Otis Jarrell unless he has to, but he had had questions to which he intended to get answers. Actually he had got only one answered: had Jarrell hired Nero Wolfe to do something? Yes. Plus its rider: had Archie Goodwin, alias Alan Green, come as Jarrell's secretary to do the something Wolfe had been hired for, or to help do it? Yes. That was all. Jarrell had told them that the something was a personal and confidential matter, with no bearing on their investigation, and that therefore they could forget it.

It was a cinch Cramer wouldn't forget it, but evidently he decided that for the present he might as well lump it, for there wasn't a peep out of him during those thirty hours.

I could see no point in Alan Green's getting back into the picture, and apparently Jarrell couldn't either, for he also reported that Alan Green was no more. He was telling the family, and also Corey Brigham, who I was and why, but was leaving the why vague. He had engaged the services of Nero Wolfe on a business matter, and Wolfe had sent me there to collect some facts he needed. He was also telling them I wouldn't be back, but on that Wolfe balked. I was going back, and I was staying until further notice. When Jarrell asked what for, Wolfe said to collect facts. When Jarrell asked what facts, Wolfe said facts that he needed. Jarrell, knowing that if I wasn't let in he would soon be letting Cramer in to ask about a gun, had to take it. When Wolfe had hung up and pushed his phone back I had asked him to give me a list of the facts he needed.

"How the devil can I," he demanded, "when I don't know what they are? If something happens I want you there, and with you there it's more likely to happen. Now that they know who you are, you are a threat, a pinch at their nerves, at least for one of them, and he may be impelled to act."

Since it was May it might have been expected that at least some of them would be leaving town for what was left of the week end, and they probably would have if their nerves weren't being pinched. Perhaps Jarrell had told them to stick around; anyway, they were all at the dinner table Saturday. Their attitude toward me, with my own name back, varied. Roger Foote thought it was a hell of a good joke, his asking Wolfe to investigate my past; he couldn't get over it, and didn't. Trella not only couldn't see the joke; she couldn't see me. Her cooing days were over as far as I was concerned. Wyman didn't visibly react one way or another. Susan went out of her way to indicate that she still regarded me as human. In the lounge at cocktail time she actually came up to me as I was mixing a Bloody Mary for Lois, and said she hoped she wouldn't forget and call me Mr. Green.

"I'm afraid," she added, almost smiling, "that my brain should have more cells. It put you and that name, Alan Green, in a cell together, and now it doesn't know what to do."

I told her it didn't matter what she called me as long as it began with G. I hadn't forgotten that she was supposed to be a snake, or that she had been the only one to bid me welcome, or that she had pulled me halfway across a room on an invisible string. That hadn't happened again, but once was enough. I didn't have her tagged yet, not by any means. As a matter of fact, I was a little surprised to see her and Wyman still there, since Jarrell had accused her of swiping his gun before witnesses. Maybe, I thought, they were staying on just to get that detail settled. Her little mouth in her little oval face could have found it hard to smile, not because it was shy but because it was stubborn.

I had supposed there would be bridge after dinner, but no. Jarrell and Trella had tickets for a show, and Wyman and Susan for another show. Nora Kent was going out, destination unspecified. Roger Foote suggested gin for an hour or so, saying that he had to turn in early because he was going to get up at six in the morning to go to Belmont. I asked what for, since there was no racing on Sunday, and he said he had to go and look at the horses. Declining his gin invitation, I approached Lois. There was no point in my staying in for the evening, since there would be no one there to have their nerves pinched except Roger, and he was soon going to bed, so I told Lois that now that my name was changed it would be both possible and agreeable to take her to the Flamingo Club. She may have had no plans because her week end had been upset, or she may have had plans but took pity on me, or my charm may simply have been too much for her. Anyhow, we went, and got home around two o'clock.

On Sunday it looked at first as if I might do fairly well as a threat. Four of them were at breakfast with me—Wyman, Susan, Lois, and Nora. Jarrell had already had his and gone out somewhere, Roger had gone to look at horses, and I gathered that Trella wasn't up yet. But the future didn't look promising. Nora was going to church and then to the Picasso show at the Modern Museum, apparently to spend the day. Susan was going to church. Wyman went to the side terrace with an armload of Sunday papers. So when Lois said she was going for a walk I said I was too and which way should I head, away from her or with her? She said we could try with and see how it worked. I found that she wouldn't walk in the park, probably on account of squirrels, so we kept to the avenues, Madison and Park. After half an hour she took a taxi to go to have lunch with friends, not named. I was invited to come along, but thought I had better go and see if there was anyone around to be threatened. On the way back I phoned Wolfe to tell him what had happened: nothing. In the reception hall, Steck told me Jarrell wanted me in the library.

He thought he had news, but I wasn't impressed. He had spent an hour at the Penguin Club with an old friend, or at least an old acquaintance, Police Commissioner Kelly, and had been assured that while the district attorney and the police would do their utmost to bring the murderer of Jarrell's former secretary to the bar of justice, there would be no officious prying into Jarrell's private affairs. Respectable citizens deserved to be treated with respect, and would be. Jarrell said he was going to ring Wolfe to tell him about it, and I said that would be fine. I didn't add that Wolfe would be even less impressed than I was. Officious prying would be no name for it if and when they learned about Jarrell's gun.

Having bought a newspaper of my own on the way back, I went to the lounge with it, finding no one there, and caught up with the world, including the latest non-news on the Eber murder. There was no mention of the startling fact that Otis Jarrell's new secretary had turned out to be no other than Nero Wolfe's man Friday,

Saturday, Sunday, Monday, Tuesday, Wednesday, and Thursday, the celebrated detective, Archie Goodwin. Evidently Cramer and the DA weren't going to give us any free publicity until and unless we were involved in murder, a typical small-minded attitude of small men, and it was up to Wolfe's public-relations department, namely me, to do something about it; and besides, I owed Lon Cohen a bone. So I went up to my room and phoned him, and wished I hadn't, since he tried to insist on a hunk of meat with it. I had no sooner hung up than a ring called me to the green phone. It was Assistant District Attorney Mandelbaum, who invited me to appear at his office at three o'clock that afternoon for a little informal chat. I told him I would be delighted, and went down to get some oats, having been informed by Steck that lunch would be at one-thirty.

Lunch wasn't very gay, since there were only three of them there—Jarrell, Wyman, and Susan. Susan said maybe thirty words altogether, as for instance, "Will you have cream, Mr. Goodwin?" When I announced that I would have to leave at two-thirty for an appointment at the district attorney's office, thinking that might pinch a nerve, Wyman merely used a thumb and forefinger to pinch his thin straight nose, whether or not meant as a vulgar insult I couldn't say, and Susan merely said that she supposed talking with an assistant district attorney was nothing for a detective but she would be frightened out of her wits. Jarrell said nothing then, but when we left the table he took me aside and wanted to know. I told him that since the police commissioner had promised that there would be no officious prying into his private affairs there was no problem. I would just tell Mandelbaum that I was part of Mr. Jarrell's private affairs and therefore a clam.

Which I did. Having stopped on the way to phone Wolfe because he always likes to know where I am, I was a little late, arriving in the anteroom at 3:02 p.m., and then I was kept waiting exactly one hour and seventeen minutes. Taken in to Mandelbaum at 4:19, I was in no mood to tell him anything whatever except that he was a little balder and a little plumper than when I had last seen him, but he surprised me. I had expected him to try to bulldoze me, or sugar me, into spilling something about my assignment at Jarrell's, but he didn't touch on that at all. Apparently Jarrell's session with the commissioner had had some effect. After apologizing for keeping me waiting, Mandelbaum wanted to know what I had seen and heard when I entered the studio at noon on Wednesday and found James L. Eber there with Mrs. Wyman Jarrell. Also whether I had seen Eber with anyone else or had heard anyone say anything about him.

Since that was about Eber and his movements and contacts the day before he was killed, I couldn't very well say that I concluded by an acceptable process of reasoning that it was irrelevant, so I obliged. I even gave him verbatim the words that had passed among Eber and Susan and me. He spent some time trying to get me to remember other words, comments that had been made in my hearing about Eber and his appearance there that day, but on that I passed. I had heard a few, chiefly at the lunch table, and had reported them to Wolfe, but none of them had indicated any desire or intention to kill him, and I saw no point in supplying them for the record.

It was for the record. A stenographer was present, and after Mandelbaum finished with me I had another wait while a statement was typed for me to sign. Reading it, I could find nothing that needed changing, so I signed it "Archie Goodwin, alias Alan Green." I thought that might as well be on record too.

Back at my threatening base at twenty minutes to six, I found that bridge was under way in the lounge, but only one table: Jarrell, Trella, Wyman, and Nora. Steck informed me, when asked, that neither Lois nor Roger had returned, and that Mrs. Wyman Jarrell was in the studio. Proceeding down the corridor and finding the studio door open, I entered.

The only light was from the corridor and the television screen. Susan was in the same chair as before, in the same spot. Since she was concentrating on the screen, with the discussion panel, "We're Asking You," it wasn't much of a setup from a professional standpoint, but personally it might be interesting. The conditions were precisely the same as formerly, and I wanted to see. If I felt another trance coming on I could make a dash for the door and safety. Not to cut her view of the screen, I circled behind her chair and took the one on the other side.

I would have liked to look at her, her profile, instead of the screen, giving her magic every chance, but she might have misunderstood, so I kept my eyes on "We're Asking You" clear to the end. I didn't learn much. They were asking what to do about extrabright children, and since I didn't have any and intended to stay as far away as I could from those I had seen and heard on TV and in the movies, I wasn't concerned.

When they got it settled and the commercial started Susan turned to me. "Shall I leave it on for the news?"

"Sure, might as well, I haven't heard the baseball scores."

I never did hear them, not on that TV set. It was Bill Brundage, the one who has the trick of rolling his eyes up, pretending he's looking for a word, when it's right there in front of him and everybody knows it. I listened with one ear while he gave us the latest on the budget, Secretary Dulles, a couple of Senatorial investigations, and so forth, and then suddenly he got both ears.

"The body of Corey Brigham, well-known socialite and man-about-town, was found this afternoon in a car parked on Thirty-ninth Street near Seventh Avenue. According to the police, he had been shot in the chest. The body was on the floor of the car in front of the rear seat, covered with a rug. It was discovered when a boy saw the toe of a shoe at the edge of the rug and notified a policeman. The windows of the car were closed and there was no gun in the car. Mr. Corey Brigham lived at the Churchill Towers. He was a bachelor and was a familiar figure in society circles and in the amusement world."

Susan's fingers had gripped my arm, with more muscle than I would have guessed she had. Apparently just realizing it, she took her hand back and said, "I beg your pardon." Her voice was low, as always, and Bill Brundage was talking, but I caught it, and that's what she said. I reached across her lap to the chair on the other side and flipped the switch on the control box.

"Corey Brigham?" she said. "He said Corey Brigham, didn't he?"

"He certainly did." I got up, went to the door, turned on lights, and came back. "I'm going to tell Mr. Jarrell. Do you want to come?"

"What?" Her face tilted up. It was shocked. "Oh, of course, tell them. You tell them."

Evidently she wasn't coming, so I left her. Going along the corridor I was thinking that the news might not be news to one of them. It was even possible that it hadn't been news to Susan. At the card table in the lounge they were in the middle of a hand, and I went and stood by until the last trick was raked in.

"I wasted my queen, damn it," Jarrell said. He turned to me. "Anything new, Goodwin?"

"Not from the district attorney," I told him. "Just routine, about the last time I saw Jim Eber—and for me the only time. Now he'll be asking about the last time I saw Corey Brigham. You too. All of you."

I had three of their faces: Jarrell, Trella, and Wyman. Nora was shuffling. None of them told me anything. There was no point in prolonging it, so I went on. "Something new on TV just now. The body of Corey Brigham has been found in a parked car. Shot. Murdered."

Jarrell said, "Good God. No!" Nora stopped shuffling and her head jerked to me. Trella's blue eyes stretched at me. Wyman said, "You wouldn't be pulling a gag, would you?"

"No gag. Your wife was there, I mean in the studio. She heard it."

Wyman shoved his chair back and was up and gone. Jarrell demanded, "Found in a car? Whose car?"

"I don't know. For what I do know I'll give you the broadcast verbatim. I'm good at that." I did so, not trying to copy Bill Brundage's delivery, just his words. At the end I added, "Now you know all I know."

Trella spoke. "You said he was murdered. That didn't say murder. He might have shot himself."

I shook my head. "No gun in the car."

"Anyway," Nora said, "he wouldn't have got under a rug. If Corey Brigham was going to shoot himself he would do it in the dining room of the Penguin Club." It wasn't as mean as it reads; she was merely stating a fact.

"He had no family," Trella said. "I guess we were his closest friends. Shouldn't you do something, Otis?"

"You don't need me," I said. "I'm sorry I had to break up your game." To Jarrell: "I'll be with Mr. Wolfe, in case."

"No." He was emphatic. "I want you here."

"You'll soon be too busy here to bother with me. First your former secretary, and now your friend Brigham. I'm afraid that calls for officious prying, and I'd rather not be in the way."

I moved, and I didn't mosey. I was surprised that someone hadn't already come, since they had got sufficiently interested in the Jarrells to collect miscellaneous facts and the collection must have included the name of Corey Brigham. The one who came might be Lieutenant Rowcliff—it was his kind of errand; and while I liked nothing better than twisting Rowcliff's ear, I wasn't in the humor for it at the moment. I wanted a word with Wolfe before twisting anybody's ear, even Rowcliff's. So I didn't mosey, leaving the premises, crossing the avenue, and getting a taxi headed downtown.

When I entered the office Wolfe was there alone, no Orrie on Sunday, and one glance at him was enough. He had a book in his hand, with a finger inserted to keep his place, but he wasn't reading, and a good caption for a picture of the face he turned to me would have been *The Gathering Storm*.

"So," I said, crossing to his desk, "I see I don't bring news. You've already heard it."

"I have," he growled. "Where were you?"

"Watching television with Susan. We heard it together. I notified Jarrell and his wife and Wyman and Nora Kent. Lois and Roger Foote weren't there. Nobody screamed. Then I beat it to come and get instructions. If I had stayed I wouldn't have known whether the time has come to let the cat out or not. Do you?"

"No."

"Do you mean you don't know or the time hasn't come?"

"Both."

I swiveled my chair around and sat. "That's impossible. If I said a thing like that you'd say I had a screw loose, only you never use that expression. I'll put it in its simplest terms. Do you wish to speak to Cramer?"

"No. I'll speak to Mr. Cramer only when it is requisite." The gathering storm had cleared some. "Archie. I'm glad you came. I confess I needed you, to say no to. Now that I have said it, I can read." He opened the book. "I will speak to no one on the phone,

and no one will enter my door, until I have more facts." His eyes
went to the book and he was reading.

I was glad he was glad I had come, but I wasn't glad, if I make
myself clear. I might as well have stayed up there and twisted
Rowcliff's ear.

11

I slept in my own bed that night for the first time in nearly a week.

That was a very interesting period, Sunday evening and part of
Monday. I suppose you noticed what Wolfe said, that he would
see no one and hear no one until he had more facts. Exactly how
he thought he would get facts, under the conditions he imposed,
seeing or hearing no one, I couldn't say. Maybe by ESP or holding a séance. However, by noon on Monday it had become evident
that he hadn't meant it that way. What he had really meant was
that he wanted no facts. If he had seen a fact coming he would have
shut his eyes, and if he had heard one coming he would have stuck
fingers in his ears.

So it was a very interesting period. There he was, a practicing
private detective with no other source of income except selling a
few orchid plants now and then, with a retainer of ten grand in
cash in the safe, with a multi-millionaire client with a bad itch,
with a fine fat fee in prospect if he got a move on and did some
first-class detecting; and he was afraid to stay in the same room
with me for fear I would tell him something. He wouldn't talk with
Jarrell on the phone. He wouldn't turn on the radio or television.
I even suspected that he didn't read the *Times* Monday morning,
though I can't swear to that because he reads the *Times* at breakfast, which is taken up to his room by Fritz on a tray. He was a
human ostrich with his head stuck in the sand, in spite of the fact
that he resembles an ostrich in physique less than any other human
I know of with the possible exception of Jackie Gleason.

All there was to it, he was in a panic. He was scared stiff that
any minute a fact might come bouncing in that would force him

to send me down to Cramer bearing gifts, and there was practically nothing on earth he wouldn't rather do, even eating ice cream with cantaloupe or putting horseradish on oysters.

I understood how he felt, and I even sympathized with him. On the phone with Jarrell, both Sunday evening and Monday morning, I did my best to string him along, telling him that Wolfe was sitting tight, which he was, God knows, and explaining why it was better for me to be out of the way, at least temporarily. It wasn't too bad. Lieutenant Rowcliff had called on the Jarrell family, as I had expected, but hadn't been too nasty about the coincidence that two of Jarrell's associates, his former secretary and a close friend, had got it within a week. He had been nasty, of course—Rowcliff would be nasty to Saint Peter if he ever got near him; but he hadn't actually snarled.

But although I sympathized with Wolfe, I'm not a genius like him, and if I was sliding into a hole too deep to crawl out of I wanted to know about it in time to get a haircut and have my pants pressed before my appearance in the line-up. Of the half a dozen possible facts that could send me over the edge there was one in particular that I wanted very much to get a line on, but it wasn't around. None of the newscasts mentioned it, Sunday night or Monday morning. It wasn't in the Monday morning papers. Lon Cohen didn't have it. There were four guys—one at headquarters, one on the DA's staff, and two on Homicide—for whom I had done favors in the past, who could have had it and who might have obliged me, but with two murders in the stew it was too risky to ask them.

So I was still factless when, ten minutes before noon, the phone rang and I got an invitation to call at the DA's office at my earliest convenience. Wolfe was still up in the plant rooms. He always came down at eleven o'clock, but hadn't shown that morning—for fear, as I said, that I would tell him something. I buzzed him on the house phone to tell him where I was going, went out and walked to Ninth Avenue, and took a taxi to Leonard Street.

That time I was kept waiting only a few minutes before I was taken in to Mandelbaum. He was polite, as usual, getting to his feet to shake hands. I was only a private detective, true, but as far as he knew I had committed neither a felony nor a misdemeanor, and the only way an assistant DA can get the "assistant" removed from his title is to have it voted off, making it DA, and I was a voter. The chair for me at the end of his desk was of course placed so I was facing a window.

What he wanted from me was the same as before, things I had seen and heard at Jarrell's place, but this time concentrating on Corey Brigham instead of James L. Eber. I had to concede that that had now become relevant, and there was more ground to cover since Brigham had been there for dinner and bridge on Monday, and again on Wednesday, and also I might have heard comments about him at other times. Mandelbaum was patient, and thorough, and didn't try to be tricky. He did double back a lot, but doubling back has been routine for so many centuries that you can't call it a trick. I didn't mention one of my contacts with Brigham, the conference at Wolfe's office Friday afternoon, and to my surprise he didn't either. I would have thought they would have dug that up by now, but apparently not.

After he told the stenographer to go and type the statement, and she went, I stood up. "It will take her quite a while," I said. "I have to run a couple of errands, and I'll drop in later and sign it. If you don't mind."

"Quite all right. Certainly. If you make it today. Say by five o'clock."

"Oh, sure." I turned to go, and turned back, and grinned at him. "By the way, you may have noticed that I didn't live up to my reputation for wisecracks."

"Yes, I noticed that. Maybe you're running out."

"I hope not. I'll do better next time. I guess my mind was too busy with something I had just heard—about the bullets."

"What bullets?"

"Why, the two bullets. Haven't you got that yet? That the bullet that killed Eber and the one that killed Brigham were fired by the same gun?"

"I thought that was—" He stopped. "Where did you hear that?"

I gave him another grin. "I know, it's being saved. Don't worry, I won't slip it out—I may not even tell Mr. Wolfe. But it won't keep long, it's too hot. The guy who told me, it was burning his tongue, and he knows me."

"Who was it? Who told you?"

"I *think* it was Commissioner Kelly. There's a wisecrack, I seem to be recovering. I suppose I shouldn't have mentioned it. Sorry. I'll be in to sign the statement before five." I was going. He called after me, wanting to know who had told me, but I said I couldn't remember, and went.

So the fact was a fact, and I had it. I hadn't risked anything. If it had turned out not to be a fact, and his reaction would have shown it, it could have been that someone had been stringing me, and of course I wouldn't have remembered who. Okay, I had it. If Wolfe had known what I was bringing home with me he would probably have locked himself in his room and not answered the phone, and I would have had to yell through the door.

He had just sat down to lunch—red snapper filets baked in butter and lemon juice and almonds—so I had to hold it. Even without the rule that business was taboo at the table, I wouldn't have had the heart to ruin his meal. But I still might want time to get a haircut and have my pants pressed, so as soon as we had crossed to the office and coffee had been poured I spoke. "I hate to bring it up right after lunch, but I think you ought to know. We're out of the frying pan. We're in the fire. At least that is my opinion."

He usually takes three little sips of coffee at its hottest before putting the cup down, but that time, knowing my tones of voice, he took only two.

"Opinion?"

"Yes, sir. It may be only that because it's an inference. For more than an hour Mandelbaum asked me what I had seen and heard from, by, to, and about Corey Brigham. I said I'd drop in later to sign the statement, got up to go, and said something. So you can form your own opinion, I'll give it to you."

I did so. His frown at the start was a double-breasted scowl at the end. He said nothing, he just scowled. It isn't often that his feelings are too strong for words.

"If you want to," I said, "you can be sore at me for fishing it up. If I hadn't worked that on him it would have been another day, possibly two, before you had to face it. But you can be sore and use your mind at the same time, I've seen you, and it looks to me as if a mind is needed. I'm assuming that your opinion is the same as mine."

He snorted. "Opinion? Bah. He might as well have certified it."

"Yes, sir."

"He's a simpleton. He should have known you were gulling him."

"Yes, sir. You can be sore at him."

"Soreness won't help. Nor will it help to use my mind—supposing that I have one. This is disaster. There is only one forlorn issue to raise: whether we should verify it before we act, and if so how."

"If you had been there I doubt if you would think it was necessary. If you could have seen his face when he said 'I thought that was—' and chopped it off."

"No doubt. He's a simpleton."

He flattened his palms on his desk and stared into space. That didn't look promising. It didn't mean he was using his mind; when he uses his mind he leans back and closes his eyes, and when he's hard at it his lips go in and out. So he wasn't working. He was merely getting set to swallow a pill that would taste bad even after it was down and dissolved. It took him a full three minutes.

Then he transferred his palms to the chair arms and spoke. "Very well. Your notebook. A letter to Mr. Jarrell, to be delivered at once by messenger. It might be best to take it yourself, to make sure he gets it without delay."

He took a breath. "Dear Mr. Jarrell. I enclose herewith my check for ten thousand dollars, returning the retainer you paid me in that amount for which I gave you a receipt. My outlay for expenses has not been large and I shall not bill you.

"Paragraph. A circumstance has transpired which makes it necessary for me to report to the proper authority some of the information I have acquired while acting on your behalf, particularly the disappearance of your Bowdoin thirty-eight revolver. Not being at liberty to specify the circumstance, I will say only that it compels me to take this step in spite of my strong inclination against it. I shall take it later this afternoon, after you have received this letter and the enclosure.

"Paragraph. I assume, naturally, that in this situation you will no longer desire my services and that our association ceases forthwith. In the unlikely event that you—"

He stopped short and I raised my eyes from the notebook. His lips were clamped tight and a muscle at the side of his neck was twitching. He was having a fit.

"No," he said. "I will not. Tear it up."

I hadn't cared much for it myself. I put the pen down, ripped two pages from the notebook, tore them across three times, and dropped them in the wastebasket.

"Get Mr. Cramer," he said.

I cared for that even less. Apparently he had decided it was too ticklish to wait even a few hours and was going to let go even before notifying the client. Of course that wasn't unethical, with two murders sizzling, but it was rather unindomitable. I would have liked to take a stand, but in the first place he was in no mood for one of my stands, and in the second place the only alternative was the letter to Jarrell and that had been torn up. So I got Cramer, who, judging from his tone, was in a mood too. He told Wolfe he could give him a minute.

"That may do," Wolfe said. "You may remember our conversation Saturday. Day before yesterday."

"Yeah, I remember it. What about it?"

"I said then that if I have reason to think I have information relevant to the crime you're investigating I am bound to give it to you. I now suspect that I have such information but I want to make sure. To do so I must proceed on the basis of knowledge that has come to me in a peculiar manner and I don't know if I can rely on it. Mr. Goodwin has learned, or thinks he has, that the markings on the bullet which killed Corey Brigham have been compared with those on the bullet which killed James L. Eber, and that they are identical. I can proceed to verify my suspicion only if I accept that as established, and I decided to consult you. Do you advise me to proceed?"

"By God," Cramer said.

"I'm afraid," Wolfe objected, "that I need something more explicit."

"Go to hell and get it there," Cramer advised. "I know where Goodwin got it, from that damn fool at Leonard Street. He wanted us to find out who had leaked it to Goodwin, and we wanted to know exactly what Goodwin had said, and he told us, and we told him if he wanted to know who leaked it to Goodwin just look in a mirror. And now you've got the gall to ask me to verify it. By God. If you've got relevant information about a murder you know where it belongs."

"I do indeed. And I'll soon know whether I have it or not if I proceed on the basis of Mr. Goodwin's news. If and when I have it you'll get it without undue delay. Do you advise me to proceed?"

"Look, Wolfe. Are you listening?"

"Yes, I'm listening."

"Okay, you want my advice. Here it is. Get the written permission of the police commissioner and the mayor too, and then proceed all you want to."

He hung up.

I did too, and swiveled, and spoke. "So that's settled. It was the same gun. And in spite of it, Jarrell's private affairs are still private, or we'd be downtown right now, both of us, and wouldn't get home for dinner. By the way, I apologize. I thought you were going to cough it up."

"I am, confound it. I'll have to. But not until I get the satisfaction of a gesture. Get Mr. Jarrell."

"Where he can talk?"

"Yes."

That took a little doing. Nora Kent answered and said he was on another phone, long distance, and also someone was with him, and I told her to have him call Wolfe for a private conversation as soon as possible. While we waited Wolfe looked around for something to take his mind off his misery, settled on the big globe, and got up and walked over to it. Presumably he was picking a spot to head for, some remote island or one of the poles, if he decided to lam. When the phone rang and I told him it was Jarrell he took his time getting to it.

"Mr. Jarrell? I have in my hand a letter which Mr. Goodwin has just typed, dictated by me, which I intended to send you at once by messenger, but on second thought I'm going to read it to you first. Here it is."

He read it. My notes were in the wastebasket, but my memory is good too, and not a word was changed. It was just as he had dictated it. He even finished the last sentence, which he had left hanging: " 'In the unlikely event that you wish me to continue to act for you, let me know at once. Sincerely.' That's the letter. It occurs to me—"

"You can't do that! What's the circumstance?"

"No, sir. As I said in the letter, I'm not at liberty to reveal it, at least not in a letter, and certainly not on the telephone. But it occurs—"

"Get this straight, Wolfe. If you give anybody information about my private affairs that you got working for me in a confidential capacity, you'll be sorry for it as long as you live!"

"I'm already sorry. I'm sorry I ever saw you, Mr. Jarrell. Let me finish, please. It occurs to me that there is a chance, however slim, that a reason can be found for ignoring the circumstance. I doubt it, but I'm willing to try. When I dictated the letter I intended to ask Mr. Cramer to visit me here at six o'clock, three hours from now. I'll postpone it on one condition, that you come at that hour and bring with you everyone who was here on Friday—except Mr. Brigham, who is dead—with the—"

"What for? What good will that do?"

"If you'll let me finish. With the understanding that you stay, all of you, until I am ready to adjourn, and that I will insist on answers to any questions I ask. I can't compel answers, but I can insist, and I may learn more from refusals to answer than from the answers I get. That's the condition. Will you come?"

"What do you want to ask about? They have already told you they didn't take my gun!"

"And you have told me that you know your daughter-in-law took it. Anyway, one of them lied, and I told them so. You'll know what I want to ask about when you hear me. Will you come?"

He balked for another five minutes, among other things demanding to know what the circumstance was that had made Wolfe write the letter, but only because he was used to being at the other end of the whip and it was a new experience for him. He had no choice and knew it.

Wolfe hung up, shook his head like a bull trying to chase a fly, and rang for beer.

12

Wolfe started it off with a bang. He surveyed them with the air of a judge about to impose a stiff one, and spoke in a tone that was meant to be offensive and succeeded.

"There is nothing to be crafty about so I won't try. When you were here on Friday my main purpose was to learn which of you had taken Mr. Jarrell's gun; today it is to learn which of you used it to kill Mr. Eber and Mr. Brigham. I am convinced that one of you did. First I'll— Don't interrupt me!"

He glared at Jarrell, but it was more the voice than the glare that stopped Jarrell with only two words out. Wolfe doesn't often bellow, and almost never at anyone but Cramer or me, but when he does he means it. Having corked the client, who was in the red leather chair, he gave the others the glare. In front were Susan, Wyman, Trella, and Lois, as before. With Brigham no longer available and me back where I belonged, there were only two in the rear, Nora Kent and Roger Foote.

"I will not be interrupted." It was as positive as the bellow, though not so loud. "I have no more patience for you people— including you, Mr. Jarrell. Especially you. First I'll explain why I am convinced that one of you is a murderer. To do so I'll have to disclose a fact that the police have discovered but are keeping to themselves. If they learn that I've told you about it and are annoyed, then they'll be annoyed. I am past regard for trivialities. The fact is that the bullets that killed Eber and Brigham came from the same gun. That, Mr. Jarrell, is the circumstance I spoke of on the phone."

"How do—"

"Don't interrupt. The technical basis of the fact is of course a comparison of the bullets in the police laboratory. How I learned it is not material. So much for the fact; now for my conclusion from it. The bullets are thirty-eights; the gun that was taken from Mr. Jarrell's desk was a thirty-eight. On Friday I appealed to all of you to help me find Mr. Jarrell's gun, and told you how, if it was innocent, it could be recovered with no stigma for anyone. Surely, if it was innocent, one of you would have acted on that appeal, but you didn't, and it was therefore a permissible conjecture that the gun had been used to kill Eber, but only a conjecture. Now it is no longer a conjecture; it has reached the status of a reasonable assumption. For Brigham was killed by a bullet from the gun that killed Eber, and those two men were both closely associated with you people. Eber lived with you for five years, and Brigham was in your familiar circle. Not only that, they were both concerned in the matter which I was hired to investigate one week ago today, the matter which took Mr. Goodwin there—"

"That'll do! You know what—"

"Don't interrupt!" It was close to a bellow again. "The matter which took Mr. Goodwin there under another name. I need not unfold that matter; enough that it was both grave and exigent, and that both Eber and Brigham were involved in it. So consider a hypothesis: that those two men were killed by some outsider with his own private motive, and it is merely a chain of coincidences that they were both in your circle, that the gun was the same caliber as Mr. Jarrell's, that Mr. Jarrell's gun was taken by one of you the day before Eber was killed, and that in spite of my appeal the gun has not been found. If you can swallow that hypothesis, I can't. I reject it, and I conclude that one of you is a murderer. That is our starting point."

"Just a minute." It was Wyman. His thin nose looked thinner, and the deep creases in his brow looked deeper. "That may be your starting point, but it's not mine. Your man Goodwin was there. What for? All this racket about a stolen gun—what if he took it? That's your kind of stunt, and his too, and of course my father was in on it. That's *my* starting point."

Wolfe didn't waste a bellow on him. He merely shook his head. "No, sir. Apparently you don't know what you're here for. You're here to give me a chance to wriggle out of a predicament. I am desperate. I dislike acting under compulsion in any case, and I abominate being obliged to divulge information about a client's affairs that I have received in confidence. The starting point is my conclusion that one of you is a murderer, not to go on from there to identify the culprit and expose him—that isn't what I was hired for—but to show you the fix I'm in. What I desperately need is not sanction for my conclusion, but plausible ground for rejecting it. I want to impeach it. As for your notion that Mr. Goodwin took the gun, in a stratagem devised by me with your father's knowledge, that is mere drivel and is no credit to your wit. If it had happened that way I would be in no predicament at all; I would produce the gun myself, demonstrate its innocence, and have a good night's sleep."

"If death ever slept," Lois blurted.

Their heads all turned to her. Not, probably, that they expected her to supply anything helpful; they were glad to have an excuse to take their eyes off Wolfe and relieve the strain. They hadn't been exchanging glances. Apparently no one felt like meeting other eyes.

"That's all," Lois said. "What are you all looking at me for? That just came out."

The heads went back to Wolfe. Trella asked, "Am I dumb? Or did you say you want us to prove you're wrong?"

"That's one way of putting it, Mrs. Jarrell. Yes."

"How do we prove it?"

Wolfe nodded. "That's the difficulty. I don't expect you to prove a negative. The simplest way would be to produce the gun, but I've abandoned hope of that. I don't intend to go through the dreary routine of inquiry on opportunity; that would take all night, and checking your answers would take an army a week, and I have no army. But I have gathered from the public reports that Eber died between two o'clock and six o'clock Thursday afternoon, and Brigham died between ten o'clock Sunday morning and three o'clock that afternoon, so it may be possible to exclude one or more of you. Has anyone an alibi for either of those periods?"

"You've stretched the periods," Roger Foote declared. "It's three to five Thursday and eleven to two Sunday."

"I gave the extremes, Mr. Foote. The extremes are the safest. You seem well informed."

"My God, I ought to be. The cops."

"No doubt. You'll soon see much more of them if we don't discredit my conclusion."

"You can start by excluding me," Otis Jarrell said. "Thursday afternoon I had business appointments, three of them, and got home a little before six. Sunday—"

"Were the appointments all at the same place?"

"No. One downtown and two midtown. Sunday morning I was with the police commissioner at the Penguin Club for an hour, from ten-thirty to eleven-thirty, went straight home, was in my library until lunch time at one-thirty, returned to the library and was there until five o'clock. So you can exclude me."

"Pfui." Wolfe was disgusted. "You can't be as fatuous as you sound, Mr. Jarrell. Your Thursday is hopeless, and your Sunday isn't much better. Not only were you loose between the Penguin

Club and your home, but what about the library? Were you alone there?"

"Most of the time, yes. But if I had gone out I would have been seen."

"Nonsense. Is there a rear entrance to your premises?"

"There's a service entrance."

"Then it isn't even worth discussing. A man with your talents and your money, resolved on murder, could certainly devise a way of getting down to the ground without exposure." Wolfe's head moved. "When I invited exclusion by alibis I didn't mean to court inanities. Can any of you furnish invulnerable proof that you must be eliminated for either of those periods?"

"On Sunday," Roger Foote said, "I went to Belmont to look at horses. I got there at nine o'clock and I didn't leave until after five."

"With company? Continuously?"

"No. I was always in sight of somebody, but a lot of different people."

"Then you're no better off than Mr. Jarrell. Does anyone else want to try, now that you know the requirements?"

Apparently nobody did. Wyman and Susan, who were holding hands, looked at each other but said nothing. Trella turned around to look at her brother and muttered something I didn't catch. Lois just sat, and so did Jarrell.

Then Nora Kent spoke. "I want to say something, Mr. Wolfe."

"Go ahead, Miss Kent. You can't make it any worse."

"I'd like to make it better—for me. If you're making an exception of me you haven't said so, and I think you should. I think you should tell them that I came to see you Friday afternoon and what I said."

"You tell them. I'll listen."

But she kept focused on him. "I came right after lunch on Friday. I told you that I had recognized the new secretary as Archie Goodwin as soon as I saw him, and I asked why you had sent him, and whether Mr. Jarrell had hired you or someone else had. I told you that the murder of Jim Eber had made me think I had better try to find out what the situation was. I told you I had discovered that Mr. Jarrell's gun was missing from the drawer of his desk, and that I had just found out that the caliber of the bullet that killed

Jim Eber was the same as Mr. Jarrell's gun. I told you that I wasn't frightened, but I didn't want to just wait and see what happened, and I wanted to hire you to protect my interests and pay you a retainer. Is that correct?"

"It is indeed, madam. And well reported. And?"

"And I wanted Mr. Jarrell to know. I wanted them all to know. And I wanted to be sure that you hadn't forgotten."

"You may be. And?"

"And I wanted it on the record. I don't think they're going to discredit your conclusion. I think you're going to tell the police about the gun, and I know what will happen then. I would appreciate it if you'll tell them that I came to see you Friday and what I said. I'll tell them myself, of course, but I wish you would. I'm not frightened, but—"

Jarrell had been controlling himself. Now he exploded. "Damn you, Nora! You saw Wolfe Friday, three days ago? And didn't tell me?"

She sent the gray eyes at him. "Don't yell at me, Mr. Jarrell. I won't have you yelling at me, not even now. Will you tell the police, Mr. Wolfe?"

"I will if I see them, Miss Kent, and I agree with you, reluctantly, that I'm probably going to." He took in the audience. "There is a third period, a brief one, which I haven't mentioned, because we covered it on Friday—from six to six-thirty Wednesday afternoon, when the gun was taken. None of you was excluded from that, either, not even Mr. Brigham, but he is now." He went to Jarrell. "I bring that up, sir, because you stated explicitly that your daughter-in-law took the gun, but you admitted that you had no proof. Have you any now?"

"No. Proof that you would accept, no."

"Have you proof that anyone would accept?"

"Certainly he hasn't." It was Wyman. He was looking, not at Wolfe, but at his father. But he said "he," not "you," though he was looking at him. "And now it's a little too much. Now it may not be just taking a gun, it may be killing two men with it. Of course he has no proof. He hates her, that's all. He wants to smear her. He made passes at her, he kept it up for a year, and she wouldn't let him touch her, and so he hates her. That's all there is to it."

Wolfe made a face. "Mrs. Jarrell. You heard what your husband said?"

Susan nodded, just perceptibly. "Yes, I heard."

"Is it true?"

"Yes. I don't want—" She closed her mouth and opened it again. "Yes, it's true."

Wolfe's head jerked left. "Mr. Jarrell. Did you make improper advances to your son's wife?"

"No!"

Wyman looked straight at his father and said distinctly, "You're a liar."

"Oh, my God," Trella said. "This is fine. This is wonderful."

If I know any man who doesn't need feeling sorry for it's Nero Wolfe, but I came close to it then. After all the trouble he had taken to get them there to help him out of his predicament, they had turned his office into a laundromat for washing dirty linen.

He turned and snapped at me, "Archie, draw a check to Mr. Jarrell for ten thousand dollars." As I got up and went to the safe for the checkbook he snapped at them, "Then it's hopeless. I was afraid it would be, but it was worth trying. I admit I made the effort chiefly for the sake of my own self-esteem, but also I felt that you deserved this last chance, at least some of you. Now you're all in for it, and one of you is doomed. Mr. Jarrell, you don't want me any more, and heaven knows I don't want you. Some of Mr. Goodwin's things are up there in the room he occupied, and he'll send or go for them. The check, Archie?"

I gave it to him, he signed it, and I went to hand it to Jarrell. I had to go to the far side of the red leather chair to keep from being bumped by Wolfe, who was on his way out and who needs plenty of room whether at rest or in motion. Jarrell was saying something, but Wolfe ignored it and kept going.

They left in a bunch, not a lively bunch. I accompanied them to the hall, and opened the door, but no one paid any attention to me except Lois, who offered a hand and frowned at me—not a hostile frown, but the kind you use instead of a smile when you are out of smiles for reasons beyond your control. I frowned back to show that there was no hard feeling as far as she was concerned.

I watched them down the stoop to the sidewalk through the one-way glass panel, and when I got back to the office Wolfe was there behind his desk. As I crossed to mine he growled at me, "Get Mr. Cramer."

"You're riled," I told him. "It might be a good idea to count ten first."

"No. Get him."

I sat and dialed WA9-8241, Manhattan Homicide West, asked for Inspector Cramer, and got Sergeant Purley Stebbins. He said Cramer was in conference downtown and not approachable. I asked how soon he would be, and Purley said he didn't know and what did I want.

Wolfe got impatient and picked up his receiver. "Mr. Stebbins? Nero Wolfe. Please tell Mr. Cramer that I shall greatly appreciate it if he will call on me this evening at half past nine—or, failing that, as soon as his convenience will permit. Tell him I have important information for him regarding the Eber and Brigham murders. . . . No, I'm sorry, but it must be Mr. Cramer. . . . I know you are, but if you come without Mr. Cramer you will not be admitted. With him you will be welcome. . . . As soon as he can make it, then."

As I hung up I spoke. "One thing, anyhow, there is no longer—"

I stopped because I had turned and seen that he had leaned back and shut his eyes, and his lips had started to go in and out. He was certainly desperate. It was only fifteen minutes until dinner time.

13

I would say that Inspector Cramer and Sergeant Stebbins weigh about the same, around one-ninety, and little or none of it is fat on either of them, so you would suppose their figures would pretty well match, but they don't. Cramer's flesh is tight-weave and Stebbins' is loose-weave. On Cramer's hands the skin follows the line of the bones, whereas on Stebbins' hands you have to take the bones for granted, and presumably they are like that all over, though I have never played with them on the beach and so can't swear to it. I'm not sure which of them would be the toughest to tangle with, but some day I may find out, even if they are officers of the law.

That was not the day, that Monday evening. They were there by invitation, to get a handout, and after greeting Wolfe and sitting —Cramer in the red leather chair and Purley near him, against the wall, on a yellow one—they wore expressions that were almost neighborly. Almost. Cramer even tried to be jovial. He asked Wolfe how he was making out with his acceptable process of reason.

"Not at all," Wolfe said. He had swiveled to face them and wasn't trying to look or sound cordial. "My reason has ceased to function. It has been swamped in a deluge of circumstance. My phone call, to tell you that I have information for you, was dictated not by reason but by misfortune. I am sunk and I am sour. I just returned a retainer of ten thousand dollars to a client. Otis Jarrell. I have no client."

You might have expected Cramer's keen gray eyes to show a gleam of glee, but they didn't. He would swallow anything that Wolfe offered only after sending it to the laboratory for the works. "That's too bad," he rumbled. "Bad for you but good for me. I can always use information. About Eber and Brigham, you said."

Wolfe nodded. "I've had it for some time, but it was only today, a few hours ago, that I was forced to acknowledge the obligation to disclose it. It concerns an event that occurred at Mr. Jarrell's home last Wednesday, witnessed by Mr. Goodwin, who reported it to me. Before I tell you about it I need answers to a question or two. I understand that you learned from Mr. Jarrell that he had hired me for a job, and that it was on that job that Mr. Goodwin went there as his secretary under another name. I also understand that he declines to tell you what the job was, on the ground that it was personal and confidential and has no relation to your inquiry; and that the police commissioner and the district attorney have accepted his position. That you have been obliged to concur is obvious, since you haven't been pestering Mr. Goodwin and me. Is that correct?"

"It's correct that I haven't been pestering you. The rest, what you understand, I can't help what you understand."

"But you don't challenge it. I understand that too. I only wanted to make it clear why I intend to tell you nothing about the job Mr. Jarrell hired me for, though he is no longer my client. I assume that the police commissioner and the district attorney wouldn't want me to, and I don't care to offend them. Another question, before I—yes, Mr. Stebbins?"

Purley hadn't said a word. He had merely snarled a little. He set his jaw.

Wolfe resumed to Cramer. "Another question. It's possible that my piece of information is bootless because your attention is elsewhere. If so, I prefer not to disclose it. Have you arrested anyone for either murder?"

"No."

"Have you passable grounds for suspicion of anyone outside of the Jarrell family?"

"No."

"Now a multiple question which can be resolved into one. I need to know if any discovered fact, not published, renders my information pointless. Was someone, presumably the murderer, not yet identified, seen entering or leaving the building where Eber lived on Thursday afternoon? The same for Brigham. According to published accounts, it is assumed that someone was with him in the back seat of his car, which was parked at some spot not under observation, that the someone shot him, covered the body with the rug, drove the car to Thirty-ninth Street near Seventh Avenue, from where the subway was easily and quickly accessible, parked the car, and decamped. Is that still the assumption? Has anyone been found who saw the car, either en route or while being parked, and can describe the driver? To resolve them into one: Have you any promising basis for inquiry that has not been published?"

Cramer grunted. "You don't want much, do you? You'd better have something. The answer to the question is no. Now let's hear it."

"When I'm ready. I am merely taking every advisable precaution. My information carries the strong probability that the two murders were committed by Otis Jarrell, his wife, Wyman Jarrell, his wife, Lois Jarrell, Nora Kent, or Roger Foote. Or two or more of them in conspiracy. So another question. Do you know anything that removes any of those people from suspicion?"

"No." Cramer's eyes had narrowed. "So that's what it's like. No wonder you got from under. No wonder you gave him back his retainer. Let's have it."

"When I'm ready," Wolfe repeated. "I want something in return. I want a cushion for my chagrin. You will be more than satisfied with what I give you, and you will not begrudge me a crumb of satisfaction for myself. After I give you my information I want some from you. I want a complete report of the movements of the seven people I named, and I want the report to cover a considerable period: from two o'clock Thursday afternoon to three o'clock Sunday afternoon. I want to know everywhere they went, with an indication of what has been verified by your staff and what has not. I'm not asking for—"

"Save it," Cramer rasped. "You asking! You're in a hell of a position to ask. You've been withholding material evidence, and it's got too hot for you and you've got to let go. Okay, let go!"

He might not have spoken as far as Wolfe was concerned. He took up where he left off. "I'm not asking for much. You already have some of that and will now be getting the rest of it, and all you need to do is let Mr. Goodwin copy the reports of their movements. That will reveal no departmental secrets, and that's all I want. I'm not haggling. If you refuse my request you'll get what you came for anyway; I have no choice. I make the request in advance only because as soon as I give you the information you'll be leaving. You'll have urgent business and you wouldn't wait to hear me. Will you oblige me?"

"I'll see. I'll consider it. Come on, spill it."

Wolfe turned to me. "Archie?"

Since I had been instructed I didn't have to ask him what to spill. I was to tell the truth, the whole truth, and nothing but the truth about the gun, and that was all. I did so, beginning with Jarrell dashing into my room at 6:20 Wednesday afternoon, and ending twenty-four hours later in Wolfe's office, with my report to him. When I finished Purley was on the edge of his chair, his jaw clamped, looking holes through me. Cramer was looking at Wolfe.

"Goddamn you," he said. "Four days. You've had this four days."

"Goodwin's had it five days," Purley said.

"Yeah." Cramer transferred to me. "Okay, go on."

I shook my head. "I'm through."

"Like hell you're through. You'll be surprised. If you—"

"Mr. Cramer," Wolfe cut in. "Now that you have it, use it. Railing at us won't help any. If you think a charge of obstructing justice will hold, get a warrant, but I advise against it. I think you'd regret it. As soon as the possibility became a probability I acted. And when it was merely a possibility I explored it. I had them all here, on Friday, including Mr. Brigham, and told them that the gun must be produced. Yesterday, when the news came about Brigham, it was touch and go. Today, when Mr. Goodwin learned about the bullets, it became highly probable, but I felt that I owed my client at least a gesture, and I had them here again. It was fruitless. I repaid Mr. Jarrell's retainer, dismissed them, and phoned you. I will not be squawked at. I have endured enough. Either get a warrant, or forget me and go to work on it."

"Four days," Cramer said. "When I think what we've been doing those four days. What are you hanging onto? What else have you got? Which one was it?"

"No, sir. If I had known that I would have called you here, not to give it up but to deliver a murderer. I would have been exalted, not mortified. I haven't the slightest notion."

"It was Jarrell himself. It was Jarrell, and he was your client, and you cut him loose, but you wouldn't deliver him on account of your goddamn pride."

Wolfe turned. "Archie. How much cash is in the safe?"

"Thirty-seven hundred dollars in the reserve and around two hundred in petty."

"Bring me three thousand."

I went and opened the door of the safe, unlocked the cash drawer and opened it, counted three grand from the reserve stack, and stepped to Wolfe's desk and handed it to him. With it in his fist he faced Cramer.

"The wager is that when this is over and the facts are known you will acknowledge that at this hour, Monday evening, I had no inkling of the identity of the murderer, except that I had surmised that it was one of the seven people I have named, and I have told you that. Three thousand dollars to three dollars. One thousand to one. You have three dollars? Mr. Stebbins can hold the stakes."

Cramer looked at Stebbins. Purley grunted. Cramer looked at me. I grinned and said, "For God's sake grab it. A thousand to one? Give me that odds and I'll bet you I did it myself."

"That's not as funny as you think it is, Goodwin. You could have." Cramer looked at Wolfe. "You know I know you. You know I never yet saw you open a bag and shake it out without hanging onto a corner that had something in it you were saving for yourself. If you're backing clear out, if you've got no client and no fee in sight, why do you want the reports on their movements from two o'clock Thursday to three o'clock Sunday?"

"To exercise my brain." Wolfe put the stack of bills on the desk and put a paperweight—a chunk of jade that a woman had once used to crack her husband's skull—on top. "It needs it, heaven knows. As I said, I want a crumb of satisfaction for myself. Do you believe in words of honor?"

"I do when the honor is there."

"Am I a man of honor?"

Cramer's eyes widened. He was flabbergasted. He started to answer and stopped. He had to consider. "You may be, at that," he allowed. "You're tricky, you're foxy, you're the best liar I know, but if anybody asked me to name something you had done that was dishonorable I'd have to think."

"Very well, think."

"Skip it. Say you're a man of honor. What about it?"

"Regarding the reports I have asked for, to exercise my brain on. I give you my word of honor that I have no knowledge, withheld from you, which can be applied to those reports; that when I inspect them I'll have no relevant facts that you don't have."

"That *sounds* good." Cramer stood up. "I was going home, and now this. I've heard you sound good before. Who's at my desk, Purley? Rowcliff?"

"Yes, sir." Stebbins was up too.

"Okay, let's get started. Come on, Goodwin, get your hat if you've got one big enough."

I knew that was coming. It would probably go on all night, and my style would be cramped because if they got exasperated Wolfe wouldn't get the reports to exercise his brain on. I didn't even remark that I didn't wear a hat when I went slumming.

14

That was twenty minutes past ten Monday night. At six o'clock Wednesday afternoon, when Wolfe came down from the plant rooms, I had just finished typing the last of the timetables and had them ready for him.

It had taken that long to fill his order, for three reasons. First, the city and county employes hadn't got started on the trails of the Jarrells until Tuesday morning, and each of the subjects was given two sittings before Cramer got the results. Second, Cramer didn't decide until Wednesday noon that he would let Wolfe have it, though I had known darned well he would, since it included nothing he wanted to save, and since he was curious to see what Wolfe wanted with it. And third, after I had been given permission to look at a selected collection of the reports, it took quite a job of digging to get what Wolfe wanted, not to mention my own contributions and the typing after I got home.

I can't tell you what Wolfe did Tuesday and Wednesday because I wasn't there to see, but if you assume that he did nothing whatever I won't argue—that is, nothing but eat, sleep, read, drink beer, and play with orchids. As for me, I was busy. Monday night they kept me at 20th Street—Rowcliff and a Sergeant Coffey—until four o'clock in the morning, going over it back and forth and across and up and down, and when they got through they knew every bit as much as Cramer and Stebbins had already known when they took me down. Rowcliff could not believe that he wasn't smart enough to maneuver me into leaking what I was at Jarrell's for, and I didn't dare to make it clear to him in words he would understand for fear he might see to it that Wolfe didn't get what he wanted for brain exercise. So daylight was trying to break through at my windows when I turned in.

And Tuesday at noon, when I had just started on my fourth griddle cake and my second cup of coffee, the phone rang to tell me that I would be welcome at the DA's office in twenty minutes.

I made it in forty, and was there five solid hours, one of them with the DA himself present, and at the end they knew everything that Rowcliff did. There was one little spot where the chances looked good for my getting booked as a material witness, but I bumped through it without having to yell for help.

My intention was, if and when I left Leonard Street a free man, to stop in at Homicide West to see if Cramer had decided to let me look at the reports, but I was interrupted. After finally being dismissed by Mandelbaum, as I was on my way down the hall from his room to the front, a door on the right opened and one of the three best dancers I had ever stepped with came out. Seeing me, she stopped.

"Oh," she said. "Hello."

An assistant DA named Riley, having opened the door for her, was there shutting it. He saw me, thought he would say something, decided not to, and closed the door. The look Lois was giving me was not an invitation to dance, far from it.

"So," she said, "you've made it nice for us, you and your fat boss."

"Then don't speak to me," I told her. "Give me an icy stare and flounce out. As for making it nice for you, wrong address. We held on till the last possible tenth of a second."

"Hooray for you. Our hero." We were moving down the hall. "Where are you bound for?"

"Home, with a stopover."

We were in the anteroom, with people there on chairs. She waited until we were in the outer hall to say, "I think I want to ask you something. If we go where we can get a drink, by the time we get there I'll know."

I looked at my wrist. Ten minutes to six. We no longer had a client to be billed for expenses, but there was a chance she would contribute something useful for the timetables, and besides, looking at her was a pleasant change after the five hours I had just spent. So I said I'd be glad to buy her a drink whether she decided to ask me something or not.

I took her to Mohan's, which was in walking distance around the corner, found an empty booth at the far end, and ordered. When the drinks came she took a sip of her Bloody Mary, made a face, took a bigger sip, and put the glass down.

"I've decided to ask you," she said. "I ought to wait until I've had a couple because my nerves have gone back on me. When I saw you there in the hall my knees were shaking."

"After you saw me or before?"

"They were already shaking. I knew I'd have to tell about it. I knew that yesterday, but I was afraid nobody would believe me. That's what I want to ask you, I want you to back me up and then they'll have to believe me. You see, I know that nobody used my father's gun to kill Jim Eber and Corey Brigham. I want you to say you were with me when I threw it in the river."

I raised my brows. "That's quite a want. God knows what you might have wanted if you waited till you had a couple. You threw your father's gun in the river?"

"Yes." She was making her eyes meet mine. "Yes, I did."

"When?"

"Thursday morning. That's how I know nobody could have used it, because Jim was killed Thursday afternoon. I got it the day before, Wednesday, you know how I got it, going in with that rug held up in front of me. I hid it—"

"How did you open the library door?"

"I had a key. Jim Eber let me have a duplicate made from his— about a year ago. Jim was rather warm on me for a while. I hid the gun in my room, under the mattress. Then I was afraid Dad might have the whole place searched and it would be found, so I got rid of it. Don't you want to know why I took it?"

"Sure, that would help."

"I took it because I was afraid something might happen. I knew how Dad felt about Susan, and I knew it was getting worse every day between him and Wyman, and I knew he had a gun in his drawer, and I hate guns anyway. I didn't think any one thing—I didn't think he would shoot Susan or Wyman would shoot him—I just thought something might happen. So Thursday morning I put it in my bag and went and got my car, and drove up the West Side Highway and onto the George Washington Bridge, and stopped on the bridge and threw the gun in the river."

She finished the drink and put the glass down. "Naturally I never intended to tell anybody. Friday morning, when the news came that Jim Eber had been shot, it never occurred to me that that had anything to do with Dad's gun. How could it, when I

knew Dad's gun was in the river? Then that afternoon at Nero
Wolfe's office I saw how wrong I was. What he suggested, that
whoever took the gun should put it out in sight somewhere,
naturally I would have done that if I could—but I was afraid that
if I told what I had done no one would believe me. It would sound
like I was just trying to explain it away. Could I have a refill?"

I caught the waiter's eye and gave him the sign.

She carried on. "Then Sunday, the news about Corey Brigham—
of course that made it worse. And then yesterday, with Nero
Wolfe again—you know how that was. And all day today, detectives and district attorneys with all of us—they were there all morning, and we have been at the district attorney's office all afternoon,
in separate rooms. Now I have to tell about it, I know that,
but I don't think they'll believe me. I'm sure they won't. But they
will if you say you went with me and saw me throw it in the river."

The waiter was coming with the refills, and I waited until he
had gone.

"You left out something," I told her. "You left out about hiring
a crew of divers to search the river bottom and offering a trip to
Hollywood and ten thousand dollars in cash to the one who found
the gun."

She surveyed me. "Are you being droll?"

"Not very. But that would give it color and would stand up just
as well. Since you've been answering questions all day, I suppose
you have accounted for your movements Thursday morning. What
did you tell them?"

She nodded. "I'll have to admit I lied, I know that. I told them
that after breakfast I was on the terrace until about half past
eleven, and then I went shopping, and then I went to lunch on the
Bolivar. Now I'll have to admit I didn't go shopping."

"Where did you tell them you went?"

"To three shoe shops."

"Did you name the shops?"

"Yes. They asked. Zussman's, and Yorio's, and Weeden's."

"Did you buy any shoes?"

"Yes, I—" She chopped it off. "Of course not, if I wasn't there.
How could I?"

I shook my head at her. "Drink up. What was the name of the

girl who hung onto the clapper so the bell couldn't ring, or was it a boy?"

"Damn it, don't be droll!"

"I'm not. You are. Beyond remarking that they'll check at those three shops, and that if you tried that mess on them they'd find that you didn't get your car from the garage that morning, there's no point in listing the dozen or so other holes. I should be sore at you for thinking I could be sap enough to play with you, but you meant well, and it's a tough trick to be both noble and nimble. So drink up and forget it—unless you want to tell me who *did* take the gun. Do you know?"

"Of course I don't!"

"Just protecting the whole bunch, including Nora?"

"I'm not protecting anybody! I just want this awful business to stop!" She touched my hand with fingertips. "Archie. So I made a mess of it, but it wouldn't be a mess if you would help me work it out. We could have done it Wednesday night. We didn't take my car, we took a taxi—or we walked to the East River and threw it in. Won't you help me?"

And there you are. What if I had lost sight of basic facts? The circumstances had been favorable. When I first saw her Monday afternoon on the terrace, as she approached with the sun full on her, I had realized that no alterations were needed anywhere, from the top of her head clear down to her toes. Talking with her, I had realized that she was fine company. At Colonna's Tuesday evening I had realized that she was good to be close to. Not to mention that by the time I was too old to provide properly for the family her father would have died and left her a mint. What if I had lost my head, made a supreme effort, rushed her off her feet, and wrapped her up? I would now be stuck with a female who got so rattled in a pinch that she thought she could sidetrack a murder investigation with a plant so half-baked it was pathetic. There you are.

But she meant well, so I let her down easy, paid for the drinks without entering it on my expense pad, helped her into a taxi, and had no hard feelings as I took another one, to 20th Street.

Nothing doing on the reports. Neither Cramer nor Stebbins was around, and all Rowcliff had for me was a glassy eye.

As I said, Cramer didn't shake loose until noon the next day, Wednesday. I lunched on sandwiches and milk at a desk he let me use, digging out what was wanted, got home with it at four o'clock and got at the typewriter, and had just finished and was putting the original and a carbon on Wolfe's desk when he came down from the plant rooms. He got arranged in his chair, picked up the original, and started his brain exercise. I give it here, from the original from the Jarrell file, not for you to exercise your brain—unless you insist on it—but for the record.

May 29, 1957
AG for NW

JARRELL TIMETABLES

(Mostly from police reports, but some from AG is included. Comments are AG's. Some items have been firmly verified by police, some partly verified, some not yet verified at all. Too complicated to try to distinguish among them, but can supply information on items considered important from my notes. OJ is Otis Jarrell, TJ is his wife, WJ is Wyman Jarrell, SJ is his wife, LJ is Lois Jarrell, NK is Nora Kent, RF is Roger Foote, AG is either Alan Green or Archie Goodwin, depending.)

OTIS JARRELL

Thursday
9:30 breakfast with WJ, LJ, NK, AG, then in library until lunch at 1:30 with TJ, SJ, & AG. Left at 2:30 for three business appointments: (1) Continental Trust Co., 287 Madison Ave., (2) Lawrence H. Eggers, 630 5th Ave., (3) Paul Abramowitz, 250 Park Ave. Exact times on these being checked. Got home at 6:00, went to his room. At 6:30 cocktails and dinner, then to library; AG joins him there at 10:35 p.m. Bed.

Friday
8:15 to AG's room to tell him Eber killed. 8:45 breakfast. 9:30 gathers everyone in library for conference about Eber. At 11:00 Lieut. Rowcliff comes, stays an hour, NK is present. Stays in library with WJ & NK; at 1:22 phone call comes from AG; at 1:40 calls AG, is told to bring everyone to NW office at 6:00. 1:45 lunch with SJ, LJ, & RF, tells them to be at NW office at 6:00. After lunch phones WJ and Corey Brigham to tell them.

Phones Clarinda Day's & leaves word for TJ to call him. She does so at 3:00 & he tells her about NW summons. Phones district attorney, whom he knows, & has friendly talk about Eber. 5:00 RF comes to library, asks for $335, doesn't get it. 5:30 is ready to leave for NW, waits till 5:50 for TJ to be ready. 6:10 arrives NW, leaves 7:10; home, dinner, long family discussion of situation, bed.

Saturday

8:30 breakfast with NK. Has everyone told to stand by because asst. DA coming at 11:00. 9:15 Herman Dietz comes on business matter, leaves at 9:45. 10:00 tells AG to make himself scarce because asst. DA coming. 10:10 WJ comes in for talk. 11:00 Mandelbaum arrives with dick stenographer; 11:15 everybody is called in, except that TJ doesn't make it until 11:45. 12:05 Cramer joins them, having just left NW. 1:35 Mandelbaum and Cramer leave. All lunch together except NK. 2:45 phones DA, can't get him. Phones Police Commissioner Kelly & arranges to meet him at Penguin Club at 10:30 Sunday. 3:40 leaves to meet WJ at Metropolitan Athletic Club for talk. 5:40 they go home together for early dinner. 8:10 to theater with TJ.

Sunday

9:00 breakfast. 10:10 leaves for Penguin Club for date with Police Commissioner Kelly, with him until 11:30, goes home & to library. 12:00 AG comes in and stays 10 minutes. 1:30 lunch with WJ, SJ, & AG. 2:30 to 5:00 in library, then bridge with TJ, WJ, & NK. At 6:10 AG comes to announce Corey Brigham's death.

TRELLA JARRELL

Thursday

Up at noon, coffee on terrace. 1:30 lunch with OJ, SJ, & AG. 2:30 to Clarinda Day's. 3:45 shopping, information about where & when confused & incomplete & being checked. 6:00 home to change for cocktails & dinner. After dinner, pinochle with RF & NK.

Friday

9:30 goes to family conference in library in negligee, returns to bed, up at noon, eats big breakfast. 1:15 goes to park, arrives 2:30 at Clarinda Day's, gets message to call OJ, does so at 3:00. 4:00 to 5:00 looks at cats in two pet shops, gets home at 5:15, ready to leave for NW at 5:50. From there on with others as under OJ.

Saturday

Told at 11:05 to come to library to join party with asst. DA, makes it at 11:45. 1:35 lunch with others. 2:30 to Clarinda Day's. 3:45 to movie at Duke's Screen Box on Park Avenue. 5:30 home to dress for early dinner. 8:10 to theater with OJ.

Sunday

Up at noon, big breakfast again. On terrace with papers. 2:00 went to park, back at 3:00, went to studio to watch television, is wakened by WJ at 5:00 for bridge with OJ, WJ, & NK. At 6:10 AG announces Corey Brigham's death.

WYMAN JARRELL

Thursday

9:30 breakfast with OJ, LJ, NK, & AG. 10:30 to 12:15, on terrace reading play in manuscript. 12:45 arrives at Sardi's and has lunch with three men to discuss financing of play he may produce (two of them have verified it). 2:45 to 4:30, auditions for casting play at Drew Theatre. 4:35 to 6:30, at Metropolitan Athletic Club, watching handball & drinking. 6:45 meets Susan at Sardi's, dinner, theater, home, bed.

Friday

9:30 family conference in library, then breakfast. Reads papers, waits around with SJ until Rowcliff has come & gone. In library with OJ & NK until 1:22, when phone call comes from AG; leaves, cashes check at bank, then to his office in Paramount Bldg. Lunch at Sardi's with same three men as on Thursday. 3:00 back to his office, gets call from OJ telling him to be at NW office at 6:00. Gets call from SJ. 3:45 SJ comes for him in Jaguar, they drive up to Briscoll's in Westchester for a drink, then back to town, arriving NW at 5:56. From there on with others as under OJ.

Saturday

9:10 breakfast with SJ, LJ, & AG. 10:10 in library with OJ until 11:00, when asst. DA arrives. 1:35 lunch with others. 3:00 meets Corey Brigham at Churchill men's bar, with him until 3:50. 4:00 to 5:40 with OJ at Metropolitan Athletic Club; they go home together, arriving at 6:00 for early dinner. 8:15 to theater with SJ.

Sunday

10:00 breakfast with SJ, LJ, NK, & AG. Reads papers and does crossword puzzles until 1:30 lunch with OJ, SJ, & AG. 2:40 leaves for Drew Theatre to hear auditions. 4:40 leaves theater, gets home at 5:00, goes to studio and wakes TJ, bridge with OJ, TJ, & NK. At 6:10 AG announces Corey Brigham's death.

SUSAN JARRELL

Thursday

10:30 breakfast alone. To Masson's, jeweler, 52nd & 5th Ave., to leave watch. Walks to park & in park, then home at 1:30 for lunch with OJ, TJ, & AG. 2:45 back to Masson's to get watch; buys stockings at Merrihew's, 58th & Madison. Arrives Clarinda Day's at 4:00, leaves at 6:30, meets WJ at Sardi's at 6:45. Dinner, theater, home, bed.

Friday

9:30 family conference in library, then breakfast. Waits around with WJ until Rowcliff has come & gone. 12:10 goes to Abingdon's, florist at 65th & Madison, to order plants for terrace. Back home. 1:45 lunch with OJ, LJ, & RF, is told to be at NW office at 6:00. Rings WJ's office three times, gets him at 3:20, gets Jaguar and goes for him. Rest of day & evening, corroborates WJ.

Saturday

9:10 breakfast with WJ, LJ, & AG. On terrace until 11:15, joins party in library with asst. DA. 1:35 lunch with others. 2:45 goes to Abingdon's to look at plants. Home at 3:45, in room until 4:40, leaves, arrives Clarinda Day's 5:05, leaves at 6:15, is late at home for early dinner. 8:15 to theater with WJ.

Sunday

10:00 breakfast with WJ, LJ, NK, & AG. 10:30 leaves for St. Thomas Church, 53rd & 5th Ave. After church walks home, arriving at 1:15. 1:30 lunch with OJ, WJ, & AG. Reads papers, looks at television, goes to room and takes nap, back to television at 5:30, is there with AG at 6:00 when news comes about Corey Brigham.

LOIS JARRELL

Thursday

9:30 breakfast with OJ, WJ, NK, & AG. 10:15 to 11:30 on terrace reading. 11:45 to 1:00 buying shoes at three shops: Zussman's, Yorio's, and Weeden's. Bought seven pairs altogether, not liking to go barefoot. 1:15 lunch at party on steamship *Bolivar* at dock in Hudson River. 3:00 got car from garage & drove to Net Club in Riverdale, tennis until 6:00. Home at 6:35 to change. Left at 7:30 for dinner and dancing with a group at Flamingo Club; wish I had been there.

Friday

Up at 7:00 for breakfast & ride on a horse in park. Home just in time for family conference in library at 9:30. Drives to Net Club for an hour of tennis, home at 1:15. 1:45 lunch with OJ, SJ, & RF, is told to be at NW office at 6:00. 3:00 to Evangeline's, 49th Street near Madison, to try on clothes. Home at 5:20, leaves at 5:30 with RF & NK to taxi to NW. From there on with others as under OJ.

Saturday

Up at 7:00 to ride in park, back for breakfast at 9:10 with WJ, SJ, & AG. Cancels tennis date because of party in library with asst. DA at 11:15. 1:35 lunch with others. 2:30 takes nap in her room. 4:15 goes for walk, goes to Abingdon's & cancels Susan's order for plants for terrace. Home at 5:45, dresses for early dinner. 8:20 goes with AG to Flamingo Club, home at 2:00 a.m.

Sunday

10:00 breakfast with WJ, SJ, NK, & AG. Goes for walk with AG, at 11:30 takes taxi to apartment of friends named Buchanan, 185 East River Drive, goes with them to Net Club for lunch, tennis, drinks. Home at 6:40, learns about Corey Brigham.

NORA KENT

Thursday

9:30 breakfast with OJ, WJ, LJ, & AG. Library all morning, lunch alone there, remains there alone until OJ returns at 6:00. After cocktails & dinner, pinochle with TJ & RF.

Friday

8:45 breakfast. 9:30 family conference in library. 11:00 with OJ when Rowcliff comes. Lunches in library, learns caliber of bullet that killed Eber, leaves at 1:45 to go to see NW. Home at 3:10, in library until 5:30, leaves with LJ & RF to go to the meeting at NW. From there on with others as under OJ.

Saturday

8:30 breakfast with OJ, then with him to library. 10:10 WJ comes for talk with OJ & she is told to beat it. In her room until 11:15, when she joins party in library with asst. DA. 1:35 lunch with others. 2:30 back to library with OJ; he leaves at 3:40. 3:45 gets phone call from Abingdon's about plants; she goes and cancels orders given by both SJ & LJ. Goes shopping, buys various personal items not specified. 5:45 gets home, dresses for early dinner. 7:50 leaves for meeting of Professional Women's League at Vassar Club, 58th Street. Home at 11:10.

Sunday

10:00 breakfast with WJ, SJ, LJ, & AG. 10:50 goes to church at 5th Ave. Presbyterian, 55th St. Lunch at Borgner's on 6th Ave., then to Picasso show at Modern Museum, 53rd St. Home at 5:00 for bridge with OJ, TJ, & WJ. At 6:10 AG announces Corey Brigham's death.

ROGER FOOTE

Thursday

7:00 breakfast alone. To Jamaica race track, loses $60 I lent him, home at 6:00. After cocktails and dinner, pinochle with TJ & NK.

Friday

9:30 family conference in library, then breakfast. On terrace & in his room until 1:45, then lunch with OJ, SJ, & LJ, is told to be at NW office at 6:00. 2:50 leaves to go to 49th Street to see if he can get into Eber's apartment to look for a record, if any, of the fact that he owed Eber $335. No luck, apartment sealed. Calls on a lawyer he knows, unnamed, to find out where he stands. Gets home at 5:00, goes to library to try to borrow $335 from OJ, is turned down. 5:30 leaves with LJ & NK for NW office.

Saturday

10:15 breakfast alone. 11:15 joins party with asst. DA in library. 1:35 lunch with others. 2:45 goes to Mitchell's Riding Academy on West 108th Street to look at a horse. 3:45 returns home and plays solitaire in his room until time for early dinner. After dinner invites AG to play gin, AG declines. Goes to bed at 9:00.

Sunday

7:00 breakfast alone. To Belmont race track to look at horses. Home at 7:00 p.m., learns about Corey Brigham. Has given police details of his day at Belmont, but they are too confused & complicated to be worth copying.

15

At a quarter past ten Thursday morning, Memorial Day, I arrived at Jamaica race track to start the damnedest four days of detecting, or non-detecting, that I have ever put in.

After Wolfe had picked up the timetables, at six o'clock Wednesday, he had read them in twenty minutes, and then had gone over them for more than an hour, until dinner time. Back in the office after dinner, he had asked a few dozen assorted questions. What did I know about Mr. and Mrs. Herman Dietz? Practically nothing. Had Trella Jarrell's hour in the park from two o'clock to three on Sunday been checked? No, and probably it never would be. If I wanted to leave a revolver in Central Park where I was reasonably certain it wouldn't be discovered for three days, but where I could get it when I wanted it, where would I hide it? I made three suggestions, none of them any good, and said I'd have to think it over. Who was Clarinda Day? She was a woman who ran an establishment on 48th Street just off Fifth Avenue where women could get almost anything done that occurred to them—to their hair, their faces, their necks, their busts, their waists, their hips, their legs, their knees, their calves, their ankles—and where they could sweat, freeze, rest, or exercise forty-two different ways. Her customers ran all the way from stenographers to multi-millionairesses.

Did Nora Kent have keys to all the files in Jarrell's library and the combination to the safes? Don't know. Had a thorough search been made of the Jarrell duplex? Yes; a regiment of experts, with Jarrell's permission, had spent all day Tuesday at it. Including the library? Yes, with Jarrell present. Who had told me so? Purley Stebbins. Where was the Metropolitan Athletic Club? Central Park South, 59th Street. How long would it take to get from where the steamship *Bolivar* was docked to Eber's apartment on 49th Street? Between ten and thirty minutes, depending on traffic. Average, say eighteen minutes. How difficult would it have been for

Nora Kent to get from the library to the street, and, later, back in again, without being observed? With luck, using the service entrance, fairly simple. Without luck, impossible.

Etc.

At ten-thirty Wolfe leaned back and said, "Instructions."

"Yes, sir."

"Before you go to bed get Saul, Fred, and Orrie, and ask them to be here at eleven in the morning."

"Yes, sir."

"Tomorrow is a holiday. I don't suppose Miss Bonner will be at her office. If possible, get her tonight and ask her to breakfast with me at eight."

I looked at him. He meant business, though what business I couldn't say. Add his opinion of women to his opinion of other detectives, and you get his opinion of female detectives. Circumstances had compelled him to use Dol Bonner a year or so back, but now he was asking for it, and even inviting her to breakfast. Fritz would be on needles.

"I have her home number," I told him, "and I'll try, but she may already be gone for the long week end. If so, is it urgent enough to dig her out?"

"Yes. I want her. Now for you. You will go early in the morning to Jamaica race track and—"

"No racing at Jamaica now. It's closed."

"What about Belmont?"

"Open. Big day tomorrow."

"Then we'll see. You will act on this hypothesis: that Roger Foote took Jarrell's gun and hid it in his room or elsewhere on the premises. Thursday afternoon he shot Eber with it. Since he intended to say he had spent the day at Jamaica, he went there so as to be seen, and he hid the gun somewhere there. To speculate as to why he hid it instead of disposing of it is pointless; we know he did hide it because it was used again on Sunday. Either he hid it at Jamaica or, having made an appearance there, he went to Belmont and hid it there. In either case, on Sunday he went and retrieved it, returned to New York, met Brigham by appointment, and killed him. Acting on that hypothesis, your job is to learn where he left the gun from Thursday to Sunday, and you may start either at Jamaica or at Belmont. It's barely possible you'll even find the gun. He may have thought he might have further use for it and went back and hid it again in the same place after killing Brigham. He didn't get home Sunday until seven o'clock."

I said—not an objection, just a fact—"Of course he had all of New York City too."

"I know, but that's hopeless. He had to go to Jamaica on Thursday and to Belmont on Sunday, to be seen, and since we know he was there we'll look there. We know little or nothing of his movements in New York City; we know of no place particularly available to him where he could hide a gun and count on getting it again. First explore the possibilities at Jamaica and Belmont."

I explored them for four straight days, equipped with five hundred bucks in small bills from cash reserve and eight pictures of Roger Foote, procured early Thursday morning from the files at the *Gazette*. I went to Jamaica first because Belmont would have such a mob on the holiday that I would merely have got trampled.

Meanwhile, throughout the four days, Wolfe presumably had the gang busy working on other hypotheses—including Dol Bonner—though he never told me who was after what, except that I gathered Saul Panzer was on Otis Jarrell himself. That was a compliment to the former client, since Saul's rate was sixty bucks a day and expenses and he was worth at least five times that. Fred Durkin was good but no Saul Panzer. Orrie Cather, whom you have seen at my desk, was yes and no. On some tricks he was unbeatable, but on others not so hot. As for Dol Bonner, I didn't know much about her first-hand, but the word around was that if you had to have a female dick she was it. She had her own office and a staff—with one of which, Sally Colt, I was acquainted.

By Sunday night I knew enough about Jamaica and Belmont, especially Belmont, to write a book, with enough left over for ten magazine articles. I knew four owners, nine trainers, seventeen stable boys, five jockeys, thirteen touts, twenty-eight miscellaneous characters, one lamb, three dogs, and six cats, to speak to. I had aroused the suspicions of two track dicks and become close friends with one. I had seen two hundred and forty-seven girls it would have been fun to talk to but was too busy. I had seen about the same number of spots where a gun could be hid, but could find no one who had seen Roger Foote near any of them. None of them held a gun at the time I called, nor could I detect any trace of oil or other evidence that a gun had been there. One of them, a hole in a tree the other side of the backstretch, was so ideal that I was tempted to hide my own gun in it. Another good place would have been the bottom of a rack outside Gallant Man's stall, but there were too many eagle eyes around. Peach Fuzz wasn't there.

Sunday night I told Wolfe there was nothing left to explore unless he wanted me to start looking in horses' mouths, and he said he would have new instructions in the morning.

But he never gave them to me, for a little after ten on Monday a call came inviting me to visit the DA's office, and, after buzzing Wolfe in the plant rooms to tell him where to find me, I went. After thirty minutes with Mandelbaum and a dick I knew one thing, that the several hundred city and county employes working on the case had got exactly as far as I had at Jamaica and Belmont. After another thirty minutes I knew another thing, that the police commissioner and the district attorney had decided it had become necessary to find out what I was doing at Jarrell's under an assumed name, no matter how Jarrell felt about it. I said I wanted to phone Mr. Wolfe and was told that all the phones were busy. At noon I was taken in to the DA himself and had forty minutes with him that did neither of us any good. At one o'clock I was allowed to take my pick of ham or turkey in a sandwich; no corned beef. I insisted on milk and got it. At two-thirty I decided it had gone far enough and was walking out, but was stopped. Held as a material witness. Then, of course, they had to let me make a phone call, and within ten minutes there was a call for Mandelbaum from Nathaniel Parker, who is Wolfe's lawyer when Wolfe is driven to the extremity of using one.

I didn't get locked up at all. The DA had another try at me and then sent me into another room with a dick named O'Leary, and in two hours I won $3.12 from him at gin. I was perfectly willing to give him a chance to get it back, but someone came and took me to Mandelbaum's room, and Nathaniel Parker was there. As I shook hands with him Mandelbaum warned me not to leave the jurisdiction, and I said I wanted it in writing, and he said to go to hell, and I said I didn't know that was in the jurisdiction, and Parker steered me out.

Down on the sidewalk I asked him, "How high am I priced this time?"

"No bail, Archie. No warrant. I persuaded Mandelbaum that the circumstances didn't call for it, and promised that you will be available when needed."

I was a little disappointed because being out on bail is good for the ego. It gives you a sense of importance, of being wanted; it makes you feel that people care. However, I didn't reproach Parker; he had acted for the best. We took a taxi together uptown, but he said he had a dinner appointment and didn't get out when we reached the old brownstone on West 35th Street. So I thanked him for the rescue and the lift. As I crossed the sidewalk to the stoop my wrist watch said 6:23.

Wolfe, at his desk reading a book, lifted his eyes to grunt a greeting and returned them to the book. I went to my desk to see if there were any memos for me, found none, sat, and inquired, "Anything happen?"

He said no, without looking up.

"Parker said to give you his regards. I am not under bail. He talked Mandelbaum out of it."

He grunted.

"They've decided that Jarrell's private affairs are no longer private. They'll be after you any time, in the morning at the latest. Do you want a report?"

He said no, without looking up.

"Any instructions?"

He lifted his eyes, said, "I'm reading, Archie," and lowered them back to the book.

The best thing to throw at him would have been the typewriter, but I didn't own it. Next best would have been the telephone, but I didn't own that, either, and the cord wasn't long enough. I got up and left, mounted the two flights to my room, showered, decided not to shave, put on a clean shirt and a lighter suit, and was sewing buttons on pajamas when Fritz called up that dinner was ready.

It was at the table that I caught on that something was up. Wolfe wasn't being crusty because the outlook was dark; he was being smug because he had tasted blood, or was expecting to. He always enjoyed his food, whether in spite of circumstances or in harmony with them, and after ten thousand meals with him I knew all the shades. The way he spread pâté on a cracker, the way he picked up the knife to slice the filet of beef in aspic, the way he used his fork on the salad, the way he made his choice from the cheese platter—no question about it, he had something or somebody by the tail, or at least the tail was in sight.

I was thinking that when we were back in the office with coffee he might think it was time to let me have a taste too, but no. After taking three sips he picked up his book. That was a little too much, and I was deciding whether to go after him head on or take him from the flank, when the doorbell rang and I went to answer it. In view of Wolfe's behavior I wouldn't have been surprised if it had been the whole gang, all seven of them, with a joint confession in triplicate signed and ready to deliver, but it was merely a middle-aged man in a light brown suit and no hat whom I had never seen before.

When I opened the door he spoke before I did. "Is this Nero Wolfe's house?"

"Right."

"Are you Archie Goodwin?"

"Right again."

"Okay." He extended a hand with a little package. "This is for Nero Wolfe."

I took it and he turned and was going. I told him to wait, but he called over his shoulder, "No receipt," and kept going. I looked at the package. It was the size of a box of kitchen matches, wrapped in brown paper, fastened with Scotch Tape, and if it bore any name or address it was in invisible ink.

I shut the door and returned to the office and told Wolfe, "The man who handed me this said it was for you, but I don't know how he knew. There's no name on it. It doesn't tick. Shall I open it under water?"

"As you please. It's hardly large enough to be dangerous."

That seemed optimistic, remembering the size of the capsule that had once exploded in that office inside a metal percolator, blowing the percolator lid at the wall, missing Wolfe's head by an inch. However, I could stand it if he could. I got out my knife to cut the tape, removed the paper wrapping, and disclosed a cardboard box with no label. Putting it on the desk midway between us, which was only fair, I eased the lid off. Cotton. I lifted the cotton, and there was more cotton, with an object resting in its center. Bending over for a close-up, I straightened and announced, "A thirty-eight bullet. Isn't that interesting?"

"Extremely." He reached for the box and gave it a look. "Very interesting. You're sure it's a thirty-eight?"

"Yes, sir. Quite a coincidence."

"It is indeed." He put the box down. "Who brought it?"

"A stranger. Too bad I didn't invite him in."

"Yes. Of course there are various possibilities—among them, that some prankster sent it."

"Yeah. So I toss it in the wastebasket?"

"I don't think so. There is at least one other possibility that can't be ignored. You've had a long day and I dislike asking it, but you might take it to Mr. Cramer, tell him how we got it, and suggest that it be compared with the bullets that killed Mr. Eber and Mr. Brigham."

"Uh-huh. In time, say in a week or so, that might have occurred to me myself. My mind's not as quick as yours." I replaced the top layer of cotton and put the lid on. "I'd better take the wrapping paper too. If the bullet matches, and it just might, he'll want it. Incidentally, he'll want me too. If I take him a thirty-eight bullet, with that suggestion, and with that story of how we got it, I'll have to shoot my way out if you want to see me again tonight."

"The devil." He was frowning. "You're quite right. That won't do." He thought a moment. "Your notebook. A letter to Mr. Cramer."

I got at my desk and took notebook and pen.

He dictated: "Dear Mr. Cramer. I send you herewith a package which was delivered at my door a few minutes ago. It bore no name or address, but the messenger told Mr. Goodwin it was for me and departed. It contains a bullet which Mr. Goodwin says is a thirty-eight. Doubtless it is merely a piece of tomfoolery, but I thought it best to send it to you. You may think it worth while to have the bullet compared with those that killed Mr. Eber and Mr. Brigham. Then discard it. Don't bother to return it. Sincerely."

"By mail?" I asked.

"No. Take it, please. Immediately. Hand it in and return at once."

"Glad to." I pulled the typewriter around.

16

That Monday night may not have been the worst night Fritz ever spent, for he has had some tough ones, but it was bad enough. When I had got back after delivering the package at 20th Street, a little after ten o'clock, Wolfe had called him to the office.

"Some instructions, Fritz."

"Yes, sir."

"Archie and I will go up to bed shortly, but we are not here and will not be here. You will answer the phone. You do not know where we are or when we will return. You do not know exactly when we left. You may be bullyragged, by Mr. Cramer or others, but you will maintain that position. You will take messages if any are given, to be delivered to us when we return. You will ignore the doorbell. You will open no outside door, stoop or basement or back, under any circumstances whatever. If you do, a search warrant may be thrust at you and the house will be overrun. A contingency might arise that will make you consider it necessary to disturb Archie or me, but I think not and hope not. Bring my breakfast an hour early, at seven o'clock. Archie will have his at seven also. I shall be sorry if you fail of a proper night's sleep, but it can't be helped. You can take a nap tomorrow."

"Yes, sir." Fritz swallowed. "If there is danger, may I suggest—" He stopped and started over. "I know you are reluctant to leave the house, that is understood, but there are times when it is better to leave a house, at least for a short time. Especially in your profession." He looked at me. "You know that, Archie."

Wolfe reassured him, "No, Fritz, there is no danger. On the contrary, this is the preamble to triumph. You understand the instructions?"

He said he did, but he wasn't happy. For years he had been expecting the day to come when Wolfe would be dragged out of the house in handcuffs, not to mention me, and he was against it. He gave me a reproachful look, which God knows I didn't deserve, and left, and Wolfe and I, not being there anyway, went up to bed.

Seven o'clock is much too early a breakfast hour unless you're a bird or a bird watcher, but I made it to the kitchen by 7:08. My glass of orange juice was there, but Fritz wasn't, and the phone was ringing. It was a temptation to take it and see how well I could imitate Fritz's voice, but I let it ring. By the time Fritz came it had given up. I told him he must have been late taking Wolfe's breakfast tray up, and he said no, he had got it there on the dot at seven, but had stayed to report on the night.

While I dealt with toast, bacon, fresh strawberry omelet, and coffee, he reported to me, referring to notes. The first call from Lieutenant Rowcliff had come at 11:32, and he had been so emphatic that Fritz had hung up on him. The second had been at 11:54, less emphatic but stubborner. At 12:21 Cramer had called, and had got both personal and technical, explaining the penalties that could be imposed on a man, Fritz for instance, for complicity in withholding evidence and obstructing justice in a murder investigation. At 12:56 the doorbell had started to ring, and at 1:03 pounding on the front door had begun. From 1:14 to a little after six peace had reigned, but at 6:09 Cramer had phoned, and at 6:27 the doorbell had started up again, and through the one-way glass panel Sergeant Stebbins had been visible. He had kept at it for five minutes and was now in a police car with a colleague out at the curb.

I got up, went to the front door for a look, came back, requested more toast, and poured more coffee. "He's still there," I told Fritz, "and there's one danger. As you know, Mr. Wolfe can't bear the idea of a hungry man in his house, and while Stebbins isn't actually in the house he's there in front and wants to be, and he looks hungry. If Mr. Wolfe sees him and suspects he hasn't had breakfast there'll be hell to pay. Could I borrow a little wild thyme honey?"

I was on the last bite of toast and honey and the last inch of coffee when the sound of Wolfe's elevator came, and by the time I was through swallowing and got to the office he was there behind his desk. We said good morning.

"So," I said, "it wasn't a prankster."

"Apparently not." With the edge of a blotter he was flipping from his desk pad dust that wasn't there. "Get Mr. Cramer."

I got at the phone and dialed, and soon had him, and Wolfe took it. I held my receiver an inch from my ear, expecting a blast, but it had gone beyond that. Cramer's voice was merely hoarse with fury.

"Where are you?" he demanded.

"I'm on an errand, no matter where. I'm calling to ask about the bullet I sent you. Does it match the others?"

"You know damn well it does. You knew it when you sent it. This is the rawest—"

"No. I suspected it, but I didn't know it. That was what I had to know before I divulged where it came from. That was why I arranged to keep its source anonymous until I knew. I would like to have it explicitly. Was the bullet I sent you fired from the same gun as those that killed Eber and Brigham?"

"By God." Cramer knew darned well he shouldn't use profanity on the phone, so he must have been upset. "You arranged! I'll arrange you! I'll arrange for you to—"

"Mr. Cramer! This is ridiculous. I'm supplying the solution of an extremely bothersome case, and you sputter at me. If you must sputter, wait until you have the facts. Will you please answer my question?"

"The answer is yes."

"Then I'm ready to deliver the murderer and the weapon, but there is the matter of procedure to consider. I can invite the district attorney to my house and give him the weapon and two excellent witnesses, and let him get the culprit. Or I can do that with you. I don't like either of those because I have been at considerable expense and I have earned a fee, and I want to be paid, and there is plenty of money in that family. I want the family to know what I have done, and how, and the most effective and impressive way to inform them is to have them present when I produce the weapon and identify the murderer. If I invite them they won't come. You can bring them. If you'll—please let me finish. If you'll have them at my house at eleven o'clock, all of them, I'll be there to receive you, and you'll get all you need and more. Three hours from now. I hope you'll oblige me because I like dealing with you better than with the district attorney."

"I ought to appreciate that," Cramer said, hoarser than ever.

"You're home now. You've been home all night. You knew damn well the bullet would match, and you knew as soon as we checked it we'd be on you, and you didn't want to be bothered until morning so you could spring this on me. In half an hour we'll have a search warrant for your house, and we'll have warrants for you and Goodwin as material witnesses."

"Indeed. Then forgive me if I ring off. I have a call to make."

"Yeah. You would. By God, you would. I let you have those reports and this is what I get for it. Who do you want there?"

"The five people named Jarrell, and Miss Kent and Mr. Foote. At eleven o'clock."

"Sure, I know. Until eleven you'll be up with your goddamn orchids. We mustn't interfere with that."

He hung up. So did we.

"You know," I said, "I think the orchids irritate him. I've noticed it before. Maybe you should get rid of them. Do I answer the phone now?"

"Yes. Miss Bonner and Saul and Fred and Orrie are going to call between nine and nine-thirty. Tell them to come at eleven. If the Jarrells are to be properly impressed they should see all of them."

"Okay. But it wouldn't hurt if I knew in advance which one to keep an eye on. I know darned well it's not Roger Foote."

He looked up at the wall clock. "It's early. Very well."

17

I had turned over the doorman-and-usher job to Saul and Orrie because I was otherwise engaged. Cramer, with Stebbins, had arrived twenty minutes early and insisted on seeing Wolfe, and I had taken them to the dining room and stayed to keep them company. They didn't want my company, they wanted Wolfe's, but I told them that if they climbed three flights to the plant rooms they would find the door locked. I offered to pass the time by telling them the story about the chorus girl and the anteater, but it didn't seem to appeal to them.

When Wolfe opened the dining-room door and said, "Good morning, gentlemen," and Cramer told him to come in and shut the door, a wrangle seemed unavoidable, but Wolfe avoided it by saying, "In the office, please," and turning and going. Cramer and Stebbins followed, and I brought up the rear.

On the three previous occasions that Otis Jarrell had been in that office he had had the seat of honor, the red leather chair, but this time Saul, following instructions, had kept it for Inspector Cramer, and the ex-client was in the front row of the audience with his wife, his son, and his daughter-in-law. Behind them were Lois, Nora Kent, Roger Foote, and Saul Panzer. On the couch, at my back when I got to my desk, were Sally Colt, of Dol Bonner's staff, and Fred Durkin and Orrie Cather. Purley Stebbins' chair was where he always put it himself if we didn't, against the wall at arm's length from Cramer.

Actually, for that particular party, the red leather chair was not the seat of honor. The seat of honor was one of the yellow chairs which had been placed at the other end of Wolfe's desk, on his right, and in it was Dol Bonner, a very attractive sight for a female dick, with her home-grown long black lashes making a curling canopy for her caramel-colored eyes. I had warned Fritz she would be there. She had once been invited to dine at the table he cooks for, and he suspects every woman who ever crosses the threshold of wanting to take over his kitchen, not to mention the rest of the house.

Inspector Cramer, standing, faced the audience and spoke. "Nero Wolfe is going to say something and you can listen along with me. You're here on police orders, so I want to make one thing clear. Any questions Wolfe asks you are his questions and not mine. Answer them or not as you please. Wolfe is not acting for the police or speaking for the police."

"I have nothing to ask, Mr. Cramer," Wolfe said. "Not a single question. I have only to report and expound."

"All right, go ahead." Cramer sat down.

"What I wish to report," Wolfe told the audience, "is how I found the weapon that killed two men, and how its finding revealed the identity of the killer. After you people left here on Monday, eight days ago, and after I had given Mr. Cramer the information I had told you I would give him, I was without a client and had no assigned function in this affair. But my curiosity was alive, my self-esteem was involved, and I wanted to be paid for the time I had spent and the ignominy I had endured. I resolved to pursue the matter."

He cleared his throat. "You people were no longer available to me for inquiry. You were through with me. I had neither the personnel nor the facilities for the various lines of routine investigation, and besides, the police were seeing to that. But there was one established fact that offered possibilities: the bullets that killed Eber and Brigham had been fired by the same gun. Assuming that they had also been fired by the same person, obviously the gun had been in his possession from Thursday afternoon, when Eber was killed, to Sunday afternoon, when Brigham was killed—or at least it had been kept where he could get it again. Where had it been kept?"

His eyes went to Cramer and back to them. "Mr. Cramer obliged me by permitting Mr. Goodwin access to the reports of your movements during that period. I was and am deeply appreciative of his cooperation; it would be churlish to suppose that he let me learn the contents of the reports only because he wanted to know what I was going to do with them. Here they are."

With a forefinger he tapped papers on his desk. "Here they are, as typed by Mr. Goodwin. I inspected and analyzed them. It was possible, of course, that the gun had been kept somewhere on the premises where you all live, but I thought it extremely unlikely. At any moment the police, learning of the disappearance of Mr. Jarrell's gun, might search the place—as they did eventually, one week ago today. It was highly probable that the gun had been kept somewhere else, and I proceeded on that theory."

"So did I," Cramer rasped.

Wolfe nodded. "No doubt. But for you it was only one of many lines of inquiry, whereas it was all I had. And not only was it a near-certainty that the gun had been kept in some available spot from Thursday afternoon to Sunday afternoon, but also there was a chance that it had been returned to that spot after Brigham was killed and was still there. On Sunday, when he left the car on Thirty-ninth Street, the murderer had the gun and had to dispose of it somehow. If he put it somewhere, anywhere, where it might be found, there was the risk that it *would* be found and would be identified both as Mr. Jarrell's gun and as the gun the bullets had come from. If he put it somewhere where it would *not* be found— for instance, at the bottom of the river—he might be seen, and besides, time was probably pressing. So it was quite possible that he had returned it, at the first opportunity, if not immediately, to the place where he had kept it for three days. Therefore my quest was for a spot not merely where the gun had been kept for the three days, but where it might still be."

He took a breath. "So I analyzed the timetables. They offered various suggestions, some promising, some far-fetched. To explore them I needed help, and I called on Mr. Saul Panzer, who is seated there beside Mr. Foote; on Mr. Fred Durkin, on the couch; on Mr. Orville Cather, on the couch beside Mr. Durkin; on Miss Theodolinda Bonner, here at my right; and on Miss Sally Colt, Miss Bonner's assistant, on the couch beside Mr. Durkin."

"Get on with it," Cramer growled.

Wolfe ignored him. "I won't detail all their explorations, but some deserve brief mention. They were all severely handicapped by the holiday and the long week end. Mr. Goodwin spent four days at the Jamaica and Belmont race tracks. Mr. Panzer traced Mr. Jarrell's movements on the Thursday when Eber was killed with extraordinary industry and acumen. Mr. Durkin performed with perseverance and ingenuity at the Metropolitan Athletic Club. Mr. Cather found three different people who had seen Mrs. Otis Jarrell in Central Park on the Sunday when Brigham was killed. But it was Miss Bonner and Miss Colt who had both ability and luck. Miss Bonner, produce the gun, please?"

Dol Bonner opened her bag, took out a revolver, said, "It's loaded," and put it on Wolfe's desk. Cramer came breezing around the front of the desk, nearly tripping on Wyman's foot, spouting as he came, and Purley Stebbins was up too. Dol Bonner told Cramer, "I tried it for prints, Inspector. There were no good ones. Look out, it's loaded."

"You loaded it?"

"No. It held two cases and four cartridges when I found it. I fired one cartridge, and that left—"

"You fired it?"

"Mr. Cramer," Wolfe said sharply. "How could we learn if it was the guilty gun without firing it? Let me finish and you can have all day."

I opened a drawer of my desk, got a heavy manila envelope, and handed it to Cramer. He picked the gun up by the trigger guard, put it in the envelope, circled Wolfe's desk to hand the envelope to Purley, said, "Go ahead and finish," and sat.

Wolfe asked, "What did you do after you found the gun, Miss Bonner?"

"Miss Colt was with me. We phoned you and got instructions and followed them. We went to my office and filed a nick in the barrel of the gun so we could identify it. We then went to my apartment, turned on the radio as loud as it would go, fired a bullet into some cushions, got the bullet, put it in a box with cotton, wrapped the box in paper, and sent it to you by messenger."

"When did you find the gun?"

"At ten minutes after six yesterday afternoon."

"Has it been continuously in your possession since then?"

"It has. Every minute. I slept with it under my pillow."

"Was Miss Colt with you when you found it?"

"Yes."

"Where did you find it?"

"In a locker on the fourth floor at Clarinda Day's on Forty-eighth Street."

Trella Jarrell let out a king-size gasp. Eyes went to her and she covered her mouth with both hands.

Wolfe went on. "Was the locker locked?"

"Yes."

"Did you break it open?"

"No. I used a key."

"I won't ask you how you got the key. You may be asked in court, but this is not a court. Was the locker one of a series?"

"Yes. There are four rows of private lockers on that floor, with twenty lockers to a row. Clarinda Day's customers put their clothes and belongings in them while they are doing exercises or getting massages. Some of them keep changes of clothing or other articles in them."

"You said private lockers. Is each locker confined to a single customer?"

"Yes. The customer has the only key, except that I suppose the management has a master key. The key I used—but I'm not to tell that now?"

"It isn't necessary. You may tell it on the witness stand. As you know, what you did is actionable, but since you discovered a weapon that was used in two murders I doubt if you will suffer any penalty. Instead, you should be rewarded and probably will be. Do you know which of Clarinda Day's customers the locker belonged to? The one you found the gun in."

"Yes. Mrs. Wyman Jarrell. Her name was on it. It also had other articles in it, and among them were letters in envelopes addressed to her."

No gasp from anyone. No anything, until Otis Jarrell muttered, barely loud enough to hear, "The snake, the snake."

Wolfe's eyes were at Susan. "Mrs. Jarrell. Do you wish to offer an explanation of how the gun got into your locker?"

Naturally, knowing what was coming, I had been watching her little oval face from a corner of my eye, and she was only four feet from me, and I swear there hadn't been a flicker. As she met Wolfe's eyes her lip muscles moved a little as if they were trying to manage a smile, but I had seen them do that before. And when she spoke it was the same voice, low, and shy or coy or wary or demure, depending on your attitude.

"I can't explain it," she said, "because I don't know. But you can't think I took it that day, that Wednesday, because I told you about that. I was upstairs in my room, and my husband was with me. Weren't you, Wy?"

She would probably have skipped that if she had turned for a good look at his face before asking it. He was paralyzed, staring at Wolfe with his jaw hanging. He looked incapable of speech, but a kind of idiot mumble came out, "I was taking a shower, a long shower, I always take a long shower."

You might think, when a man is hit so hard with the realization that his wife is a murderess that he lets something out which will help to sink her, he would at least give it some tone, some quality. That's a hell of a speech in a crisis like that: "I was taking a shower, a long shower, I always take a long shower."

As Wolfe would say, pfui.

18

As it turned out, when Otis Jarrell's private affairs, at least some of them, became public, it was out of his own mouth on the witness stand. While it is true that evidence of motive is not legally essential in a murder case, it helps a lot, and for that the DA had to have Jarrell. The theory was that Susan had worked on Jim Eber and got information from him, specifically about the claim on the shipping company, and passed it along to Corey Brigham, who had acted on it. After Eber was fired he had learned about Brigham's clean-up on the deal, suspected he had been fired because Jarrell thought he had given the information to Brigham, remembered he had told Susan about it, suspected her of telling Brigham, and told her, probably just before I entered the studio that day, that he was going to tell Jarrell. To support the theory Jarrell was needed, though they had other items, the strongest one being that they found two hundred thousand dollars in cash in a safe-deposit box Susan had rented about that time, and she couldn't remember where she had got it.

Brigham's death was out of it as far as the trial was concerned, since she was being tried for Eber, but the theory was that he had suspected her of killing Eber and had told her so, and take your pick. Either he had disapproved of murder so strongly that he was going to pass it on, or he wanted something for not passing it on— possibly the two hundred grand back, possibly something more personal.

None of the rest of them was called to testify by either side. The defense put neither Susan nor Wyman on, and that probably hurt. Susan's having a key to the library was no problem, since her husband had one and she slept in the same room with him. As for whether they'll ever get her to the chair, you'll have to watch the papers. The jury convicted her of the big one, with no recommendation, but to get a woman actually in that seat, especially a young one with a little oval face, takes a lot of doing.

Wolfe took Jarrell's money, a check this time, and a very attractive one, and that's all right, he earned it. But that was all he wanted from that specimen, or me either. He said it for both of us the day after Susan was indicted, when Jarrell phoned to say he was going to mail a check for a certain amount and would that be satisfactory, and when Wolfe said it would Jarrell went on: "And I was right, Wolfe. She's a snake. You didn't believe me the day I came to hire you, and neither did Goodwin, but now you know I was right, and that gives me a lot of satisfaction. She's a snake."

"No, sir." Wolfe was curt. "I do not know you were right. She is a murderess, a hellcat, and a wretch, but you have furnished no evidence that she is a snake. I still do not believe you. I will be glad to get the check."

He hung up and so did I.

Before Midnight

1

Not that our small talk that Tuesday evening in April had any important bearing on the matter, but it will do for an overture, and it will help to explain a couple of reactions Nero Wolfe had later. After a dinner that was featured by one of Fritz's best dishes, squabs with sausage and sauerkraut, in the dining room of the old brownstone house on West Thirty-fifth Street, I followed Wolfe across the hall to the office, and, as he got some magazines from the table near the big globe and went to his chair behind his desk, asked if there were any chores. That was insurance. I had notified him that I intended to take Thursday afternoon off for the opening of the baseball season at the Polo Grounds, and when Thursday came I didn't want any beefing about my letting things pile up.

He said no, no chores, got all his vast bulk adjusted in the chair, the only chair on earth he approved of, and opened a magazine. He allotted around twenty minutes a week for looking at advertisements. I went to my desk, sat, and reached for the phone, then changed my mind, deciding a little more insurance wouldn't hurt. Swiveling and seeing that he was scowling at the open magazine, I got up and circled around near enough to see what he was focused on. It was a full-page ad, black and white, that I and many millions of my fellow citizens knew by heart—though it didn't require much study, since there were only six words in it, not counting repetitions. At the center near the top was a distinguished-looking small bottle, labeled in fancy script *Pour Amour*, with the *Amour* beneath the *Pour*. Right below it were two more of the same, also centered, and below them three more, and then four more, and so on down the page. At the bottom seven bottles stretched clear across, making the base of a twenty-eight-bottle pyramid. In the space at the top left was the statement:

Pour Amour

means

For Love

and at top right it said:

Pour Amour

is

for love

"There are two things about that ad," I said.

Wolfe grunted and turned a page.

"One thing," I said, "is the name itself. To sixty-four and seventenths per cent of the women seeing it, it will suggest 'paramour,' and the percentage would be higher if more of them knew what a paramour is. I won't decry American womanhood. Some of my best friends are women. Very few of them want to be or have paramours, so you couldn't come right out and name a perfume that. Put it this way. They see the ad, and they think, So they have the nerve to suggest their snazzy old perfume will get me a paramour! I'll show 'em! What do they think I am? Half an ounce, ten bucks. The other thing—"

"One's enough," he growled.

"Yes, sir. The second thing, so many bottles. That's against the rules. The big idea in a perfume ad is to show only one bottle, to give the impression that it's a scarce article and you'd better hurry up and get yours. Not Pour Amour. They say, Come on, we've got plenty and it's a free country and every woman has a right to a paramour, and if you don't want one prove it. It's an entirely new approach, one hundred per cent American, and it seems to be paying off, it and the contest together."

I had expected to get the desired results by that time, but all he did was sit and turn pages. I took a breath.

"The contest, as you probably know since you look at ads some, is a pip. A million dollars in cash prizes. Each week for nearly five months they have furnished a description of a woman—I might as well give you the exact specifications, since you've been training my memory for years—'a woman recorded in non-fictional history in any of its forms, including biography, as having used cosmetics.' Twenty of them in twenty weeks. This was the description of Number One:

> *"Though Caesar fought to give me power*
> *And I had Antony in my grasp,*
> *My bosom, in the fatal hour,*
> *Welcomed the fatal asp.*

"Of course that was pie. Cleopatra. Number Two was just as easy:

> *"Married to one named Aragon,*
> *I listened to Columbus' tales,*
> *And offered all my gems to pawn*
> *To buy him ships and sails.*

"I didn't remember ever reading that Queen Isabella used cosmetics, but since nobody ever bathed in the fifteenth century she must have. I could also give you Numbers Three, Four, and Five, but after that they began to get tough, and by Number Ten I wasn't even bothering to read them. God knows what they were like by the time they got to Twenty—to give you an example, here's Number Seven or Eight, I forget which:

> *"My eldest son became a peer*
> *Although I couldn't write my name;*
> *As Mr. Brown's son's fondest dear*
> *I earned enduring fame.*

"I call that fudging. Considering how many Mr. Browns have had sons in the course of history, and how many of the sons—"

"Pah." Wolfe turned a page. "Nell Gwynn, the English actress."

I stared. "Yeah, I've heard of her. How come? One of her boy friends may have been named Brown or Brownson, but that wasn't what made her famous. It was some king."

"Charles the Second." He was smug. "He made his son by her a duke. His father, Charles the First, on a trip to Spain in his youth,

had assumed the name of Mr. Brown. And of course Nell Gwynn
was the mistress of Charles the Second."

"I prefer paramour. Okay, so you've read ten thousand books.
What about this one—I think it was Number Nine:

> *"By the law himself had earlier made*
> *I could not be his legal wife;*
> *The law he properly obeyed*
> *And loved me all my life."*

I flipped a hand. "Name her."

"Archie." His head turned to me. "You have somewhere to go?"

"No, sir, not tonight. Lily Rowan has a table at the Flamingo
Room and thought I might drop in for a dance, but I told her you
might need me, and she knows how indispensable I—"

"Pfui." He started to glare and decided it wasn't worth the trouble. "You intended to go, and undertook to shift the responsibility
for your absence by pestering me into suggesting it. You have succeeded. I suggest that you go somewhere at once."

There were three or four things I could have said, but he sighed
and went back to the magazine, so I skipped it. As I headed for the
hall his voice told my back, "You shaved and changed your clothes
before dinner."

That's the trouble with working for and living with a really great
detective.

2

Since I got home late that night and there was nothing urgent on,
it was after nine Wednesday morning before I got down to the
kitchen for my snack of grapefruit, oatmeal, griddle cakes, bacon,
blackberry jam, and coffee. Wolfe had of course breakfasted in
his room as usual and gone up to the plant rooms on the roof for
his morning session with the orchids.

"It is a good thing, Archie," Fritz remarked, spooning batter,
his own batter, onto the griddle for my fourth cake, "to see you

break your fast with proper leisure. Disturbed by no interruptions."

I finished a paragraph in the *Times* on the rack before me, swallowed, sipped some coffee, and spoke. "Fritz, I'll be honest with you. There's no one else on earth I could stand in the same room while I'm eating breakfast and reading the morning paper. When you speak you leave it entirely up to me whether I reply, or even whether I listen. However, you should know that I understand you. Take what you just said. What you meant was that no interruptions means no clients and no cases, and you're wondering if the bank account is getting too low for comfort. Right?"

"Yes." He flipped the thick golden-brown disc onto my plate. "But if you think I am worried, no. It is never a question of worry here. With Mr. Wolfe and you—"

The phone rang. I took it there on the kitchen extension, and a deep baritone voice told me it was Rudolph Hansen and wanted to speak to Nero Wolfe. I said Mr. Wolfe wouldn't be available until eleven o'clock but I would take a message. He said he had to see him immediately and would be there in fifteen minutes. I said nothing doing before eleven unless he told me why it was so urgent. He said he would arrive in fifteen minutes and hung up.

Meanwhile Fritz had ditched the cake because it had been off the griddle too long, and started another one.

Ordinarily when a stranger has made an appointment I do a little research on him in advance, but I wouldn't have got very far in a quarter of an hour, and anyway I had another cake and cup of coffee coming. I had just finished and gone to the office with the *Times* to put it on my desk when the doorbell rang. When I went to the hall I saw out on the stoop, through the one-way glass panel in the door, not one stranger but four—three middle-aged men and one who had been, all well dressed and two with homburgs.

I opened the door the two inches that the chain bolt allowed and spoke through the crack. "Your names, please?"

"I'm Rudolph Hansen. I telephoned."

"And the others?"

"This is ridiculous! Open the door!"

"It only seems ridiculous, Mr. Hansen. There are at least a hundred people within a hundred miles, which takes in Sing Sing, who would like to tell Mr. Wolfe what they think of him and maybe prove it. I admit you're not hoods, but with four of you—names, please?"

"I'm an attorney-at-law. These are clients of mine. Mr. Oliver Buff. Mr. Patrick O'Garro. Mr. Vernon Assa."

The names were certainly no help, but I had had time to size them up, and if I knew anything at all about faces they had come not to make trouble but to get out from under some. So I opened the door, helped them put their hats and coats on the big old walnut rack, ushered them into the office and onto chairs, sat at my desk, and told them:

"I'm sorry, gentlemen, but that's the way it is. Mr. Wolfe never comes to the office until eleven. The rule has been broken, but it takes a lot of breaking. The only way would be for you to tell me all about it and persuade me to tackle him, and then for me to go and tell him all about it and try to persuade him. Even if I succeeded, all that would take twenty-five minutes, and it's now twenty-five to eleven, so you might as well relax."

"Your name's Goodwin," Hansen stated. His baritone didn't sound as deep as it had on the phone. I had awarded him the red leather chair near the end of Wolfe's desk, but, with his long thin neck and gray skin and big ears, he clashed with it. A straight-backed painted job with no upholstery would have suited him better.

"Mr. Goodwin," he said, "this is a confidential matter of imperative urgency. I insist that you tell Mr. Wolfe we must see him at once."

"We all do," one of the clients said in an executive tone. Another had popped up from his chair as soon as he sat down and was pacing the floor. The third was trying to keep a match steady enough to light a cigarette. Seeing that I was in for a pointless wrangle, I said politely, "Okay, I'll see what I can do," and got up and left the room.

In the kitchen, Fritz, who was cleaning up after breakfast and who would never have presumed to ask in words if it looked like business, asked it with a glance as I entered and went to the table where the phones were. I lifted my brows at him, took the house phone, and buzzed the plant rooms.

In a minute Wolfe growled in my ear. "Well?"

"I'm calling from the kitchen. In the office are four men with Sulka shirts and Firman shoes in a panic. They say they must see you at once."

"Confound it—"

"Yes, sir. I'm merely notifying you that we have company. I told them I'd see what I can do, and that's what I can do." I hung up before he could, took the other phone, and dialed a number.

Nathaniel Parker, the lawyer Wolfe always calls on when he is driven to that extremity, wasn't in, but his clerk, Sol Ehrlich, was, and he had heard of Rudolph Hansen. All he knew was that Hansen was a senior partner in one of the big midtown firms with a fat practice, and that he had quite a reputation as a smooth operator. When I hung up I told Fritz that there was a pretty good prospect of snaring a fee that would pay our wages for several months, provided he would finish waking me up by supplying another cup of coffee.

When the sound came, at eleven o'clock on the dot, of Wolfe's elevator starting down, I went to the hall, met him as he emerged, reported on Hansen, and followed him into the office. As usual, I waited to pronounce names until he had reached his chair behind his desk, because he doesn't like to shake hands with strangers, and then Hansen beat me to it. He arose to put a card on Wolfe's desk and sat down again.

"My card," he said. "I'm Rudolph Hansen, attorney-at-law. These gentlemen are clients of mine—that is, their firm is. Mr. Oliver Buff. Mr. Patrick O'Garro. Mr. Vernon Assa. We've lost some valuable time waiting for you. We must see you privately."

Wolfe was frowning. The first few minutes with prospective clients are always tough for him. Possibly there will be no decent excuse for turning them down, and if not he'll have to go to work. He shook his head. "This is private. You glance at Mr. Goodwin. He may not be indispensable, but he is irremovable."

"We prefer to see you alone."

"Then I'm sorry, sir. You have indeed lost time."

He looked at his clients, and so did I. Oliver Buff, the one who had finished with middle age, had a round red face that made his hair look whiter, and his hair made his face look redder. He and Hansen wore the homburgs. Patrick O'Garro was brown all over—eyes, hair, suit, tie, shoes, and socks. Of course his shirt was white. The eyes were bright, quick, and clever. Vernon Assa was short and a little plump, with fat shoulders, and either he had just got back from a month in Florida or he hadn't needed to go. The brown getup would have gone fine with his skin, but he was in gray with black shoes.

"What the hell," he muttered.

"Go ahead," Buff told Hansen.

The lawyer returned to Wolfe. "Mr. Goodwin is your employee, of course?"

"He is."

"He is present at this conversation in his capacity as your agent?"

"Agent? Very well. Yes."

"Then that's understood. First I would like to suggest that you engage me as your counsel and hand me one dollar as a retaining fee."

I opened my eyes at him. The guy must be cuckoo. For fee shipments that office was strictly a one-way street.

"Not an appealing suggestion," Wolfe said drily. "You have a brief for it?"

"Certainly. As you know, a conversation between a lawyer and his client is a privileged communication and its disclosure may not be compelled. I wish to establish that confidential relationship with you, lawyer and client, and then tell you of certain circumstances which have led these gentlemen to seek your help. Obviously that will be no protection against voluntary disclosure by you, since you may end the relationship at any moment, but you will be able to refuse a disclosure at the demand of any authority without incurring any penalty. They and I will be at your mercy, but your record and reputation give us complete confidence in your integrity and discretion. I suggest that you retain me for a specific function: to advise you on the desirability of taking a case about to be offered to you by the firm of Lippert, Buff and Assa."

"What is that firm?"

"You must have heard of it. The advertising agency."

Wolfe's lips were going left to right and back again. It was his kind of smile. "Very ingenious. I congratulate you. But as you say, you will be at my mercy. I may end the relationship at any moment, with no commitment whatever."

"Just a minute," O'Garro put in, his clever bright brown eyes darting from Wolfe to Hansen. "Must it be like that?"

"It's the only way, Pat," the lawyer told him. "If you hire him, you either trust him or you don't."

"I don't like it . . . but if it's the only way . . ."

"It is. Oliver?"

Buff said yes.

"Vern?"

Assa nodded.

"Then you retain me, Mr. Wolfe? As specified?"

"Yes. —Archie, give Mr. Hansen a dollar."

I got one from my wallet, suppressing a pointed comment which the transaction certainly deserved, crossed to the attorney-at-law, and handed it over.

"I give you this," I told him formally, "as the agent for Mr. Nero Wolfe."

3

"It's a long story," Hansen told Wolfe, "but we'll have to make it as short as possible. These gentlemen have appointments at the District Attorney's office. I speak as your counsel of matters pertinent to the case to be offered you about which you seek my advice. Have you heard of the murder of Louis Dahlmann?"

"No."

"It was on the radio."

"I don't listen to the radio in the morning. Neither does Mr. Goodwin."

"To hell with the radio," Assa snapped. "Get on, Rudolph."

"I am. One of LBA's big accounts—we call Lippert, Buff and Assa LBA—is Heery Products, Incorporated. One of the Heery products is the line of cosmetics that they call Pour Amour. They introduced it some years ago and it was doing fairly well. Last spring a young man on the LBA staff named Louis Dahlmann conceived an idea for promoting it, and he finally succeeded in getting enough approval of the idea to have it submitted to the Heery people, and they decided they liked it, and it was scheduled to start the twenty-seventh of September. It was a prize contest, the biggest in history, with a first prize of five hundred thousand dollars in cash, second prize two hundred and fifty thousand, third prize one hundred thousand, and fifty-seven smaller prizes. I have to explain it to you. Each week for twenty weeks there appeared in newspapers and magazines a four-line verse, from which—"

"I can save you that," Wolfe told him. "I know about it."

"Did you enter?" O'Garro demanded.

"Enter the contest? Good heavens, no."

"Get on," Assa snapped.

Hansen did so. "The deadline was February fourteenth. The answers had to be postmarked before midnight February fourteenth. There were over two million contestants, and Dahlmann had trained three hundred men and women to handle the checking and recording. When they finished they had seventy-two contestants who had identified all twenty of the women correctly. Dahlmann had more verses ready, and on March twenty-eighth he sent five of them to each of the seventy-two contestants, by airmail to those at a distance, and the answers had to be postmarked before midnight April fourth. It came out a quintuple tie. Five of them correctly identified the five new ones, and Dahlmann telephoned them and arranged for them to come to New York. They would land the first three prizes, the big three, and also two of the ten-thousand-dollar prizes. They came, and last evening he had them to dinner in a private room at the Churchill. Talbott Heery of Heery Products was there, and so were Vernon Assa and Patrick O'Garro. Dahlmann was going to give them five more verses, with a week to solve them, but a woman who lives in Los Angeles objected that she wanted to work at home and would have to take part of the week getting there, so it was arranged to stagger the deadlines for the postmarks according to how long it would take each one to get home. The meeting ended shortly before eleven o'clock, and they left and separated. Four of them, from out of town, had rooms at the Churchill. One who lives in New York, a young woman named Susan Tescher, presumably went home."

"Get on, damn it," Assa snapped.

"I'm making it as brief as possible, Vern. —Dahlmann also presumably went home. He was a bachelor and lived alone in an apartment on Perry Street. A woman came at seven in the morning to get his breakfast, and when she got there this morning he was on the floor of the living room, dead. He was shot through the heart, from the back, and a cushion from a divan was used to muffle the sound. She ran and got the building superintendent, and the police were notified, and they came and went to work. You may need more facts about the murder when they're available—he was found only four hours ago—but you may not, because that's not what you're needed for. You're needed for something more urgent than murder."

I uncrossed my legs. Something more urgent than murder called for muscles set to go.

Hansen was leaning forward, his palms on his knees. "Here's the crux of it. No one knew the answers in that contest but Louis Dahlmann. He had written all the verses himself—the original twenty, the five to break the first tie, with seventy-two contestants, and the five to break the second tie, with five contestants. Of course the answers for the first twenty had to be known to the crew of checkers and recorders, after the deadline had passed and they started to work, but he himself checked the answers of the seventy-two who were in the first tie. With the third group, the five in the second tie, he guarded the verses themselves almost as strictly as the answers. He typed the verses personally and made only seven copies. One copy was placed in a safe deposit vault, one he kept—I'm not sure where—and the other five were given by him last evening to the five contestants at the meeting."

"He kept it in his wallet," O'Garro said.

Hansen ignored it. "Anyway, the point is not the verses but the answers. I speak of the answers to the last group of five verses— the others don't matter now. Of course it was merely the names of five women, with an explanation of the fitness of the verses for them. There was supposed to be only one copy in existence. It had been typed by Dahlmann on an LBA letterhead, signed by him and initialed by Buff, O'Garro, and Assa, with the answers covered so they couldn't see them, and then put in the safe deposit vault, in a sealed envelope, with five men present. So as I said, no one knew the answers but Dahlmann."

"As far as we know," Oliver Buff put in.

"Certainly," the lawyer agreed. "To our knowledge."

"My God, reach the point," Assa rapped out.

"I am. But at the meeting last evening Dahlmann did an extremely reckless thing. When he—"

"Worse than reckless," Buff declared. "Irresponsible! Criminal!"

"That may be a little strong. But it was certainly ill-advised. When he was ready to hand out the new group of verses he took some envelopes from his inside breast pocket, and other things came with them—other papers and his wallet. He passed the envelopes around, and then—you tell it, Pat, you were there."

O'Garro obliged. "After he gave them the envelopes he started to return the other stuff to his pocket, then he hesitated a moment, smiled around at them, opened the wallet, took a piece of folded paper from it and held it up, and told them he wanted to make—"

"No. Exactly what he said."

"He said, 'I just wanted to make sure I wasn't leaving this here on the table. It's the names of the women who fit the verses I just gave you.' Then he slipped the paper back in the wallet and put it in his pocket."

"Criminal!" Buff blurted.

"How soon after that did the meeting end?"

"Almost immediately. They were so anxious to take a look at the verses we couldn't have held them if we had wanted to, and we didn't."

Hansen leaned to Wolfe. "There it is. When Dahlmann's body was found he was fully dressed, in the same clothes. Everything was in his pockets, including a roll of bills, several hundred dollars, except one thing. The wallet was gone. We want—Lippert, Buff and Assa want you to find out which one of those five people took it, and today if possible. They're in New York. Four of them were going to take planes this morning, but we stopped them by telling them that the police will have to see them." He glanced at his wrist watch. "We have appointments at the District Attorney's office, but they can wait. What do you need to get started fast?"

"Quite a little." Wolfe sighed. "Am I being engaged by the firm of Lippert, Buff and Assa? Is that correct?"

Hansen turned his head. "Oliver?"

"Yes," Buff said, "that's correct."

"I charge extravagantly. The amount of the fee is left open?"
"Yes."

"To hell with the fee," Assa said, a noble attitude.

"Where," Wolfe asked, "is Mr. Lippert?"

"There is no Lippert. He died ten years ago."

"Then he's through with perfume contests. —You said, Mr. Hansen, that you want me to find out which of those five people took the wallet. I won't undertake it. It's too restricted. What if none of them did?"

"For God's sake." Hansen stared. "Who else?"

"I don't know. From what you have told me I think it highly probable it was one of them, indeed it seems almost conclusive, but I won't be bound like that. At least three others knew that paper was in the wallet: Mr. Heery, Mr. O'Garro, and Mr. Assa."

Assa snorted with impatience. O'Garro said, "You're absolutely right. And from a booth in the Churchill I phoned Hansen and Buff and told them about it. Hansen said nothing could be done. Buff wanted me to see Dahlmann and persuade him to destroy the paper, but I talked him out of it."

"All right," Hansen conceded, "it's immaterial anyway. Put it that the job is to find out who took the wallet and got the paper. Is that satisfactory?"

"It is," Wolfe agreed. "It is understood that I am not engaging to expose the murderer."

"No. I mean it's understood. That's for the police, and I must make it clear. Nothing has been said to the police about Dahlmann's displaying that paper from his wallet last evening, and nothing is going to be said by any of us, including Mr. Heery. The paper has not been mentioned and will not be. The police will of course question the five contestants, probably they already are, and it might be thought certain that some of them will tell about the paper, but I think it doubtful. —What you said, Pat?"

O'Garro nodded. "I only said, from seeing them last evening, they're not fools. They're anything but fools, and there's half a million dollars at stake, not to mention the other prizes. My guess is none of them will mention it. What do you think, Vern?"

"The same," Assa agreed, "except possibly that old hellcat, the Frazee woman. God knows what she'll say."

"But," Hansen told Wolfe, "even if they do mention it, and the police ask us why we didn't, the answer is that we didn't think it worth mentioning because it was so obvious that Dahlmann was only joking. At least it was obvious to us, and we assumed it was to the others. If the police don't accept that, we shall nevertheless utterly reject the notion that Dahlmann had the answers to those five verses on a paper in his wallet, and the corollary that someone killed him to get it. The police are disposed to be discreet, and they often are, but a thing like that would certainly get out."

He had slid so far forward in the red leather chair that he would certainly slide off. He went on, "You may not fully realize how desperate it is. This contest is the most spectacular promotion of the century. A million in prizes with two million contestants, and the whole country is waiting to see the winner. Naturally we have thought of calling in those verses and preparing five new ones, but that would be risky. It would be an admission that we suspect one of them has secured the answers to those verses by killing Dahlmann, implying an admission that Dahlman had the answers in his wallet. Any one or all of the five contestants could refuse to surrender the verses on the ground that they had accepted them in good faith, and that would be a frightful mess. If LBA declined to proceed as agreed they could sue and almost certainly collect."

He took a piece of paper from his pocket and unfolded it. "This is a schedule of which each one of them has a copy.

"*Susan Tescher, New York City, before noon April nineteenth.*
"*Carol Wheelock, Richmond, Virginia, before midnight April nineteenth.*
"*Philip Younger, Chicago, Illinois, before midnight April nineteenth*
"*Harold Rollins, Burlington, Iowa, before midnight April nineteenth.*
"*Gertrude Frazee, Los Angeles, California, before midnight April twentieth.*"

He returned the paper to his pocket and slid back in the chair, which was a relief. "That's the postmark deadline for their answers, staggered as I said. It favors Miss Frazee, who was going to take a plane, but she held out for it. Since they're being held in New York they might agree on an extension, but what if Miss

Tescher, who lives here, refused? What if she went ahead and sent in her answers before her deadline? Where would we be?"

Wolfe grunted. "In a pickle."

"We certainly would. There's only one possible way out, to learn who got that paper, today or tomorrow if possible, but absolutely before midnight April twentieth, the last deadline. With proof of that we'll have them licked. We can say to them, One of you—and we name him—stole the answers. That makes it impossible to proceed with those verses. Surrender them or not, as you please, but we're going to give you five new verses and new deadlines, and award the prizes on the basis of your answers to them. They'll have to take it. Under those circumstances they would have no alternative. Would they?"

"No," Wolfe conceded. "But the one exposed as the purloiner of the answers wouldn't have much opportunity for research. He would be jailed on a charge of murder."

"That's his lookout."

"True. Also your guile would be disclosed. The police would know you had lied when you told them that you thought Dahlmann's display of that paper last night was only a joke."

"That can't be helped. Anyway, they'll have the murderer."

"True again. Also," Wolfe persisted, "you're taking an excessive risk in assuming that I will find the thief, with evidence, within a week. I may not. If I don't, you're not in a pickle, you're sunk. Before midnight April twentieth? I have only this"—he tapped his forehead—"and Mr. Goodwin and a few men I can rely on. Whereas the police have thousands of men and vast resources and connections. I must suggest that you consider taking your problem to them just as you have brought it to me."

"We have considered it. That wouldn't even be risky, it would be certain. By tomorrow morning it would have got out that the answers to the contest had been stolen, and it would be a national scandal, and LBA would have a black eye they might never recover from."

Wolfe was stubborn. "I must be sure you have thought it through. Even if I get the culprit before the deadline it will likewise come out that the answers were stolen."

"Yes, but then we will have the thief, and we'll have arranged to decide the contest in a way agreed to by everybody else concerned. A totally different situation. LBA will be admired and congratulated for dealing with a crisis promptly, boldly, and brilliantly."

"Not by the police."

"No. But by the advertising and business world, the press, and the American people."

"I suppose so." Wolfe's head turned. "I would like to make sure of the decision to dodge with the police. You concur in it, Mr. Buff?"

Buff's big red face had been getting redder, and his brow was moist. "I do," he said. "Because I have to."

"Mr. O'Garro?"

"Yes. We had that out before we came to you."

"Mr. Assa?"

"Yes. You're wasting time!"

"No. If it were a simple matter of catching a murderer—but it isn't. This is full of complexities, and I must know things." Wolfe turned a palm up. "For example. If I were sure that the one who took the wallet actually got the paper with the answers, that would help. But what if he didn't? What if the paper Dahlmann displayed was something else, and it was in fact a hoax, and the thief got nothing for his pains? That would make my job much more difficult and would require a completely different procedure."

"Don't worry," O'Garro assured him. "It was the answers all right. I was there and saw him. Vern?"

"I would say twenty to one," Assa declared. "Louis would get a kick out of showing them the paper with the answers, but just faking it, no. What do you think, Oliver?"

"You know quite well what I think." Buff was grim. "It was strictly in character. At the age of thirty-two Louis Dahlmann was a great creative genius, and in another ten years he would have been a dominant figure in American advertising, another Lasker. That's what we all thought, didn't we? But he had that lunatic streak in him. Of course that paper was the answers; there's not the slightest doubt. After you phoned me last night, Pat, I would have gone down to his place myself, but what was the use? Even if he had destroyed the paper to humor me, after I left he could have sat down and written another one just like it, and he probably would have. But now I wish I had. Right now the future of

LBA is in more danger than at any time in the thirty-eight years I've been with it. On account of him! If he were here now, alive, I tell you it would be hard for me to—" He tightened his lips and let the sentence hang.

Wolfe went to the lawyer. "Are you also convinced, Mr. Hansen, that it was no hoax?"

"I am."

"Then I'll proceed on that assumption until it is disproved. I must first see the five contestants, preferably not together, even though time is pressing." He glanced up at the wall clock. "They may already be engaged with the police, but we'll try. One of you will phone and arrange for one of them to be here at twelve-thirty, and arrange also for the others—one at three, one at six, one at—"

"Why six?" Assa demanded. "Good God, you won't need three hours!"

"I hope not. One should be plenty. But from four to six I'll be occupied with other matters, and—"

"There are no other matters! That's preposterous!"

Wolfe eyed him. "Your firm hasn't hired me by the hour, Mr. Assa. My schedule isn't subject to direction. I work as I work. One of them at three o'clock, one at six, one at seven, and one at eight. You can tell them that their detention in the city has created certain problems in connection with the contest and that you would like them to confer with me as your firm's representative. You will of course not mention the paper Mr. Dahlmann displayed last evening. I'll have dinner at nine o'clock, and any time after ten-thirty you may call on me for a report."

"I'd like to be present at the interviews," Hansen said. "But I can't at twelve-thirty."

"You can't at all, sir. They're going to be ticklish enough as it is, and I may even banish Mr. Goodwin. He will have an errand, by the way. Where is the safe deposit vault in which the answers were placed?"

"The Forty-seventh Street office of the Continental Trust Company."

"One of you will please meet Mr. Goodwin there at two-thirty, take him to the vault, open the envelopes containing the last five verses and the last five answers, and let him copy them and bring the copies to me. Return the originals to the vault."

"Impossible," O'Garro said positively. "Those envelopes must not be opened."

"Nonsense." Wolfe was beginning to get touchy, as usual when he was compelled to start things moving in his skull. "Why not? Those verses and answers are done for. No matter what happens, they can't possibly be the basis for awarding the prizes. They might, if we could get apodictic proof that there was no paper in Dahlmann's wallet containing the answers, but we can't. Can any of you describe any circumstances in which those verses and answers can now be used? Try it."

They exchanged glances. Wolfe waited.

"You're right," Buff admitted for the firm.

"Then it can do no harm for me to have them, provided Mr. Goodwin and I keep them to ourselves, and it may do some good. I have an idea for using them which may be worth developing. Will one of you meet him at two-thirty?"

"Yes," Buff agreed. "Probably two of us. Those envelopes have been untouchable. Mr. Heery will have to know about it. He may want to be present."

"As you please. By the way, since his firm is as deeply concerned as yours, what about him? Does he know you're hiring me? Does he approve your strategy?"

"Completely."

"Then that will do for now. Please use the phone on Mr. Goodwin's desk. Do you want him to get a number for you?"

They didn't, which was the best proof yet of how desperate they were. Since those birds were up around the top, the top numbers in one of the three biggest agencies in the country, with corner rooms at least twenty by twenty and incomes in six figures, it had of course been years since any of them had personally dialed a number in an office. To expect them to would be against all reason. But when I vacated my chair O'Garro came and took it, asked me for the number of the Churchill, and went ahead and dialed it as if it were a natural and normal procedure. I thought, There you are, a man with eyes as clever as that can do anything.

It took a while. After the rest of us had sat and listened for some minutes he finally hung up and told us, "Two of them were out. Rollins was just leaving for an appointment at Homicide West. Miss Frazee will be here at twelve-thirty."

Hansen, on his feet, said, "We must go, we'll be half an hour late. We'll get them later."

But Wolfe kept them for one more thing, information about the five contestants. They only had enough to fill one page of my notebook, which wasn't much to go on. I went to the hall with them to see that nobody took my topcoat by mistake, let them out, and returned to the office. Wolfe was sitting with his eyes closed and his palms flattened on the desk. I went to my desk and wheeled the machine to me and got out paper, to type the meager dope on the suspects. At the sound of footsteps I turned to see Fritz enter with beer on a tray.

"No," I said firmly. "Take it back, Fritz."

"A woman is coming!" Wolfe bellowed.

"That's only an excuse. The real trouble is that you hate a job with a deadline, especially when you stand about one chance in four thousand. I admit that before midnight April twentieth is one hell of an order, but on January nineteenth at three-twenty-seven p.m. you told me that if you ever rang for beer before lunch I should cancel it and disregard your protests, if any. I don't blame you for losing control, since we're almost certainly going to get our noses bumped, but no beer until after lunch. However, we don't want to embarrass Mr. Brenner."

I went and took the tray from Fritz and convoyed it to the kitchen.

4

If I had known what was on the way to him in the shape of Miss Gertrude Frazee of Los Angeles, founder and president of the Women's Nature League, I wouldn't have had the heart to hijack the beer. And if Wolfe had known, he probably would have refused the case and sent LBA and their counselor on their way.

I should try to describe her outfit, but I won't; I will only say she had swiped it from a museum. As for describing her, it's hard to believe. The inside corners of her eyes were trying to touch above a long thin nose, and nearly made it. Only an inch of brow was visible because straggles of gray hair flopped down over the rest. The left half of her mouth slanted up and the right half slanted down, and that made you think her chin was lower on one side than on the other, though maybe it wasn't. She was exactly my height, five feet eleven, and she strode.

She sat halfway back in the red leather chair, with both hands on her bag in her lap and her back straight and stiff. "I fail to see," she told Wolfe, "that the death of that man has any effect on the contest. Murder or not. There was nothing in the rules about anybody dying."

When she spoke her lips wanted to move perpendicular to the slant, but her jaw preferred straight up and down. You might have thought that after so many years, at least sixty, they would have come to an understanding, but nothing doing.

Wolfe was taking her in. "Certainly, madam, the rules did not contemplate sudden and violent death, and made no provision for it. The contest is affected, not by the death itself, but by the action of the police in asking the contestants not to leave the city until further—"

"They didn't ask me! They told me! They said if I left I would be brought back and arrested for murder!"

I shook my head. So she was that kind. No homicide cop and no assistant DA could possibly have said anything of the sort.

"They are sometimes ebullient," Wolfe told her. "Anyhow, I wanted to discuss not only the contest, but also you. After the prizes are awarded there will be great demand for information about the winners, and my clients want to be able to supply it. The enforced delay gives us this opportunity. My assistant, Mr. Goodwin, will take notes. I assume that you have never married, Miss Frazee?"

"I have not. And I won't." Her eyes took in my notebook. "I want to see anything that's going to be printed about me."

"You will. Have you ever won a prize in a contest?"

"I have never entered a contest. I despise contests."

"Indeed. Didn't you enter this one?"

"Of course I did. That's a stupid question."

"No doubt." Wolfe was polite. "But surely that's an interesting paradox—you despise contests, but you entered one. There must have been a compelling motive?"

"I fail to see that my motive is anybody's business, but I certainly am not ashamed of it. Ten years ago I founded the Women's Nature League of America. We have many thousand members, too many to count. What is your opinion of women who smear themselves with grease and soot and paint and stink themselves up with stuff made from black tar and decayed vegetable matter and tumors from male deer?"

"I haven't formulated one, madam."

"Of course you have. You're a male." Her eyes darted to me. "What's yours, young man?"

"It depends," I told her. "The tumor part sounds bad."

"It smells bad. It's been used for thirty centuries. Musk. In the Garden of Eden, when Eve's face was dirty what did she do? She washed it with good clean water. What do women do today? They rub it in with grease! Look at their lips and fingernails and toes and eyelashes—and other places. The Women's Nature League is the champion and the friend of the natural woman, and the natural woman was Eve, Eve the way God made her. The only true beauty is natural beauty, and I know, because I was denied that wondrous gift. I am not merely unlovely, I am ugly. The well-favored ones have no right to pollute the beauty of nature. I know!"

Her back had bowed a little, and she straightened it. "That knowledge came to me early, and it has been my staff and my banner all my life. I have always had to work for my bread, but I saved some money, and ten years ago I used some of it to start the League. We have many members, over three thousand, but the dues are small and we are severely limited. Last fall, last September, when I saw the advertisement of the contest, I thought again what I had thought many times before, that it was hopeless because there was too much money against us, millions and millions, and then, sitting there looking at the advertisement, the idea came to me. Why not use *their* money for *us?* I considered it and approved of it. A majority of our members live in or near Los Angeles, and most of them are cultured and educated women. I phoned to some and asked them to phone others, and all of them were enthusiastic about it and wanted to help. I organized it, and you don't have to be beautiful to know how to organize. Within two weeks there were over three hundred of us working at it. We had no serious trouble with any of the original twenty, the twenty that were published—except Number Eighteen, and we finally got that. With the second group, to break the tie, with those we had to get five in less than a week, which was unfair because the verses were all mailed at the same time in New York and it took longer for them to get to me, and they were harder, much harder, but we got them, and I mailed them ten hours before the deadline. We're going to get these too." She tapped her bag, in her lap. "No question about it. No question at all. We're going to get it, no matter how hard they are. Half a million dollars. For the League."

Wolfe was regarding her, trying not to frown and nearly succeeding. "Not necessarily half a million, madam. You have four competitors."

"The first prize," she said confidently. "Half a million." Suddenly she leaned forward. "Do you ever have a flash?"

The frown won. "Of what? Anger? Wit?"

"Just a flash—of what is coming. I had two of them long ago, when I was young, and then never any more until the day I saw the advertisement. It came on me, into me, so swiftly that I only knew it was there—the certainty that we would get their money. Certainty can be a very sweet thing, very beautiful, and that day it filled me from head to foot, and I went to a mirror to see if I could see it. I couldn't, but it was there, so there has never been any question about it. The first prize. Our budget committee is already working on projects, what to do with it."

"Indeed." The frown was there to stay. "The five new verses, those that Mr. Dahlmann gave you last evening—how did you send them to your colleagues? Telephone or telegraph or airmail?"

"Ha," she said. Apparently that was all.

"Because," Wolfe observed matter-of-factly, "you have sent them, naturally, so they could go to work. Haven't you?"

Her back was straight again. "I fail to see that that is anybody's business. There is nothing in the rules about getting assistance. Nothing was said about it last night. This morning I telephoned my vice-president, Mrs. Charles Draper, because I had to, to tell her I couldn't return today and I didn't know when I could. It was a private conversation."

Evidently it was going to stay private. Wolfe dropped it and switched. "Another reason for seeing you, Miss Frazee, was to apologize on behalf of Lippert, Buff and Assa, my clients, for the foolish joke that Mr. Dahlmann indulged in last evening—when he exhibited a paper and said it was the answers to the verses he had just given you. Not only was it witless, it was in bad taste. I tender you the apologies of his associates."

"So that's how it is," she said. "I thought it would be something like that, that's why I came, to find out." Her chin went up and her voice hardened. "It won't work. Tell them that. That's all I wanted to know." She stood up. "You think because I'm ugly I haven't got any brains. They'll regret it. I'll see that they regret it."

"Sit down, madam. I don't know what you're talking about."

"Ha. You're supposed to have brains too. They know that one of them went there and killed him and took the paper, and now they're going—"

"Please! Your pronouns. Are you saying that one of my clients took the paper?"

"Of course not. One of the contestants. That would put them in a hole they couldn't get out of unless they could prove which one took it, so they're going to say it was a joke, there was no such paper, and when we send in the answers they'll award the prizes, and they think that will settle it unless the police catch the murderer, and maybe they never will. But it won't work. The murderer will have the right answers, all five of them, and he'll have to explain how he got them, and he won't be able to. These five are going to be very difficult, and nobody can get them by spending a few hours in a library."

"I see. But you could explain how you got them. Your colleagues at home are working on them now. You're going?"

She had headed for the door, but turned. "I'm going back to the hotel for an appointment with a policeman. I use my brains with them too, and I know my rights. I told them I didn't have to go to see them, they could come to see me unless they arrested me, and they don't dare. I wouldn't let them search my room or my belongings. I've told them what I've seen and heard, and that's all I'm going to tell them. They want to know what I thought! They want to know if I thought the paper he showed us really had the answers on it! I fail to see why I should tell them what I thought—but I'll certainly tell you and you can tell your clients . . ."

She came back to the chair and was sitting down, so I held on to my notebook, but as her fanny touched the leather she said abruptly, "No, I have an appointment," got erect, and strode from the room. By the time I got to the rack in the hall she had her coat on, and I had to move to get to the doorknob before her.

When I returned to the office Wolfe was sitting slumped, taking air in through his nose and letting it out through his mouth, audibly. I stuck my hands in my pockets and looked down at him.

"So she told the cops about Dahlmann showing the paper," I said. "That'll help. Twenty minutes to lunch. Beer? I'll make an exception."

He made a face.

"I could probably," I suggested, "get Los Angeles phone information to dig up a Mrs. Charles Draper, and you could ask her how they're making out with the verses."

"Pointless," he growled. "If she killed him and got the answers, she would certainly have made the call and given her friends the verses. She admits she has brains. If I had had the answers I might . . . but no, that would have been premature. You have an appointment at two-thirty."

"Right. Since expenses are on the house it wouldn't cost you anything to get Saul and Fred and Orrie and Johnny and Bill and hang tails on them, but with four of them living at the Churchill it would be a hell of a job—"

"Useless. If anything is to be learned by that kind of routine the police will get it long before we can. They probably—"

The phone rang. I got it at my desk, heard a deep gruff voice that needed filing, an old familiar voice, asked it to hold on, and told Wolfe that Sergeant Purley Stebbins wished to speak to him. He reached for his instrument, and since I am supposed to stay on unless I am told not to, I did so.

"This is Nero Wolfe, Mr. Stebbins. How do you do."

"So-so. I'd like to drop in to see you—say three o'clock?"

"I'm sorry, I'll be engaged."

"Three-thirty?"

"I'll still be engaged."

"Well . . . I guess it can wait until six. Make it six o'clock?"

Purley knew that Wolfe's schedule, four to six up in the plant rooms, might be changed for an H-bomb, but nothing much short of that.

"I'm sorry, Mr. Stebbins, but I'll have no time today or this evening. Perhaps you can tell me—"

"Sure, I can tell you. Just a little friendly talk, that's all. I want to get your slant on a murder case."

"I have no slant on any murder case."

"No? Then why the hell—" He bit it off. He went on, "Look, I know you and you know me. I'm no fancy dancer. But how about this, at half-past twelve a woman named Gertrude Frazee entered your premises and as far as I know she's still there. And you have no slant on the murder of a man named Louis Dahlmann? Tell it to Goodwin. I'm not trying to get a piece of hide, I just want to come and ask you some questions. Six o'clock?"

"Mr. Stebbins." Wolfe was controlling himself. "I have no commission to investigate the murder of Louis Dahlmann, or any other. On past occasions you and your associates have resented my presumption in undertaking to investigate a homicide. You have bullied me and harried me. When I offend again I shall expect you upon me again, but this time I am not invading your territory, so for heaven's sake let me alone."

He hung up and so did I, synchronizing with him. I spoke. "I admit that was neat and a chance not to be passed up, but wait till he tells Cramer."

"I know." He sounded better. "Is the chain bolt on?"

I went to the hall to make sure, and then to the kitchen to tell Fritz we were under siege.

5

I could merely report that I kept my two-thirty appointment and got the verses and answers, and let it go at that, but I think it's about time you had the pleasure of meeting Mr. Talbott Heery. He was quite a surprise to me, I don't know why, unless I had unconsciously decided what a perfume tycoon should look like and he didn't match. Nor did he smell. He was over six feet, broader than me and some ten years older, and his clear smooth skin, stretched tight over the bones, didn't look as if it had ever needed to be shaved. Nor was there any sign of grease or soot or paint. He might have been a member of the Men's Nature League.

Buff and O'Garro were with him, but not Assa. They had to do some explaining to get me admitted to the vault. Buff and Heery and I went to a small room, and soon O'Garro and an attendant came with the box, only about five by three and eighteen inches long, evidently rented for this purpose exclusively. The attendant left, and O'Garro unlocked the box and opened it, and took out some envelopes, six of them. The sealed flaps had gobs of sealing wax. Four of them had been cut open. He asked me, "You want only the last group of five?"

I told him yes, and he handed me the two uncut envelopes. One of them was inscribed, "Verses, second group of five, Pour Amour Contest," and the other, "Answers, second group of five, Pour Amour Contest." As I got out my knife to slit them open O'Garro said, "I don't want to see them," and backed up against the end wall, and the others followed suit. From that distance they couldn't read typing, but they could watch me, and they did. There were pencils and paper pads on the table, but I preferred my pen and notebook, and sat down and used them. The five four-line verses were all on one sheet, and so were the answers—the names of five women, with brief explanations of the references in the verses.

It didn't take long. As I was folding the sheets and returning them to the envelopes, Buff spoke. "Your name is Archie Goodwin?"

"Right."

"Please write on each envelope, 'Opened, and the contents copied, by Archie Goodwin, on April thirteenth, nineteen-fifty-five, in the presence of Talbott Heery, Oliver Buff, and Patrick O'Garro,' and sign it."

I gave it a thought. "I don't like it," I told him. "I don't want to sign anything so closely connected with a million dollars. How about this: I'll write 'Opened, and the contents copied, by Archie Goodwin, on April thirteenth, nineteen-fifty-five, with our consent and in our presence,' and you gentlemen sign it."

They decided that would do, and I wrote, and they signed, and O'Garro returned the envelopes to the box and locked it, and went out with it. Soon he rejoined us, and the four of us went up a broad flight of marble steps and out to the street. On the sidewalk Heery asked where they were bound for, and they said their office, which was around the corner, and he turned to me. "You, Goodwin?"

I told him West Thirty-fifth Street, and he said he was going downtown and would give me a lift. The others went, and he flagged a taxi and we got in, and I told the driver Thirty-fifth and Ninth Avenue. My watch said ten to three, so I should make it by the time the second customer arrived.

As we stopped for a red light at Fifth Avenue, headed west on Forty-seventh Street, Heery said, "I have some spare time and I think I'll stop in for a talk with Nero Wolfe."

"Not right now," I told him. "He's tied up."

"But now is when I have the time."

"Too bad, but it'll have to be later—in fact, much later. He has appointments that run right through until late this evening, to ten-thirty or eleven."

"I want to see him now."

"Sorry. I'll tell him, and he'll be sorry too. If you want to give me your number I'll ring you and tell you when."

He got a wallet from his pocket, fingered in it, and came up with a crisp new twenty. "Here," he said. "I don't need long. Probably ten minutes will do it."

I felt flattered. A finiff would have been at the market, and a sawbuck would have been lavish. "I deeply appreciate it," I said with feeling, "but I'm not the doorman or receptionist. Mr. Wolfe has different men for different functions, and mine is to collect poetry out of safe deposit boxes. That's all I do."

Returning the bill neatly to the wallet, he stated, with no change whatever in tone or manner, "At a better time and place I'll knock your goddam block off." You see why I wanted you to meet him. That ended the conversation. To pass the time as we weaved along with the traffic I thought of three or four things to say, but after all it was his taxi and it had been nice of him to make it a twenty. When the cab stopped at Thirty-fifth Street I only said, "See you at a better time and place," as I got out.

At the corner drugstore I went to the phone booth, dialed our number, got Wolfe, and was told that no company had come. It may have been a minor point, whether Homicide had tails on all five of them or was giving Miss Frazee special attention, but it wouldn't hurt to find out, so I went down the block to Doc Vollmer's place, thirty yards from Wolfe's, and stepped down into the areaway, from where I could see our stoop. My watch said ten past three. I was of course expecting a taxi and wasn't interested in pedestrians, until I happened to send a glance to the east and saw a figure approaching that I could name. I swiveled my head to look west, and saw a female mounting the seven steps to our stoop. So I moved up to the sidewalk into the path of the approaching figure —Art Whipple of Homicide West. He stopped on his heels, opened his mouth, and closed it.

"I won't tell her," I assured him. "Unless you want me to give her a message?"

"Go chin yourself," he suggested.

"At a better time and place. She'll probably be with us nearly an hour. If you want to go to Tony's around the corner I'll give you a ring just before she leaves. Luck."

I went on to our stoop, and as I was mounting the steps the door opened a crack and Fritz's voice came through it. "Your name, please, madam?"

I said okay, and he slipped the bolt and opened up, and I told the visitor to enter. While Fritz attended to the door I offered to take her coat, a brown wool number that would have appreciated a little freshening up, but she said she would keep it and her name was Wheelock.

I ushered her to the office and told Wolfe, "Mrs. James R. Wheelock, of Richmond, Virginia." Then I went and opened the safe, took the four leaves from my notebook that I had written on, put them in the inner compartment, closed that door and twirled the knob of the combination, and closed the outer door. By the time I got to my desk Carol Wheelock was in the red leather chair, with her coat draped over the back.

According to the information she was a housewife, but if so her house was nearly out of wife. She looked as if she hadn't eaten for a week and hadn't slept for a month. Properly fed and rested for a good long stretch, filled in from her hundred pounds to around a hundred and twenty, she might have been a pleasant sight and a very satisfactory wife for a man who was sold on the wife idea, but it took some imagination to realize it. The only thing was her eyes. They were dark, set in deep, and there was fire back of them.

"I ought to tell you," she said in a low even voice, "that I didn't want to come here, but Mr. O'Garro said it was absolutely necessary. I have decided I shouldn't say anything to anybody. But if you have something to tell me—go ahead."

Wolfe was glowering at her, and I would have liked to tell her that it meant nothing personal, it was only that the sight of a hungry human was painful to him, and the sight of one who must have been hungry for months was intolerable. He spoke. "You understand, Mrs. Wheelock, that I am acting for the firm of Lippert, Buff and Assa, which is handling the contest for Heery Products, Incorporated."

"Yes, Mr. O'Garro told me."

"I do have a little to tell you, but not much. For one item, I have had a talk with one of the contestants, Miss Gertrude Frazee. You may know that she is the founder and president of an organization called the Women's Nature League. She says that some three hundred of its members have helped her in the contest, which is not an infraction of the rules. She does not say that she has telephoned to them the verses that were distributed last evening, and that they are now working on them, but it wouldn't be fanciful to assume that she has and they are. Have you any comment?"

She was staring at him, her mouth working.

"Three hundred," she said.

Wolfe nodded.

"That's cheating. That's—she can't do that. You can't let her get away with it."

"We may be helpless. If she has violated no rule and nothing that was agreed upon last evening, what then? This is one aspect of the grotesque situation created by the murder of Louis Dahlmann."

"I'll see the others." The fire behind her eyes was showing through. "We won't permit it. We'll refuse to go ahead with those verses. We'll insist on new ones when we're allowed to go home."

"That would suit Miss Frazee perfectly. She would send in her answers before the agreed deadline and demand the first prize, and if she didn't get it she could sue and probably collect. You'll have to do better than that if you want to head her off—emulate her, perhaps. Of course you've had help too—your husband, your friends; get them started."

"I've had no help."

She started to tremble, first her hands and then her shoulders, and I thought we were in for it, but she pulled one that I had never expected to see. Women of all ages and shapes and sizes have started to have a fit in that office. Some I have caught in time with a good shot of brandy, some I have stopped with a smack or other physical contact, and some I have had to ride out—with Wolfe gone because he can't stand it. I left my chair and started for her, but she stuck her tongue out at me. So I thought, but that wasn't it. She was only getting the tongue between her teeth and clamping down on it. Its end bulged and curled up and was purple, but she only clamped harder. It wasn't pretty, but it worked. She stopped trembling, opened her fists and closed them and opened them again, and got her shoulders set, rigid. Then she retrieved her tongue. I had a notion to give her a pat before returning to my chair, in recognition of an outstanding performance, but decided that a woman who could stand off a fit like that in ten seconds flat probably didn't care for pats.

"I beg your pardon," she said.

"Brandy," Wolfe told me.

"No," she said, "I'm all right. I couldn't drink brandy. I guess what did it was what you said about help. I haven't had any. The first few weeks weren't bad, but after that they got harder, and later, when they got really hard . . . I don't know how I did it. I said I wasn't going to say anything, but after what you said about Miss Frazee having three hundred women helping her . . . well. I'm thirty-two years old, and I have two children, and my husband is a bookkeeper and makes fifty dollars a week. I was a schoolteacher before I married. I had been going along for years, just taking it, and I saw this contest and decided to win it. I'm going to have a nice home and a car—two cars, one for my husband and one for me—and I'm going to have some clothes, and I'm going to send my husband to school and make him a CPA if he has it in him. That day I saw the contest, I took charge that day. You know what I mean."

"Indeed I do," Wolfe muttered.

"So when they got hard there was no one I could ask for help, and anyway, if I had got help I would have had to share the prize. I didn't do much eating or sleeping the last seven weeks of the main contest, but the worst was when they sent us five to do in a week to break the tie. I didn't go to bed that week, and I was afraid I had one of them wrong, and I didn't get them mailed until just before midnight—I went to the post office and made them let me see them stamp the envelope. After all that, do you think I'm going to let somebody get it by cheating? With three hundred women working at it while we're not allowed to go home?"

After seeing her handle the fit I didn't think she was going to let somebody get anything she had made up her mind to have, with or without cheating.

"It is manifestly unfair," Wolfe conceded, "but I doubt if it can be called cheating, at least in the legal sense. And as for cheating, it's conceivable that someone else had a bolder idea than Miss Frazee and acted upon it. By killing Mr. Dahlmann in order to get the answers."

"I'm not going to say anything about that," she declared. "I've decided not to."

"The police have talked with you, of course."

"Yes. They certainly have. For hours."

"And they asked you what you thought last evening when Mr. Dahlmann displayed a paper and said it contained the answers. What did you tell them?"

"I'm not going to talk about it."

"Did you tell the police that? That you wouldn't talk about it?"

"No. I hadn't decided then. I decided later."

"After consultation with someone?"

She shook her head. "With whom would I consult?"

"I don't know. A lawyer. A phone call to your husband."

"I haven't got a lawyer. I wouldn't call my husband—I know what he'd say. He thinks I'm crazy. I couldn't pay a lawyer anyway because I haven't got any money. They paid for the trip here, and the hotel, but nothing for incidentals. I was late for my appointment with you because I got on the wrong bus. I haven't consulted anybody. I made the decision myself."

"So you told the police what you thought when Mr. Dahlmann displayed the paper?"

"Yes."

"Then why not tell me? I assure you, madam, that I have only one interest in the matter, on behalf of my clients, to make sure that the prizes are fairly and honestly awarded. You see, of course, that that will be extremely difficult if in fact one of the contestants took that paper from Mr. Dahlmann and it contains the answers. You see that."

"Yes."

"However, it is the belief of my clients—and their contention—that the paper did not contain the answers, that Mr. Dahlmann was only jesting; and that therefore the secrecy of the answers is still intact. Do you challenge that contention?"

"No."

"You accept it?"

"Yes."

"Then you must have told the police that when Mr. Dahlmann displayed the paper you regarded it as a joke, and the sequel is plain: it would be absurd to suspect you of going to his apartment and killing him to get it. So it is reasonable to suppose that you are not suspected. —Archie, your phone call from the corner. Did you see anyone?"

"Yes, sir. Art Whipple. He was here on the Heller case."

"Tell Mrs. Wheelock about it."

I met her eyes. "I was hanging out up the street when you came, and a Homicide detective was following you. I exchanged a few words with him. If you want to spot him when you leave, he's about my size, drags his feet a little, and is wearing a dark gray suit and a gray snap-brim hat."

"He was following me?"

"Right."

Her eyes left me for Wolfe. "Isn't that what they do?" But her left hand had started to tremble, and she had to grasp it with the other one and squeeze it. Wolfe shut his eyes, probably expecting some more tongue control. Instead, she arose abruptly and asked, "May I have—a bathroom?"

I told her certainly, and went and opened the door of the one partitioned off in the far corner, to the left of my desk, and she came and passed through, closing the door behind her.

She was in there a good quarter of an hour without making a sound. The partitions, like all the inner walls on the ground floor, are soundproofed, but I have sharp ears and heard nothing whatever. I said something to Wolfe, but he only grunted. After a little he looked up at the clock: twenty to four. Thereafter he looked at it every two minutes; at four sharp he would leave for the plant rooms. There were just nine minutes to go when the door in the partition opened and she was back with us.

She came and stood at Wolfe's desk, across from him. "I beg your pardon," she said in her low even voice. "I had to take some pills. The food at the hotel is quite good, but I simply can't eat. I haven't eaten much for quite a while. Do you want to tell me anything else?"

"Milk toast," Wolfe said gruffly. "My cook, Fritz Brenner, makes it superbly. Sit down."

"I couldn't swallow it. Really."

"Then hot bouillon. Our own. It can be ready in eight minutes. I have to leave you, but Mr. Goodwin—"

"I couldn't. I'm going back to the hotel and see the others about Miss Frazee—I think I am—I'll think about it on the bus. That's cheating." She had moved to get her coat from the back of the chair, and I went and held it for her.

Knowing what bus crowds were at that time of day, and thinking it wouldn't break LBA, I made her take a buck for taxi fare, but had to explain it would go on the expense list before she would take it. When, in the hall, I had let her out and bolted the door and turned, Wolfe was there, opening the door of his elevator.

"You put the answers in the safe," he stated.

"Yes, sir, inner compartment. I told you on the phone that Buff and O'Garro and Talbott Heery were there, but I didn't report that Heery brought me downtown in a taxi so he could offer me twenty bucks to get him in to see you right away. I told him—"

"Verbatim, please."

I gave it to him, which was nothing, considering that he will ask for a whole afternoon's interviews with five or six people verbatim, and get it. At the end I added, "For a footnote, Heery couldn't knock my block off unless he got someone to hold me. Do you want to squeeze him in somewhere?"

He said no, Heery could wait, and entered the elevator and shut the door, and I went to the office. There were a few daily chores which hadn't been attended to, and also my notes of the talks with Miss Frazee and Mrs. Wheelock had to be typed. Not that it seemed to me there was anything in them that would make history. I admitted that Wolfe was only going fishing, hoping to scare up a word or fact that would give him a start, and that he had got some spectacular results from that method more than once before, but in this case genius might have been expected to find a short cut. There were five of them, which would take a lot of time, and the time was strictly rationed. Before midnight April twentieth.

I was in the middle of the Frazee notes when the phone interrupted me, and when I told it, "Nero Wolfe's office, Archie Goodwin speaking," a male voice said, "I want to speak to Mr. Wolfe. This is Patrick O'Garro."

They were certainly popping the precedents. He should have told his secretary, and she should have got me and spent five minutes trying to lobby me into putting Wolfe on. The best explanation was that they were playing it so close to their chins they were even keeping it from the staff that they had hired Nero Wolfe.

"He's engaged," I said, "and if I disengage him for a phone call it would have to be good. Can't you use me for a relay?"

"I want to ask him if he's made any progress."

"If he has it's in his head. He told you he would report later this evening. He has seen Miss Frazee and Mrs. Wheelock. How about the others?"

"That's why I'm calling. Susan Tescher will be there at six, and Harold Rollins at seven, but Younger can't come. He's in bed at the hotel with heart flutters. They sent him up from the District Attorney's office in an ambulance. He wouldn't go to a hospital. My doctor saw him and says it's not serious, but he's staying in bed until the doctor sees him tomorrow."

I said I'd tell Wolfe and got the number of Younger's room. After I hung up I got at the house phone and buzzed the plant rooms, and in a minute Wolfe's voice blurted at me, "Well?"

"O'Garro just phoned. One's coming at six and one at seven, but at the DA's office Philip Younger's heart began to flutter and he's at the hotel in bed. Shall I go up and sit with him?"

"You must be back by six o'clock."

I said I would and the connection went.

There was a slight problem. Years before, after a certain episode, I had made myself promise that I would never go on any errand connected with a murder case without a gun, but this wasn't

a murder case by the terms agreed upon. The job was to nail
a thief. I decided that was quibbling, got my shoulder holster from
the drawer and put it on, got the Marley .32 and loaded it and
slipped it into the holster, went to the hall, and called to Fritz to
come and bolt the door after me.

6

It was safe to assume that the floor clerk on the eighteenth floor of
the Churchill would be stubborn about it, since journalists were
certainly stalking the quintet, so I anticipated her by first finding
Tim Evarts, the hotel's first assistant security officer, not to be
called a house dick, who owed me a little courtesy from past
events. He obliged by phoning her, after I promised to set no fires
and find no corpses, and all she did was look at both sides of my
card and one side of me and wave me on.

Eighteen-twenty-six was about halfway down a long corridor.
There was no one in sight anywhere except a chambermaid with
towels, and I concluded that the city employees hadn't invaded the
hotel itself for surveillance. My first knock on the door of eighteen-
twenty-six got me an invitation to come in, not too audible, and I
opened the door and entered, and saw that LBA had done well by
their guests. It was the fifteen-dollar size, with the twin beds
headed against the wall at the left. On one of them, under the covers, was Old King Cole with a hangover, his mop of white hair
tousled and his eyes sick.

I approached. "My name's Archie Goodwin," I told him.
"From Nero Wolfe, on behalf of Lippert, Buff and Assa." There
was a chair there, and I sat. "We need to clear up a few little points
about the contest."

"Crap," he said.

"That won't do it," I stated. "Not just that one word. Is the contest crap, or am I, or what?"

He shut his eyes. "I'm sick." He opened them. "I'll be all right
tomorrow."

"Are you too sick to talk? I don't want to make you worse. I don't know how serious a heart flutter is."

"I haven't got a heart flutter. I've got paroxysmal tachycardia, and it is never serious. I'd be up and around right now if it wasn't for one thing—there are too many fools. The discomfort of paroxysmal tachycardia is increased by fear and anxiety and apprehension and nervousness, and I've got all of 'em on account of fools."

He raised himself on an elbow, reached to the bedstand for a glass of water, drank about a spoonful, and put the glass back. He bounced around and settled on his side, facing me.

"What kind of fools?" I asked politely.

"You're one of 'em. Didn't you come to ask me where I got the gun I shot that man Dahlmann with?"

"No, sir. Speaking for Nero Wolfe, we're not interested in the death of Dahlmann except as it affects the contest and raises points that have to be dealt with."

He snorted. "There you are. Crap. Why should it affect the contest at all? It happened to be last night that someone went there and shot him—some jealous woman or someone who hated him or was afraid of him or wanted to get even with him—and just because it happened last night they think it was connected with the contest. They even think one of us did it. Only a fool would think that. Suppose when he held up that paper, suppose I believed him when he said it was the answers, and I decided to kill him and get it. Finding out where he lived would have been easy enough, even the phone book. So I went there, and getting him to let me in was just as easy, I could tell him there was something about the agreement that I thought ought to be changed and I wanted to discuss it with him. Getting a chance to shoot him might be a little harder, since he might have a faint suspicion I had come to try to get the paper, but it could be managed. So I kill him and take the paper and get back to my hotel room, and where am I?"

I shook my head. "You're telling it."

"I've dug a hole and jumped in. If they go on with the contest on the basis of those answers, I've ruined my chances, because they'll hold us here in the jurisdiction, or if I leave for Chicago before the body is found they'll invite me back and I'll have to come, and if I send in the right answers before my deadline I couldn't explain how I got 'em. If they don't go on with those answers, if

they void them and give us new verses, all I've got for killing a
man is the prospect of being electrocuted. So they're fools for
thinking one of us did it. Crap."

"There's another possibility," I objected. "What if you were a
fool yourself? I admit your analysis is absolutely sound, but what
if the sight of that paper and the thought of half a million dollars
carried you away, and you went ahead and did it and didn't bother
with the analysis until afterward? Then when you did analyze it and
saw where you were, for instance in the District Attorney's office, I should think your heart would flutter no matter what name
you gave it. I know mine would."

He turned over on his back and shut his eyes. I sat and looked
at him. He was breathing a little faster than normal, and a muscle
in his neck twitched a couple of times, but there was no indication
of a crisis. I had not scared him to death, and anyway, I had only
promised Tim Evarts that I wouldn't find a corpse, not that I
wouldn't make one.

He turned back on his side. "For some reason," he said, "I feel
like offering you a drink. You look a little like my son-in-law, that
may be it. There's a bottle of scotch in my suitcase that he gave
me. Help yourself. I don't want any."

"Thanks, but I guess not. Another time."

"As you please. About my being a fool, I was one once, twenty-
six years ago, back in nineteen-twenty-nine. I had stacked up a
couple of million dollars and it all went. Fifty million others were
fools along with me, but that didn't help any. I decided I had had
enough and got a job selling adding machines, and never touched
the market again. A few years ago my son-in-law made me quit
work because he was doing very well as an architect, and that was
all right, I was comfortable, but I always wanted something to do,
and one day I saw the advertisement of this contest, and the first
thing I knew I was in it up to my neck. I decided to make my
daughter and son-in-law a very handsome present."

He coughed, and shut his eyes and breathed a little, then went
on. "The point is that it's been twenty-six years since I made a fool
of myself, and if you and those other fools only knew it, once was
enough. There's only one thing you can tell me that I'm interested
in, and that's this, what are they going to do about the contest? As
it stands now it's a giveaway, and I'll fight it. That young woman,
Susan Tescher—she lives here in New York and she's a researcher

for *Clock* magazine. She's working on it right now—and here I am.
I'll fight it."

"Fight it how?" I asked.

"That's the question." He passed his fingertips over his right
cheek and then over his left one. "I haven't shaved today. I don't
see why I shouldn't tell you one idea I had."

"Neither do I."

He had his eyes steady on me, and they didn't look so sick.
"You strike me as a sensible young man."

"I am."

"It's just possible that Miss Tescher is a sensible young woman.
If she tries to bull it through on the basis of what was agreed last
night, after what has happened, she may end up by wishing she'd
never heard of the damn contest. I think the rest of us might get
together with her and suggest that we split it up five ways. The first
five prizes total eight hundred and seventy thousand dollars, so
that would make it one hundred and seventy-four thousand apiece.
That ought to satisfy everybody, and I don't see why you people
would object to it. As it stands now—was that a knock at the door?"

"It sounded like it."

"I told them I didn't want . . . oh well. Come in!"

The door opened slowly and there was Carol Wheelock, without
coat or hat. As I left my chair she stopped, and apparently was
about to turn and scoot, but I spoke. "Hello there. Come on in."

"Leave the door open," Younger said.

"I'm here," I told him.

"I know you are. With a woman in my hotel room the door stays
open."

"I shouldn't have come." She stood. "I should have phoned, but
with all the wiretapping—"

"It's all right." I was moving another chair up. "Mr. Younger
is resting because he had a little paroxysm, nothing serious."

"Crap," Younger said. "Sit down. I want to talk to you anyway."

She still hesitated, then came on and sat. If she had eaten anything there was no noticeable result. She looked at me. "Does he
know about Miss Frazee?"

I shook my head. "I hadn't got to that yet."

She looked at Younger. "I couldn't reach Miss Tescher, and
I wanted to speak to you before Mr. Rollins. You know Miss

Frazee is the head of the Women's Nature League. You remember it was mentioned last evening, and Mr. Dahlmann was very witty about it. He thought it would be amusing for her to win a prize, and of course she was going to, one of the first five."

"I didn't think he was witty," Younger declared.

She didn't press it. "Well, he thought he was. What I wanted to tell you, three hundred women, members of her league, have been working with Miss Frazee on the contest, and she has sent them the verses we got last night by long distance telephone, and they're working on them now—three hundred of them."

"Just a minute," I put in. "As Mr. Wolfe told you, she said they helped her, but not that they have the new verses. That's an assumption. I admit it has four legs."

Younger had raised himself to an elbow, and the open front of his pajama top showed a hairy chest. "Three hundred women?" he demanded.

"Right. So I doubt if you can sell Miss Frazee on your plan to split it five ways. You'll have to think up—"

"Get out!" he commanded. Not me; it was for Mrs. Wheelock. "Get out of here. I'm getting up and I haven't got any pants on. —Wait a minute! You'll be in your room? Stay in your room until you hear from me. I'm going to find Rollins and the three of us are going to fight. We'll blow it so high they won't find any pieces. Stay in your room!"

He gave the covers a kick, proving he had been right about the pants, and she ran. I looked at my watch, and took my hat from the back of the chair.

"I have an appointment," I told him, "and anyway, you're going to be busy."

7

Up in the plant rooms on the roof it was Cattleya mossiae time. In the cool room, the first one you enter from the vestibule, the Odontoglossums were sporting their sprays, and in the middle room, the tropical room, two benches of Phalaenopsis, the hardest of all to grow well, were crowding the aisle with racemes two feet long, but at mossiae time the big show was in the third room. Of Wolfe's fourteen varieties of mossiae my favorite was reineckiana, with its white, yellow, lilac, and violet. But then, passing through, I only had time for a glance at them.

Wolfe, in the potting-room, washing his hands at the sink and talking with Theodore, growled at me. "Couldn't it wait?"

"Just rhetoric," I said. "It's ten to six and Miss Tescher may be there when you come down, and you might want a report on Younger before you see her. If not, I'll go look at orchids."

"Very well. Since you're here."

I gave it to him verbatim. He had no questions and no comments. By the time I finished he had his hands and nails clean and had moved to the workbench to frown at a bedraggled specimen in a pot.

"Look at this Oncidium varicosum," he grumbled. "Dry rot in April. It has never happened before and there is no explanation. Theodore is certain—"

The buzz of the house phone kept me from learning what Theodore was certain of. Instead, I learned what had upset Fritz downstairs: "Archie, you only told me to admit a Miss Susan Tescher. She has come, but there are three men with her. What do I do?"

"Are they in?"

"Of course not. They're out on the stoop and it has started to rain."

I said I'd be right down, told Wolfe Miss Tescher had arrived with outriders, and beat it. I rarely use the elevator, and never squeeze in together with Wolfe's bulk. Descending the three flights to the main hall, and taking a look through the one-way glass panel, I saw that Fritz's count was accurate. One female and three males were standing in the April shower, glaring in my direction but not seeing me. The men were strangers but not dicks unless they had changed brands without telling me, and it seemed unnecessary to let them get any wetter, so I went and unbolted the door and swung it open, and in they came. A remark about rain being wet might have been expected from the males, but they started removing their coats with no remarks at all. The female said in a clear strong capable voice, "I'm Susan Tescher."

I told her who I was and hung her coat up for her. She was fairly tall, slender but not thin, and not at all poorly furnished with features. From a first glance, and I try to make first glances count, everything about her was smart, with the exception of the earrings, which were enameled clock dials the size of a quarter. She had gray eyes and brassy hair and very good skin and lipstick.

As we were starting for the office the elevator door opened and Wolfe emerged. He stopped, facing her.

"I'm Susan Tescher," she said.

He bowed. "I'm Nero Wolfe. And these gentlemen?"

She used a hand. "Mr. Hibbard, of the legal staff of *Clock*." Mr. Hibbard was tall and skinny. "Mr. Schultz, an associate editor of *Clock*." Mr. Schultz was tall and broad. "Mr. Knudsen, a senior editor of *Clock*." Mr. Knudsen was tall and bony.

I had edged on ahead, to be there to get her into the red leather chair, which was where Wolfe always wanted the target, without any fuss. There was no problem. The men were perfectly satisfied with the three smaller chairs I placed for them, off to my right and facing Wolfe at his desk. All three crossed their legs, settled back, and clasped their hands. When I got out my notebook Schultz called Hibbard's attention, and Hibbard called Knudsen's attention, but there was no comment.

"If you please," Wolfe asked, "in what capacity are these gentlemen present?"

He was looking at them, but Miss Tescher answered. "I suppose you know that I am assistant director of research at *Clock*."

"At least I know it now."

"The publicity about the contest, after what happened last night and this morning, and my connection with it, was discussed at a conference this afternoon. I can tell you confidentially that Mr. Tite himself was there. I thought I would be fired, but Mr. Tite is a very fair man and very loyal to his employees. All my work on the contest was done on my own time—of course I'm a highly trained researcher. So it was decided that Mr. Hibbard and Mr. Knudsen and Mr. Schultz should come with me here. They want to be available for advice if I need it."

"Mr. Hibbard is a counselor-at-law?"

"Yes."

"Is he your attorney?"

"Why—I don't—" She looked at Hibbard. He moved his head, once to the left and back again. "No," she said, "he isn't." She cocked her head. "I want to say something."

"Go ahead."

"I came here only as a favor to Lippert, Buff and Assa, because Mr. Assa asked me to. The conditions for breaking the tie in the contest were agreed to last evening by all of us, and they can be changed only by changing the agreement, and it remains the same. So there is really nothing to discuss. That's the way it looks to me and I wanted you to understand it."

Wolfe grunted. She went on, "But of course there's nothing personal about it—I mean personal towards you. I happen to know a lot about you because I researched you two years ago, when you were on the list of cover prospects for *Clock,* but don't ask me why they didn't use you because I don't know. Of course there are always dozens on the list, and they can't all—"

Knudsen cleared his throat, rather loud, and she looked at him. There was no additional signal that I caught, but evidently she didn't need one. She let it lay. Returning to Wolfe, "So," she said, "it's not personal. It's just that there is nothing to discuss."

"From your point of view," Wolfe conceded, "there probably isn't. And naturally, for you, as a consequence of the peculiar constitution of the human ego, your point of view is paramount. But your ego is bound to be jostled by other egos, and efforts to counteract the jostling by ignoring it have rarely succeeded. It is frequently advisable, and sometimes necessary, to give a little ground. For example, suppose I ask you for information in which you have no monopoly because it is shared with others. Suppose I ask you: at the meeting last evening, after Mr. Dahlmann displayed a paper and said it contained the answers, what remarks were made about it by any of the contestants? What did you say, and what did you hear any of them say?"

"Are you supposing or asking?"

"I'm asking."

She looked at Knudsen. His head moved. At Schultz. His head moved. At Hibbard. His head moved. She returned to Wolfe. "When Mr. Assa asked me to come to see you he said it was about the contest, and that has no bearing on it."

"Then you decline to answer?"

"Yes, I think I should."

"The police must have asked you. Did you decline to answer?"

"I don't think I should tell you anything about what the police asked me or what I said to them."

"Nor, evidently, anything about what the other contestants have said to you or you have said to them."

"My contact with the other contestants has been very limited. Just that meeting last evening."

Wolfe lifted a hand and ran a fingertip along the side of his nose a few times. He was being patient. "I may say, Miss Tescher, that my contact with the other contestants, mine and Mr. Goodwin's, has been a little broader. Several courses have been suggested. One was that all five of you agree that the first five prizes be pooled, and that each of you accept one-fifth of the total as your share. The suggestion was not made by my clients or by me; I am merely asking you, without prejudice, would you consider such a proposal?"

She didn't need guidance on that one. "Of course I wouldn't. Why should I?"

"So you don't concede that the manner of Mr. Dahlmann's death, and the circumstances, call for a reconsideration of anything whatever connected with the contest?"

She pushed her head forward, and it reminded me of something, I couldn't remember what. She said slowly and distinctly and positively, "I don't concede anything at all, Mr. Wolfe."

She pulled her head back, and I remembered. A vulture I had seen at the zoo—exactly the same movement. Aside from the movement there was no resemblance; certainly the vulture hadn't looked anything like as smart as she did, and had no lipstick, no earrings, and no hair on its head.

"All the same," Wolfe persisted, "there are the other egos and other viewpoints. I accept the validity of yours, but theirs cannot be brushed aside. Each of you has made a huge investment of time and energy and ingenuity. How much time have you spent on it since the beginning?"

"I don't know. Hundreds and hundreds of hours."

"The rules didn't forbid help. Have you had any?"

"No. A friend of mine with a large library let me use it nights and early mornings before I went to work, but she didn't help.

I'm very expert at researching. When they gave us five to do in one week, to break the tie—that was on March twenty-eighth—I took a week off without pay."

Wolfe nodded. "And of course the others made similar sacrifices and endured similar strains. Look at them now. They are detained here willy-nilly, far from their base of operations, by no fault of their own—except possibly for one of them, but that's moot. Whereas you're at home and can proceed as usual. You have an overwhelming advantage and it is fortuitous. Can you pursue it without a qualm? Can you justify it?"

"I don't have to justify it. We made an agreement and I'm not breaking it. And I can't proceed as usual—if I could I'd be at the library now, working. I've got another week off, but I had to spend today with the police and the conference at the office and now here with you. I'll work tonight, but I don't know what tomorrow will be like."

"Would you accept an invitation to meet with the others and discuss a new arrangement?"

"I would not. There's nothing to discuss."

"You are admirably single-minded, Miss Tescher." Wolfe leaned back with his elbows on the chair arms and matched his fingertips. "I must tell you about Miss Frazee—she is in a situation comparable to yours. Her home is in Los Angeles, where three hundred of her friends, fellow members of a league of which she is president, have worked with her on the contest throughout. It is presumed, though not established, that she has telephoned them the verses that were distributed last evening, and that they are busy with them. A situation comparable to yours, though by no means identical. Have you any comment?"

She was staring at him, speechless.

"Because," Wolfe went on, "while there may be no infraction of the rules or the agreement, it is surely an unfair advantage—even against you, since you have already lost a day and there's no telling how much you'll be harassed the rest of the week; but Miss Frazee's friends can proceed unhampered. Don't you think that's worth discussing?"

From the look on Susan's face she would have liked to discuss it with Miss Frazee herself, with fingernails and teeth at ten inches. Before she found any words Knudsen arose, crooked his finger at the other two men and at Susan, and headed for the door. They all got up and followed. Wolfe sat and gazed at their receding backs. Not knowing whether they were adjourning or only taking a recess, I sat pat until I saw that Schultz, out last, was shutting the door to the hall, then I thought I'd better investigate, put down my notebook, went to the door and opened it, and crossed the sill. The quartet was in a close huddle over by the big walnut rack.

"Need any help?" I asked brightly.

"No," Susan said. "We're conferring."

I re-entered the office, closed the door, and told Wolfe, "They're in conference. If I go in the front room and put my ear to the keyhole of the door to the hall I can catch it. After all, it's your house."

"Pfui," he said, and shut his eyes. I treated myself to a good yawn and stretch, and looked at my wrist. Twenty to seven.

For the second time that day we had a king-size wait. At six-forty-five I turned on the radio to see how the Giants had made out with the Phillies, and got no glow out of that. I would have gone to the kitchen for a glass of milk, since dinner would be late, but the only route was through the rear of the hall, and I didn't want to disturb the conference. At six-fifty-five I reminded Wolfe that Harold Rollins was due in five minutes, and he only nodded without opening his eyes. At seven-two the doorbell rang, and I went.

Still in a huddle at the rack, they broke off as I appeared and gave me their faces. Out on the stoop was a lone male. I went on by the huddle, opened the door, and said, "Mr. Rollins? Come in."

My own idea would have been to put him in the front room until the conference was over and we had got the score, but if Wolfe had wanted that he would have said so, and I'm perfectly willing to let him have things his way unless his ego is jostling mine. So I took Rollins' hat and coat and ushered him along to the office. I was inside too and was shutting the door when Susan's voice came. "Mr. Goodwin!"

I pulled the door to with me on the hall side. As I approached she asked, "Wasn't that one of them? The one named Rollins?"

"Right. Harold Rollins, Burlington, Iowa, professor of history at Bemis College."

She looked at her pals. Their heads all moved, an inch to the left and back again. She looked at me. "Mr. Wolfe asked me if I had any comment about what he told me about Miss Frazee. He asked me if I thought it was worth discussing. I have no comment now, but I will have. It's absolutely outrageous to expect—"

A quick tug at her sleeve by Knudsen stopped her. She shot him a glance and then pushed her head forward at me. "No comment!" she shrilled, and turned to reach to the rack for her coat. The men simultaneously reached for theirs.

"If you gentlemen don't mind," I said, perfectly friendly, "my grandmother out in Ohio used to ask me if the cat had my tongue. I've always wondered about it. Was it a cat in your case?"

No soap. Not a peep. I gave up and opened the door to let them out.

8

Back in the office, I attended to the lights before going to my desk. There are eight different lights—one in the ceiling above a big bowl of banded Oriental alabaster, which is on the wall switch, one on the wall behind Wolfe's chair, one on his desk, one on my desk, one flooding the big globe, and three for the book shelves. The one on Wolfe's desk is strictly for business, like crossword puzzles. The one on the wall behind him is for reading. He likes all the others turned on, and after making the rounds I sat, picked up my notebook, and gave Harold Rollins a look.

"They have gone?" Wolfe asked.

"Yes, sir. No comment."

Rollins was comfortable in the red leather chair, right at home, though one about half the size would have been better for him. He hadn't shrunk from underfeeding like Carol Wheelock; he looked healthy enough, what there was of him. Nor was there much to his face except a wide flexible mouth and glasses in thick black frames. You didn't see his nose and chin at all unless you concentrated.

It's hard to tell with glasses like those, but apparently he was returning my regard. "Your name's Goodwin, isn't it?" he asked.

I admitted it.

"Then it was you who sicked that man Younger on me. You don't expect me to be grateful, do you? I'm not." He switched to Wolfe. "We might as well start right. I made this appointment, and kept it, only to pass the time. I'm in this grotesque imbroglio, with no discoverable chance of emerging with honor and dignity, so why miss an opportunity of meeting an eminent bloodhound?" He smiled and shook his head. "No offense intended. I am hardly in a position to offend anybody. What are we going to talk about?"

Wolfe was contemplating him. "I suggest, Mr. Rollins, that your despair is excessive. My client is the firm of Lippert, Buff and Assa, but in many respects your interest runs with theirs, and their honor and dignity are involved with yours. Both may be salvaged; and in addition, you may get a substantial amount of money. You didn't like what Mr. Younger proposed?"

He was still smiling. "Of course I know I should make allowances."

"For Mr. Younger?"

"For all of you. Your frame of reference is utterly different from mine, in fact to me it seems quite contemptible, but it was my own thoughtlessness that got me entangled in it. I dug my own grave, that's true; but, realizing and confessing it, I may still resent the slime and the worms. Can you get me back my job?"

"Job?"

"Yes. I am a professor of history at Bemis College, but I won't be very long. It will amuse you to hear—no, that's not the right way to look at it. It will amuse me to tell you; that's better. One day last September a colleague showed me an advertisement of this contest, and said facetiously that as a student and teacher of history I should be interested. As a puzzle the thing was so obvious it was inane, and so was the second one, which my colleague also showed me. I was curious as to how long the inanity would be maintained, and got others as they appeared, and before long I found I was being challenged. I made a point of getting them without referring to any book, but the twelfth one so distracted me that I broke that ban just to get rid of it."

He screwed up his lips. "Have I said that I hadn't entered the contest?"

"No."

"Well, I hadn't. I regarded it as a diversion, an amusing toy. But after I had solved the twentieth and last, which I must confess was rather ingenious, I sent in an entry blank with my answers. If you were to ask me why I did so I would be at a loss. I suppose in the lower strata of my psyche the primitive lusts are slopping around in the mire, and somehow they managed it; they are not in direct communication with me. The next day I was appalled at what I had done. I had a professorship at the age of thirty-six; I was a serious and able scholar with two books to my credit; and I had well-defined ambitions which I was determined to realize. If I won a prize in a perfume contest—a perfume called *Pour Amour*— it would be a blemish on my career, and if I won a sensational one, a half or quarter of a million, I would never live it down."

He smiled and shook his head. "But you won't believe I was appalled, because when I was notified that I was in a tie with seventy-one others, and was sent five new verses to solve in a week, I had the answers in four days and sent them in. I can only plead that schizophrenia must have many forms and manifestations, or I could resort to demonology. I was once much impressed by Roskoff's *Geschichte des Teufels*. Anyhow, I sent the answers, and was asked to come to New York, and arrived just twenty-four hours ago; and now I'm involved not only in a perfume contest— Pour Amour Rollins they'll call me—but in a murder, a nation-wide *cause célèbre*. I am done for. If I don't resign I'll be fired. Can you get me a job?"

I was wishing he would take his glasses off so I could see his eyes. From his easy posture and his voice and his superior smile he was taking it well, a manly and gallant bozo refusing to squirt blood under the wheels of calamity. But without more sales pressure I wasn't buying the notion that one definition of "calamity" was half a million bucks, even for a man as highly educated as him, and I wanted to see his eyes. All I could see was the reflection of the ceiling light from the lenses.

"You're in a fix," Wolfe admitted, "but I still think your despair is excessive. Establish academic scholarships with your prize money."

"I've thought of that. It wouldn't help much." He smiled. "The simplest way would be to confess to the murder. That would do it."

"Not without corroboration. Could you furnish any?"

"I'm afraid not. I couldn't describe his apartment, and I don't know what kind of gun was used."

"Then it would be hopeless. Perhaps a better expedient, expose the murderer and become a public hero. The acclaim would smother the infamy. You are not a bloodhound by profession, I know, but you have cerebral resources. You could start by recalling all the details of the meeting last evening. How did they act and talk? What signs of greed or zealotry did they display? Particularly, what did they say and do when Mr. Dahlmann showed the paper and said it was the answers?"

"Nothing. Nothing whatever."

"It was a shock, naturally. But afterward?"

"Not afterward either." The smile was getting more superior. "I would suppose you wouldn't need to be told what the atmosphere was like. We were tigers crouching to spring upon the same prey. Vultures circling to swoop and be first on the carcass to get the heart and liver. The amenities were forced and forged. We separated immediately after the meeting, each clutching his envelope, each wishing the others some crippling misfortune, anything up to death."

"Then you have no idea which of them, if any, thought Mr. Dahlmann was joking."

"Not the faintest."

"Did you?"

"Ah." Rollins looked pleased. "This is more like it, only I thought you would be more subtle. The police wouldn't believe my answer, and you won't either. I really don't know. I was in a sort of nightmare. My demon had brought me there with the single purpose of winning the contest by my own wit and ingenuity. Whether the paper he showed us held the answers or not was a matter of complete indifference to me. If careless chance had put it in my way I would have burned it without looking at it, at the dictate not of conscience, but of pride. I'm sorry to disappoint you, but I can't say if I thought Dahlmann was joking or not because I didn't think one way or the other. Now you want to know what I did last evening after the meeting."

Wolfe shook his head. "Not especially. You have told the police, of course, and they're much better equipped to trace movements and check alibis than I am. And I'm not investigating the murder."

"Exactly what are you doing?"

"I'm trying to find a way to settle the contest in a manner acceptable to all parties. You say Mr. Younger spoke to you? What did he say?"

"He told me what Goodwin told him about Miss Frazee, and he wanted Mrs. Wheelock and me to join him in getting a lawyer and starting legal action. But also he wanted us to propose to Miss Tescher and Miss Frazee that the amount of the first five prizes will be divided equally among us. I told him we couldn't very well do both."

"Which do you prefer?"

"Neither. Since I have to pay the piper I'm going to dance. Dahlmann said these verses are much more obscure than any of the others, and I believe him. I doubt if Miss Frazee's friends can get any of them, and I'll be surprised if Miss Tescher can. When I leave here I'm going to one of the finest private libraries in New York and spend the night there, and I already know which book I'll go to first. This is one of the verses:

> "From Jack I learned love all the way,
>   And to the altar would be led;
>   But on my happy wedding day
>   I married Charles instead."

He lifted a hand to his glasses, but only shifted them a little on his nose. "Does that suggest anything to you?"

"No," Wolfe said emphatically.

"It does to me. Not any detail of it, but the flavor. I have no idea what her name was, but I think I know where to find her. I may be wrong, but I doubt it, and if not, there's one right off."

He probably had it. Either he had had a lucky hunch, or he knew a lot about flavors, or he had got the paper from Dahlmann's wallet and was preparing the ground for a later explanation of how and where he got the answers. I could certainly have impressed him by asking if the book he would go to first would be Jacques Casanova's *Memoirs,* but he might have suspected me if

I had also told him her name was Christine and he should try Volume Two, pages one hundred seventy-two to two hundred one, of the Aventuros edition.

Wolfe said abruptly, "Then I mustn't keep you, if you're going to work. I wouldn't care to stir the choler of a demon." He put his hands on the desk edge to push his chair back, and arose. "I hope to see you again, Mr. Rollins, but I shall try to interfere as little as may be with your labors. You will excuse me." He headed for the door and was gone.

Rollins looked at me. "What was that, pique? Or did I betray myself and he has gone for handcuffs?"

"Forget it." I stood up. "Don't you smell anything?"

He sniffed. "Nothing in particular. What is it?"

"Of course," I conceded, "you're not a bloodhound. It's shad roe in casserole with parsley, chervil, shallot, marjoram, bay leaf, and cream. That's his demon, or one of them. He has an assortment. You're going? If you don't mind, what was Number Nine? I think it was. It goes:

> *"By the law himself had earlier made*
> *I could not be his legal wife;*
> *The law he properly obeyed*
> *And loved me all my life."*

He had turned at the door, and his smile was super-superior. "That was palpable. Aspasia and Pericles."

"Oh, sure. I should have known."

We went to the hall and I held his coat. As I opened the door he inquired, "Wasn't that Miss Tescher here when I came?"

I told him yes.

"Who were the three men?"

"Advisers she brought along. You should have heard them. They talked Mr. Wolfe into a corner."

He thought he was going to ask me more, vetoed it, and went. I shut the door and started for the kitchen to tell Wolfe about Aspasia and Pericles, but the phone ringing pulled me into the office. I answered it, had a brief exchange with the caller, and then went to the kitchen, where Wolfe was in conference with Fritz, and told him:

"Talbott Heery will be here at a quarter past nine."

Already on edge, he roared. "I will not gallop through my dinner!"

I told him, apologetically, that I was afraid he'd have to. He only had an hour and a half.

9

The subject of discussion at Wolfe's dinner table, whether we had company or not, might be anything from politics to polio, so long as it wasn't current business. Business was out. That evening was no exception, strictly speaking, but it came close. Apparently at some time during the day Wolfe had found time to gallop through the encyclopedia article on cosmetics, and at dinner he saw fit, intermittently, to share it with me. He started, when we had finished the chestnut soup and were waiting for Fritz to bring the casserole, by quoting verbatim a bill which he said had been introduced into the English Parliament in 1770. It ran, he said:

"All women of whatever age, rank, profession, or degree, whether virgins, maids, or widows, that shall, from and after this Act, impose upon, seduce, and betray into matrimony, any of His Majesty's subjects, by the scents, paints, cosmetic washes, artificial teeth, false hair, Spanish wool, iron stays, hoops, high heeled shoes, bolstered hips, shall incur the penalty of the law in force against witchcraft and like misdemeanors and the marriage, upon conviction, shall stand null and void."

I asked him what Spanish wool was, and had him. He didn't know, and because he can't stand not knowing the meaning of any word or phrase he sees or hears, I asked why he hadn't looked in the dictionary, and he said he had but it wasn't there. Another item was that Mary Queen of Scots bathed in wine regularly, and so did the elder ladies of the court, but the younger ones couldn't afford it and had to use milk. Another was that when they found unguent vases in old Egyptian tombs they had dug into, the aromatics in them were still fragrant, after thirty-five hundred years. Another, that Roman fashion leaders at the time of Caesar's wife bleached their hair with a kind of soap that came from Gaul. Another, that Napoleon liked Josephine to use cosmetics and got them for her from Martinique. Another, that Cleopatra and other Egyptian babes painted the under side of their eyes green, and the lid, lashes, and eyebrows black. For the black they used kohl, and put it on with an ivory stick.

I admitted it was very interesting, and made no remark about how helpful it would be in finding out who had swiped Dahlmann's wallet, since that would have touched on business. Even after we finished with cheese and coffee and left the dining room to cross the hall to the office, I let him digest in peace, and went to my desk and dialed Lily Rowan's number. When I told her I wouldn't be able to make it to the Polo Grounds tomorrow, she began to call Wolfe names, and thought of several new ones that showed her wide experience and fine feeling for words. While we were talking the doorbell rang, but Fritz had been told about Heery, so I went ahead and finished the conversation properly. When I hung up and swiveled, Heery was in the red leather chair.

He measured up to it, both vertically and horizontally, much better than either Rollins or Mrs. Wheelock. In a dinner jacket, with the expanse of white shirt front, he looked broader even than before. Apparently he had been glancing around, for he was saying, "This is a very nice room. Very personal. You like yellow, don't you?"

"Evidently," Wolfe muttered. Such remarks irritate him. Since the drapes and couch cover and cushions and five visible chairs were yellow, it did seem a little obvious.

"Yellow is a problem," Heery declared. "It has great advantages, but also it has a lot of drawbacks. Yellow streak. Yellow journalism. Yellow fever. It's very popular for packaging, but Louis Dahlmann wouldn't let me use it. Formerly I used it a great deal. Seeing all your yellow made me think of him."

"I doubt," Wolfe said drily, "if you needed my décor to remind you of Mr. Dahlmann at this juncture."

"That's funny," Heery said, perfectly serious.

"It wasn't meant to be."

"Anyway, it is, because it's wrong. That's the first time I've thought of him today. Ten seconds after I heard he was dead, and how he had died, I was in a stew about the effect on the contest and my business, and I'm still in it. I haven't had any room for thinking about Louis Dahlmann. Have you seen all the contestants?"

"Four of them. Mr. Goodwin saw Mr. Younger."

"Have you got anywhere?"

Wolfe hated to work right after dinner. He said testily, "I report only to my client, Mr. Heery."

"That's funny too. Your client is Lippert, Buff and Assa. I'm one of their biggest accounts—their commission on my business last year was over half a million. I'm paying all the expenses of the contest, and of course the prizes. And you won't even tell me if you've got anywhere?"

"Certainly not." Wolfe frowned at him. "Are you really as silly as you sound? You know quite well what my obligation to my client is. You have a simple recourse: get one of them on the phone and have me instructed—preferably Mr. Buff or Mr. Assa."

It seemed a good spot for Heery to offer to knock his block off, but instead he got to his feet, stuck his hands in his pockets, and looked around, apparently for something to look at, for he marched across to the globe and stood there staring at it. His back looked even broader than his front. Pretty soon he turned and came back and sat down.

"Have they paid you a retainer?" he asked.

"No, sir."

He took a thin black leather case from his breast pocket, opened it and tore off a strip of blue paper, produced a midget fountain pen, put the paper on the table at his elbow, and wrote. After putting the pen and case away he reached to send the paper fluttering onto Wolfe's desk and said, "There's ten thousand dollars. I'm your client now, or my firm is. If you want more say so."

Wolfe reached for the check, tore it across, again, again, and leaned to the right to drop it in the wastebasket. He straightened up. "Mr. Heery, I am never too complaisant when my digestion is interrupted, and you are trying me. You might as well go."

I'll be damned if Heery didn't look at me. Wanting to save him the embarrassment of offering me a twenty, possibly even a C, to put him back on the track, and getting another turndown, and also thinking that if Wolfe wanted his nose pushed in I might as well help, I met his eyes and told him, "When you do go, if you're still looking for a better time and place there's a little yard out back."

He burst out laughing—a real good hearty laugh. He stopped long enough to say, "You're a team, you two," and then laughed some more. We sat and looked at him. He took out a folded hand-kerchief and coughed into it a couple of times, and was sober.

"All right," he said, "I'll tell you how it is."

"I know how it is." Wolfe was good and sore.

"No, you don't. I went about it the wrong way, so I'll start over. LBA has a good deal at stake in this mess, I know that, but I have more. If this contest explodes in my face it could ruin me. Will you listen?"

Wolfe was leaning back with his eyes closed. "I'm listening," he muttered.

"You have to know the background. I started my business twenty years ago on a shoestring. I worked hard, but I had some luck, and my biggest piece of luck was that a man named Lippert, an advertising man, got interested. The firm's name then was McDade and Lippert. My product was good, but Lippert was better than good, he was great, and in ten years my company was leading the field in dollar volume. It was sensational. Then Lippert died. Momentum kept us on the rise for a couple of years, and then we started to sag. Not badly, we had some ups too, but it was mostly downs. I still had a good organization and a good product, but Lippert was gone, and that was the answer."

He looked at his folded handkerchief as if he wondered what it was for, and stuck it back in his pocket. "In nineteen-fifty the LBA people submitted some names for a new line we were getting ready to start, and from the list I picked Pour Amour. I didn't learn until later that that name had been suggested by a young man named Louis Dahlmann who hadn't been with them long. Do you know anything about the agency game?"

"No."

"It's very tough, especially with the big ones. The men who have made it, who have got up around the top, most of them spend a lot of their time kicking the faces of the ones who are trying to climb. Of course that's more or less true in any game because it's how people are made, but advertising agencies are about the worst, I mean the big ones. It took me two years to find out who thought of that name Pour Amour, and it was another year before Dahlmann was allowed to confer with me on my account. By that time he had shown so much stuff there was no holding him. There was a lot of talk—you may have heard of him?"

"No."

"He wasn't very likable. He was too cocky, and if he thought you were a goddam fool he said so, but he had real brains and there's no substitute for brains, and his were a special kind. I don't say that Oliver Buff and Pat O'Garro and Vern Assa haven't got brains. Buff has some real ability. He's a good front man. Lippert trained him and knew what he was good for. Now he's the senior member of the firm. For presenting an outline for an institutional campaign to the heads of a big national corporation, he's as good as anybody and better than most, but that kind of approach never has sold cosmetics and never will. I've been one of the firm's big accounts for years, and he has never personally come up with an idea that was worth a dime."

Heery turned a hand over. "There's Pat O'Garro. He knows about as much about advertising, my kind, as I know about Sanskrit, but he's at the very top as a salesman. He could sell a hot-water bottle to a man on his way to hell, and most of the accounts LBA has today, big and little, were landed by him, but that's nothing in my pocket. I don't need someone to sell me on LBA, I need someone who can keep my products sliding over the counters from Boston to Los Angeles and New Orleans to Chicago, and O'Garro's not the man. Neither is Vern Assa. He started in as a copy writer, and that's where he shines. He has a big reputation, and now he's a member of the firm—so is O'Garro of course. I did a lot of analyzing of Vern and his stuff during the years after Lippert died, and it had real quality, I recognize that, but there was something lacking—the old Lippert touch wasn't there. It's not just words, you've got to have ideas before you're ready for words, and LBA didn't have any that were worth a damn until Louis Dahlmann came along."

He shook his head. "I thought my worries were over for good. I admit I didn't like him, but there are plenty of people to like. He was young, and within a year he would have been a member of the firm—he could have forced it whenever he pleased—and before too long he would be running the show, and he had a real personal interest in my account because it appealed to him. Now he's dead, and I'm through with LBA. I've decided on that, I'm through with them, but this goddam contest mess has got to be cleaned up. This morning, when they suggested hiring you, I didn't have my thoughts in order and I told them to go ahead, but with the situation the way it is and me deciding to cut loose from them as soon as this is straightened out it doesn't make sense for LBA to be your client. It will be my money you'll get anyhow. You were a little too quick tearing up that check."

"Not under the circumstances," Wolfe said.

"You didn't know all the circumstances. Now you do—at least the main points. Another point, some important decision about this contest thing may have to be made at any minute, and be made quick, about what you do or don't do, and as it stands now they hired you and they'll decide it. I won't have it that way. I've got more at stake than they have." He took the black leather case from his pocket. "What shall I make it? Ten thousand all right?"

"It can't be done that way," Wolfe objected. "You know it can't. You have a valid point, but you admit you told them to come and hire me. There's a simple way out: get them on the phone and tell them you wish to replace them as my client, and if they acquiesce they can speak to me and tell me so."

Heery looked at him. He put his palms on the chair arms, and spread his fingers and held them stiff. "That would be difficult," he said. "My relations with them the past year or so, especially Buff, have been a little—" He let it hang, and in a moment finished positively, "No, I can't do that."

Wolfe grunted. "I might be willing to phone them myself and tell them what you want. At your request."

"That would be just as bad. It would be worse. You understand, I've got to avoid an open break right now."

"I suppose so. Then I'm afraid you'll have to accept the status quo. I have sympathy with your position, Mr. Heery. Your interest is as deeply engaged as theirs, and as you say, the money they pay me will have come from you. At a minimum you have a claim to get my reports firsthand. Do you want me to phone them for authority to give them to you? That shouldn't be an intolerable strain

on the thread of your relations. I shall tell them that it seems to me
your desire is natural and proper."

"It would be something," Heery said grudgingly.

"Shall I proceed?"

"Yes."

The phone rang. I answered it, exchanged some words with the
caller, asked him to hold on, and turned to tell Wolfe that Rudolph
Hansen wished to speak to him. He reached for his instrument,
changed his mind, left his chair, and made for the door. As he
rounded the corner of his desk he pushed air down with his palm,
which meant that I was to hang up when he was on—presumably
to leave me free to chat with the company. A faint squeak that
came via the hall reminded me that I had forgotten to oil the
kitchen door. When I heard Wolfe's voice in my ear I cradled the
phone.

Heery and I didn't chat. He looked preoccupied, and I didn't
want to take his mind off his troubles. We passed some minutes
in silent partnership before Wolfe returned, crossed to his chair,
and sat.

He addressed Heery. "Mr. Hansen was with Mr. Buff, Mr.
O'Garro, and Mr. Assa. They wanted my report and I gave it to
them. They have no objection to my reporting to you freely, at any
time."

"That's damned sweet of them," Heery said, not appreciatively.
"Did *they* have anything to report?"

"Nothing of any consequence."

"Then I'm back where I started. Have you got anywhere?"

"Now I can answer you. No."

"Why not?"

Wolfe stirred. "Mr. Heery. I tell you precisely what I told Mr.
Hansen. If my talks with the contestants had led me to any conclusions, I might be ready to disclose them and I might not, but I
have formed no conclusions. Conjectures, if I have any, are not
fit matter for a report unless I need help in testing them, and
I don't. You interrupted the digestion not only of my dinner, but
also of the information and impressions I have gathered in a long
and laborious day. Those four men wanted to come here. I told
them either to let me alone until I have something worth discussing
or hire somebody else."

"But there's no time! What do you do next?"

It took another five minutes to get rid of him, but finally he went. After escorting him to the door I went back to my desk, got at the typewriter, and resumed where I had left off on my notes of the Frazee interview. They should all be done before I went to bed, and it was after ten o'clock, so I hammered away. There were one or two remarks I had for Wolfe, and several questions I wanted to ask, but I was too busy, and besides, he was deep in a book. When I returned after seeing Heery out he had already been to the bookshelves and was back at his desk, with *Beauty for Ashes,* by Christopher La Farge, opened to his place, and the wall light turned on. That may not be the way you go about settling down to work on a hard job with a close deadline, but you're not a genius.

I had finished Frazee and was well along with Wheelock when the doorbell rang. As I started for the hall I offered five to one that it was LBA and their lawyer, disregarding Wolfe's demand to be let alone, but I was wrong. When I flipped the switch of the stoop light, one glance through the panel was enough. Stepping back into the office, I told Wolfe:

"Too bad to disturb you—"

"No one," he growled. "No one on earth."

"Okay. It's Cramer."

He lowered the book, with his lips tightened. Slowly and neatly, he dog-eared a page and closed the book on the desk. "Very well," he said grimly. "Let him in."

The doorbell rang again.

10

Wolfe and Inspector Cramer of Manhattan Homicide West have never actually come to blows, though there have been times when Cramer's big red seamy face has gone almost white, and his burly broad shoulders have seemed to shrink, under the strain. I can always tell what the tone is going to be, at least for the kickoff, by the way he greets me when I let him in. If he calls me Archie, which doesn't happen often, he wants something he can expect to get only as a favor and has determined to forget old sores and keep it friendly. If he calls me Goodwin and asks how I am, he still is after a favor but thinks he is entitled to it. If he calls me Goodwin but shows no interest in my health, he has come for what he would call co-operation and intends to get it. If he calls me nothing at all, he's ready to shoot from the hip and look out.

That time it wasn't Archie, but he asked how I was, and after he got into the red leather chair he accepted an offer of beer from Wolfe, and apologized for coming so late without phoning. As Fritz served the beer I went to the kitchen to get a glass of milk for myself. When I returned Cramer had a half-empty glass in his hand and was licking foam from his lips.

"I hope," he said, "that I didn't interrupt anything important." He was gruff, but he would be gruff saying his prayers.

"I'm on a case," Wolfe said, "and I was working." *Beauty for Ashes,* by Christopher La Farge, is a novel written in verse, the scene of the action being Rhode Island. I don't read novels in verse, but I doubt if there's anything in it about perfume contests, or even any kind of cosmetics. If it were *Ashes for Beauty* that might have been different.

"Yeah," Cramer said. "The Dahlmann murder."

"No, sir." Wolfe poured beer. "I'm aware of your disapproval of private detectives concerning themselves with murders in your jurisdiction—heaven knows I should be—and it pleases me to know that I'm not incurring it. I am not investigating a murder."

"That's fine. Would you mind telling me who your client is? This case you're on?"

"As a boon?"

"I don't care what you call it, just tell me."

"There's no reason why I shouldn't, in confidence of course. A firm, an advertising agency, called Lippert, Buff and Assa."

I raised my brows. Evidently Cramer wasn't the only one in favor of favors. Wolfe was being almost neighborly.

"I've heard of them," Cramer said. "Just today, in fact. That's the firm Louis Dahlmann was with."

"That's right."

"When did they hire you?"

"Today."

"Uh-huh. And also today four people have come to see you, not counting your clients, who were at a dinner meeting with Dahlmann last night, and Goodwin has called on another one at his hotel. But you're not investigating a murder?"

"No, sir."

"Nuts."

It looked as if the honeymoon was over and before long fur would be flying, but Cramer took the curse off his lunge with a diversion. He drank beer, and put his empty glass down. "Look," he said, "I've heard you do a lot of beefing about people being rational. Okay. If anyone who knew you, and knew who has been coming here today—if he didn't think you were working on the murder would he be rational? You know damn well he wouldn't. I'm being rational. If you want to try to talk me out of it, go ahead."

Wolfe made a noise which he may have thought was a friendly chuckle. "That would be a new experience, Mr. Cramer. There have been times when I have tried to talk you *into* being rational. I can only tell you, also in confidence, what my job is. Of course you know about the perfume contest, and about the wallet that was missing from Mr. Dahlmann's pocket. I'm going to provide for a satisfactory settlement of the contest by learning who took the wallet, and what was in it, to demonstrate that none of its contents had any bearing on the contest. I'm also going to arrange that certain events, especially the detention of four of the contestants in New York, shall not prevent the fair and equitable distribution of the prizes. If you ask why I'm being so outspoken with you, it's because our interests touch but do not conflict. If and when I get anything you might need you shall have it."

"Quite a job." Cramer was eying him, not as a neighbor. "How are you going to learn who took the wallet without tagging the murderer?"

"Perhaps I can't. That's where our interests touch. But the murder is not my concern."

"I see. Just a by-product. And you say that the paper Dahlmann showed them and put back in his wallet didn't have the answers on it."

"Well." Wolfe pursed his lips. "Not categorically. On that point I am restrained. That is what my clients have told you, and it would be uncivil for me to contradict them. In any case, that illustrates the difference between your objective and mine. Since one of my purposes is to achieve a fair and satisfactory distribution of the prizes, the contents of that paper are of the first importance to me. But to you that is of no importance at all. What matters to you is not whether the paper contained the answers, but whether the contestants thought it did. If you had good evidence that one of them thought that Dahlmann was only hoaxing them, you'd have to eliminate him as a suspect. By the way, have you any such evidence?"

"No. Have you?"

"No, sir. I have no evidence of anything whatever."

"Do you believe that one of the contestants killed him?"

Wolfe shook his head. "I've told you, I'm not working on a murder. I think it likely that one of them took the wallet—only a conjecture, not a belief."

"Are you saying there might have been two of them—one killed him and one took the wallet?"

"Not at all. Of course my information is scanty. I haven't even read the account in the evening paper, knowing it couldn't be relied on. Have you reason to think there were two?"

"No."

"You are assuming that whoever killed him took the wallet?"

"Yes."

"Then so am I. As I said, there's no conflict. You agree?"

There was some beer left in Cramer's bottle, and he poured it, waited a little for the foam to go down, drank, put the glass down, and licked his lips.

He looked at Wolfe. "I'll tell you. I have never yet bumped into you in the course of my duties without conflict before I was through, but I don't say it couldn't possibly happen. As it stands now, if I take you at your word—I say if—I think we might get along. I think your clients are holding out on us. I think they're worried more about what happens to their goddam contest than what happens to a murderer, and that's why I'm willing to believe your job is what you say it is. I think they have probably given it to you straight, and I'd like to know exactly what they've told you, but I certainly don't expect you to tell me. I think that on the contest part, especially the paper Dahlmann had in his wallet, you're on the inside track, and you know things or you'll learn things that

we don't know and maybe can't learn. God knows I don't expect
to pump them out of you, but I do expect you to realize that it
won't hurt you a damn bit to loosen up with anything I could use."

"It's a pity," Wolfe said.

"What's a pity?"

"That you choose this occasion for an appeal instead of the
usual bludgeon, because this time I'm armored. Mr. Rudolph
Hansen, who is a member of the bar, made our conversation a
privileged communication by taking a dollar from me as a retainer.
I'm his client. It's a pity you don't give me a chance to raise my
shield."

Cramer snorted. "A lot you need it. I've had enough goes at
you without a shield. But this is a new one. You can't tell me anything because it's all privileged, huh?"

"No, sir." Wolfe was a little hurt. "I acquiesced in Mr. Hansen's subterfuge only to humor him. What I was told under the
cloak of privilege may be of help in connection with the contest,
but it wouldn't help you to find the murderer—since you know
about the wallet and the paper. The same is true of my conversations with the contestants, except to add that I have not been led
to conclude that any one of them did not take the wallet. I think
any one of them might have done so, and, as a corollary, might
have killed Dahlmann to get it. Beyond that I have nothing but
a medley of conjectures which I was sorting out when you interrupted me. None of them is worth discussing—at least not until
I look them over. I'll make this engagement: when I reach an
assumption I like you'll hear from me before I act on it. Meanwhile, it would simplify matters if I knew a few details."

"Yeah. You haven't even read the papers?"

"No, sir."

"I'll be glad to save you the trouble and maybe throw in a few
extras. He was killed between eleven-thirty and three o'clock,
shot once from behind, with a cushion for a muffler, with a .32
revolver. That's from the bullet; we haven't found the gun. The
building has a self-service elevator and no doorman, and we
haven't dug up anyone who saw Dahlmann come home or saw
anyone else coming to see him. Do you want all the negatives?"

"I like positives better."

"So do I, but we haven't got any, or damn few. No fingerprints that have helped so far, no other clues from the premises, nothing in his papers or other effects, no hackie that took somebody there, no phone call to that number from the hotel, and so on right through the routine. But you already knew that. If routine had got us anywhere I wouldn't be here keeping you from your work."

"Your routine is impeccable," Wolfe said politely.

"Much obliged. As for alibis, nobody is out completely. Getting out of a big hotel, and back in again, without being observed, isn't hard to do if you've got a good reason for it. The Tescher woman says that after the meeting she went to the library of a friend of hers and worked there on the contest until four o'clock, but nobody was in the room with her and everyone in the house was asleep. This leads to the point that really brought me here—the chief point. We're finding out that there were quite a few people around town who had it in for Louis Dahlmann—three or more women for personal reasons, two or three men for personal reasons, and several of both sexes for business reasons. Even some of his own business associates. We're looking into them, checking on where they were last night and so on, but the fact that his wallet was taken, and nothing else, may mean that it's a waste of time and talent. There was no money in the wallet; he carried bills in a roll in another pocket. The wallet was more of a card case, driver's license and so on."

Speaking of pockets must have reminded him. He reached to his breast pocket and took out a cigar, and wrapped his fingers around it. "So," he said, "I thought you might answer a question. Now that you've told me what you're after, I think so even more. Was he killed in order to get the wallet, or not? If so, it was one of the contestants and we can more or less forget the others, for now anyway, and it was on account of the contest, and as I said, you've got the inside track on that. I'm not asking for Goodwin's notes of your talk with your clients and that lawyer. I'm only asking your opinion, if he was killed to get the wallet."

"I repeat, Mr. Cramer, I am not investigating the murder."

"Damn it, who said you were? How do you want me to put it?"

Wolfe's shoulders went up and down. "It doesn't matter. You only want my opinion. I am strongly inclined to think that your man, the murderer, and my man, the thief, are one and the same.

It would seem to follow, therefore, that the answer to your question is yes. Does that satisfy you?"

From the look on Cramer's face, it didn't. "I don't like that 'strongly inclined,'" he objected. "You know damn well what's on my mind. And this privileged communication dodge. Why couldn't it be like this: after the meeting last night Dahlmann's associates talked it over, and they decided it was dangerous for him to have that paper in his wallet, and one of them went to his place to get it or destroy it. When he got there the door wasn't locked, and he went in and found Dahlmann on the floor, dead. He took the wallet from his pocket and beat it. Don't ask me why he didn't notify the police, ask him; he could have thought he would be suspected. Anyhow he didn't, but of course he had to tell his associates, and they all got hold of their lawyer and told him, and after talking it over they decided to hire you."

"To do what?"

"To figure out a way of handling it so the contest wouldn't blow them all sky high. Of course the contestants would learn not only that Dahlmann had been killed but also that the wallet was missing, and they would suspect each other of getting the answers, and it would be a hell of a mess. But I'm not going to try to juggle that around, that's their lookout, and yours. My lookout is that if it happened that way the contestants are not my meat at all because he wasn't killed to get the wallet. And can you give me a reason why it couldn't have happened that way?"

"No, sir."

"And the lawyer fixing it so that what he told you was privileged —wouldn't that fit in?"

"Yes," Wolfe conceded. "But it is a fact, not an opinion, that if it did happen that way I am not privy to it. I have been told that none of Mr. Dahlmann's associates went to his apartment last night, and have had no reason to suspect that they were gulling me. If they were they're a pack of fools."

"You state that as a fact."

"I do."

"Well," Cramer allowed, "it's not your kind of a lie." He was suddenly flustered, realizing that wasn't the way to keep it clean. He blurted, "You know what I mean." He stuck the cigar between his teeth and chewed on it. If he couldn't chew Wolfe the cigar would have to do. I've never seen him light one.

"Yes," Wolfe said indulgently, "I know what you mean."

Cramer took the cigar from his mouth. "You asked me a while ago if I assumed that whoever killed him took the wallet, and I said yes, but I should have said maybe. This other angle has got a bite. If I got some grounds to believe that one or more of Dahlmann's associates went to his place last night that would make it a different story entirely, because that would account for the missing wallet, and I could stop concentrating on the contestants. I tell you frankly I have no such grounds. None of them—Buff, O'Garro, Assa, Heery, Hansen the lawyer—no one of that bunch can prove he didn't go down to Perry Street some time last night, but I haven't got anything to back up a claim that one of them did. You understand I'm not itching to slap a murder charge on him; as I said, he could have found Dahlmann dead and took the wallet. In that case he would be the one you're interested in, and I'd have an open field to find the murderer."

"Satisfactory all around," Wolfe said drily.

"Yeah. You say if one of them went there last night you know nothing about it, and I believe you, but what if they held that out on you? Wouldn't they? Naturally?"

"Not if they expected me to earn my fee." Wolfe looked up at the clock. "It's midnight. Mr. Cramer. I can only say that I reject your theory utterly. Not only for certain reasons of my own—as you say, I'm on the inside track on the contest—but also from other considerations. If one of those men went there last night and found Dahlmann dead, why was he ass enough to take the wallet, when he knew it would be missed, and that that would make a botch of the contest? He had to have the paper, of course, since if it were left on the corpse it would be seen by policemen, and possibly by reporters too, but why didn't he just take the paper and leave the wallet?"

"By God," Cramer said, "you were lying after all."

"Yes? Why?"

"Because that's dumb and you're not dumb. He goes in and finds a corpse, and he's nervous. It makes people nervous to find a corpse. He wants to turn and run like hell, they all do, especially if there's the slightest reason for them to be suspected, but he makes himself get the wallet from the corpse's pocket. He may even intend to take the paper and put the wallet back and start looking for the paper, but he thinks of fingerprints. Maybe he can wipe the wallet off before he puts it back, but he might miss one. Even so, he might try, if he calmly considered all the consequences of taking the wallet, but he's not calm and there's no time and he has to get out of there. So he gets, with the wallet. Excuse me for taking up your valuable time with kindergarten stuff, but you asked for it."

He stood up, looked at the cigar in his hand, threw it at my wastebasket, and missed. He glared at it and then at Wolfe. "If that's the best you can do I'll be going." He turned.

"Manifestly," Wolfe said, "you don't believe Mr. Hansen and the others when they profess their conviction that Mr. Dahlmann's display of the paper was only a hoax?"

Cramer turned at the door long enough to growl, "Nuts. Do you?"

When I returned to the office after seeing him out Wolfe was still at his desk, pinching the lobe of his ear with a thumb and forefinger, staring at nothing. I put my empty milk glass on one of the beer trays, took them to the kitchen, washed and wiped the glasses, disposed of the bottles, and put the trays away. Fritz goes to bed at eleven unless he has been asked not to. Back in the office, the ear massage was still under way. I spoke. "I can finish the typing tonight if there are other errands for the morning. Have I got a program?"

"No."

"Oh well," I said cheerfully, "there's no rush. April twentieth is a week off. You can read twenty books in a week."

He grunted. "Get Saul and ask him to breakfast with me in my room at eight o'clock. Give me two hundred dollars for him —no, make it three hundred—and lock the safe and go to bed. I want some quiet."

I obeyed, of course, but I wondered. Could he be tossing a couple of C's—no, three—of LBA money to the breeze just to make me think he had hatched something? Saul Panzer was the best man in the city of New York for any kind of a job, but what was it? Tailing five people, hardly. If tailing one, who and why? If not tailing, then what? For me, nothing we had heard or seen had pointed in anyone's direction. For him, I didn't believe it. He wanted company for breakfast, and not me. Okay.

I got Saul at his apartment on East Thirty-eighth Street, signed him up for the morning, got the money from the cash drawer in the safe and locked the safe, gave Wolfe the dough, and asked him, "Then I don't do the typing tonight?"

"No. Go to bed. I have work to do."

I went. Up one flight I stopped on the landing, thinking it might help if I tiptoed back down and went in and caught him with his book up, but decided it would only make him so stubborn he'd read all night.

11

My morning paper is usually the *Times,* with the *Gazette* for a side dish, but that Thursday I gave the *Gazette* a bigger play because it has a keener sense of the importance of homicide. Its by-line piece on the career and personality of the brilliant young advertising genius who had been shot in the back did not say that there were at least a hundred beautiful and glamorous females in the metropolitan area who might have had reason to erase him, but it gave that impression without naming names.

However, that was only a tactful little bone tossed to the sex hounds for them to gnaw on. The main story was the contest, and they did it proud, with their main source of information Miss Gertrude Frazee of Los Angeles. There was a picture of her on page three which made her unique combination of rare features more picturesque than in the flesh, and harder to believe. She had briefed the reporter thoroughly on the Women's Nature League, told him all about the dinner meeting Tuesday evening, including Dahlmann's display of the paper and what he said, and spoken at length of her rights as a contestant under the rules and the agreement.

Of the other contestants, Susan Tescher of *Clock* magazine had been inaccessible to journalists, presumably after consulting her three windbags. Harold Rollins had been reached but had refused any information or comment; he hadn't even explained why winning half a million bucks would be a fatal blow to him. Mrs. Wheelock, who was living on pills, and Philip Younger, who had paroxysms to contend with, had apparently been almost as talkative as Miss Frazee. They were both indignant, bitter, and pugnacious, but on one point their minds had not met. Younger thought that the only fair way out of the mess was to split the prize money five ways, whereas Mrs. Wheelock did not. She was holding out for the big one, and said the five verses should be scrapped and five new ones substituted, under circumstances that would give each of them an equal opportunity.

Perhaps I should have confined my reading to the contest part, since we hadn't been hired for the murder, but only Fritz was in the kitchen with me and he wouldn't blab. There were a lot of facts that Cramer hadn't furnished—that Dahlmann was wearing a dark blue suit; that he had taken a taxi from the Churchill to his apartment and arrived a little before 11:30; that the woman who found him when she came to get his breakfast was named Elga Johnson; that his apartment was two rooms and bath; that the bullet had hit a rib after passing through the heart; and many other details equally helpful. The name of the murderer wasn't given.

Having got an early start, I was through with breakfast and the papers and was in the office at the typewriter when Saul Panzer came. Saul is not a natural for Mr. America. His nose is twice as big as he needs, he never looks as if he had just shaved, one shoulder is half an inch higher than the other and they both slope, and his coat sleeves are too short. But if and when I find myself up a tree with a circle of man-eating tigers crouching on the ground below, and a squad of beavers starting to gnaw at the trunk of the tree, the sight of Saul approaching would be absolutely beautiful. I have never seen him fazed.

He came at eight sharp and went right upstairs, and I went back to the typewriter. At five to nine he came back down but I didn't hear him until he called to me from the door to the hall. "Want to come and bolt me out?"

I swiveled. "With pleasure. That's what the bolt's for, such as you." I arose. "Have a good breakfast?"

"You know I did."

I was with him. "Need any professional coaching?"

"I sure do." He was at the rack getting his things. "I'll start at the bottom and work down."

"That's the spirit." I opened the door. "If you get your throat cut or something just give me a ring."

"Glad to, Archie. You'd be the one all right."

"Okay. Keep your gloves on."

He went, and I shut the door and went back to work. There had been a day when I got a little peeved if Wolfe gave Saul a chore without telling me what it was, and also told him not to tell me, but that was long past. It didn't peeve me any more; it merely bit me because I couldn't guess it. I sat at my desk a good ten minutes trying to figure it, then realized that was about as useful as reading a novel in verse, and hit the typewriter.

My speed at typing notes of interviews depends on the circumstances. Once in a real pinch I did ten pages an hour for three hours, but my average is around six or seven, and I have been known to mosey along at four or five. That morning I stepped on it, to get as much done as possible before Wolfe came down from the plant rooms at eleven o'clock, since he would certainly have some errands ready for me. I was interrupted by phone calls—one from Rudolph Hansen, wanting a progress report, one from Oliver Buff, wanting the same, one from Philip Younger, wanting me to arrange an appointment for him with the LBA crowd and getting sore when I stalled him, and one from Lon Cohen of the *Gazette*, wanting to know if I felt like giving him something hot on the Dahlmann murder. Being busy, I didn't start an argument by saying we weren't working on the murder; I just told him he'd have to stand in line, and didn't bother to ask him how he knew we were in the play. Probably Miss Frazee. In spite of the interruptions, I had finished Wheelock and Younger and Tescher by eleven o'clock, and started on Rollins.

The sound of Wolfe's elevator came, and he appeared, told me good morning, crossed to his chair and got his poundage adjusted, and spoke. "I left my papers in my room. May I have yours?"

I should have put them on his desk, since I knew he had had company for breakfast. I took them to him and then resumed at the typewriter. He glanced through the morning mail, which was

mostly circulars and requests from worthy causes, then settled back
with the news. That was okay, since there could have been an
item that might affect the program for the day. He is not a fast
reader, and I pounded along in high so as to be finished by the
time he was ready. It was still before noon by ten minutes when
I rolled the last page of Rollins from the machine, and after col-
lating the originals and carbons I turned for a glance at him.

He had put the papers down and was deep in *Beauty for Ashes*.
No commonplace crack would fit the situation. It was serious
and could be critical. I stapled the reports, labeled a folder
"Lippert, Buff and Assa" and put them in it, went and put the
folder in the cabinet, came back to my desk and put things away,
turned to him and announced, "I'm all set. Hansen and Buff
phoned to ask how we're coming, and I told them there was no
use crowding. Philip Younger wants you to get him a conference
with LBA, and I said maybe later. Lon Cohen wants the murderer's name with a picture by five o'clock. That's the crop. I'm ready
for instructions."

He finished a paragraph—no, it was verse. He finished something, then his eyes came at me over the top of the book. "I haven't
any," he stated.

"Oh. Tomorrow, maybe? Or some day next week?"

"I don't know. I gave it some thought last night, and I don't
know."

I stared at him. "This is your finest hour," I said emphatically.
"This is the rawest you have ever pulled. You took the case just
twenty-four hours ago. Why didn't you turn it down? That you
have the gall to sit there on your fanny and read poetry is bad
enough, but that you tell me to do likewise . . ." I stood up. "I
quit."

"I haven't told you to read poetry."

"You might as well. I'm quitting, and I'm going to the ball
game."

He shook his head. "You can't quit in the middle of a case, and
you can't go to the ball game because I couldn't get you if you were
suddenly needed."

"Needed for what? Bring you beer?"

"No." He put the book down, drew a long deep sigh, and

leaned back. "I suppose this has to be. You're enraged because I haven't devised a list of sallies and exploits for you. You have of course pondered the situation, as I have. I sympathize with your eagerness to do something. What would you suggest?"

"It's not up to me. If I did the suggesting around here, that would be my desk and this would be yours."

"Nevertheless, I put it to you. Please sit down so I can look at you without stretching my neck. Thank you. There is nothing you can do about any of those people that the police have not already done, and are doing, with incomparably greater resources and numbers. Keeping them under surveillance, investigating their past, learning if any of them had a gun, checking their alibis, harassing them by prolonged and repetitive inquisition—do you want to compete with the police on any of those?"

"You know damn well I don't. I want you to go to work and come up with instructions for me. Unless Saul is handling it?"

"Saul has been given a little task I didn't want to spare you for. You will accept my decision that at the moment there is nothing to be done by either you or me. That condition may continue for a week, until after the deadline has come and gone. Messrs. Hansen and Buff and O'Garro and Assa—and Mr. Heery too—are quite wrong in thinking that the culprit must be exposed before the deadline; on the contrary, it will be much more feasible after the deadline, unless—"

"That won't do us any good. You can't stall them that long. They'll bounce you."

"I doubt it. I'd have something to say about it. And anyway, I was saying that it will be more feasible after the deadline unless something happens, and I rather think that something will. The tension is extremely severe, not only for the culprit, but also for the others, in one way or another. That's why you can't go to the ball game; you must be at hand. Also for the phone calls. They'll get increasingly exigent and must be handled discreetly but firmly. I could help some with them, but it would be best for me to be so deeply engaged with the problem that I am unavailable. Of course they are not to be told that I think the solution may have to wait until after the deadline."

"Say by the Fourth of July," I suggested bitterly.

"Sooner than that or not at all." He was tolerant. "Commonly I take your badgering as a necessary evil; it has on occasion served a purpose; but this may go on for a while and I wish to be spared. I assure you, Archie—"

The phone rang. I answered it, and a trained female voice told me that Mr. O'Garro wanted to speak with Mr. Wolfe. Evidently they were reverting to type up at LBA. I told her Mr. Wolfe was engaged, but Mr. O'Garro could speak with Mr. Goodwin if he cared to. She said he wanted Mr. Wolfe, and I said I was sorry he couldn't have him. She told me to hold on, and after a wait resumed by asking me to put Mr. Goodwin on, and I said he was on. Then I got a male voice: "Hello, Goodwin? This is Pat O'Garro. I want to speak to Wolfe!"

"So I understand, but I have strict instructions not to disturb him, and I don't dare to. When he's buried in a case, as he is right now in yours, it's not only bad for me if I interrupt him, it's bad for the case. You've given him a tough one to crack, and you'd better leave him alone with it."

"My God, we've got to know what he's doing!"

"No, sir. Excuse me, but you're dead wrong. You either rely on him to get it or you don't. When he's working as hard as he is on this he never tells anybody what he's doing, and it's a big mistake to ask him. As soon as there's anything you'd like to know or need to know or can help with, you'll hear without delay. I told Mr. Hansen, and also Mr. Buff, about Inspector Cramer calling on us last night."

"I know you did. What time this afternoon can I drop in?"

"Any time that suits you. I'll be here, and you can look at the transcripts of the talks with the contestants if you want to. Mr. Wolfe will be upstairs and not available. When he's sunk in a thing as he is in this it's a job to get him to eat."

"But damn it, what's he doing?"

"He's using the brain you hired. Didn't you gentlemen decide you needed a special kind of brain? All right, you got one."

"We certainly did. I'll see you this afternoon."

I told him that would be fine, and hung up, and turned to ask Wolfe if that would do, but he had lifted his book and opened it and I didn't want to disturb him.

12

Thank the Lord those next four days are behind me instead of ahead. I admit that there are operations and situations where the best you can do is set a trap and then wait patiently for the victim to spring it, and in such a case I can wait as patiently as the next one, but we had set no trap. Waiting for the victim to make the trap himself and then spring it called for more patience than I had in stock.

Wolfe had asked me what I would suggest, and I spent part of the time from Thursday noon to Friday noon, in between phone calls and personal appearances of LBA personnel and Talbott Heery, trying to hit on something. I had to agree with him that there was no point in tagging along after the cops on any of the routines. Altogether, while sitting at my desk or on the stool in the kitchen, or brushing my teeth, or shaving, or looking out the window, I conceived at least a dozen bright ideas, none of them worth a damn when you turned them over. I did submit one of them to Wolfe after dinner Thursday evening: to get the five contestants together in the office, and tell them it had been thought that Dahlmann had put the answers to the last five verses in a safe deposit box, but evidently he hadn't, since none could be found, and there was no authentic list of answers against which their solutions could be checked, and therefore other verses, not yet devised, would have to replace the ones they had. He asked what good it would do. I said we would get their reactions. He said we already had their reactions, and besides, LBA would properly reject a procedure that made them out a bunch of bungling boobies.

There was nothing in Friday's papers that struck a spark, but at least they didn't announce that Cramer had got his man and the case was solved. Just the contrary. No one had been tapped even as a material witness, and it was plain, from the way the *Gazette* handled it, that the field was still wide open. Lon Cohen phoned again around noon to ask what Wolfe was waiting for, and I told him for a flash. He asked what kind of flash, and I told him to ask Miss Frazee.

The climax of the phone calls from the clients began soon after lunch Friday. Wolfe was up in his room to be away from the turmoil. He had finished *Beauty for Ashes* and started on *Party of One,* not in verse, by Clifton Fadiman. The climax was in three scenes, the hero of the first one being Patrick O'Garro. It was the third call from him in the twenty-four hours, and he made it short and to the point. He asked to speak to Wolfe and I gave him the usual dose. He asked if I had anything to report and I said no.

"All right," he said, "that's enough. This is formal notice that our agreement with him is canceled and he is no longer representing Lippert, Buff and Assa. This conversation is being recorded. He can send a bill for services to date. Did you hear me?"

"Sure I hear you. I'd like to say more because my phone conversations don't get recorded very often, but there's nothing to say. Goodbye."

I went to the hall, up the flight of stairs to Wolfe's room, tapped on the door, and entered. He was in the big chair by the window, in his shirt sleeves with his vest unbuttoned, with his book.

"You look nice and comfortable," I said approvingly, "but you prefer the chair downstairs and you can come on down if you want to. O'Garro just phoned and canceled the order. We're fired. He said the conversation was being recorded. I wonder why it makes a man feel important to have what he says on the phone recorded? I don't mean him, I mean me."

"Bosh," he said.

"No, really, it *did* make me feel important."

"Shut up." He closed his eyes. In a minute he opened them. "Very well. I'll be down shortly. It's a confounded nuisance."

I agreed and left him. As I went back downstairs my feelings were mixed. Getting tossed out on our ear would certainly be no fun, it wouldn't help our prestige any, and it would reduce our bill by about ninety-five per cent to a mere exorbitant charge for consultation, but I did not burst into tears as I began strolling around the office to wait for developments. At least the fat son of a gun would have to snap out of it and show something. At least his eyes would get a rest from the strain of constant reading. At least I wouldn't have to try to dig up more ways of explaining why they couldn't speak to a genius while he was fermenting.

The phone rang, and I answered it, and was told by a baritone that I recognized, "This is Rudolph Hansen. I want to speak to Mr. Wolfe."

I didn't bother. I said curtly, "Nothing doing. Orders not to disturb."

"Nonsense. He has already been disturbed by the message from Mr. O'Garro. Let me speak to him."

"I haven't given him the message from O'Garro. When he tells me to disturb him on no account he means it."

"You haven't given him that message?"

"No, sir."

"Why not?"

"My God, how many times must I say it? Do . . . not . . . disturb."

"That certainly is a strange way of—no matter. It's just as well. Mr. O'Garro was too impetuous. His message is hereby canceled, on my authority as counsel for the firm of Lippert, Buff and Assa. Mr. Wolfe is too highhanded and we would like to be kept better informed, but we have full confidence in him and we want him to go on. Tell him that—no, I'll tell him. I'll drop in a little later. I'm tied up here for the present."

I thanked him for calling, hung up, and mounted the stairs again to Wolfe's room; and by gum, he wasn't reading. He had put the book down and was sitting there looking imposed upon.

"I said I'd be down shortly," he growled.

"Yeah, but you don't have to. Go right on working. Hansen phoned as counsel for the firm. O'Garro was too impetuous, he said. They have full confidence in you, which shows how little—oh well. You're to keep at it. I didn't ask him if the conversation was recorded."

He picked up his book. "Very well. Now you may reasonably expect a respite."

"Not for long. Hansen's dropping in later."

He grunted and I left him.

The respite was a good ten minutes, maybe eleven, and it was ended at the worst possible moment. I had turned on the television and got the ball game, Giants and Dodgers, and Willie Mays was at bat in the fourth inning with a count of two and one, when the phone rang. Dialing the sound off but not the picture, I got at the phone, and received a double jolt. With my ears I heard Oliver Buff saying that both O'Garro and Hansen were too impetuous and had it wrong, and going on from there, and simultaneously with my eyes I saw Mays pop a soft blooper into short center field that I could have caught on the tip of my nose. I turned my back on that, but the rest of Buff I had to take. When he was through I went and turned off the TV, and once again ascended the stairs.

Wolfe frowned at me suspiciously. "Is this flummery?" he demanded.

"Not to my knowledge," I told him. "It sounds like their voices."

"Pfui. I mean you. The call by Mr. Hansen voided the one by Mr. O'Garro. You could have invented both of them; it would be typical."

"Sure I could, but I didn't. You asked for a cease-fire on badgering and got it. This time it was Buff. LBA seems to be tossing coins and giving me a play-by-play report. Buff voided both O'Garro and Hansen. He says they have been conferring and just reached a decision. They want a report by you personally on progress to date, and they're all at the LBA office, including Talbott Heery, and can't leave to come here, so you're to go there. At once. Otherwise the deal is off. I told him, first, that you never go outdoors on business, and second, that I wasn't supposed to disturb you and I wasn't going to. He had heard that before. He said you would be there by four o'clock, or else. It is now a quarter past three. May I offer a suggestion?"

"What?"

"If you ever take another job for that outfit, even to find out who's stealing the paper clips, get it in writing, signed by everybody. I'm tired out running up and down stairs."

He didn't hear me. With his elbow on the chair arm, he was pulling gently at the tip of his nose with thumb and forefinger. After a little he spoke. "As I said yesterday, the tension is extremely severe, and something had to snap. I doubt if this is it. This is probably merely the froth of frustration, but it may be suggestive to watch the bubbles. How long will it take you to get there?"

"This time of day, fifteen to twenty minutes."

"Ample. Get them together. All of them."

"Sure. Do I just tell them I'm you, or shall I borrow one of your suits and some pillows?"

"You are yourself, Archie. But I must define your position. You've been demanding instructions and here they are. Sit down."

I moved a chair up.

13

My visit to their office that afternoon probably cost LBA around three grand, maybe even five, for I found occasion later to describe the layout to Wolfe, thinking he should have it in mind when he was deciding on the amount of his bill, which he surely did if I know him.

From the directory in the lobby of the modern midtown skyscraper I learned that LBA had six floors, which opened my eyes and made me pick one. Choosing twenty-two because it was marked *Executive,* I found the proper elevator, was lifted, and emerged into a chamber that would have been fine for badminton if you took up the rugs. With upholstered chairs here and there sort of carelessly, and spots of light from modern lamps, it was a very cultured atmosphere. Two or three of the chairs were occupied, and at the far side, facing the elevators, an aristocratic brunette with nice little ears was seated at an executive desk eight feet long. When I approached she asked if she could help me, and I told her my name and said I wanted to see Mr. Buff.

"Do you have an appointment, Mr. Goodwin?"

"Yes, but under an alias, Nero Wolfe."

That only confused her and made her suspicious, but I finally got it straightened out and she used the phone and asked me to wait. I was crossing to a chair when a door opened and Vernon Assa appeared. He stood a moment, wiping his brow and neck with a handkerchief, and then came to me. Short plump men are inclined to sweat, but it did seem that an LBA top executive might have finished wiping before entering the reception room.

"Where's Mr. Wolfe?" he asked.

"At home. I'll report. To all of you."

"I don't think—" He hesitated. "Come with me."

We passed through into a wide carpeted hall. The third door on the left was standing open and we turned in. It was a fairly large room and would be a handsome one after the cleaning women had been around, but at present it was messy. The gleaming top of the big mahogany table in the center had most of its gleam spotted with cigarette ashes and stray pieces of paper, and the nine or ten executive-size chairs were every which way. A cigar butt had spilled out of an ash tray onto the mahogany.

Three men, not counting Assa, looked at me, and I looked at them. Talbott Heery wasn't so broad and tall when he had slid so far forward in his chair that most of him was underneath the table. Buff's white hair was touseled, and his round red face was puffy. He was seated across from Heery and had to twist around to look at me. Rudolph Hansen's long thin neck had a big smudge below the right ear. He was standing to one side with his arms folded and his narrow shoulders slumped.

"Goodwin says he'll report," Assa told them. "We can hear what he has to say."

"To all of you," I said, not aggressively. "Including Mr. O'Garro."

"He's in a meeting and can't be here."

"Then I'll wait." I sat down. "He canceled the agreement, and it wouldn't do much good to come to an understanding with you if he phones as soon as I get back and cancels it."

"That was on his own initiative," Buff said, "and unauthorized."

"Isn't he a member of the firm?"

"Yes."

"Okay. I'll wait. If I'm in the way here, tell me where."

"Get him in here," Heery demanded. "He can get the goddam toothpaste account any time."

They all started clawing, not at me but at each other. I sat and watched the bubbles, and heard them. LBA was certainly boiling over, and I tried to take it in, knowing that Wolfe would want a verbatim report, but it got a little confused. Finally they got it decided, I didn't know exactly how, and Buff got at a phone and talked, and pretty soon the door opened and Patrick O'Garro was with us. He was still brown all over, and his quick brown eyes were blazing.

"Are you all feeble-minded?" he blurted. "I said I'd go along with whatever you decided. I don't intend—"

I cut in. "Hold it, Mr. O'Garro. It's my fault. I came to report for Mr. Wolfe, and you have got to be present. I'm willing to wait, but they're in a hurry—some of them."

He said something cutting to Heery, and the others chimed in, and I thought the boiling was going to start again, but Buff got up and took O'Garro's arm and eased him to a chair. Then Buff returned to his own chair, which was next to me at the left.

"All right, Goodwin," he said. "Go ahead."

I took a paper from my pocket and unfolded it. "First," I announced, "here is a letter to Mr. Hansen, signed by Mr. Wolfe. It's only one sentence. It says, 'I herewith dismiss you as my attorney and instruct you not to represent me in any matter whatsoever.' Mr. Wolfe told me to deliver it before witnesses." I handed it to Assa, he handed it to O'Garro, and he handed it to Hansen. Hansen glanced at it, folded it, and put it in his pocket.

"Proceed," he said stiffly.

"Yes, sir. There are three points to consider. The first is the job itself and how you people have handled it. In the years I have been with Mr. Wolfe he has had a lot of damn fools for clients, but you have come pretty close to the record. Apparently you—"

"For God's sake," O'Garro demanded, "do you call that reporting? We want to know what he's done!"

"Well, you're not going to. Apparently you haven't stopped to realize what the job's like. I'll put it this way: if he knew right now who went there and stole the wallet—and killed Dahlmann, put that in too—and all he needed was one additional piece of evidence and he knew he was going to get it tonight—if he knew all that, he wouldn't tell any of you one single damn thing about it. Not before he had it absolutely sewed up. In the condition of panic you're in, all of you except Mr. Hansen, I don't know how much you can understand, but maybe you can understand that."

"I can't," Buff said. "It sounds preposterous. We hired him and we'll pay him."

"Then I'll spell it out. What would happen if he kept you posted on exactly what he had done and was doing and intended to do?

God only knows, but judging from the way you've been acting this afternoon there would be a riot. One or another of you would be calling every ten minutes to cancel what the last one said and give him new instructions. Mr. Wolfe doesn't take instructions, he takes a job, and you should have known that before you hired him. —You did, didn't you, Mr. Hansen? You said that all of you would be at his mercy."

"Not precisely in that sense." The lawyer's eyes, meeting mine, were cold and steady. "But I knew of Wolfe's methods and manners, yes. I grant that the conflicting messages from us this afternoon were ill-advised, but we are under great pressure. We need to know at least whether any progress is being made."

"You will, when he is ready to tell you. He's under pressure too. You have to consider that he's not working for you . . . or you . . . or you . . . or you . . . or you. He's working for the firm of Lippert, Buff and Assa. I can say this, if the men authorized to speak for the firm want to call it off, it may be possible to make another arrangement. Just a suggestion: do you want to ask Mr. Heery if he cares to take over and have Mr. Wolfe represent him instead of LBA?"

"No!" O'Garro blurted. Assa looked at Hansen and the lawyer shook his head. Buff said, "I can't see that that would improve the situation any. Our interests are identical." Heery, sending his eyes around, said, "If you want it that way, say so."

Nobody said so. I gave them four seconds and went on. "Another point. I've told you that Inspector Cramer of Homicide came to see Mr. Wolfe last night. I'm not quoting him, but when he left, Mr. Wolfe's main impression was that he wasn't completely sold on the idea that one of the contestants killed Dahlmann to get the paper in the wallet. Someone could have killed him for a quite different reason and didn't take the wallet or anything else, and later one of you went there to see him and found him dead. You looked to see if the wallet was in his pocket, and it was, and you didn't want it found on his body on account of the risk that what was on the paper might possibly be made public, so you took the wallet and beat it. That would—"

They all broke in. Hansen said, "Absurd. Mr. Wolfe certainly wasn't—"

"Just a minute," I stopped him. "Mr. Wolfe told Cramer that he thought it likely that one of the contestants took the wallet, and that he was assuming that whoever killed Dahlmann took the wallet, but that doesn't mean he can toss Cramer's idea in the garbage as a pipe dream. He has no proof it didn't happen like that; all he has is what you men told him. So if he doesn't want to run the risk of being made a monkey of, which he doesn't, believe me, he has to keep that on the list of possibles, and in that case how can he tell you what he's doing and going to do? Tell who? His client is Lippert, Buff and Assa, but there's no such person as Lippert, Buff and Assa, it would have to be one of you, and it might be the very guy who went to Dahlmann's place and retrieved the wallet. Therefore—"

"It's absurd on the face of it," Hansen said. "It would—"

"Let me finish. Therefore Mr. Wolfe has a double reason not to keep you posted on every move—first, he never does with anybody, and second, one of you could be holding out on him and set to spike him. I don't think he thinks you are, but it's a cinch he wouldn't take that chance. There's no use trying to persuade me it's absurd, because Mr. Wolfe is the expert on absurdity, not me, and I wouldn't undertake to pass it on. That about covers the situation, except this, that he's fed up with your shoving. I had to disturb him to tell him about the performance you have put on this afternoon because I had to ask him if he wanted me to come up here, and I am now reporting that he is fed up. He is willing to go on with the job only with the understanding that what he is committed to get for you is results as they were outlined, as quickly and satisfactorily as possible, using his best ability and judgment. If you want him to continue on that basis, okay. If not, he might be willing to take on the job for Mr. Heery, but I doubt it, without the consent and approval of LBA, because you're all in it together."

"What then?" Hansen asked, colder than ever. "He has dismissed me as his attorney. What would he do?"

"I don't know, but I can give you a guess, and I know him fairly well. I think he would give Inspector Cramer the whole story as he knows it, including whatever he may have learned since he talked with you people, and forget it."

"Let him!" O'Garro barked. "To hell with him!"

Buff said, "Take it easy, Pat."

"I think we're overlooking something," Assa said. "We've let our personal feelings get involved, and that's wrong. The one thing we all want is to save the contest, and what we've got to ask ourselves is whether we're more likely to do that with Wolfe or without him. Let me ask you this, Goodwin. I agree with Mr. Hansen that Inspector Cramer's idea is absurd, but just suppose that Wolfe did find evidence, or thought he did, that one of us went to Dahlmann's apartment and found him dead and took the wallet. Whom would he report it to?"

"That would depend. If LBA was still his client, to LBA. He was hired—these were Hansen's words—*to find out who took the wallet and got the paper*. If he did what he was hired to do, or thought he had, naturally he would tell his client and no one else. There would be two offenses involved, swiping a wallet and failing to report discovery of a dead body, but that wouldn't bother him. But he couldn't report to a client if he no longer had one, and my guess is he would just empty the bag for Cramer."

"That," Hansen said, "is an unmistakable threat."

"Is it?" I grinned at him. "That's bad. I thought I was just answering a question. I withdraw it."

Talbott Heery, across the mahogany top from me, suddenly was up and on his feet, in all his height and breadth, glaring around with no favorites. "If I ever saw a bunch of lightweights," he told them, "this is it. You know goddam well Nero Wolfe is our only hope of getting out of this without losing most of our hide, and listen to you!" He put two fists on the table. "I'll tell you this right now: at the end of the contract you're done with Heery Products! If I had had any sense—"

"Tape it, Tal." O'Garro's voice was raised, with a sneer in it. "Go downstairs and tape it! We'll get along without you and without Nero Wolfe too! I don't—"

The others joined in and they were boiling again. I was perfectly willing to sit and watch the bubbles, but Oliver Buff arose and took my sleeve and practically pulled me to my feet, and was steering me to the door. His teeth were set on his lower lip, but had to release it for speech. "If you'll wait outside," he said, pushing me into the hall. "We'll send for you." He shut the door.

Outside could have meant right there, but eavesdropping is vulgar if you can't distinguish words, and I soon found that I couldn't, so I moseyed down the wide carpeted hall and on through into the reception room. A couple of the upholstered chairs had customers, but not the same ones as when I had arrived. When I lingered instead of pushing the elevator button the aristocratic brunette at the desk gave me a look, and, not wanting her to worry, I went and told her the evidence was all in and I was waiting for the verdict. She had a notion to give me a smile—I was wearing a dark brown pin-stripe that was a good fit, with a solid tan shirt and a soft wool medium-brown tie—but decided it would be better to wait until we heard the verdict. I decided she was too cagey for one of my temperament, and crossed the rugs over to a battery of large cabinets with glass fronts that covered all of a wall and part of two others. They were filled with an assortment of objects of all sizes, shapes, colors, and materials.

Being a detective, I soon detected what they were: samples of the products of LBA clients, past and present. I thought it was very democratic to have them here in the executive reception room instead of down on a lower floor with the riffraff. Altogether there must have been several thousand different items, from spark plugs to ocean liners to paper drinking cups to pharmaceuticals—though in the case of the liners and trucks and refrigerators, and other bulky items, they had settled for photographs instead of the real thing. There was an elegant little model of a completely equipped super-modern kitchen, about eighteen inches long, that I would have taken home for a doll's house, if I had had a wife and we had had a child and the child had been a girl and the girl had liked dolls. I was having a second look at the Heery Products section, which alone had over a hundred specimens, and was trying to decide what I thought of yellow for packaging, when the brunette called my named and I turned.

"You may go in," she said, and darned if the smile didn't nearly break through. Of course she had had plenty of time to inspect me from behind, and I never had a suit that fitted better. I repaid her with a friendly glance that spoke volumes as I stepped to the door to the inner hall.

In the executive committee room, I suppose it was, I couldn't tell from their expressions who or what had won. Certainly nobody looked happy or even hopeful. Heery was at a window with his back to us, which I thought was tactful since technically he was not a party. The others eyed me without love as I approached the big table.

Hansen spoke. "We have decided to have Nero Wolfe continue with the case, using his best ability and judgment as you stated, without prejudice to any of our rights and privileges. Including the right to be informed on matters affecting our interests, but leaving that to his discretion for the present."

I had my notebook out and was jotting it down. That done, I asked, "Unanimous? Mr. Wolfe will want to know. Do you concur, Mr. Buff?"

"Yes," he said firmly.

"Mr. Assa?"

"Yes," he said wearily.

"Mr. O'Garro?"

"Yes," he said rudely.

"Good." I returned the notebook to my pocket. "I'll do my best to persuade Mr. Wolfe to carry on, and if you don't hear from me within an hour you'll know it's okay. I'd like to add one little point: as his confidential assistant I'm in it too somewhat, and it interferes with my chores to spend half my time answering your phone calls, so I personally request you to keep your shirts on."

I turned to go, but Buff caught my sleeve. "You understand, Goodwin, that the time element is vital. Only five days. And we hope Wolfe understands it."

"Sure he does. Before midnight Wednesday. That's why he can't bear to be disturbed."

I left them to their misery. Passing through the reception room I paused to tell the brunette, "Guilty on all counts. See you up the river." It was a shock for her.

14

The next two days, Saturday and Sunday, I found that my personal request had been a mistake. Thursday and Friday had been bad enough, but at least their phone calls had given me something to do now and then, and with them muzzled, or nearly so, my patience got a tougher test than ever. You might think that after putting up with Wolfe for so long I would be acclimatized, and I am up to a point, but he keeps breaking records. After I reported to him in full on my session at LBA, including a description of the premises, there was practically no mention of the case for more than sixty hours. By Monday morning I was willing to believe he had really meant it when he said it would be more feasible after the deadline, and I had to admit that at least it was an original idea to use a deadline for a starting barrier.

I spent most of the week end prowling around the house, but was allowed to go out occasionally to walk myself around the block, and even made a couple of calls. Saturday afternoon I dropped in at Manhattan Homicide West on Twentieth Street for a little visit with Sergeant Purley Stebbins. Naturally he was suspicious, thinking that Wolfe had sent me to pry something loose, if only a desk and a couple of chairs, but he also thought I might have something to peddle, so we chatted a while. When I got up to go he actually said there was no hurry. Later, back home, when I reported to Wolfe and told him I was offering twenty to one that the cops were as cold as we were, his only comment was an indifferent grunt.

Late Sunday afternoon I spent six bucks of LBA money buying drinks for Lon Cohen at Yaden's bar. I told him I wanted the total lowdown on all aspects of the Dahlmann case, and he offered to autograph a copy of yesterday's *Gazette* for me. He was a great help. Among the items of unprinted scuttlebutt were these: Dahlmann had welshed on a ninety-thousand-dollar poker debt. His wallet had contained an assortment of snapshots of society women, undressed. He had double-crossed a prominent politician on a publicity deal. All the members of his firm had hated his guts and ganged up on him. The name of one of the several dozen women he had played games with was Ellen Heery, the wife of Talbott. He had been a Russian spy. He had got something on a certain philanthropist and been blackmailing him. And so on. The usual crop, Lon said, with a few fancy touches as tributes to Dahlmann's outstanding personality. Lon would of course not believe that Wolfe wasn't working on the murder, and almost refused to accept another drink when he was convinced that I had no handout for him.

I gave Wolfe the scuttlebutt, but apparently he wasn't listening. It was Sunday evening, when he especially enjoys turning the television off. Of course he has to turn it on first, intermittently throughout the evening, and that takes a lot of exertion, but he has provided for it by installing a remote control panel at his desk. That way he can turn off as many as twenty programs in an evening without overdoing. Ordinarily I am not there, since I spend most of my Sunday evenings trying to give pleasure to some fellow being, no matter who she is provided she meets certain specifications, but that Sunday I stuck around. If something did snap on account of the extremely severe tension, as Wolfe had claimed he thought it might, I was going to be there. When I went up to bed, early, he was turning off *Silver Linings*.

The snap, if that's the right word for it, came a little after ten o'clock Monday morning, in the shape of a phone call, not for Wolfe but for me.

"You don't sound like Archie Goodwin," a male voice said.

"Well, I am. You do sound like Philip Younger."

"I ought to. You're Goodwin?"

"Yes. The one who turned down your scotch."

"That sounds better. I want to see you right away. I'm in my room at the Churchill. Get here as fast as you can."

"Coming. Hold everything."

That shows the condition I was in. I should have asked him what was up. I should at least have learned if a gun was being leveled at him. Speaking of guns, I should have followed my rule to take one along. But I was so damn sick and tired of nothing I was in favor of anything, and quick. I dived into the kitchen to tell Fritz to tell Wolfe where I was going, grabbed my hat and coat as I passed the rack, ran down the stoop steps, and hoofed it double quick to Tenth Avenue for a taxi, through the scattered drops of the beginning of an April shower.

As we were crawling uptown with the thousand-wheeled worm I muttered to the hackie, "Try the sidewalk."

"It's only Monday," he said gloomily. "Got a whole week."

We finally made it to the Churchill, and I went in and took an elevator, ignored the floor clerk on the eighteenth, went to the door of eighteen-twenty-six, knocked, and was told to come in. Younger, looking a little less like Old King Cole when up and dressed, wanted to shake hands and I had no objection.

"It took you long enough," he complained. "I know, I know, I live in Chicago. Sit down. I want to ask you something."

I thought, my God, all for nothing, he's got another idea about splitting the pot and yanked me up here to sell it. I took a chair and he sat on the edge of the bed, which hadn't been made.

"I just got something in the mail," he said, "and I'm not sure what to do with it. I could give it to the police, but I don't want to. The ones I've seen haven't impressed me. Do you know a Lieutenant Rowcliff?"

"I sure do. You can have him."

"I don't want him. Then there's those advertising men with Dahlmann at that meeting, that's where I met them, but I've seen them since, and they don't impress me either. I was going to phone a man I know in Chicago, a lawyer, but it would take a lot of explaining on the phone, the whole mess. So I thought of you. You know all about it, and when you were here the other day I offered you a drink. When I offer a man a drink without thinking, that's a good sign. I can go by that as well as anything. I've got to do something about this and do it quick, and the first thing is show it to you and see what you say."

He took an envelope from his pocket, looked at it, looked at me, and handed it over. I inspected the envelope of ordinary cheap white paper, which had jagged edges where it had been torn open. Typewritten address to Mr. Philip Younger, Churchill Hotel. No return address front or back. Three-cent stamp, postmarked Grand Central Station 11:00 PM APR 17 1955. It contained a single sheet of folded paper, and I took it out and unfolded it. It was medium-grade sulphide bond, with nothing printed on it, but with plenty of something typewritten. It was headed at the top in caps: ANSWERS TO THE FIVE VERSES DISTRIBUTED ON APRIL 12TH. Below were the names of five women, with a brief commentary on each. I kept my face deadpan as I ran over them and saw that they were the real McCoy.

"Well," I said, "this is interesting. What is it, a gag?"

"That's the trouble—or one trouble. I'm not sure. I think it's the real answers, but I don't know. I'd have to go to a library and check. I was going to, and then I thought this is dynamite, and I thought of you. Isn't that the first—hey, I want that! That's mine!"

I had absent-mindedly folded the paper and put it in the envelope and was sticking it in my pocket. "Sure," I said, "take it." He took it. "It's somewhat of a problem. Let me think." I sat and thought a minute. "It looks to me," I said, "that you're probably right, the first thing to do is to check it. But the police are probably still tailing all of you. Have you been going to libraries the last few days?"

"No. I decided not to. I don't know my way around in any library here, and those two women, Frazee and Tescher, have got too big an advantage. I decided to fight it instead."

I nodded sympathetically. "Then if a cop tails you to a library now, only two days to the deadline, they'll wonder why you started in all of a sudden, and they'll want to know. The man I work for, Nero Wolfe, is quite a reader and he has quite a library. I noticed the titles of the books mentioned on that thing, and I wouldn't be surprised if he has all of them. Also it wouldn't hurt any for you to consult him about this."

"I'm consulting you."

"Yeah, but I haven't got the library with me. And if a cop tails you to his place it won't matter. They know he's representing Lippert, Buff and Assa about the contest, and all the contestants have been there except you."

"That's what I don't like. He's representing them and I'm fighting them."

"Then you shouldn't have showed it to me. I work for Mr. Wolfe, and if you think I won't tell him about it you'll have to take back what you said the other day about not making a fool of yourself for twenty-six years. Crap."

He looked pleased. "See," he said, "you remembered that."

"I remember everything. So the choice is merely whether I tell Mr. Wolfe or you tell him, and if you do you can use his library."

He was no wobbler. He went and opened a closet door and got out a hat and topcoat. As he was putting an arm in he said, "I don't suppose you drink in the morning."

"No, thanks." I was headed for the door. "But if you want one go ahead."

"I quit twenty-six years ago." He motioned for me to precede him, followed, pulled the door shut, and tried it to make sure it was locked. "But," he added, "now that I can afford little luxuries, thanks to my son-in-law, I like to have some around for other people." As we turned the corner of the hall he finished, "*Some* other people." On the way down in the elevator it occurred to me that he would want the verses to refer to, and I asked if he had them with him, and he said yes.

To make sure whether your taxi is being followed in mid-town traffic takes a lot of maneuvering, which takes time, and Younger and I decided we didn't really give a damn, so except for a few backward glances out of curiosity we skipped it. At the curb in front of the old brownstone on West Thirty-fifth I paid the driver, got out, led the way up the steps to the stoop, and pushed the button. In a moment the door was opened by Fritz, who, as I was taking Younger's coat, made sure I saw his extended forefinger, meaning that a visitor was in the office with Wolfe. Acknowledging it with a nod, I ushered Younger across the hall into the front room, told him it would be a short wait, and, instead of using the connecting door to the office, which was soundproofed, went around by way of the hall.

Wolfe was in his chair, with half a dozen books in front of him on his desk, but he wasn't reading. He was frowning at Mrs. James R. Wheelock of Richmond, Virginia, who was in the red leather chair, frowning back at him. The frowns switched to me as I approached. I was a little slow meeting them because it took me a second to get the title of the book on top of the pile: *The Letters of Dorothy Osborne to Sir William Temple.* With that, which was enough, I told Mrs. Wheelock good morning, informed Wolfe that Fritz wanted him in the kitchen for something, and walked out.

When he joined me in the kitchen the frown was gone and there was a gleam in his eye. I spoke first. "I just wanted to ask you if she has any idea who mailed her the answers."

It got him for half a second. Then he said, "Oh. Mr. Younger got them too?"

"He did. That's what he wanted to see me about. He's in the front room. He wanted to find out if the answers are the real thing, and I told him he could use your library, but I see Mrs. Wheelock had the same idea."

"No. She merely wished to tell me, and consult me. I suggested looking at the books; luckily I had all of them. I hadn't hoped for anything as provocative as this. Very satisfactory."

"Yeah. Worth waiting for. A slight comedown for me, to bring home a slab of bacon and find you're already slicing one just like it, but anyhow we've got it. Shall I send mine back?"

"By no means." He pursed his lips, and in a moment continued, "I'll tell her. You tell him. Bring him in in three minutes." He was gone.

I returned to the front room and found Younger on a chair by a window with a sheet of paper in each hand, one presumably being the verses. "You're not the only one," I told him. "Mrs. Wheelock got it too, and came to show it to Mr. Wolfe. She's in there with him now. He has the books, and they've checked the answers, and it's not a gag."

He squinted at me. "She got—just like this?"

"I haven't seen it, but of course it is."

"And they've checked it?"

"Right."

He stood up. "I want to see hers. Where is she?"

"You will." I looked at my wrist. "In one minute and twenty seconds."

"I'll be damned. Then it's not a frame. That was one thing I thought, that someone was trying to frame me, but I couldn't see how. She got it in the mail this morning?"

I told him she would no doubt be glad to supply all details, and right at the deadline crossed to open the door to the office and invited him in. He brushed on by, went straight to Mrs. Wheelock, and demanded, "Where's the one you got?"

I went and took his elbow, called his attention to Wolfe, steered him to a chair, and told Wolfe, "Mr. Younger wants details. Is hers like his and when did she get it and so on."

Wolfe lifted a sheet of paper from his desk blotter. Younger popped up from his chair and went to him. I joined them, and so did Mrs. Wheelock. It didn't take much comparing to see that hers was a carbon copy of his. The envelopes, including the postmarks, were the same except for the names. When Younger had satisfied himself on those points he picked up one of the books, Casanova's *Memoirs,* and opened it. Mrs. Wheelock told him that wasn't necessary, they were the right answers, no question about it. She didn't look as if she had changed her attitude to the food at the Churchill, but the fire back of her dark deep-set eyes was shining through in her excitement. Younger went ahead anyway, finding a page in the book, and we were still grouped at Wolfe's desk when the phone rang.

I went to my desk to answer it, and got from the receiver the same old refrain. "I want to speak to Mr. Wolfe. This is Talbott Heery."

But the lid was off, maybe. I told Wolfe, and he took his instrument, and I kept mine.

"This is Nero Wolfe. Yes, Mr. Heery?"

"I'm calling from my office. Harold Rollins, one of the contestants, is here. He just came, a few minutes ago, to show me something he received in the mail this morning. I have it here in my hand. It's a typewritten sheet of paper, headed, 'Answers to the five verses distributed on April twelfth,' and then the names of five women and comments on each. Of course I don't know whether they are the correct answers or not, but Rollins says they are. He says he came to me because this nullifies the contest, and my company is responsible. I'll consult my lawyer on that—not Rudolph Hansen—but I'm calling you first. What have you got to say?"

"Not much offhand. Mr. Rollins is with you?"

"He's in my office. I came to another room to phone. By God, this does it. Now what?"

"That needs a little thought. You may tell Mr. Rollins that he was not singled out. Mrs. Wheelock and Mr. Younger also received sheets in the mail like the one you describe. They are here on my desk—that is, the sheets are. Mrs. Wheelock and Mr. Younger are here with me. Probably all five—"

"We've got to do something! We've got—"

"Please, Mr. Heery." For years I have studied Wolfe's trick of stopping a man without raising his voice, but I still don't get it. "Something must indeed be done, I agree, but this doesn't heighten the urgency. Rather the contrary. I can't discuss it now, and anyway I'm not working for you, but I think this will require a conference of everyone concerned. Please tell Mr. Rollins that he will be expected at a meeting at my office at nine o'clock this evening. I'll invite the others, and I invite you now. At my office at nine o'clock, unless you hear otherwise."

"But what are we going—"

"No, Mr. Heery. You must excuse me. I'm busy. Goodbye, sir."

We hung up, and he turned to the company. "Mr. Rollins got one too and took it to Mr. Heery. It may reasonably be presumed that the other two—Miss Frazee and Miss Tescher—were not excluded. You heard what I said about a meeting here at nine o'clock this evening, and we shall want you with us. You'll come?"

"We're here now," Younger said. "This blows the whole thing sky high and you know it. Why put it off? Get them here now!"

"I don't want to wait until this evening," Mrs. Wheelock said, her voice so tense that I inspected her for signs of trembling, but saw none.

"You'll have to, madam." Wolfe was blunt. "I have to digest this strange finesse, and consult my clients." He looked up at the clock. "Only nine hours."

"You never answered my question," she complained. "Must I show this to the police and let them take it?" Her sheet was in her hand, and Younger had his.

"As you please—or rather, as you will. If you don't, when they learn that you got it, as of course they will, they'll be ruffled, but they are already. Suit yourself."

I was up and halfway to the door, to escort them out, but they weren't coming. They wanted to know what was what, then and there. Younger was so stubborn that I finally had to take his arm and put a little pressure on, and by the time I got him to the front, with his hat and coat on, and over the threshold to the stoop, he was in no humor to offer me a drink. They left together, and I hoped Younger would give Mrs. Wheelock a lift back to the hotel. She didn't have the physique or the vigor for a midtown bus.

I returned to the office and told Wolfe, "I know you like to do your own digesting, but one thing occurs to me. As far as the contest is concerned, it no longer matters who lifted the wallet. They've all got the answers now and there'll have to be a new deal, so what's left of our job?"

He grunted. "We still have it. You know what I was hired to do."

"Yes, sir. I ought to. But what if the client has lost interest in what you were hired to do?"

"We'll handle that contingency when we face it. For the immediate present there is enough to occupy us. I told you that with such tension something was sure to snap, though I must confess that I hadn't listed this among the possibilities. You will phone the others, all of them, and notify them of the meeting this evening, but from the kitchen or your room. I have to work. I haven't the slightest idea what course to take at the meeting, and I must contrive one. Now that this has happened we must move quickly, or you will be quite right—there will be no job left. I may need—confound it!"

The phone was ringing. I had it off the cradle automatically before remembering that my base of operations had been moved. An urgent male voice gave me not a request but an order, and I covered the transmitter and turned to Wolfe. "Buff. Exploding. You and only you."

He reached for his receiver. I stayed with mine.

15

"Nero Wolfe spea—"

"This is Buff. Is your wire tapped?"

"Not to my knowledge. I think we must assume it isn't, just as we assume an atom bomb won't interrupt us. Otherwise life becomes—"

"I couldn't reach Hansen so I got you." Buff's words were piling up. "A city detective is here, a Lieutenant Rowcliff, in my office. I came to another room to phone. He says that they have information that one of the contestants, Susan Tescher, received in the mail this morning a list of the answers to the five verses. Before he told me that he had asked me how many copies of the answers were in existence, and I told him what we have been telling them all along, just the one in the safe deposit box as far as we know.

We haven't mentioned the copy Goodwin took. But with that woman getting a copy in the mail, the police—"

"One moment, Mr. Buff. Three of the other contestants also received copies in the mail, and I suppose—"

"Three others! Then what—who sent them?"

"I don't know. I didn't, and Mr. Goodwin didn't."

"Where's the copy he took?"

"In the inner compartment of my safe. That's where he put it, and it must still be there. Hold the wire a moment while he looks."

I put my receiver down, went to the safe, swung the outer door open, and got at the dial of the four-way combination of the inner door. It takes a little time. Opening the door, there on top of the stack of papers I saw the leaves from my notebook. I took them out, made sure all four were there, returned them, shut the door and the outer door, announced to Wolfe, "Intact," and went back to my chair and picked up the receiver.

Wolfe spoke. "Mr. Buff? Mr. Goodwin's copy has remained in my safe and is there now. Mrs. Wheelock and Mr. Younger have been to see me, and Mr. Heery has phoned me that Mr. Rollins was in his office. Have you heard from Mr. Heery?"

"Yes. He phoned Assa. We were just going to call you when this detective came. What's this about a meeting?"

"There will be one at nine o'clock this evening, at my office, for all those concerned. Mr. Goodwin was going—"

"That can wait." Buff was sounding more like a top executive than he had before. "What about the police? We've lied to them. We've told them that we know of no copy except the one in the safe deposit box. I have just repeated it to this detective. He's waiting in my office. What about it?"

"Well." Wolfe was judicious. "You were not under oath. The police have been lied to informally many times by many people, including me. The right to lie in the service of your own interests is highly valued and frequently exercised. However, the police are investigating a murder, and now the number of extant copies of the answers will be of vital concern to them. Hitherto they would have been annoyed at the discovery of your lie; if you fail to disclose it now and they discover it later they will be enraged. I suggest that you disclose it immediately."

"Admit we all lied?"

"Certainly. There is no depravity attached and there can be no penalty. No man should tell a lie unless he is shrewd enough to recognize the time for renouncing it, if and when it comes, and knows how to renounce it gracefully. About the meeting this evening—"

"We can discuss that later. I'll call you."

He was off. Wolfe cradled the receiver, pushed the phone to one side, heaved a sigh clear down to where a strip of his yellow shirt showed between his vest and pants, as usual, leaned back, and shut his eyes.

"Of course you know," I said, "that that will bring us company."

"It can't be helped," he muttered.

Since the phone numbers of LBA and the Churchill were in my head, the only ones I had to scribble in my notebook were *Clock* magazine and Hansen's and Heery's offices. That done, I went to the kitchen, where Fritz was putting some lamb hearts to soak in sour milk and an assortment of herbs and spices, asked if I could use his phone, and started in. Four of them—Wheelock, Younger, Heery, and Buff—had already been invited and would get a reminder call later. Presumably Rollins had also been invited, but that had to be checked. I got two of them without much difficulty, O'Garro and Assa, on one call, but had a hell of a time with the others. Four different calls to Gertrude Frazee's room, eighteen-fourteen, at the Churchill, in a period of forty minutes, got me no answer. Three calls failed to land Rudolph Hansen, but he finally called back, and of course had to speak to Wolfe. I stood pat that he couldn't, and though he refused to accept the invitation to the meeting, I knew nothing could keep him away. I also got Harold Rollins, who told me in one short superior sentence that he would be present and hung up.

Susan Tescher was a tough one. First *Clock* told me she was in conference. Then *Clock* said she wasn't there today. I asked for Mr. Knudsen, the tall and bony one, but he had stepped out. I asked for Mr. Schultz, the tall and broad one, and he was engaged. I asked for Mr. Hibbard, the tall and skinny one, of the legal staff, and darned if I didn't get him. I told him about the meeting, and who would be there, and said that if Miss Tescher didn't come she might find herself tomorrow morning confronted with a *fait accompli,* knowing as I did that any lawyer would feel that a guy who used words like *fait accompli* was a man to be reckoned with. As I was starting to dial the Churchill number for another stab at Miss Frazee, the doorbell rang. I went to the hall for a look through the panel, then opened the door to the office. Apparently Wolfe hadn't moved a muscle.

I announced, "Stebbins."

He opened his eyes. "At least it's better than Mr. Cramer. Bring him in."

I went and unbolted the door, swung it wide, and said hospitably, "Hello there. We've been waiting for you."

"I'll bet you have." He marched on by me, making quite an air wash, and on by the rack, removing his hat as he entered the office. By the time I attended to the door and caught up he was standing in front of Wolfe's desk and talking. ". . . the copy of the contest answers that Goodwin made last Wednesday. Where is it?"

If you want to see Purley Stebbins at his worst you should see him with Nero Wolfe. He knows that on the record of the evidence, of which there is plenty, Wolfe is more than a match for him and Cramer put together, and by his training and experience evidence is all that counts, but he can't believe it and he won't. The result is that he talks too loud and too fast. I have seen Purley at work with different kinds of characters, taking his time with both his head and his tongue, and he's not bad at all. He hates to come at Wolfe, so he always comes himself instead of passing the buck.

Wolfe muttered at him, "Sit down, Mr. Stebbins. As you know, I don't like to stretch my neck."

That was the sort of thing. Purley would have liked to say, "To hell with your neck," and nearly did, but blocked it and lowered himself onto a chair. He never took the red leather one.

Wolfe looked at me. "Archie, tell him about the copy you made."

I obliged. "Last Wednesday I went to the safe deposit vault with Buff, O'Garro, and Heery. They got the box and opened it. I cut the two envelopes open, one with the verses and one with the answers, and made copies on four sheets from my notebook. The originals were returned to the envelopes, and the envelopes to the box, and the box to the vault. I came straight home with my copies and put them in the safe as soon as I got here, and they've been there ever since and are there now."

"I want to see them," Purley rasped.

Wolfe answered him. "No, sir. It would serve no purpose unless you handled and inspected them, and if you got hold of them you wouldn't let go. It would be meaningless anyway. Since Mr. Buff decided to tell about them we knew you would be coming, and if anything had happened to them Mr. Goodwin could have made duplicates and put them in the safe. No. We tell you they are there."

"They've been there all the time since Goodwin put them there last Wednesday?"

"Yes. Continuously."

"You haven't had them out once?"

"No."

Purley turned his big weathered face to me. "Have you?"

"Nope. —Wait a minute, I have too. An hour ago. Buff was on the phone and asked where they were, and Mr. Wolfe told me to take a look to make sure. I took them out and glanced over them, and put them right back. That was the only time I've had them out of the safe since I put them in."

His head jerked back to Wolfe and he barked, "Then what the hell did you get 'em for?"

Wolfe nodded. "That's a good question. To answer it adequately I would have to go back to that day and recall all of my impressions and surmises and tentative designs, and I'm busy and haven't time. So I'll only say that I had certain vague notions which never ripened. That will have to do you."

Purley's jaw was working. "What I think," he said.

"I beg your pardon?"

"I said, what I think. So does the Inspector. He wanted to come, but he was late for an appointment with the Commissioner, so he sent me. We think you sent the copies of the answers to the contestants." He clamped the jaw. He released it. "Or we think you might have, and we want to know. I don't have to tell you what it means to this murder investigation, whether you did or not—hell, I don't have to tell you anything. I ask you a straight question: did you send copies of those answers to the contestants?"

"No, sir."

"Do you know who did?"

"No, sir."

Purley came to me. "Did you send them?"

"No."

"Do you know who did?"

"No."

"I think you're both lying," he growled. That was an instance. He was talking too fast.

Wolfe lifted his shoulders and dropped them. "After that," he said, "conversation becomes pointless."

"Yeah, I know it does." Purley swallowed. "I take it back. I take it back because I want to ask a favor. The Inspector told me not to. He said if Goodwin typed those copies he wouldn't have used his machine here, and he may be right, but I hereby request you to let me type something on that typewriter"—he aimed a thumb—"and take it with me. Well?"

"Certainly," Wolfe agreed. "It's rather impudent, but I prefer that to prolonging the conversation. I'm busy and it's nearly lunch time. Archie?"

I pulled the machine to me, rolled some paper in, and vacated the chair, and Purley came and took it and started banging. He used forefingers only but made fair time. I stood back of his shoulder and watched him run it off:

Many minimum men came running and the quick brown fox jumped over the lazy moon and now is the time for all good men to come to the aid of the party 234567890-ASDFGHJKL:QWERTYUIOPZXCVBNM?

When he had rolled it out and was folding it I said helpfully, "By the way, I've got an old machine up in my room that I use sometimes. You should have a sample of that too. Come on."

That was a mistake, because if I hadn't said it I probably would have had the pleasure of hearing him thank Wolfe for something, which would have been a first. Instead, "Hang 'em on your nose and snap at 'em," he told me, retrieved his hat from the floor beside his chair, and tramped out. By the time I got to the hall he had the front door open. He didn't pull it shut after him, which I thought was rather petty for a sergeant. I went and closed and bolted it, and returned to the office.

Wolfe was at the bookshelves, returning Casanova and Dorothy Osborne and the others to their places. Since it was only ten minutes to lunch time, he couldn't have been expected to get back to work. I stood and watched him.

"Apparently," I said, "the rules have been changed, but you might have told me. It has never been put into words, but I have always understood that when you want to keep something to yourself you may choke me off with a smoke screen but you don't tell me a direct lie. You may lie to others in my presence, and often have, but not to me when we're alone. So I believed you when you said the contestants getting the answers in the mail was a surprise to you. I'm not griping, I'm just saying I think it would be a good idea to let me know when you change the rules."

He finished slipping the last book in, nice and even with the edge of the shelf, and turned. "I haven't changed the rules."

"Then have I been wrong all along? Is it okay for you to tell me a direct lie when we're alone?"

"No. It never has been."

"And it isn't now?"

"No."

"You haven't lied to me about the answers?"

"No."

"I see. Then I'd better keep everybody off your neck this afternoon. If you haven't already got a program for tonight's meeting, and evidently you haven't, I'm glad it's up to you and not me."

I went to my desk and rolled the typewriter back in place, to have something to do. I like to think I can see straight, and during the past hour or so I had completely sold myself on the idea that I knew now what Saul Panzer's errand had been; and I don't like to buy a phony, especially from myself. Pushing the typewriter stand back, I banged it against the edge of my desk, not intentionally, and Wolfe looked at me in surprise.

16

By four o'clock everybody was set for the evening party with one exception. Wheelock, Younger, Buff, and Heery had been reminded. O'Garro, Assa, Rollins, and Hansen didn't need to be. As for Susan Tescher, Hibbard had called and said she would be present provided he could come along, and I said we'd be glad to have him. The exception was Gertrude Frazee. I tried her five times after lunch, three times from the kitchen and twice from my room, and didn't get her.

When, at four o'clock, Fritz and I heard Wolfe's elevator ascending to the roof, we went to the office and made some preliminary preparations. There would be ten of them, eleven if I got Frazee, so chairs had to be brought from the front room and dining room. Wolfe had said there should be refreshments, so a table had to be placed at the end of the couch, covered with a yellow linen cloth, with napkins and other accessories. Fritz had already started on canapés and other snacks and filling the vacuum bucket with ice cubes. There was no need to check the supply of liquids, since Wolfe does that himself at least once a week. He hates to have anybody, even a policeman or a woman, ask for something he hasn't got. When we had things under control Fritz returned to the kitchen and I went to my desk and got at the phone for another try for Frazee.

By gum, I got her, no trouble at all. Her own voice, and she admitted she remembered me. She was a little frosty, asking me what I wanted, but I overlooked it.

"I'm calling," I said, "to ask you to join us at a gathering at Mr. Wolfe's office at nine o'clock this evening. The other contestants will be here, and Mr. Heery, and members of the firm of Lippert, Buff and Assa."

"What's it for?"

"To discuss the situation as it stands now. Since the contestants have received a list of the answers from some unknown source, there must be—"

"I haven't received any answers from any source, known or unknown. I'm expecting word Wednesday morning from my friends at home, and I'll have my answers in by the deadline. I've heard enough of this trick."

She was gone.

I cradled the phone, sat and gave it a thought, buzzed the plant rooms on the house phone, and got Wolfe.

"Do you want Miss Frazee here tonight?" I asked him.

"I want all of them here. I said so."

"Yeah, I heard you. Then I'll have to go get her. She just told me on the phone that she hasn't received any answers and she's heard enough of this trick. And hung up. If she's clean, she tore up the envelope and paper and flushed them down the toilet, and she's standing pat. Do you want her?"

"Yes. Phone again?"

"No good. She's not in a mood to chat."

"Then you'll have to go."

I said okay, went to the kitchen to ask Fritz to come and bolt after me, got my hat and coat, and left.

The clock above the bank of elevators at the Churchill said five-seventeen. On the way up in the taxi I had considered three different approaches and hadn't cared much for any of them, so my mind was occupied and I didn't notice the guy who entered the elevator just before the door closed and backed up against me. But when he got out at the eighteenth, as I did, and crossed over to the floor clerk and told her, "Miss Frazee, eighteen-fourteen," I took a look and recognized him. It was Bill Lurick of the *Gazette,* who is assigned to milder matters than homicide only when there are no homicides on tap. I thought, By God, she's been croaked, and stepped on it to catch up with him, on his way down the hall, and told him hello.

He stopped. "Hi, Goodwin. You in on this? What's up?"

"Search me. I'm taking magazine subscriptions. What brought you?"

"Always cagey. The subtle elusive type. Not me, ask me a question I answer it." He moved on. "We got word that Miss Gertrude Frazee would hold a press conference."

Of course that was a gag, but when we turned the corner and came to eighteen-fourteen, and I got a look inside through the open door, it wasn't. There were three males and one female in sight, and I knew two of them: Al Riordan of the Associated Press and Missy Coburn of the *World-Telegram.* Lurick asked a man standing just inside if he had missed anything, and the man said no, she insisted on waiting until the *Times* got there, and Lurick said that was proper, they wouldn't start Judgment Day until the *Times* was set to cover. A man approached down the hall and exchanged greetings, and entered, and somebody said, "All right, Miss Frazee. This is Charles Winston of the *Times*."

Her voice came: "The *New York Times?*"

"Correct. All others are imitations. Do you think one of the contestants killed Louis Dahlmann?"

"I don't know and I don't care." I couldn't see her, but she kept her voice up and spoke distinctly. "I asked you to come here because the American public ought to know, especially American women, that a gigantic swindle is being perpetrated. I have been accused by three people of getting a list of the contest answers in the mail, and it's not true. They say the other contestants got lists of the answers too, and I don't know whether they did or not, but they have no right to accuse me. It's an insult to American women. It's a trick to wreck the contest and get out of paying the prizes to those who have earned them, and it's a despicable thing to do. And it's me they want to cheat. They're afraid of all the publicity the Women's Nature League is getting at last, they're afraid American women will begin to listen to our great message—"

"Excuse me, Miss Frazee. We need the facts. Who are the three people that accused you?"

"One was a policeman, not in uniform, I don't know his name. One was a man named Hansen, a lawyer, I think his first name is Rudolph, he represents the contest people. The third was a man named Goodwin, Archie Goodwin, he works for that detective, Nero Wolfe. They're all in it together. It's a dirty conspiracy to—"

I had my notebook out, along with the journalists, chiefly for the novelty of participating in a press conference without paying dues to the American Newspaper Guild, and I got it all down, but I doubt if it's worth passing on. It developed into a seesaw. She wanted to concentrate on the Women's Nature League, of which they had already had several doses, and they wanted to know about the alleged list of answers received by the contestants, which would have rated the front page on account of its bearing on the murder if they could nail it down. But they couldn't very well get the nail from her, since she was claiming she had never got such a list and knew nothing about it. They kept working on her anyway until Lurick suddenly exclaimed, "Hey, Goodwin's right here!" and headed for the door.

Instead of retreating, I crossed the sill and got my back against the open door, since the main point was to make sure that it didn't get closed with me on the wrong side. They all came at me and hemmed me in so that I didn't have elbow room to put my notebook in my pocket, all demanding to know if the contestants had received a list of the answers, and if so, when and how and from whom?

I regarded them as friends. It is always best to regard journalists as friends if they are not actually standing on your nose. "Hold everything," I said. "What kind of a position is a man in when he is being tugged in two directions?"

Charles Winston of the *Times* said, "Anomalous."

"Thanks. That's the word I wanted. I would love to get my name in the paper, and my employer's name, Nero Wolfe, spelled with an e on the end, and this is a swell chance, but I'll have to pass it up. As you all saw at once, if the contestants have been sent a list of the answers by somebody it would be a hot item in a murder case, and it would be improper for me to tell you about it. That's the function of the police and the District Attorney."

"Oh, come off it, Archie," Missy Coburn said.

"Spit out the gum," Bill Lurick said.

"Is it your contention," Charles Winston of the *Times* asked courteously but firmly, "that a private citizen should refuse to furnish the press with any information regarding a murder case and that the sole source of such information for the public should be the duly constituted authorities?"

I didn't want to get the *Times* sore. "Listen, folks," I said, "there is a story to be had, but you're not going to get it from me, for reasons which I reserve for the present, so don't waste time and breath on me. Try Inspector Cramer or the DA's office. You heard Miss Frazee mention Rudolph Hansen, the lawyer. I've told you there's a story, so that's settled, but you'll have to take it from there. Cigarettes on my bare toes will get you no more from me."

They hung on some, but pretty soon one of them broke away and headed down the hall, and of course the others didn't want him to gobble it so they made after him. I stayed in the doorway until the last of them had disappeared around the corner, then, leaving the door open, turned and went on in. Gertrude Frazee, in the same museum outfit she had worn five days previously, minus the hat, was in an upholstered armchair backed up against the wall, with a cold eye on me.

She spoke. "I have nothing to say to you. You can go. Please shut the door."

I had forgotten that her lips moving at right angles to their slant, and her jaw moving straight up and down, made an anomalous situation, and I had to jerk my attention to her words. "You must admit one thing, Miss Frazee," I said earnestly. "I didn't try to spoil your press conference, did I? I kept out of it, and when they came at me what did I do? I refused to tell them a single thing, because I thought it wouldn't be fair to you. It was your conference and I had no right to horn in."

She didn't thaw any. "What do you want?"

"Nothing now, I guess. I was going to explain why I thought you might want to come to the meeting this evening at Mr. Wolfe's office, but now I suppose you wouldn't be interested."

"Why not?"

"Because you've already got your lick in. Not only that, you've spilled the beans. Outsiders weren't supposed to know about the meeting, especially not the press, but now those reporters will be after everybody, and they're sure to find out, and they'll be camping on Mr. Wolfe's stoop. I wouldn't be surprised if they even got invited in. The others will know they've heard your side of the story, and naturally they'll want to get theirs in too. So if you were there it might get into a wrangle in front of the reporters, and you wouldn't want that. Anyhow, as I say, you've already got your lick in."

With her unique facial design nothing could be certain, but I was pretty sure I had her, so I finished, "So I guess you wouldn't be interested and I've made the trip for nothing. Sorry to bother you. If you care at all to know what happens at the meeting see the morning papers, especially the *Times.*" I was turning to go.

Her voice halted me. "Young man."

I faced her.

"What time is this meeting?"

"Nine o'clock."

"I'll be there."

"Sure, Miss Frazee, if you want to, but under the circumstances I doubt—"

"I'll be there."

I grinned at her. "I promised my grandmother I'd never argue with a lady. See you later then."

Leaving, I took the door along, pulling it shut gently until the lock clicked.

By the time I got home it was after six and Wolfe should have been down from the plant rooms, but he wasn't. I went to the kitchen, where Fritz was arranging two plump ducklings on the rack of a roasting pan, asked what was up, and was told that Wolfe had descended from the roof but had left the elevator one flight up and gone to his room. That was unusual but not alarming, and I proceeded with another step of the preparations for the meeting. When I got through the table at the end of the couch in the office was ready for business: eight brands of whisky, two of gin, two of cognac, a decanter of port, cream sherry, armagnac, four fruit brandies, and a wide assortment of cordials and liqueurs. The dry sherry was in the refrigerator, as were the cherries, olives, onions, and lemon peel, where they would remain until after dinner. As I was arranging the bottles I caught myself wondering which one the murderer would fancy, but corrected it hastily to wallet thief, since we weren't interested in the murder.

At six-thirty I thought I'd better find out if Wolfe had busted a shoestring or what, and, mounting a flight and tapping on his door and hearing him grunt, entered. I stopped and stared. Fully dressed, with his shoes on, he was lying on the bed, on top of the black silk coverlet. Absolutely unheard of.

"What have you got?" I demanded.

"Nothing," he growled.

"Shall I get Doc Vollmer?"

"No."

I approached for a close-up. He looked sour, but he had never died of that. "Miss Frazee is coming," I told him. "She was holding a press conference. Do you want to hear about it?"

"No."

"Excuse me for disturbing you," I said icily, and turned to go, but in three steps he called my name and I halted. He raised himself to his elbows, swung his legs over the edge, got upright, and took a deep breath.

"I've made a bad mistake," he said.

I waited.

He took another breath. "What time is it?"

I told him twenty-five to seven.

"Two hours and a half and dinner to eat. I was confident that this development would of itself supply me with ample material for an effective stratagem, and I was wrong. I don't say I was an ass. I relied overmuch on my ingenuity and resourcefulness, though on the solid basis of experience. But I did make a mistake. Various people have been trying to see me all afternoon, and I have declined to see them. I thought I could devise a stroke without any hint or stimulant from them, but I haven't. I should have seen them. Oh, I can proceed; I am not without expedients; I may even bring something off; but I blundered. Just now you asked me if I wanted to hear about Miss Frazee, and I said no. That was fatuous. Tell me."

"Yes, sir. As I said, she was holding a press conference. When I got there—"

The sound of the doorbell came up and in to us. I lifted my brows at Wolfe. He snapped at me, "Go! Anybody!"

17

It was Vernon Assa.

He wasn't as much of a misfit for the red leather chair as Mrs. Wheelock, at least he was plump, and his deep tan went well with the red, but he was much too short. I have surveyed a lot of people in that chair, and there has only been one who was exactly right for it. I must tell about him some time.

You might have thought, after what had just been said upstairs, that Wolfe would have been spreading butter on the caller, but he wasn't. When he came down, after brushing his hair and tucking his shirt in, he crossed to his chair, sat, and said brusquely, "I can spare a few minutes, Mr. Assa. What can I do for you?"

Assa looked at me. I thought he was going to start the old routine about seeing Wolfe privately, but apparently he only wanted something attractive to look at while he got his words collected. I remembered that at the first visit of the LBA bunch he had been the impatient one, snapping at Hansen to get on and telling Wolfe he was wasting time, but now he seemed to feel that deliberation was better.

He looked at Wolfe. "About the meeting this evening. You'll have to call it off."

"Indeed." Wolfe cocked his head. "Under what compulsion?"

"Well . . . it's obvious. Isn't it?"

"Not to me. I'm afraid you'll have to elaborate."

Assa shifted in the chair. I had noticed that he seemed to be having trouble getting comfortably adjusted. "You realize," he said, "that our main problem is solved, thanks to you. The problem that brought us to you last Wednesday in a state of panic. There was no chance of finishing the contest without confusion and some discord after what happened to Dahlmann, and the wallet gone, but as it looked when we came to you we were headed for complete disaster, and you have prevented it. Hansen is certain that legally we are in the clear. With the contestants receiving the answers as they have, and it won't do Miss Frazee any good to deny she got them, if we repudiate those verses and replace them with others, as of course we will, our position would be upheld by any court in the land. There is still serious embarrassment, but that couldn't be helped. You have rescued the contest from utter ruin by a brilliant stroke and are to be congratulated."

"Mr. Assa." Wolfe's eyes, on him, were half closed. "Are you speaking for my client, the firm of Lippert, Buff and Assa, or for yourself?"

"Well . . . I am a member of the firm, as you know, but I came here on my own initiative and responsibility."

"Do your associates know you're here and what for?"

"No. I didn't want to start a long and complicated discussion. I decided to come only half an hour ago. Your meeting starts at nine, and it's nearly seven now."

"I see. And you are assuming that I sent the answers to the contestants—or had them sent."

Assa passed his tongue over his lips. "I didn't put it baldly like that, but I suppose it doesn't matter. Goodwin is in your confi-

dence anyway. It was impossible to figure why one of the contestants would have sent them, if he had killed Dahlmann and got
them from the wallet, and that leaves only you."

"Not impossible," Wolfe objected. "Not if he found to his dis-
may that in the situation he had created they were worse than useless to him."

Assa nodded. "I considered that, of course, but still thought
it impossible. Another reason I didn't mention my coming to my
associates was that I realize you can't acknowledge what you did
to save us. I don't expect you to acknowledge it even to me, and
you certainly wouldn't if one or two of them had come along,
especially Hansen. We wouldn't want you to acknowledge it anyhow, because we've hired you, and the legal position would probably be that we did it ourselves, and that would be disastrous. So
you see why I didn't put it baldly."

"Thank you for your forbearance," Wolfe said drily. "But why
must the meeting be called off?"

"Because it can't do any good and may do harm. What good
can it do?"

Wolfe's eyes were still half closed. "It can help me to earn a
fee. I accepted Mr. Hansen's definition of my job: 'to find out who
took the wallet and got the paper.' It remains to be performed."

"It doesn't have to be performed, not now, since the contest
problem is solved. You've earned your fee and you'll get it."

"You've admitted, Mr. Assa, that you're speaking only for
yourself."

The red tip of his tongue showed again, flicking his lips. "I'll
guarantee the fee," he said.

Wolfe shook his head. "I'm afraid that's not acceptable. My
responsibility is to my client, and his reciprocal responsibility, to
pay me, is not transferable. As for canceling the meeting, that's out
of the question. If such a request came unanimously from Messrs.
Buff, O'Garro, Hansen, Heery—and you, and cogent reasons were
given, I might consider it, but would probably refuse. As it is, I
won't even consider it."

Assa looked at me. He glanced at the refreshment table, came
back to me, and said, "There's a bottle of Pernod there. That's my
drink. Could I have some?"

I said certainly and asked if he wanted ice, and he said no. I took him the Pernod and an Old-Fashioned glass, and he poured two fingers as plump as his own, and darned if he didn't toss it off as if it were a jigger of bourbon. I'm not a Pernod drinker, but there is such a thing as common sense. Not only that, he poured again, this time only one finger, and then, without taking a sip, put the glass down on the little table at his elbow, beside the bottle.

He swallowed a couple of times for a chaser. "That's a high-handed attitude, Mr. Wolfe," he said. He paused to collect more words. "Frankly, I don't see what you expect to accomplish. You'll get your fee, and from our standpoint, as far as the contest is concerned, it no longer matters who got the wallet. Of course it may still be a factor in the murder, but you weren't hired to investigate the murder. That's up to the police. Why do you insist on this meeting?"

"To finish my job. What I engaged to do."

"But you're more apt to undo what you've already done. The police know now—they were told on your advice—that you have had a copy of the answers in your possession since last Wednesday. How far the discretion of the police can be trusted I don't know, but it's conceivable that one or more of the contestants have learned about it, and if so, God only knows what would happen at the meeting. You might even find yourself backed into a corner where you had to admit you had mailed the answers to them, and LBA would be responsible, and we'd be in a deeper hole than ever."

"You would indeed," Wolfe conceded. "But if that's your fear, dismiss it. There will be no such admission by me."

"What will there be?"

"I couldn't tell you if I would. I have formed certain conjectures and I intend to explore them. That's what the meeting is for, and I shall not abandon it."

Assa regarded him in silence, steadily, for a full half a minute. At length he broke it. "When your man Goodwin came to our office on Friday and got the word for you to go ahead, he wanted it unanimous. He polled us, and I voted yes with the others. Now I don't, so it's no longer unanimous. I ask you to suspend operations until I have conferred with my associates—say until tomorrow noon. I not only ask you, I direct you."

Wolfe was shaking his head. "I'm afraid I can't oblige you, Mr. Assa. Time's important now, now that the spark has been struck and the fire started. It's too late."

"Too late for what?"

"To stop."

Assa's eyes dropped. He gazed at his right palm, saw nothing there to encourage him, tried the left, and there was nothing there either. "Very well," he said, and arose, in no haste, and started for the door. Considering the turn things had taken, I wouldn't have been astonished if Wolfe had told me to fasten onto him and lock him in the front room until nine o'clock, but he didn't, so I got up and followed the guest into the hall. I didn't resent his not thanking me for holding his topcoat and opening the door, since he was obviously preoccupied.

Back in the office, I stood and looked down at Wolfe. "I suppose," I observed, "it doesn't matter who struck the spark as long as it caught."

"Yes. Get Mr. Cramer."

I sat at my desk and dialed. It was a bad time of day to get Cramer ordinarily, but when something big was stirring, or refusing to stir, he sometimes ate at his desk instead of going home for what he called supper. That was one of the times. From the way he growled at me, it was very much one of the times.

Wolfe took it. "Mr. Cramer? I thought you might be interested in a meeting at my office this evening. We're going to discuss the Dahlmann case. It will—"

"Who's going to discuss it?"

"Everyone concerned—that is, everyone I know about. It will of course be confined to the theft of the wallet, since that's what I'm investigating, but it will inevitably touch upon points that affect you, so I'm inviting you to come—as an observer."

Silence. Cramer could have been chewing a bite of a corned beef sandwich, or he could have been chewing what he had heard.

"What have you got?" he demanded.

"For myself, a reasonable expectation. For you, the possibility of a suitable disclosure. Have I ever wasted your time on frivolity?"

"No. Not on frivolity. There's no use asking you on the phone. . . . Stebbins will be there in ten minutes."

"No, sir. Nor you. I need a little time to arrange the inside of

my head, and my dinner will be ready shortly. The meeting will
be at nine o'clock."

"I'll bring Stebbins with me."

"By all means. Do so."

We hung up.

"You know darned well," I said, "that Purley will bring handcuffs, and he hates to take them back empty—"

I stopped because he was leaning back and closing his eyes,
and his lips were starting to move, pushing out and then in, out
and in. . . . He was working at last. I went across the hall for
two more chairs.

18

If a successful party is one where everybody comes, there was no
question about that one. In fact, some came too early. Gertrude
Frazee showed up at eight-thirty-five, when Wolfe and I were still
in the dining room, and I was having coffee in the office with her
when Philip Younger arrived, and a minute later Talbott Heery.
Patrick O'Garro and Oliver Buff came together, and almost on
their heels Professor Harold Rollins. When Inspector Cramer and
Sergeant Stebbins got there it was still ten minutes short of nine.
They wanted to see Wolfe immediately, of course, and I took them
to the dining room and shut them in there with him. Back at the
front door, I opened it for Vernon Assa, who was still in no frame
of mind to thank anybody for anything, and then for Susan Tescher,
of *Clock* magazine. I had been sort of hoping to see Mr. Tite himself, but all she had along was Mr. Hibbard, the tall and skinny
one. It was nine on the dot when Mrs. Wheelock appeared, and
not more than thirty seconds later here came Rudolph Hansen.
Not only did everybody come, they all beat the bell except Hansen,
and he just shaved it.

I went to glance in at the office door and saw that Fritz had
things under control at the refreshment table. Evidently they had
all been thirsty, or else they didn't want to talk and were drinking

instead. Pleased that the party was starting well, I crossed to the dining room to tell Wolfe we had a full house and were set for his entrance, but, entering, I shut the door and stood. Cramer, sitting with his big rough fist tapping the table, was reading Wolfe the riot act, with Purley standing behind his shoulder looking satisfied. I approached. What seemed to be biting Cramer was that he did not intend to let Wolfe call a meeting of murder suspects and expect him, Cramer, to sit and take it in like a goddam stenographer (Cramer's words, not mine; I have known at least three stenographers who were absolutely—anyway, I have known stenographers).

I had heard Cramer lose that argument with Wolfe some twenty times. What he wanted was the moon. He wanted, first, to know in advance exactly what Wolfe was going to say, which was ridiculous because most of the time Wolfe didn't know himself. Second, he wanted it understood that he would be free to take over at any point, bound by no commitment, whereas Wolfe demanded a pledge that the proceedings would be left to him short of extreme provocation, such as gunplay or hair pulling. Since it was a cinch that Cramer wouldn't have been there at all if he hadn't thought Wolfe had something he badly needed, he might as well have given up on that one for good, but he never did. All he accomplished that Monday evening was holding up the start of the meeting by a quarter of an hour. I cut in on the squabble to announce that the audience was ready and waiting, and then went to the office.

A few details needed attention. Miss Frazee had copped the red leather chair, which was reserved for Inspector Cramer, and I had to talk her into moving. Buff and Hansen were in a huddle at the wall end of the couch, where Wolfe would have to look through me to see them, and I got them to transfer to chairs, Buff stopping on the way for a refill of his highball glass. Hibbard was seated beside Miss Tescher in the front row, and when I asked him to move to the rear I thought he was going to speak at last, but he controlled it and went without a word. Vernon Assa bothered me. He was standing backed up against the far wall, staring straight ahead, an Old-Fashioned glass in his hand, presumably holding Pernod. When I went to him he turned his eyes on me and I didn't like them. He could have been high, too high, but when I suggested that he come and take a chair he said in a perfectly good voice that he was all right where he was. As I turned to leave him Wolfe and Cramer and Stebbins entered.

Wolfe walked across to his desk. Cramer stood a moment taking in the crowd and then went to the red leather chair and sat. I had put a chair for Purley against the wall, so he would be facing the audience, and he didn't need to be told it was his. The talking had stopped, and all eyes went to Wolfe as he rested his clasped hands on the desk and moved his head from left to right and back again.

He took a breath. "Ladies and gentlemen. I must first explain the presence of Inspector Cramer of the New York Police Department. He is here by invitation, not to—"

Two sounds came almost simultaneously from the rear of the room—first from a throat, part gurgle and part scream, and then a bang as something hit the floor. Everybody jerked around by reflex, so we all saw Vernon Assa stagger toward us with the fingers of both hands clutching at his mouth, and then he went down. By the time he touched the floor I was there, but Purley Stebbins was right behind me, and Cramer behind him, so I dived back to my desk for the phone and dialed Doc Vollmer's number. At the second buzz he answered and I told him to come on the jump. As I hung up Cramer called to me to get a doctor and I told him I had one. He stood up, saw Susan Tescher and Hibbard crossing the sill into the hall, and sang out, "Get back in here!" He came to me. "I'll call downtown. Put 'em all in the dining room and stay there with 'em. Understand? No gags." He was at the phone.

I looked around. They were behaving pretty well, except Susan Tescher and her silent partner, who had apparently had the notion of fading. There had been no shrieks. Wolfe was sitting straight, his lips pressed tight, his eyes narrowed to slits. He didn't meet my glance. O'Garro and Heery and Hansen had gone to the prostrate Assa, but Purley, kneeling there, had ordered them back. I went to the doorway to the hall and turned.

"Everybody this way," I said. No one moved. "I'd rather not yell," I said, "because the inspector's phoning. He wants you out of this room, and four of the men will please bring chairs."

That helped, giving them something to do. Philip Younger picked up a chair and came, and the others after him. I opened the door to the dining room, and they filed across and in. Fritz was at my elbow, and I told him there would be lots of company and he might as well leave the bolt off. The doorbell rang, and he went and admitted Doc Vollmer, and I waved Doc to the office.

Leaving the door from the dining room to the hall wide open and standing just inside, I surveyed my herd. Mrs. Wheelock had flopped onto a chair, and so had Philip Younger. I hoped Younger wasn't having a paroxysm. Most of the others were standing, and I told them they might as well sit down.

The only one who put up a squawk was Rudolph Hansen. He confronted me. "Vernon Assa is my client and my friend, and I have a right to see that he gets proper—"

"He's already got. A doctor's here, and a good one." I raised my voice. "Just take it easy, everybody, and it would be better if you'd shut up."

"What happened to him?" Gertrude Frazee demanded.

"I don't know. But if you want something to occupy your minds, just before Mr. Wolfe entered he was standing by the wall with a glass in his hand and there was liquid in the glass. You heard the glass hit the floor, but I saw no sign of spilled liquid. You might turn that over and see what you think of it."

"It was Pernod in the glass," Patrick O'Garro said. "I saw him pour it. He always drank Pernod. He put the glass down on the table when Hansen called to him, and went—"

"Hold it, Pat," Hansen snapped at him. "This may be—I hope not—but this may be a very grave matter."

"You see," I told the herd. "I advised you to shut up, and Mr. Hansen, who is a lawyer, agrees with me."

"I want to telephone," Heery said.

"The phone's busy. Anyway, I'm just a temporary watchdog. I'll be getting a relief, and you can—"

I broke it off to stretch my neck for a look at the newcomers Fritz was admitting—two city employees in uniform. They came down the hall and headed for me, but I pointed across to the office and they right-angled. From there on it was a parade. A minute later two more in uniform came, and then three in their own clothes, two of whom I knew, and before long one with a little black bag. My herd had more or less settled down, and I had decided I didn't need to catch Doc Vollmer on his way out for a look at Younger. Two more arrived, and when I saw one of them was Lieutenant Rowcliff a little flutter ran over my biceps. He affects me that way. He and his pal went to the office, but pretty soon appeared again, heading for the dining room, and I sidestepped to keep from being trampled.

They entered, and the pal closed the door, and Rowcliff faced the herd. "You will remain here under surveillance until otherwise notified. Vernon Assa is dead. I am Lieutenant George Rowcliff, and for the present you are in my custody as material witnesses."

That was like him. In fact, it was him. What the hell did they care whether he was George Rowcliff or Cuthbert Rowcliff? Also he had said it wrong. If they were in his custody they were under arrest, and in that case they could demand to be allowed to communicate with their lawyers before answering any questions as a matter of ordinary prudence, which would stop the wheels of justice for hours. I was surprised that neither Hansen nor Hibbard picked it up, but they could have thought it would sound like soliciting business and didn't want to be unethical. Lawyers are very delicate.

I was in an anomalous position again. I wanted to open the door to leave, (a) to see if Wolfe wanted me, (b) to watch the scientists at work, and (c) to get a rise out of Rowcliff in case he had the notion that I was in his custody too, but on the other hand it seemed likely that a specimen who had had the nerve to commit a murder in Wolfe's office, right under his nose, was there in the dining room, and I didn't like to leave him with only a baboon like Rowcliff to keep an eye on him. I was propped against the wall, considering it, when the door opened and Inspector Cramer walked in. Short of the table he stopped and sent his eyes around.

"Mr. Buff," he said. "Buff and O'Garro and Hansen—and I guess Heery. You four men come here please." They moved. "Stand there in front of me. I'm going to show you something and ask if you can identify it. Look at it as close as you want to, but don't touch it. You understand? Don't touch it."

They said they understood, and he lifted a hand. The thumb and forefinger were pinching the corner of a brown leather wallet. The quartet gazed at it. O'Garro's hand started toward it and he jerked it back. No one spoke.

"The initials 'LD' are stamped on the inside," Cramer said, "and it contained items with Louis Dahlmann's name on them, but I'm asking if you can identify it as the wallet Dahlmann was carrying at that meeting last Tuesday evening."

"Of course not," Hansen said curtly. "Positively identify it? Certainly not."

A voice came from behind him: "It looks like it." Gertrude Frazee had stepped up to help. Rowcliff got her elbow to ease her back, but she made it stronger. "It looks exactly like it!"

"Okay," Cramer said, "I'm not asking you to swear to it, but you can tell me this, is it enough like the wallet he had at that meeting that you can't see any difference? I ask you that, Mr. Hansen."

"I can't answer. I wasn't at the meeting. Neither was Mr. Buff."

"Oh." Cramer wasn't fazed. Even an inspector can't remember everything. "You, Mr. O'Garro? You heard the question."

"Yes," O'Garro said.

"Mr. Heery?"

"It looks like it. Assa had it?"

Cramer nodded. "In his breast pocket."

"I knew it!" Miss Frazee cried. "A trick! A cheat! I knew all the time—"

Rowcliff gripped her arm, and she whirled and used the other one to smack him in the face, and I made a note to send a contribution to the Women's Nature League. Others started to ask Cramer things, or tell him, but he showed them a palm. "You'll all get a chance to talk before you leave here. Plenty. Stay here until you're sent for."

"Are we under arrest?" Harold Rollins asked, as superior as ever.

"No. You're being detained by police authority at the scene of a violent death in your presence. Anyone who prefers to be arrested will be accommodated." He turned, looked around for me, found me, said, "Come with me, Goodwin," and made for the door.

19

I supposed he was taking me to the office, but no, he told me to wait in the hall, and anyway there wasn't room for me in the office. A mob of experts was expertizing in every direction, and Fritz was seated in Wolfe's chair behind his desk, watching them. Wolfe was nowhere in sight. From the door I saw Cramer go to one sitting at my desk and deliver the wallet by depositing it gently in a little box. Then he passed a few orders around, came to me and said, "Wolfe's up in his room," and headed up the stairs. I followed.

Wolfe's door was closed, but Cramer opened it without bothering to knock, and walked in. That was bad manners. He was unquestionably in command of the office, since a man had just died there violently with him present, but not the rest of the house. However, it wasn't the best possible moment to read him the Bill of Rights, so I followed him in and shut the door.

At least Wolfe hadn't gone to bed. He was in the big chair under the reading lamp with a book. Lifting his eyes to us, he put the book on the table, and as I moved a chair up for Cramer I caught its title: *Montaigne's Essays.* It was one of a few dozen he kept on the shelves there in his room, so he hadn't removed anything from the office, which might have been interfering with justice.

"Was he dead when you left?" Cramer asked.

Wolfe nodded. "Yes, sir. I stayed for that."

"He's still dead." Cramer is not a wag; he was just stating a fact. He pushed his chair back an inch, wrinkling the carpet. "It was cyanide. To be verified, but it was. We found a crumpled paper on the floor under the end of the couch. Toilet paper. Not the kind in your bathroom."

"Thank you," Wolfe said drily.

"Yeah, I know. You didn't do it. You were with me. Goodwin wasn't, not all the time, but I'm willing to be realistic. There was white powder left on the paper, and when we put a drop of water on a spot it had the cyanide smell. The glass seemed to have it too, but there was the smell of the drink." He looked up at me. "Sit down, Goodwin. Do you know what the drink was?"

"No," I replied, "but O'Garro said it was Pernod. He said he saw him pour it and put it down on the table when Hansen called to him. And when—"

"Damn you," Cramer exploded, "you had the nerve to start in on them? You know damn well—"

"Nuts," I said distinctly. "I asked no questions. He volunteered it. And when Assa was here this evening just before dinner he drank Pernod—or rather, he gulped it, and said it was his drink."

"He was here? Before dinner?"

"Right. Unless Mr. Wolfe says he wasn't."

"What did he want?"

"Ask Mr. Wolfe."

"No," Wolfe said emphatically. "My brain is fuddled. Tell Mr. Cramer what Mr. Assa said and what I said. All of it."

I got a chair and sat, and shut my eyes for a moment to get my brain arranged. I had had a long and strict training, but the past hour had shoved other details to the rear, and I had to adjust. I did so, opened my eyes, and reported. When I had got to the end, with Assa saying, "Very well," and departing, I added, "That's it. If we had a tape of it I'd welcome a comparison. Any questions?"

No reply. Cramer had stuck a cigar in his mouth and was chewing on it. "Go down to the office," he said, "and get your typewriter and some paper. Tell Stebbins I said so, and take it somewhere and type that. All of it."

"That can wait," Wolfe said gruffly, "until we're through here. I want him here."

Cramer didn't press it. He took the cigar from his mouth and said, "And then you phoned me."

"Yes. As soon as Mr. Assa was out of the house."

"Too bad you didn't tell me what had happened. Assa would still be alive."

"Perhaps."

Cramer goggled. "By God, you admit it?"

"I'll admit anything you please. I have had cause for chagrin before now, Mr. Cramer, but nothing to compare with this. I didn't know that mortification could cut so deeply. One more stab and it would have got the bone. If Mr. Assa had had the wallet in his possession, actually on his person—then it would have been consummate. That would have finished me."

"He did."

"He did what?"

"He had the wallet. In his breast pocket. It has been identified as the one Dahlmann was carrying—sufficiently identified. There was no paper in it containing the answers."

Wolfe swallowed. He swallowed again. "I am humiliated beyond expression, Mr. Cramer. Go and get the murderer. But lock me in here; I would only botch it for you. The rest of the house is yours."

Cramer and I regarded him, not with pity. We both knew him too well. Naturally he was bitter, since he had got the stage all set for one of his major performances, with him as the star, and had actually started his act, only to have a prominent member of the cast, presumably the villain, up and die on him, there before his eyes. It was certainly upsetting, but neither Cramer nor I was sap enough to believe that he was humiliated beyond expression—or anything else beyond expression.

Cramer didn't go to pat his shoulder. He merely asked, "What if he wasn't murdered? What if he dosed his drink himself?"

"Pfui," Wolfe said, and I lifted a hand to hide a grin. He went on, "If he did, he had the paper of cyanide in his pocket when he left wherever he was to come here. With a choice of places for ending his life, I refuse to believe he selected the audience he knew he would have in my office—and with that wallet in his pocket."

"Something might have happened after he got here."

"I don't believe it. He had had ample opportunity to talk with his associates beforehand."

"He might have wanted to throw suspicion on someone."

"Then for an intelligent man he was remarkably clumsy about it. Unless you have details unknown to me?"

"No. I think he was murdered." Cramer dumped that by turning his hand over. "If I understand you, after he came and tried to get you to call off the meeting you assumed he had killed Dahlmann and taken the wallet, and you intended to screw it out of him tonight. Was that it?"

"No, sir. You forget that I was not interested in the murder. I assumed, of course, that points relevant to the murder would be broached, and that was why I invited you to come. I also assumed that Assa had taken the wallet, because—"

"Sure you did," Cramer blurted. "Naturally. Because he was certain you had sent the answers to the contestants, so he knew nobody else could have sent them, and the only way he could have known that was obvious."

"Nothing of the sort." Wolfe didn't sound humiliated, but I'm not saying he hadn't been. It was just that he had a good repair department. "On the contrary. Because he was eager to give me the credit for sending the answers, though he knew I hadn't. If he hadn't known who had sent them he wouldn't have risked such a move, so he had sent them himself, getting them from the paper in Dahlmann's wallet. I rejected the remote possibility that he had got them from the originals in the safe deposit vault, since he wouldn't have dared go there alone and ask for that box. The brilliant stroke that saved the contest, for which he heaped praise on me, was his own. Therefore he had either taken the wallet himself or he knew who had, and the former was the more probable, since he said he had come to me on his own initiative and responsibility without consulting his associates. And of course he wanted the meeting canceled."

"Why not?" Cramer demanded. "Why didn't you cancel it?"

"Because I had a double obligation, and not to him. One was my obligation to my client, the firm of Lippert, Buff and Assa, to do the job I had been hired for, and the other was my obligation to myself, not to be hoodwinked." He stopped short, tightened his lips, and half closed his eyes. "Not to be hoodwinked," he said bitterly, "and look at me."

He opened his eyes. "Hoodwinked, however, not by a Mr. Assa trying to save a perfume contest, but by a man who had already murdered once and was ready to murder again. I was assuming that Assa had taken Dahlmann's wallet, but not that he had killed him; and anyway, that was your affair. Now it's quite different. To assume that Assa was killed merely because someone knew he had taken the wallet and sent the answers to the contestants would be infantile. To assume that Assa knew that Hansen or Buff or O'Garro or Heery had taken the wallet and sent the answers, and that one of them killed him to forestall disclosure, would be witless. The only tolerable assumption is that Assa knew, or had reason to believe, that one of them had killed Dahlmann. That would be worth killing for, but by heaven, not in my office!"

"Yeah, that was cheeky." Cramer took the cigar from his mouth, what was left of it. "Why just those four? What about the contestants?"

"Nonsense. Not worth considering. Send them home. Can you possibly think them worth discussing?"

"No," Cramer conceded, "but I'm not sending them home. They were there when the poison was put in the drink. They're being questioned now, separately. I thought you wouldn't mind if we used the rooms on that floor and the basement."

"I am in no position to mind anything whatever." It *had* cut deep. "I respect your routine, Mr. Cramer, question them by all means, but I doubt if he was inept enough to let himself be observed. Also you may get more than you want. Miss Frazee may well declare that she saw each of them in turn, including the other contestants, putting something into his drink. I advise you not to let her know that the paper was found. —By the way. You told me last Wednesday that none of those five men—you were including Assa—could prove he hadn't gone to Dahlmann's place the night he was killed. Does that still hold?"

"Yes. Why?"

"I wanted to know."

"What for? You looking for a murderer now? By God, I *could* lock you in!"

"I still have my job, to find out who took the wallet. Those who may suppose I'll now be satisfied that Mr. Assa took it will be wrong." All of a sudden, with no warning, Wolfe blew. He opened his mouth and roared, "Confound it, can a man kill with impunity in my office, with my liquor in my glass?"

"A goddam shame," Cramer said. "But you stick to your job and let mine alone. I'd hate to see you humiliated again. I wouldn't mind humiliating you myself some day, but not by a stranger and a murderer. Anyway, if it's down to those four, two of them are your clients."

"No. My client is a business firm."

"Okay, but keep off. I don't like the look on your face, but I seldom do. Other things I don't like. You seem positive the contestants are out of it."

"I am."

"Why? What do you know that you haven't told me?"

"Nothing of any substance."

"Do you know of any motive any of those four men had for killing Dahlmann?"

"No. Only that apparently they all envied him. Do you know of any?"

"None that has looked good enough. Now we'll look closer.

Have you any information at all that points in any way to one of them?"

"No one more than another."

"If you get any I want it. You keep off. Another thing I don't like, this client stuff. I have known you—come in!"

Bad manners again. It wasn't his door that was knocked on. It opened and a dick stepped in.

"Inspector, the lieutenant wants you. He's in the kitchen with one of the women."

Cramer said he'd be right down, and arose. The dick left. Cramer addressed me. "Get your machine and type that talk with Assa. Bring it up and do it here so you can keep an eye on your boss. We don't want him humiliated again." He walked out.

I faced Wolfe and he faced me. I wouldn't have liked his look either if his expression of cold fury had been meant for me. "Any instructions?" I asked.

"Not at present. I may call on you any time during the night. I won't try to sleep. With a murderer roaming my house, and me empty-handed and empty-headed . . ."

"He's not roaming. You ought to squeeze in a nap, with your door locked of course. I'll stick around until the company leaves— and incidentally, what about refreshments? With the gate-crashers there won't be enough marinated mushrooms and almond balls. Sandwiches and coffee?"

"Yes." He shut his eyes. "Archie. Let me alone."

"Glad to."

I left him and went downstairs. Opening the door to the kitchen to tell Fritz sandwiches and coffee, I saw only Cramer and Rowcliff and Susan Tescher and Hibbard, and backed out. Three guests in uniform were in the hall, one in charge of the front door. The doors to the dining room and front room were closed. The one to the office was also closed, and I opened it and entered. The corpse was gone. Half a dozen scientists were still researching, and Purley Stebbins and a dick from the DA's office had Patrick O'Garro between them over by the refreshment table. That could last all night, bringing each one in separately to tell who was where and when. Fritz was still perched behind Wolfe's desk and I went to him.

"Nice party."

"It's nothing to joke about, Archie. *Cochon!*"

"I never joke. I'm relieving you. Evidently nothing in this room is available, including the refreshments, so I guess you'll have to produce sandwiches and coffee. You'll find characters in the kitchen, but ignore them. If they complain tell them you're under orders. Don't bother taking anything up to Mr. Wolfe. He's chewing nails and doesn't want to be disturbed."

Fritz said he should have some beer, and I said okay if he wanted to risk it, and he departed. As for me, I was relieving Fritz on guard duty, and furthermore, the day had not come for me to tell Purley that Cramer had ordered me to remove my typewriter to another room and would he kindly permit me to do so; and I didn't want to lug it up two flights anyway; and it would be interesting and instructive to watch trained detectives solving a crime.

Speaking of trained detectives, I was supposed to be one, but I certainly wasn't bragging. I went to my desk and took my gun from the holster and put it in the drawer, and locked the drawer. In this report I could have omitted any mention of it, but I didn't want to fudge, and I preferred not to skip the way I felt when, after going around armed for several days, I thoughtfully set it up for a homicide right there in the office—and a lot of good my gun did. To hell with it. It would have made it perfect if, soon after ditching it, I had really needed it, but I didn't get even that satisfaction.

I got paper and carbon from another drawer, rolled the typewriter stand around to the rear of Wolfe's desk, sat in Wolfe's chair, and started tapping.

20

I would appreciate it if they would call a halt on all their devoted efforts to find a way to abolish war or eliminate disease or run trains with atoms or extend the span of human life to a couple of centuries, and everybody concentrate for a while on how to wake me up in the morning without my resenting it. It may be that a bevy of beautiful maidens in pure silk yellow very sheer gowns, barefooted, singing *Oh, What a Beautiful Morning* and scattering rose petals over me would do the trick, but I'd have to try it.

That Tuesday morning it was terrible. I had been in bed only three hours, and what woke me was the phone, about the worst way of all. I rolled over, opened my eyes to see the alarm clock at seven-twenty-five, reached, and yanked the damn thing off the cradle.

"Yeah?"

"Good morning, Archie. Can you be down in thirty minutes? I'm breakfasting with Saul, Fred, Orrie, and Bill."

That woke me all right, though it had no effect on the resentment. I told Wolfe I'd try, rolled out, and headed for the bathroom. Usually I yawn around for a couple of minutes before digging in, but there wasn't time. As I shaved I wished I had asked him what kind of a program it was, so I would know what to dress for, but if it had been anything special he would have said so, and I just grabbed the shirt on top.

When I made it to the ground floor, in thirty minutes flat, they were in the dining room with coffee. As I greeted them Fritz came with my orange juice, and I sat and took a healthy swallow.

"This is a hell of a time," I said, still resenting, "to spring a surprise party on me."

Bill Gore laughed. I said something funny to him once back in 1948, and ever since he has had a policy of laughing whenever I open my trap. Bill is not too smart to live, but he's tough and hangs on. Orrie Cather is smarter and is not ashamed of it, and since he got rid of the idea that it would be a good plan for him to take over my job, some years ago, he has helped Wolfe with some very neat errands when called upon. Fred Durkin is just Fred Durkin and knows it. He thinks Wolfe could prove who killed Cock Robin any time he felt like spending half an hour on it. He thinks Wolfe could prove anything whatever. You've met Saul Panzer, the one and only.

As I finished my orange juice and started on griddle cakes, Wolfe expounded. He said the surprise was incidental; he had phoned them after I had gone to bed, when he had conceived a procedure.

"Fine," I approved, spreading butter to melt, "we've got a procedure. For these gentlemen?"

"For all of us," he said. "I have described the situation to them, as much as they'll need. It is a procedure of desperation, with perhaps one chance in twenty of success. After hours on it, most of the night, this was the best I could do. As you know, I was assuming that one of four men—Hansen, Buff, O'Garro, Heery—had killed Dahlmann and taken the wallet, and that because Assa had learned of it or suspected it he had been killed too."

"I know that's what you told Cramer."

"It's also what I told myself."

"Why would one of them kill Dahlmann?"

"I don't know, but if he did he had a reason. That remains, along with his identity. To search into motives would take long and toilsome investigation, and even then motive alone is nothing. I preferred to focus on identity. Which of the four? I went over and over every word they have uttered, to you and to me; all their tones and glances and postures. There was no hint—at least, not for me. I considered all possible lines of inquiry, and found that all of them either had already been pursued by the police, or were now being pursued, or were hopelessly tenuous. All I had left, at five o'clock this morning, that gave the slightest promise of some result without a prolonged and laborious siege, was the possibility of a satisfactory answer to the question: where did he get the poison?"

Chewing griddle cake and ham, I looked at him. "Good lord, if that's the best we can do. Cramer has an army on it right now. There are six of us and we have no badges, and if—" I stopped because I saw his eyes. "You've got something?"

"Yes. A straw to grab at. Can't it be reasonably supposed that the decision to kill Mr. Assa was made only yesterday afternoon, resulting from the situation caused by the contestants' receipt of the answers by mail? Various circumstances support such—"

"Don't bother. I've gone over it too a little. I'll buy that."

"Then some time yesterday afternoon, not before, he decided that Mr. Assa would have to be killed, and he conceived the idea of using cyanide and putting it in his drink. Correct?"

"Yes."

"Then where the devil did he get the cyanide?"

"I couldn't—oh. That does make it a little special."

"It does indeed. Did he choose cyanide as something he knew to be lightning-swift and go out and buy some? Hardly. He could of course have procured it easily—a photographic supply house, for one—but he was not an imbecile. No. He knew where some was, handy; he knew where he could get some without being observed. Where? There are a thousand possibilities, and it may have been any one of them, but I didn't bother speculating about them because one of them was looking at me—or rather, at you. I hadn't seen it, but you had."

"Hold it." I put my coffee cup down. "I've seen it?"

"Yes."

"And told you about it?"

"Yes."

"That's interesting." I closed my eyes, opened them, and slapped the table. "Oh, sure. The display cases at the LBA office. I might have thought of it myself if I had stayed up all night—but I don't remember seeing any cyanide."

"You weren't looking for it. You said there are thousands of items from hundreds of firms. We're going to look for it."

"After it's gone? If he took it, it's not there."

"All the better. If he took only what he needed of it we'll find the residue. If he took it all yesterday or has removed the residue since, we'll find where it was—or we won't. There must be a list of the contents of those cases. There's no point in our trying to intrude before office hours, so there's plenty of time. Now for the details. I'll be with you, but you should know what I have in mind for the various eventualities—all of you. Fritz! Coffee!"

He gave us details.

If anyone considers this incident an exception to Wolfe's rule never to leave the house on business, I say no. It was not business. He was after the man who had abused his hospitality, which was unforgivable, and made him eat crow in front of Cramer, which was outrageous. I have evidence. On a later day, when he was going over the expense account I had prepared for LBA, he left in the fare for one taxi that morning, the one that Fred and Orrie and Bill took, but took out the other, the one that had carried him and Saul and me.

It lacked a minute of nine-thirty when the six of us entered an elevator in the modern midtown skyscraper, but when we got out at the twenty-second floor the aristocratic brunette with nice little ears was there on the job behind her eight-foot desk. The sudden appearance of a gang of half a dozen males startled her a little, but as I approached and she recognized me she recovered.

I told her good morning. "I'm afraid we'll be making a little disturbance, but we've got a job to do. This is Mr. Nero Wolfe."

Wolfe, at my elbow, nodded. "We have to inventory the contents of the cabinets. The death of Mr. Assa—of course you know of it."

"Yes, I . . . I know."

"That makes it necessary to proceed without delay."

She looked beyond us, and I turned to do likewise. The squad was certainly proceeding without delay. Saul Panzer had slid open the glass front of the end cabinet at the left wall and had his notebook out. Fred Durkin was at the end cabinet at the right wall, and Bill and Orrie were at the far wall, which was solid with cabinets, a stretch of some fifty feet. It was a relief to see that they all had doors open. I had seen no locks on my former visit, but there could have been tricky ones. We had brought along an assortment of keys, but using them would have made it complicated.

"I know nothing about this," the brunette said. "Who told you to do it?"

"It's part of a job," Wolfe told her, "that was given me by Messrs. Buff, O'Garro, and Assa last Wednesday. I refer you to them. —Come, Archie."

We headed for the cabinets at the right wall, those nearest the elevators, and as we reached them Fred left and went to join Saul at the left wall. That was according to the plan of battle as outlined at headquarters. I didn't bother to get out my notebook, wanting both hands free for moving things when necessary. For the first cabinet it wasn't necessary. It held a picture of an ocean liner, some miniature bags of a line of fertilizers, cartons of cigarettes, a vacuum cleaner, and various other items. The bottom shelf of the second cabinet was no more promising, with an outboard motor, soaps and detergents, canned soup, and beer in both bottles and cans, but the second shelf had packaged goods and got more attention. It didn't seem likely that cyanide would have fitted in with cereals and cake mixes and noodles, but the program said to look at each and every package. I was doing so, with Wolfe standing behind me, when an authoritative voice sounded.

"Are you Nero Wolfe? What's going on?"

I straightened and turned. A six-foot executive with a jutting jaw was facing Wolfe and wanted no nonsense. Since he hadn't emerged from an elevator, he must have been inside and the brunette had summoned him.

"I've explained," Wolfe said, "to the woman at the desk."

"I know what you told her and it sounds fishy. Get away from these cabinets and stay away until I can check."

Wolfe shook his head. "I'm sorry, Mr. . . ."

"My name's Falk."

"I'm sorry we can't oblige you, Mr. Falk. I was hired by Mr. Buff and Mr. O'Garro—and Mr. Assa, who is dead. We've started and we're going to finish. You look truculent, but I advise you to consult Mr. Buff or Mr. O'Garro. Where are they?"

"They're not here."

"You must know where they are. Phone them."

"I'm going to, and you're going to stay away from these cabinets until I do."

"No, sir." Wolfe was firm but unruffled. "I make allowances for your state of mind, Mr. Falk, after what happened last night, but you must know I'm not a bandit and these men are working for me. It shouldn't take long to get Mr. Buff or Mr. O'Garro. Do so by all means."

One test of a good executive is how long it takes him to realize he has lost an argument, and Falk passed it. He turned on his heel and left, striding across the carpet to the door leading to the inside corridor. Wolfe and I resumed, finishing with the shelf of packages and going on to the next one—buckets and cans of paint, electric irons, and so forth.

During the next half hour the elevators delivered eight or nine people, not more than that, and took most of them away again, but nobody bothered us. On the whole it was a nice quiet place to work. Once Wolfe and I thought we might be getting hot, when we came to the display of Jonas Hibben & Co., Pharmaceuticals, but it seemed to be intact, with no vacant spot, and there was no box or bottle from which someone could have removed a dose of cyanide. We gave it up finally, and moved on, and were at the last cabinet on that wall when Saul called to us to come and look at something, and we crossed the room to him, where he and Fred were focusing on the second shelf of the last cabinet in their battery.

The dignified little card—they were all dignified and little— identified it as the exhibit of the Allcoran Laboratories, Inc. There were a couple of dozen boxes, small and large, with the small ones in front and the large ones in the rear, and three rows of brown bottles, all the same size, I would say about a pint.

Saul said, "Middle row, fourth bottle from the left. You have to tip the one in front to see the label."

Wolfe stepped closer. Instead of tipping the one in front he lifted it with a thumb and forefinger, to get a clear view, and I got one too over his shoulder. No squinting was required. At the top of the label was printed in black, in large type, KCN. At the bottom was printed in red, also in large type, POISON. In between, and below the POISON there was some stuff in smaller type, but I didn't strain to get it. The bottle was so dark it would have to be lifted out and held up to the light for a look at the contents, and that wouldn't do, but you could see there was something white in it, almost up to the neck.

"Today's daily double," I said. "It was here, and we found it."

Wolfe returned the bottle he had lifted, gently and carefully. "Did you touch it?" he asked Saul. He knew darned well he hadn't, since our orders had been not to touch anything until we knew what it was, or at least that it wasn't what we were looking for. Saul said no, and Wolfe called to Bill and Orrie to come and bring chairs along, and Saul and Fred also went and got chairs. They lined the four chairs up in a row in front of the cabinet, their backs to it, and the quartet sat, facing the room and the elevators. They looked pretty impressive that way, the four of them, and no bottle of poison was ever better guarded.

That was the sight that met four pairs of eyes when Oliver Buff, Patrick O'Garro, Rudolph Hansen, and Talbott Heery stepped from an elevator into the reception room.

"Good morning, gentlemen!" Wolfe sang out, in about as nasty a tone as I had ever known him to use.

They headed for us.

21

It rarely gets you anywhere, practically never, but you always do it. When four men enter a room and one of them sees six men grouped in front of a cabinet which has in it a bottle of poison out of which he has recently shaken a spoonful onto a piece of toilet paper, to be used for killing a man, you try to watch all their faces like a hawk for some sign of which one it is. That time it was more useless than usual. They had all had a hard and probably sleepless night, and maybe hadn't been to bed at all. They looked it, and certainly none of them liked what he saw. Three of them—Buff, O'Garro, and Hansen—all spoke at once. They wanted to know who and what and why and when, oblivious of the presence of a customer who was seated across the room.

Wolfe was incisive. "It would be better, I think, to retire somewhere. This is rather public."

"Who are these men?" Buff demanded.

"They are working for the firm of Lippert, Buff and Assa, through me. They are now—"

"Get them out of here!"

"No. They're guarding an object in that cabinet. I intend shortly to tell the police to come and get the object, and meanwhile these four men will stay. They're all armed, so I—"

"Why, goddam you—" O'Garro blurted, but Hansen gripped his arm and said, "Let's go inside," and turned him around. Buff seemed about to choke, but controlled it, and led the way, with his partner and lawyer following, then Heery, then Wolfe, and then me. As I passed through the door to the corridor I turned for a glance at the four sentries, and Orrie winked at me.

The executive committee room was much more presentable than it had been before, with everything in order. The second the door was shut O'Garro started yapping, but Hansen got his arm again and steered him around to a chair at the far side of the big table, and took one there himself, so they had the windows back of them. Wolfe and I took the near side, with Heery at one end, on Wolfe's left, and Buff at the other, on my right.

"What's this object in a cabinet?" O'Garro demanded as Wolfe sat. "What are you trying to pull?"

"It will be better," Wolfe said, "if you let me describe the situation. Then we can—"

"We know the situation," Hansen put in. "We want to know what you think you're doing."

"That's simple. I'm preparing to learn which of you four men killed Louis Dahlmann, and took the wallet, and killed Vernon Assa."

Three of them stared. Heery said, "Jesus. Is that simple?"

Hansen said, "I advise you, Mr. Wolfe, to choose your words —and also your acts. With more care. This could cost you your license and much of your reputation, and possibly more. Let's have the facts. What is the object in the cabinet?"

"A bottle of cyanide of potassium, in the display of Allcoran Laboratories, with the cap seal broken and almost certainly some of the contents removed. That can be determined."

"There in that cabinet?" Hansen couldn't believe it.

"Yes, sir."

"A deadly poison there on public display?"

"Oh, come, Mr. Hansen. Don't feign an ignorance you can't possibly own. Dozens of deadly poisons are available to the public at thousands of counters, including cyanide with its many uses. You must know that, but if you want it on the record that you were astonished by my announcement you have witnesses. Shall I ask the others if they were astonished too?"

"No. —I advise you, Oliver, and you too, Pat, to say nothing whatever and answer no questions. This man is treacherous."

Wolfe skipped the tribute. "That will expedite matters," he said approvingly. His eyes moved. "I must tell the police about that bottle of poison reasonably soon, so the less I'm interrupted the better, but if you all refuse to say anything whatever I'll be wasting my time and might as well phone them now. There are one or two things I should know—for example, can I narrow it down? Of course Mr. Buff and Mr. O'Garro were on these premises yesterday afternoon. Were you, Mr. Hansen?"

"Yes."

"When?"

"Roughly, from four o'clock until after six."

"Were you, Mr. Heery?"

"I was here twice. I stopped in for a few minutes when I went to lunch, and around four-thirty I was here for half an hour."

"That's too bad." Wolfe put his palms on the table. "Now, gentlemen, I'll be as brief as may be. When I'm through we can consider whether I have to enter a defense against Mr. Hansen's charge of treachery. Until the moment of Mr. Assa's collapse in my office last evening I was concerned only with the job I had been hired for, not with murder. I invited Mr. Cramer to the meeting because I expected that developments to be contrived by me would remove both the contestants and yourselves as primary targets of his inquiry, which was surely desirable. My first objective was to demonstrate to the contestants that their receipt of the answers by mail had made it impossible to proceed with the verses that had been given them last week, and it would be futile for them to resist the inevitable; and to get their unanimous agreement to the distribution of new verses as soon as their freedom of movement was restored."

"You say that now." Hansen was buying nothing.

"It will be supported. I was confident I could do that, for they had no feasible alternative. Then I would be through with them and they would leave, and I would pursue the second objective with the rest of you. I confess that the second objective was not at all clear, and the path to it was poorly mapped, until nearly seven o'clock last evening, when Mr. Assa called. —Mr. Hansen, did you know that Mr. Assa came to see me at that hour yesterday?"

"No. I don't know it now."

"Did you, Mr. Buff?"

"No."

"Mr. O'Garro?"

"No!"

"Mr. Heery?"

"I did not."

Wolfe nodded. "One of you is lying, and that may help. He came and we talked. Mr. Goodwin was present, and he has typed a transcript of the conversation for Mr. Cramer. He could report it to you now, but it would take too long, so I'll summarize it. Mr.

Assa said he was speaking for himself, not for the firm; that he had not consulted his associates. He congratulated me for what he called my brilliant stroke in sending the answers to the contestants and thereby rescuing the contest from ruin. He offered his personal guarantee for payment of my fee. He took a drink of Pernod and poured another. And he began and ended with a demand that I call off the meeting for last evening. As for me, I denied sending the answers to the contestants, and I refused to call off the meeting. He left in a huff."

Wolfe took a breath. "That was all I needed. Mr. Assa's pretended certainty that I had sent the answers, and his eagerness to give me credit for it privately, could only mean that he had sent them himself, having got them from the paper in Dahlmann's wallet, or that he knew who had. The former was much more probable. Now the second objective of the meeting, and the path to it, were quite clear. I would proceed as planned with the contestants, get their consent to a new agreement, and then dismiss them. After they had gone I would tackle Mr. Assa and the rest of you, in the presence of Mr. Cramer. I wasn't assuming that Assa had killed Dahlmann; on the contrary, I was assuming that he hadn't, since in that case he would hardly have dared expose himself as he did in coming to me. My supposition was that Assa had gone to Dahlmann's apartment, found him dead, and took the wallet—one of Mr. Cramer's theories, as you know. If so, it had to be disclosed to Mr. Cramer, and the sooner the better—the better not only for the demands of justice, but for my client, the firm of Lippert, Buff and Assa. It would embarrass an individual, Vernon Assa, but it would be to the advantage of everyone else. It would eliminate the contestants as murder suspects, and would substantially lessen the burden of suspicion for the rest of you. I intended to expound that position to all of you and get you to help me exert pressure on Mr. Assa, and I expected to succeed."

He took another deep breath, deeper. "I am, as you see, confessing to an egregious blunder. It came from my failure to consider sufficiently the possibility that Mr. Assa had himself been duped or had miscalculated. I now condemn myself, but on the other hand, if I had known at nine o'clock last evening exactly what—"

"You can omit the if's," Hansen said coldly. "Apologize to yourself, we're not interested. How did Assa miscalculate?"

"By thinking that the man who had admitted to him that he had taken Dahlmann's wallet was telling the truth when he said that he had found Dahlmann dead. By dismissing the possibility that in fact he had killed Dahlmann."

"Wait a minute," Heery objected. "You thought that yourself about Assa."

"But Assa had come to me, and besides, I have said I blundered. It was painfully obvious, of course, when Assa died before my eyes. No effort was required to learn what had happened; the only question was, which one of you had made it happen. Which one—"

"Not obvious to me," O'Garro said.

"Then I'll describe it." Wolfe shifted in the chair, which was almost big enough but not used to him. "Since that bottle is under guard, with great assurance. Yesterday afternoon Assa learned somehow that one of you had Dahlmann's wallet in your possession. Whether he learned it by chance or by enterprise doesn't matter; he learned it, and he confronted you. You—"

Heery put in, "You just said that you assumed Assa took the wallet from Dahlmann himself. And he had it in his pocket."

"Pfui." Wolfe was getting testy. "If Assa took it, who killed him and what for? His death changed everything, including my assumptions. He confronted one of you with his knowledge that you had the wallet. You explained that you had gone to Dahlmann's apartment that night, found him dead, and took the wallet, and Assa believed you. Either you told him that you had sent the answers to the contestants, or that you hadn't. If the former, Assa conceived the stratagem of giving me credit for it as a blind; if the latter, he really thought I had done it. You two discussed the situation and decided what to do, or perhaps you didn't; Assa may have discussed it only with himself and made his own plans. It would be interesting to know whether he insisted on keeping the wallet or you insisted on his taking it. If I knew that I would have a better guess who you are."

Wolfe's tone sharpened. "Whether or not you knew of his visit to me beforehand, you knew its result. He told you that I had refused to cancel the meeting and that both of you would of course have to come. This raises an interesting point. If it was his report of his talk with me that so heightened your alarm that you decided to kill him, then you went to the cabinet to get the poison after seven o'clock. If your fatal resolve was formed earlier, before he came to me, you might have gone to the cabinet earlier. The former seems more likely. Dread feeds on itself. At first you were satisfied that Assa believed you, that he had no slight suspicion that you had killed Dahlmann, but that sort of satisfaction is infested with cancer—the cancer of mortal fear. The fear that Assa might himself suspect you, or already did; the fear that if he didn't suspect you, I would; the fear that if I didn't suspect you, the police would. When Assa told you of his failure to persuade me to cancel the meeting, the fear became terror; though you believed him when he said that he had given me no hint of his knowledge regarding the wallet, there was no telling what he would do or say under pressure from me with the others present. As I said, it seems likely that it was then, when fear had festered into the panic of terror, that you resolved to kill him. Therefore it—"

"This is drivel," Hansen said curtly. "Pure speculation. If you have a fact, what is it?"

"Out there, Mr. Hansen." Wolfe aimed a thumb over his shoulder at the door. "It could even be conclusive if that bottle has identifiable fingerprints, but I doubt if you—one of you—had lost his mind utterly. That's my fact, and it justifies a question. Mr. Assa left my office yesterday at ten minutes past seven. Who was on these premises later than that? Were you, Mr. Hansen?"

"No. I told you. I was here from four o'clock on, but left before six-thirty."

"Were you, Mr. Heery?"

"No. I told you when I was here."

"Mr. O'Garro?"

"Don't answer, Pat," Hansen commanded him.

"Pah." Wolfe was disgusted. "Something so easy to explore? If you prefer the plague—"

"I prefer," O'Garro said, "to have this out with you here and now." His bluster was gone. He was being very careful and keeping his eyes straight at Wolfe. "I was here all yesterday afternoon. I saw Assa and spoke with him several times, but always with others present. Buff and I left together around half-past seven and met Assa at a restaurant. We ate something and went from there to your place—Buff and I did. Assa stopped off for an errand and came on alone."

"What was his errand?"

"I don't know. He didn't say."

"At the restaurant, what did he say about his visit to me?"

"Nothing. He didn't mention it. The first I heard of it was here from you."

"When did you make the appointment to meet him at the restaurant?"

"I didn't make it."

"Who did?"

O'Garro's jaw worked. His eyes hadn't left Wolfe. "I'll reserve that," he said.

"You preferred," Wolfe reminded him, "to have it out here and now."

"That will do," Hansen said, with authority. "As your counsel, Pat, I instruct you, and you too, Oliver, to answer no more questions. I said this man is treacherous and I repeat it. He was in your employ in a confidential capacity, and he is trying to put you in jeopardy on a capital charge. Don't answer him. —If you have anything else to say, Wolfe, we're listening."

Wolfe ignored him and looked at Buff. "Fortunately, Mr. Buff, Mr. O'Garro has spared me the effort of persuading you to disobey your attorney, since he has told me that you left here with him around seven-thirty." His eyes moved. "I deny that I am treacherous. My client is a business entity called Lippert, Buff and Assa. Until the moment of Mr. Assa's death I devoted myself exclusively to my client's interests by working on the job that had been given me. Indeed, I am still doing so, but the circumstances have altered. The question is, what will best serve the interests of that business entity under these new circumstances? Its corollary is, how can I finish my job and learn who took the wallet without exposing the murderer? I can't."

He flattened his palms on the desk. "Mr. Dahlmann, who was apparently equipped to furnish the vitality and vigor formerly supplied by Mr. Lippert, has been killed—by one of you. Mr. Assa, who rashly incurred great personal risk for the sake of the firm, has also been killed—by one of you. Who, then, is the traitor? Who has reduced the firm to a strait from which it may never recover? If it is reasonable for you to expect me to regard my client's interests as paramount, as it is, it is equally reasonable for me to expect you to do the same; and you are simpletons if you don't see that those interests demand the exposure of the murderer as quickly and surely as possible."

His eyes fixed on the lawyer. "Mr. Hansen. You are counsel for the firm of Lippert, Buff and Assa?"

"I am."

"Are you Mr. Buff's personal attorney?"

"Of record? No."

"Or Mr. O'Garro's?"

"No."

"Then I charge you with treachery to your client. I assert that you betray your client's vital interests when you instruct these men to withhold answers to my questions. —No no, don't bother to reply. Draft a twenty-page brief tomorrow at your leisure." He left him for the members of the firm. "I have noted that you have not raised the question of motive. I myself have not broached it because I know little or nothing about it—that is, the motive for killing Dahlmann. Mr. Cramer of course has a stack of them, good, bad, and indifferent. I have nothing at all for Mr. Hansen and next to nothing for Mr. Heery, and anyway the timetable shelves them tentatively. For Mr. O'Garro, nothing. For Mr. Buff, nothing conclusive, but material for speculation. I have gathered that he more or less inherited his eminence in the firm on the death of Mr. Lippert, who had trained him; that since Mr. Lippert's death he has gloried in his status of senior partner and clung to it tenaciously; that his abilities are negligible except for one narrow field; and that there was a widespread expectation that before long Mr. Dahlmann would become the master instead of the servant. I don't know how severely that prospect galled Mr. Buff, but you must know." He focused on the senior partner. "Especially you, Mr. Buff. Would you care to tell me?"

Buff darted a glance at Hansen, but the lawyer had no instructions, and he went to Wolfe. His round red face was puffy and flabby, and a strand of his white hair, dangling over his brow, had been annoying me and I had been tempted to tell him to brush it back. Around the corner at the end of the table, at my right, he was close enough for me to do it myself.

He wasn't indignant. He was a big man and an important man, and this was a very serious matter. "Your attempt to give me a motive," he told Wolfe, "is not very successful. We all resented Dahlmann a little. He got on our nerves. I think some of us hated him —for instance, O'Garro here. O'Garro always did hate him. But in trying to give me a motive you're overlooking something. If I killed him to keep him from crowding me out at LBA, I must have been crazy, because why did I take the wallet? Taking the wallet was what got LBA into these grave difficulties. Was I crazy?"

"By no means." Wolfe met his eyes. "You may have gone there merely to get the wallet, and took the gun along because you were determined to get it, and the opportunity to get rid of him became irresistible after you were with him. Leaving, you would certainly take the wallet. That was what you had gone for; and in any case, you didn't want it found on his body with that paper in it. You were not in a state of mind to consider calmly the consequences of your taking it. By the way, what have you done with the paper? It must have been in the wallet, since you sent the answers to the contestants."

"That's going too far, Wolfe." Buff's voice raised a little. "You only suggested a motive, but now you're accusing me. With witnesses here, don't forget that. But what you said about the vital interests of this firm, that they are paramount, that made sense and I agree with you. At a time like this personal considerations are of no account. So I must tell you of a little mistake O'Garro made —I don't say he did it deliberately, it may have slipped his mind that he did make the appointment for us to meet Assa at the restaurant. He was in his office, and he came to my office and said that Assa had phoned and he had arranged for us to meet him at Grainger's at a quarter to eight."

I thought O'Garro was going to plug him, and O'Garro thought so too. He was across from me, at Buff's right, and he was out of his chair, his eyes blazing, with two fists ready, but he didn't swing.

He put his fists on the table and leaned on them, toward Buff, until his face was only a foot away from the senior partner's.

"You're too old to hit," he said, grinding it out between his teeth. "Too old and too goddam dirty. You said I hated Dahlmann. Maybe I didn't love him, but I didn't hate him. You did. Seeing him coming up on his way to take over and boot you out—no wonder you hated him—and by God, I felt sorry for you!"

O'Garro straightened up and looked at us. "I felt sorry for him, gentlemen. That's how clever I was. I felt sorry for him." He looked at Wolfe. "You asked me who made the appointment with Assa and I said I'd reserve it. Buff made it, and came to my room and told me. Any more questions?"

"One or two for Mr. Buff." Wolfe regarded him with half-closed eyes. "Mr. Buff. When were you alone with Mr. Assa yesterday afternoon, and where and for how long?"

"I refuse to answer." Buff was having trouble with his voice. "I decline to answer on advice of counsel."

"Who is your counsel?"

"Rudolph Hansen."

"He says he isn't." Wolfe's eyes moved. "Mr. Hansen? Are you now counsel for Mr. Buff?"

"No." It sounded final. "As it stands now I couldn't be even if I wanted to, because of a possible conflict of interest. His attorney is named Arnold Duffen, with an office a few blocks from here."

Buff looked at him. The round red face was puffier. "Arnold may not be immediately available, Rudolph. I want to consult you privately. Now."

"No. Impossible."

"Then I must try to get him." Buff was leaving his chair. "Not here. From my room."

I stopped him by taking his arm. He was going to pull away, but I don't take a murderer's arm the way I do a nymph's, and he ended back in his chair. I released him, but got up and stood beside him.

"I wish," Wolfe said, "to extend you gentlemen all possible courtesy, but I must transfer the responsibility for that bottle of poison as soon as may be. Need I wait longer?"

For three seconds no one spoke, and then O'Garro said, "Use the phone on your left."

22

The most important result from the standpoint of the People of the State of New York came a couple of months later, in June, when Oliver Buff was tried and convicted of the first degree murder of Vernon Assa, Cramer and the DA's office having collected a batch of evidence which did, after all, include one good fingerprint from the KCN bottle. But from our standpoint the most important result came much earlier, in fact the very next day, when Rudolph Hansen phoned after lunch and made a date for him and O'Garro and Heery to see Wolfe at six o'clock. They came right on the dot, just as Wolfe got down from the plant rooms. When I took them to the office I saw that O'Garro got the red leather chair, thinking he rated it as the surviving partner. Probably his name would now go into the firm's title. They sure needed some new ones.

They still looked as if they could use some sleep, say about a week, but at least they had their hair combed. They were gloomy but polite. After some recent developments had been mentioned, such as a statement by Buff's secretary that on Monday afternoon she had seen Assa in Buff's room, talking with him, with a brown wallet in his hand, Hansen opened up. He said that in spite of everything it would be a great relief to proceed with the contest in a manner that would leave no loopholes for contention or litigation, and in connection with that process they wanted Wolfe's help. Wolfe asked him how.

"We want you to handle it," Hansen said. "We want you to write the verses, give them to the contestants, and set the conditions and deadline, and, when the answers are received, check them and award the prizes. We want to leave the whole thing to you. Heery refuses to let LBA handle it, and in the circumstances we can't blame him, and it's his money. You'll have full authority. There'll be no interference from anybody. For this service LBA will agree to pay you fifty thousand dollars, plus expenses."

"I won't do it," Wolfe said flatly.

"Damn it, you must!" Heery rapped out.

"No, sir. I must not. I have stretched my dignity pretty thin on occasion to keep myself going, but I will not write verses for a perfume contest. That is not to impugn the dignity of any other man who may undertake it. Dignities are like faces; no two are the same. I beg you not to insist; I won't consider it. I confess that my refusal might give me a sharper twinge but for the fact that I am about to send the firm of Lippert, Buff and Assa a bill for precisely that amount—fifty thousand dollars. Plus expenses."

"What for?" Hansen was cold.

"For the job I was hired for and have completed."

"We've discussed that," O'Garro said. "We don't see it."

"You didn't do the job," Hansen said, settling it.

"No? Who did?"

"Nobody. Circumstances beyond your control and out of your control. If anybody did it, it was Buff himself, when he sent the answers to the contestants. Also Assa learning that Buff had the wallet, but the main thing was the contestants getting the answers. That was what saved the contest."

"You acknowledge that?"

"Certainly we acknowledge it. It's obvious."

"Very well. I suppose this was unavoidable." Wolfe turned. "Archie, give Mr. Hansen a dollar."

I got one out and went and proffered it, but Hansen didn't take it. "What's this?" he demanded.

"I am retaining you as my attorney, as before. I wish what I am going to tell you to have the protection of a confidential relationship between you and me. Since the interest of Mr. O'Garro and Mr. Heery runs with mine I'll trust their discretion. You may end the relationship at any moment. That's what you told me. You and I began with a privileged communication; we'll end with one."

Hansen took the dollar, not enthusiastically, and I returned to my desk. "Go ahead," he said.

"You're gouging this out of me." Wolfe was frowning. "I would have preferred to keep it to myself, but rather this than a prolonged wrangle. When you get the list of expenses accompanying my bill there will be an item on it, 'One second-hand Underwood typewriter, eighty-two dollars.' It is now at the bottom of the river, because I wanted to exclude all possibility of a slip, but I have several pages that were typed on it—or rather, I know where they are and can easily get them—and if you will secure from Inspector Cramer one of the sheets of answers that were received by the contestants, or a good facsimile, I'll arrange an opportunity for you to make a comparison. You'll find that the answers sent to the contestants were typed on the machine charged for in my expense list."

Heery burst out laughing. In the pressure of events I had forgotten what a good laugher he was, and that time he really meant it. After a few healthy roars he stopped to blurt, "You amazing sonofabitch!" and then roared some more. Hansen and O'Garro were staring, O'Garro with a deep frown, chewing at it.

When Heery had subsided enough for a normal voice to be heard Hansen spoke. "You're saying that you sent the answers to the contestants?"

"They were sent by a man in my employ. I can produce him if you insist, but I would prefer not to name him."

"I think we won't insist. Pat?"

"No." O'Garro's frown was going. "I will be damned."

"No wonder," Hansen told Wolfe, "you wanted it a privileged communication. This changes things."

"It should," Wolfe said drily. "Since you have just declared that sending the answers to the contestants saved the contest. It was to their advantage too, most of them. That was one of my objects, and the other, of course, was to spur somebody into doing something. I didn't know who or what, but I thought that would stimulate action, and it did."

"It certainly did," O'Garro agreed. "Too much action, but you couldn't help it."

"I should have helped it. Mr. Assa should be alive. I blundered." Wolfe tightened his lips. He released them. "Do you want me to get the pages that were typed on that machine for comparison?"

"No," Hansen said. "Pat?"

"No."

"But," Hansen told Wolfe, "we still want you to handle the contest. The payment will of course be in addition to the bill you're sending. It won't be—"

"No!" Wolfe bellowed, and I didn't blame him. Turning down fifty grand just once to keep your dignity in order is tough enough, and to be compelled to keep on turning it down is too much. They tried to insist, and Heery especially wouldn't let go, but finally they had to give it up. When they left and I went to the hall with them they corralled me by the rack and tried to sell me the idea of talking him into it, with some broad hints that it wouldn't cost me anything, but I gave them no hope. My mind wasn't really on their problem at all. It was on one of my own, and when I had closed the door behind them and returned to the office I tackled it without preamble.

"Okay," I told Wolfe, "it was a brilliant stroke. It was a masterpiece. It was a honey. But not only did you change the rules and tell me a direct lie, you also piled another one on by telling me that you had *not* changed the rules. How's that for a confidential relationship? Why do I ever have to believe anything you say?"

His mouth twisted. He thought he was smiling. "You can always believe me, Archie. With your memory, which is matchless, you can recall my words. I made just two categorical statements to you, when we were alone, on that matter. I said, first, *I hadn't hoped for anything as provocative as this.* That was true; I hadn't hoped for it; I was sure of it, since I had arranged it. I said, second, *I hadn't listed this among the possibilities.* That was likewise true; it wasn't a possibility, it was a certainty. I have never told you a direct lie and never will—and if I quibbled it was only to save you the necessity of telling one to Mr. Stebbins or any one else who might challenge you. Have I quoted myself correctly?"

I grunted. I couldn't very well repudiate my matchless memory.

"Are you suggesting," he demanded, "that verbal dodges are no longer to be permitted in our private conversations? By either of us?"

"No, sir."

He snorted. "You'd better not. We wouldn't last a week."

He rang for beer.